The Gladiator Wolf King

book - 3

J.W.G. Stout

J.W.G. Stout

Copyright © 2023 J.W.G. Stout

All rights reserved

The characters and events portrayed in this book are fictitious. Any similarity to real persons, living or dead, is coincidental and not intended by the author.

No part of this book may be reproduced, or stored in a retrieval system, or transmitted in any form or by any means, electronic, mechanical, photocopying, recording, or otherwise, without express written permission of the publisher.

ISBN-13: 9798364951908
ISBN-10: 1477123456

Cover design by: Art Painter
Library of Congress Control Number: 2018675309
Printed in the United States of America

*This book is dedicated in memory of
Jeffrey Michael Kern
Even the brightest of flames struggle to stay lit.*

***

*All it takes is a beautiful fake smile
to hide an injured soul
and they will never notice how broken
you really are
- Robin Williams*

Contents

Title Page
Copyright
Dedication
Chapter 1 – Waking Up ... 1
Chapter 2 – Land Ho! ... 11
Chapter 3 – Sweltering ... 20
Chapter 4 – A Knights first Quest ... 30
Chapter 5 – The Babysitter ... 39
Chapter 6 – My Reality ... 48
Chapter 7 – His Games, Her Torture ... 56
Chapter 8 – Teal the Alpha ... 65
Chapter 9 – First Blood ... 74
Chapter 10 – The Brother ... 83
Chapter 11 – A Face from the Past ... 91
Chapter 12 – Fake it till you make it ... 101
Chapter 13 – Respect ... 110
Chapter 14 – Game Day ... 119
Chapter 15 – Let the Games Begin ... 127
Chapter 16 – Let the Games Begin Part 2 ... 136
Chapter 17 – The Horrifying Truth ... 145

Chapter 18 – A Beautiful Truth	155
Chapter 19 – A Deal with the Devil	166
Chapter 20 – Fear not, the Despair	178
Chapter 21 – Beauty Under the Moon	187
Chapter 22 – Time to Watch	198
Chapter 23 – Jonda	208
Chapter 24 - Darrius	218
Chapter 25 – We meet Again	228
Chapter 26 – An unexpected Bite	237
Chapter 27 – A Vile Wolf & A Red Wolf	248
Chapter 28 – The First Gift	258
Chapter 29 – The Roar of a King	267
Chapter 30 – Closer	277
Chapter 31 – Lies upon Lies	288
Chapter 32 – The Second Gift	299
Chapter 33 – The Death of Kellen	310
Chapter 34 – The Queen and the fourth Knight	319
Chapter 35 – The Bond of the Knights	330
Chapter 36 – The Third Gift	339
The story of: INANNA & CONRI	349
Chapter 37 – My Hero	352
Chapter 38 – Adam	362
Chapter 39 - The Plan	371
Chapter 40 – Sealed with a Kiss	382
Chapter 41 – Finding Friends	392
Chapter 42 – The Distraction	402
Chapter 43 – A Pack of Gladiators	411
Chapter 44 – His Red Wolf	421

Chapter 45 – A Fate Worse than Death	431
Chapter 46 – Why the Witch?	441
Chapter 47 – A Painting of Old	451
Chapter 48 – The Sister	461
Chapter 49 – Luna Siobhan	471
Chapter 50 – The Queen of Shifters	481
Chapter 51 – The Next Generation	492
Chapter 52 – Happy Birthday	502
Chapter 53 – Blood Lust	512
Chapter 54 – The Road Traveled Before	521
Chapter 55 – What Future Might It Hold	530
Chapter 56 – EPILOGUE-ISH	541
Chapter 57 – Epilogue 2	552
BONUS CHAPTER FOR BOOK 4 – HUNJI A BROKEN WOLF & the witch of Andora	562
About The Author	573
Books In This Series	575

Chapter 1 – Waking Up

KING KELLEN

I opened my eyes and a nauseating feeling rose from my stomach right up to my throat.

My insides were sloshing and my vision was blurry. I blinked twice, adjusting my eyes to the dark. The only light was from a low-hanging bulb, a dim light that was swaying to and fro, not helping the churning of my gut.

The smell of salty water and damp, rusty mold hit my nose. I gagged as the scents curdled my stomach even more. My whole body ached and I went to shift my position, only to be met with the clanking sound of chains and resistance at my wrists.

Holy hell. Either I had the worst hangover in history and Mike left me tied up somewhere dumb again, or…

I didn't get to finish my thought as the bang of something metal, large and sliding, disturbed me. "Mike what the fuck…" my dry throat rasped out but was cut off by the sound of a deep, menacing chuckle.

"Ahh, you are awake. I was told to watch you. Darius, we got one awake, sort it out, ya?" I couldn't focus on his face, but I could smell his stale and pungent scent of wine and bread and make out the shape of a man's round gut and stained white shirt. His voice was hoarse and his accent was one I hadn't heard before.

The lash came out of nowhere, tearing through my skin. "Argghhh!" I yelled as I felt my back rip open. I felt the deep cuts open immediately and the sting of wolfsbane seeped through the gashes.

"Argghh!" I cried out again. This time there were two quick whips, and the lashes they left were agonizing.

I wasn't in silver but I had no strength to break the chains, try as I might. I couldn't stand on my own even before they lashed me.

I twisted in agony. What the fuck was this? I opened my mouth to ask what the hell was going on, who they were, or to command them to let me go, but the brutal lashing came again.

I reached out for Conri, my wolf, but I was met with silence. Whatever I had been drugged with had knocked my wolf out.

This could seriously not be happening to me.

The last thing I remember was... what? I closed my eyes, screwing them shut. What happened to me? Think, think, Kellen.

Crack!

Another lash wracked through my body and I clamped my jaw tight, gritting my teeth together, trying to bear the pain and not cry out. I couldn't give them the satisfaction, whoever 'they' were.

"Let me go and I will spare your lives." I heavily breathed out. The whooshing in my stomach churned again and bile rose. I began spewing. My stomach contents splashed to the floor and hit my bare feet, where my toes barely touched the metal floor.

Where the fuck were my shoes? Where the fuck were my clothes? All I had on was a pair of black boxer briefs.

I remember we won the battle of Riocht. Mathias killed Orion. Lamia, her emerald-green eyes flashing in my mind, became queen. They became king and queen, they were crowned.

My head was becoming fuzzy again. My lips were *so* dry and the smell of my puke made me want to vomit again.

Crack!

"Arggghh" I yelled out, the whip's force taking me by surprise. Who were these idiots? Did they not know who I was? Didn't they realize they were going to die for this?

"Easy Darius, this one's worth a lot of money. We wouldn't want to deliver him half dead now would we? Jack wouldn't like that. Got a lot of money riding on this one." The stale-smelling man said, breathing his rotting stench of a mouth right by my ear. "Right little prince? You will make fine entertainment." He laughed and then moved away, his footsteps clanging against the metal floor.

I remember leaving Riocht, hugging Lamia goodbye. I would see her soon. Mike left with me, we were in a car, and we stopped.

That's where it got hazy again.

The whip came down again and again; I lost count of how many times I felt the bite on my back and the sting of the wolfsbane. Blood ran down my torn skin, the red liquid dripping onto the metal ground beneath me, its coppery smell mixing with my bile and the rusty mold.

Thoughts and images of Lamia flitted through my head, focusing on something other than the pain. I smiled at her image until my thoughts shifted.

Is this how she felt when she woke up in the dungeons of MacTire? Lost... Confused...

The smell of the salty water, coupled with my empty stomach, made me queasy and dizzy. I tried to look around at my surroundings, but my sight was becoming a blur again.

I felt the sweat bead on my forehead and felt the crack of another lash opening my bareback even more. The pain was heightened by the wolfsbane and the fact that my wolf was AWOL right now.

I needed to remember what happened to me.

I called to my wolf again. Nothing. I opened my mind to Lamia and the other three knights. Nothing. I tried to feel her, sense her, but I was met with nothing.

I had no energy to cry out again, so I hung there as lash after lash tore me open. They didn't stop until I passed out.
At least when I passed out, I didn't feel it anymore. So much for going easy on me.

"Lamia," I whispered her name on my parched lips, praying she heard me as my eyes fluttered and closed, casting me back into darkness.

The next time I woke, it was with a bucket of saltwater being thrown over me, the salt stinging the lacerations on my back that had not healed yet.

"Wakeey, wakeey, little prince." That gravelly voice pierced my eardrums. His attempt at singing the words just made the throbbing in my head and wounds feel much more intense.

I felt the chains tighten, the cuffs pulling taut on my wrists. They then loosened and my body crashed to the floor, crumpling in a pile of aching limbs. The sickly stench of the man surrounding me and my head still swaying with dizziness wasn't helping.

And again I emptied my stomach, what little was left in it.

At least now I wasn't hanging, but the sloshing of my stomach became worse. I blinked my eyes a few times trying to rid them of the saltwater. Slowly, my vision became clearer and I took in my surroundings. I was in a metal box with cages, the walls were painted in a dim blue, and the paint was peeling to show the dank metal beneath.

I was on a boat, caged in the hull of what I assumed was a large ship of some kind.

What the fuck has happened to me? And more importantly, where the fuck was I going?

I opened my mind yet again, envisioning Lamia, then Mike, Hunji, and Rhett.

'Goddess damn Conri!' I yelled in my mind at him when I couldn't even create a link. What the fuck did they do to my wolf?

I was starting to realize that I was not in a good situation, as if the whipping wasn't enough of an indication to begin with.

I was more worried that my wolf might not come back.

I had no idea how to get out of this situation either - and who the fuck was Jack? The name wasn't ringing a bell. What the hell did this guy mean *'worth money'*?

At this point, I was confused, tired, hurting, and frustrated. I needed to figure this shit out and find a way to get out of my current situation, fast!

*****

For three days they bought me food, if you could call it

that. Although, I didn't expect them to bring me anything and I really shouldn't complain considering the situation I was in.

I had yet to feel Conri stir in even the slightest way, but that didn't stop me from trying to reach out to Lamia or the other guys whenever I found the strength to try. And even though I knew my efforts were in vain, I still held out hope.

They *had* to be looking for me. I knew they would. I just couldn't understand how I got here, my memories are still blurry. I could remember leaving Lonely City with Mike and I remembered that we stopped at some rundown diner... and that's where everything went blank.

They gave me porridge. I knew the disgusting, watery substance that tasted like bland glue was laced with something that was keeping my wolf at bay. I just didn't know what.

I ate the gluey food only because if I had any chance of getting out of this mess, I needed food to keep up what little strength I had.

At least now I was coherent and could think straight. Despite Conri's absence, I could at least form a thought.

I knew I was in a large cargo boat of sorts. The smell of the saltwater that surrounded me and the dizzy swaying I would feel now and then from the lurch of the boat told me I was in open water.

Where though?

It would be frivolous to try and escape while in this metal box. Who's to say if I did manage to get out of this cage that I wouldn't be stuck, my efforts wasted, just to find out I was in the middle of the ocean?

If I jumped into the ocean, my chances of survival were

slim. No one could last in the wide-open waters, not for any extended amount of time. I would either drown or get eaten by some creature.

I let out a low growl of frustration, the growl sounding weak without my counterpart to fuel my anger at being in this goddess-forsaken situation.

I would have to wait until we pulled into a port somewhere, wherever my final destination was.

By the fourth day of being held in this 10x8 cell, I had refused the porridge. I would rather go hungry if there was any chance of getting my wolf to come back. I would need him, more than the food, if I planned to escape anytime soon.

Refusing to eat earned me another twenty lashes, they were painful, but I endured them. Not giving them the satisfaction of hearing my pain, I bit my cheek and remained silent. I gritted down each throbbing sting as the single-tail whip doused in wolfsbane cracked against my open wounded back.

The lacerations from the first whipping hadn't closed up completely, and the lashes I received this time opened them all up again.

The man, Darrius as I had heard him called, laughed after the last blow he administered. "You must be a strong 'un, to take this kind of beating. Jack said you were exceptional and to not take any chances. Look at ya' now though." He came closer to me and bent to my level. His disgusting, hot breath made me sick. I could taste the smell of his rotten teeth.

"My name is Kellen Moon, Alpha of the New Moon Pack, and King of the Werewolves. There has been a mistake." I had tried several times to get these men to listen to me. Each time I was met with laughter as they jeered at my title.

"I'm a king! Look at me! Not so high and mighty now, eh?" The fat, stale-smelling one mocked in a childlike taunt, his feet kicking my legs from under me.

"A weak wolf with no future. Not sure where you came from, but where you're going... you will wish you 'ad died on this boat. Wished we 'ad fed ya to the sharks." He cackled as he left my cage.

The click of the padlock and his retreating footsteps left me back in silence. Save for the odd call of a gull or the straining sound of the creaking hull as the waves lapped at the side of the boat.

Saliva mixed with blood strung from my mouth as he left me there hanging. My arms were held high by the metal chains and my knees bent, barely touching the cold metal floor. I didn't have the strength to stand up. I let the chains take my weight, causing the cuffs to bite into my already raw and bleeding wrists.

On the fifth day, the loud and invading blow of the boat's horn woke me from another blackout. I blinked my eyes open, straining them towards the door of the hull. I could see a streak of light shining through from somewhere.

That one beam of yellow warmth lit up the dank hull. I wished I could reach out and touch it, feel the sun's warmth radiate on my skin. I closed my eyes and imagined I was by the lake, lying out on the mossy rocks, with the sun beating down on me.

The horn blew again, startling me from my daydreaming. I heard a commotion from above, then the thump and clank of footsteps coming down metal stairs. In no time the bald, dirty fat shit of a man, with the same stained white shirt, came through the hull's door that was opposite my cage. He was followed by Darrius and a large, burly-looking man.

I lifted my nose to scent the new guy. I could get no scent from him except for sweat and alcohol. If I had to take a guess, by his size, I would say he was a bear shifter. He wore a bright and menacing smile on his face.

"Prince-ee!" He beamed like we were old friends. "So sorry you had to be locked up like some dangerous rogue or criminal, but ya know, we gotta do what we gotta do!" He smirked. "We don't want you running away before we can get you to your new home now do we?"

I looked at him puzzled and without amusement. Who the fuck was this guy? Was he the one running the show here?

As if reading my mind, he clicked his tongue and narrowed his blue eyes at me. Folding his hands behind his back, he stepped closer to the cage and leaned in. "I'm insulted that you don't recognize me, but not to worry. I'm sure your little queen would recognize me, all the times I fucked her while in the dungeons of MacTire. A nice piece of pussy that one. Wouldn't you say so?" His mocking voice was berating and I let out a low growl.

The man laughed at me and clicked his tongue again when I pulled and shook the chains. Realization dawned on me, that this was one of the men that violated Lamia three years ago when she was kidnapped and held at MacTire.

If I had my wolf, we would have broken free from these chains, from this cage, and I would have ripped his heart out without mercy.

"Jack's the name and trafficking is my game. And you, Prince-ee, are going to make me a lotta money." He introduced himself and gave me a mock bow. That stupid, condescending smirk was still plastered on his face.

He turned away and began to walk out of the hull, but not

before calling back to the man named Darrius. "Get him in the cuffs, we dock in thirty minutes. Oh, and just in case, give him a little extra of the Cartbanamol serum. Don't want him wolfing out on us."

Chapter 2 – Land Ho!

KELLEN

The pull of the boat had my guts sloshing around again as I felt it come to a slow and begin to turn. The heavy creaking sound of the metal and the crash of shallow waves made the large transport sway, and in turn, my body was tugged left and right. My restraints rubbed harder on my sore joints and dug into my bleeding wrists more as I attempted to stay upright and on my feet.

Darrius unlocked my cage and, wearing a thick pair of gloves, produced two pairs of silver, thick cuffs with spikes on the inside of them.

I immediately recognized what they were. Lamia and Mike had given me detailed descriptions of the spiked cuff things they used to restrain Lamia and keep her wolf subdued.

He clamped them first around my ankles, making sure they were tight. The heavy chain connecting the two cuffs rattled as he placed them.

The spikes pierced through my skin and the silver burned. He tightened them more until I could feel those sharp points digging into my bone. I bit back the hiss that threatened to leave my lungs as the foreign objects made pain radiate from my ankles.

He then released my arms from the hook that the metal chains were shackled to, pulled my arms behind my back, and securely fastened similar spiked restraints on my wrists. My already raw skin began itching and burning from the contact with the silver. The prongs penetrated through the bone like hot skewers.

No sooner did Darrius have the new restraints fastened tightly on me, than he brought out a needle ready to inject me with a liquid that held a slight green tinge to it, otherwise clear.

I bucked my body and swiveled around, trying to avoid being pricked by it. My movements were still limited, and he overpowered me easily. I threw a head butt at him when he grabbed my arms, managing to bust his nose, but he recovered quickly and stuck the needle into my neck.

I dropped to the floor like my body had suddenly been weighted down. The heaviness of my limbs grew by the second and my head began to pound, my sight dazed.

I wasn't knocked out, but I felt like a zombie - like I was jacked up on copious amounts of belladonna and alcohol.

"Fucking ranked wolves," I heard Darrius groan viciously. His hand was over his nose as he retreated from the cage, mumbling something about not being paid enough.

I slumped into the corner, drained of energy, with a depleted life force. I was utterly screwed and I was losing hope.

My thoughts again went back to Lamia and the time when she had been kidnapped by Silas, recollecting how long it took us to find her and the fact that we only found her due to a lucky break. They had to find me, right? How would a king go missing and no one notice? Someone had to see or know how I got on this boat.

I just hoped Mike would figure out where I was before it

was too late. Because Goddess knows, I had no clue where I was or even what continent we would be docking at.

I couldn't make sense of any of this.

A little while later, after the boat had been still for a while and I could see the beam of light begin to fade, the sound of heavy clanking footsteps reached my ears again and the dim lighting from the single bulb began to give out a low, yellow glow.

"Get the cage open Darrius, the sooner this fucking wolf is off my boat, the better." The man with the stained shirt and stale breath huffed to my tormentor.

"Aye Pete, with pleasure." Darrius crowed.

So that was his name, Pete. If I lived through whatever the fuck this shit is, I promised myself right there, that I would come back for Pete and Darrius.

Darrius came in with his thick gloves, unlocked the cage, grabbed the metal chain that linked the two cuffs on my wrists, and yanked me harshly to my feet. After a few stumbles and being dragged out of the cage I had been in for the past few days, I managed to find my footing.

He pulled me out of the hull and into a long corridor, then pushed me towards the metal set of stairs that sat in the middle of it.

"Up." He gave the command, pushing me again to walk up the steps.

At the top stood two men, holding what looked to be long cattle prods, ready to corral or tase my naked ass if I thought of stepping out of line or fighting back. I highly assumed these prods carried a much higher voltage than that of the ones I knew of and would most definitely put me on my ass in an instant without the presence of my wolf.

I was led up and out through a gangway and onto a metal walkway that connected to the docks. The fresh air was heaven to my senses and I gulped it up, briefly letting my eyes close before I was prodded in the back and shoved forward.

My skin relished the warm night air. The slight breeze made me acutely aware of my open wounds, but I didn't care, I was happy to be out of that cage.

The docks were quiet this time of night; the usual hustle and bustle of cargo loaders and workers, I assumed, had gone home for the night. I had only visited a port once when my father took me with him on a business trip. We had gone to a large harbor city to oversee some export goods that were being shipped out and my father had some business to take care of with one of our import/export companies.

Darrius pulled me along until I was standing next to four other men and a group of around eight women, who were huddled together and equally as naked. I lifted my nose and scented them discretely. They were a mixed group; at least three wolves, two cats, and a bear. The other two held the scent of humans.

The four men smelled like wolves but were weak, so I assumed they were omegas, lesser-ranking wolves.

I bit my cheek in anger, wanting to lash out at the fuckers who had kidnapped these women and men. Without Conri, it was no use, I would just be putting myself and the other captives in harm's way if I tried anything. Despite not being able to punish these fuckers, I was still seething. It made my blood boil.

If I ever - no... when I got out of this mess, I would personally see to having this type of bullshit stop. I would shut it the fuck down. I was honestly not just bat shit angry but disgusted that this type of thing – trafficking, was happening in my kingdom.

As we were made to walk along the dock, the women, men, and I were being corralled that way by pushing, shoving, and threats. I noticed a few men standing ahead by some transport trucks. At first I didn't pay much attention, but as we neared the men and trucks, I recognized the man who called himself Jack.

The man who seemed to know me and had been one of Lamia's tormentors.

I gave him a sneer and leered at the other men. The one standing next to Jack looked familiar even with his back turned to me, and I got a sense of déjà vu, a tedious familiarity from him.

The man turned around and I recognized him immediately. I could never forget his face; it was ingrained into my brain. All the time pouring over reports and files on this guy, trying to track him down, countless pictures of him, yet I had never found him.

My eyes were wide and my mouth slack. I had been looking for him for three years, more so recently after the Royal Pack was attacked and my parents died. At first I was in disbelief that I would find him now, then it turned to raw, unadulterated anger.

Not only could I not get my hands on him and squeeze the life out of him, but I was also in these damn cuffs because of him.

"You mother fucker!" I growled at the man next to Jack. Oliver.

I pulled on the chains, stepped out of line, and made a move toward him. I didn't care, I just wanted to hurt him. Any way I could.

"I will fucking kill you! You piece of shit!" I screamed, trying to get to him.

Oliver looked unphased, not even a tremble. He turned his head towards Jack. "Are we sure his wolf is dormant?" he asked. Jack chuckled at his question.

"All good Ollie, no worries," he told his comrade.

"Do you hear me, Oliver? I will fucking kill you if it's the last thing I do!" I began to shout, still tugging on the cuffs and chains that linked them. I lunged forward. "You piece of shit cowar.... ARGGGHHHH"

The unpleasant sting of what felt like 100 volts ripped through my body, my teeth clenched together, and my body began to convulse. It was like lighting ripping through me and setting every nerve on edge all at once.

I fell to the ground when they did it again. My limbs stiffened and my mouth dried up, the excruciating pain shooting through me shook my brain like a lone peanut in a jar.

"Prince-ee, why you gotta hate Ollie? He's just doing the job he was paid to do." Jack crouched down next to me, the fucking smirk back on his face. He enjoyed watching my torment. "Aw, you're just pissed because he got the better of you." He began to laugh.

I looked towards Oliver. His hazel eyes trained on me. For a second, I thought I saw fear in his eyes before they flashed to a yellowy-orange, and then it was gone. Now he looked at me with no expression, his hands behind his back and facial features relaxed. Just watching the show.

I swear to the Moon Goddess, I will kill him.

"Ughhhh" I was shocked by the prod again. This time my vision became blurry and dark. My tongue felt like it swelled ten times larger and became slack.

I heard Jack's voice, "Get him up and in the truck. The sooner he ain't our problem the better." He sounded a million miles away, but I knew he was still standing beside me.

My body was hoisted up and someone began to drag me. I felt two men lift my stiff and useless frame up and then toss me onto a hard metal floor. They closed the doors, and everything went black.

I tried to adjust my eyes, but my body gave out and I must have passed out again.

When I came to, I was still shrouded in darkness. The rumbling of an engine let me know I was in the back of one of those transport trucks. I groaned and tried to sit up straight, my body still feeling stiff.

"Man, you are awake. I thought for sure you be dead after they hit you with those prods that many times." A voice with a thick accent came from the darkness, some words rolling from his tongue. His dialect was close to the shifters who come from the jungle of Tolba, a territory south of the Cat Kingdom.

"I would have liked to have seen him break out of these cuffs," another man's voice piped up, "I was hoping you would." His accent sounded more like my own.

I sat up straighter, leaning my back against the side of the moving vehicle. For a twenty-year-old, I felt like I was seventy. Everything on me hurt.

My voice was gravelly and rough when I spoke, probably due to the cattle prods and lack of fluids. "Where…" I shook my head, trying to get my thoughts right. "Can someone explain to me how we got here and where we are going?"

I was hoping at least one of these men could tell me. Give

me something, anything.

"You've been sold young wolf." The man with the thick jungle accent told me.

"Sold?" I questioned, not to him in particular, more to myself.

Sold. I was still trying to wrap my brain around it, make sense of it. Oliver kidnapped me and sold me. But how?

"My name is Ajani. I was Beta of the Hallow Rock Tribe. They took me when I was out patrolling. Shipped me down south." He explained. "You are a ranked wolf; I can smell your power and feel your aura."

"Do you have your wolf?" I asked, surprised. I could scent their were-race, but other than that I had lost all other senses and hadn't felt Conri since before I woke up in the hull of the boat.

"You must have caused some problems for them to fuck you up like they have." The second man said. "Your senses will come back; it took me a week before I could even speak with my wolf."

My head shot up, looking for the man in the darkness, his words piquing my interest. "Your wolf came back?" I asked, excited and hopeful.

"Yeah, I can feel him, but that's it. I'm not ranked, so I don't communicate with him much anyway." The man said in a nonchalant tone. "But my sight and smell came back as strong as before." He said with a little more pep.

"What is your name, young wolf?" Ajani questioned me.

"Kellen," I rasped. "King Kellen of the New Moon and the Royal Pack of Werewolves. Knight to the Queen of Shifters," I said proudly, then dropped my tone when I realized that meant nothing right now. "Or at least I was."

"Your Majesty, it is a great honor to be in your presence," Ajani said.

I scoffed out loud, leaning my head in my hands, feeling helpless. "It doesn't mean anything right now though, does it," I said more to myself than the men in the dark.

"If only I had my wolf…" I sighed. I was starting to feel defeated.

Chapter 3 – Sweltering

<u>KELLEN</u>

The smell of the ocean was long gone.

In its place was a dry heat, the scent of dusty dirt surrounded and invaded the truck we had been traveling in for two days.

Seven days I had been gone. Seven days since Oliver and Jack had kidnapped me. Now, according to Ajani, I had been sold.

Who had they sold me to? When I got there, would they realize who I was and that they had made a grave mistake?

We had not been given any food or water and my lips were cracked and dry, my attempt to wet them using my saliva and tongue was useless. I had sweated out any extra fluids my body held but the dehydration had left my muscles stiff, and along came a lack of stamina and the loss of more strength.

My lacerations had begun to heal, which meant Conri was still with me. I just couldn't feel or communicate with him. Either way, it was a good sign.

The small holes dotted along the metal wall of the truck gave us little air to breathe, the truck became like a hot box. The stiflingly thick, warm air made it hard to take oxygen into our lungs.

The truck seemed to rumble and bounce along for what

seemed like forever and my listlessness had started turning to irritability. Being stuck in this sweltering box, not knowing where my final destination was, and the fact that I had been taken so easily was starting to grate on my nerves.

I started tapping my fingers on my leg, feeling restless, when suddenly the sounds from outside changed and the scent of shifters reached my nose. I could hear distant voices, the sounds of cars, and the smell changed to one that I familiarized with the Royal Pack's city.

After a few minutes, the truck came to a rumbling stop. Were we here? Was this my final destination?

I looked at Ajani. His black skin looked pale, probably from dehydration, and his brown eyes looked defeated and sunken. He shook his head at me as if to say he didn't know.

"Will your alpha not come looking for you?" I asked him, in hopes that someone, anyone would come looking for us. That his alpha would come looking for his beta.

"No." He shook his head again, tilting it to the floor. His long braids fell over his face. "We are a small pack, and my alpha does not have the strength or numbers to find me." He sounded dejected and ashamed.

"Surely someone must be looking for you, any of you?" I said to him, then cast my eyes towards the other two men who had shared this journey.

"I am an omega, no one cares about me." The younger one said. "And this one was a rogue, so yah, no one will come looking for us." Despite our situation, this man seemed to be taking everything in his stride, like he had accepted his fate and destiny. The rogue wolf that was stuck with us had not said a word the whole journey.

"What's his deal?" I asked of the rogue.

The rogue lifted his head towards me and opened his mouth, attempting to stick out his tongue. Instead, all that was left was a small stump, showing that at some point he had had his tongue cut out. I had to assume it had been done to him because I couldn't think of any reason why someone would do that to themselves.

The doors to the back of the truck opened and a bright light came bursting through. I squinted my eyes against the harsh invasion, letting them adjust for a moment, until a skinny-looking man who I had not seen before began yelling at us to get out.

"Come on slaves!" He yelled. "Get a move on, I ain't got all day! Fucking filthy slave rogues." He grumbled at us.

Rogues? Who was he calling a rogue? He looked and smelt more like one than the rogue we were traveling with.

I hopped down from the bed of the truck, followed by Ajani and the two other men. I looked around, taking in my surroundings as they ushered us around the truck and towards a scantily looking building.

The bare, almost sand-like ground beneath my feet was hot and unforgiving, burning the soles of my feet. The heat on my back was sweltering.

"Move it!" The man said while yanking my chains. Another prodded me forward using the cattle prod as a threat that if I didn't start walking, I would be stunned - again. It wasn't fun the first few times.

I started walking to where they were ushering me, towards a red sandstone building. The entranceway was a long, caged-in walkway, and barbwire hung from the top and was around the sides, preventing either escape or intrusion. Or both.

Before we reached the building, I took in my surroundings. All of the buildings were made of the same sandstone, a much darker color than the bricks used for the Royal Palace.

I could see a market of sorts where patrons were eagerly trading and the owners of the stall called out various products that they sold. People were dressed in lighter colored clothes and mostly in a thin cotton material. Unlike the fashion of my kingdom, it seemed - simpler clothing was preferred. Probably because it was so hot out here.

When I heard a woman cry out, I spun around to see a man lifting a whip and bringing it down hard across a female I recognized from one of the other trucks. She lifted her arms in defense and cried out, "I'm sorry!"

"Fucking whore!" The man shouted as he hit her again. "Know your place, or we will be happy to make sure you know it."

The smell of her blood reached my nose, she smelled like a human. The man lifted the whip again, bringing it down equally as hard as the first time. The sound of the snapping tail connecting to her skin made me cringe and my blood boil. Without thinking I stepped out of line, ready to defend the poor girl.

I was met with resistance as I felt a hand on my bicep pulling me back.

"Young king, it is best for us to not interfere. It will do you... nor her any good." Ajani calmly spoke.

I took a step back and glanced at the poor, half-naked girl, wanting desperately to step in and give the assailant a taste of his own medicine. Ajani was right though, I could make things worse not just for myself but the girl as well. I hated to think what her fate was, but deep down I already knew.

"Are you a new fighter?" I heard the small voice that broke me from my thoughts and looked down at the young boy. His eyes were bright with wonderment and excitement.

"I don't know. Could you tell me where we are? And then maybe I can answer you." I said softly.

"You are in Bhakhil, sir. I hope I get to see you fight. You look strong." His smile spread across his face.

"Maybe you will," I replied and patted him on the head, wondering what he meant about getting to see me fight.

At the entrance of the caged walkway was a woman who was handing out small, cotton sacks. She turned to the young boy and called to him, "Nicolai! Leave them be. We are not allowed to speak to them. Alpha will have me punished!"

I furrowed my brows at her words and the expression of pure terror in her eyes. What kind of place was this where the Alpha would punish a mother and son for speaking to someone kindly? Or that they would hold fear of speaking with the... what was I, a slave? That's what I was. A slave.

What was more confusing was that when I came up to the woman, whose son was now standing by her side, I was handed one of the sacks. I peered into it to find a bottle of water, an apple, a chunk of bread, and a toothbrush with a small tube of toothpaste.

I guess they wanted us to have nice teeth, I thought. Goddess, I felt like I had stepped into a time warp, another realm, yet I was only on the other continent. How could things be this different here compared to home?

As I thanked the woman for the bag and supplies, I leaned in close to her and lowered my voice to a barely audible whisper.

"Please... If there is any way you can contact Queen Lamia

of Riocht or MacTire, please tell her where I am. My name is Kellen." I left out my rank, my gut telling me it would be wise to omit that little piece of information right now.

The woman gave a small gasp at the mention of Lamia's name. "The Queen of Shifters?" she asked in a hushed tone, her hazel eyes wide and darting around us. Then her face turned to stone as she peered over my shoulder, and she cleared her throat. "Please move on, we are not allowed to talk to common slaves." She said it loudly enough for the guards to hear, then turned her back to me.

I sighed and moved along the walkway. I didn't know if she could or even would try to reach out to Lamia for me. I knew I was taking a chance by asking a stranger, but I had to try.

At least she recognized Lamia's name. As every shifter should.

When Lamia and Mathias were crowned, a wave of change rippled across the realm and every shifter's counterpart felt the transfer of power to the new King and Queen of Shifters. Not everyone would be a friend or be happy about it, but they would know, and their animal counterpart would acknowledge their crowning.

We were shoved through the walkway and the hair on the back of my neck began to stand up. I had a feeling I wasn't going to like what came next, even less than being in my current situation. I watched the mute rogue step up to the doorway of the building first before they dragged him inside.

His mute cries could be heard from outside. I looked towards Ajani, whose eyes were shifting from left to right, trying to find a way out. He, too, was more than worried about what we were about to encounter.

Next was the omega, then it was my turn. When I stepped up to the doorway, two guards grabbed an arm each and a third used a cattle prod to shock me. It wasn't enough to knock me out, but just enough for my limbs to become slack.

A fourth man stood in front of me. He was a big guy, older, but at some point he must have held a rank. I could smell beta on him. He held up a large, metal syringe. "You are now the property of Alpha Vargr of the Dessert Moon Pack. Your life belongs to him for as long as you are useful or until he tires of you." He said without any emotion, but then a sick smirk curled up on the grimy-looking man's face as he edged closer with the needle. His peppered scruff hid the deep lines that marred him, which made him look all the more sinister.

I didn't have time to react when the third man grabbed my hair to yank my head down and the syringe was plunged into my neck.

A deep, burning sensation spread throughout my neck and into my head. The men let go of me as I grabbed the sides of my face, trying not to yell out at the agonizing feeling. It was like my head was literally ready to explode, and I fell to my knees with excruciating pain.

I then felt the silver cuffs being removed from my wrists. The spiked prongs pulled from the skin and I rubbed them, pushing the pounding and searing pain in my head to the side. The ones on my ankles came off and I sighed at the relief.

'Kellen...' I heard Conri call out to me, but all too soon he was gone again. His voice in my mind sounded panicked and pained, much like I was feeling. I called to him and again was met with silence.

What the fuck did they do to me?

Soon the pain began to subside; I hadn't even noticed that they had dragged me towards the back of the building and were shoving me into a cell. They tossed me in without another word, throwing the small sack in after me.

At least now I knew where I was and who owned me. Now all I had to do was somehow get the fuck out of here. I rubbed the back of my neck where they had injected me and felt a small, raised lump. My neck and head still throbbed and burned from whatever the substance was. I then began to rub my wrists and ankles again.

Looking down, I noticed they had already started to heal and close up. The lacerations on my back were a little slower to heal, but I could feel the wounds begin to close and the skin start threading itself back together.

They had tossed the rogue, omega, and Ajani in cells as small as mine, next to me.

"Get some sleep slave fighters. Tomorrow, you travel to the Dessert Moon Pack where your new destiny begins." The man began to laugh heartily, like this was a game or some big joke to him. He laughed like he knew something we didn't.

The rogue and omega wolves both curled up and found sleep fast, worn out from the lack of food and water and whatever it was that they just did us. I looked at Ajani; he looked tired, but like me, I knew he would either fight the sleep or sleep would never claim him.

"A few years back, my alpha and I had heard about a bear king named Orion and this Alpha Vargr's daughter, Shayna, who had made an implant that could control your spirit animal... amongst various other things. I had not believed it to be true until now." He sighed while rubbing the back of his neck.

"Orion and the bitch are dead," I told him. I was surprised to hear him mention Orion, and then when he told me about this alpha's daughter who had supposedly bought us, I put two and two together. Shayna was the bitch who attacked

Lamia and Mike killed her, right before he almost killed Finnegan.

"I watched his body burn after the battle of Riocht." I explained. He nodded his head in acknowledgment.

"This is a good thing. I had heard the tales of this king who stole young shifters and turned them into monsters. This Alpha Vargr, I do not know much, but I have been told he buys shifters and half breeds for his entertainment... for his pleasure. His Luna is said to be deranged and just as cruel." He whispered the information to me, eyes full of sorrow and a hint of fear glistened in them as he recanted the story. I wondered what exactly we were going to face when we arrived at the Dessert Moon Pack.

"I am the Queen's Knight, they will come looking for me," I told him, mustering as much confidence in my words as I could, even though I wasn't holding much of my own right now.

I hoped to offer him some aspirations.

The day turned to night and as the sun went down, the air became chilled. I looked towards the small window and could just make out the night sky, full of twinkling stars. The sky was so vast and bright, again reminding me of nights when Mike, Lamia, and I would sit in the royal gardens and lay underneath the stars. Talking about our futures and what we had wished would come to pass.

That time seemed so far away now, our lives taking different paths than what we had thought. Especially Lamia's.

I closed my eyes and opened my mind, thinking of her and the other three knights. Just one second of connection through the link was all I needed. I felt a pressure building behind my eyes and blew out a breath in frustration as I was met with blankness.

'I am here.' The faint whisper of Conri was heard and I perked up.

'Conri? Thank goddess!' I mentally exclaimed to my wolf.

'I am weak, but I am here. I need to heal,' he replied before retreating again.

A new hope rose within me, and for the first time in seven days I felt a little clarity. For the first time since my parents had died, a small smile crept onto my face.

Conri was not gone, he was still with me. I would need him and his strength to get out of here; I just had to give him time to heal. Then we could show these asshats my true rank and power.

Chapter 4 – A Knights first Quest

LAMIA
5 DAYS AFTER KELLEN DISAPPEARED

I was the strongest wolf in the realm. One of the most skilled battle strategists known! I was strong!

At least I was physically… but mentally?

I exhaled a long, slow breath.

Mentally I wasn't strong, not when it came to matters of the heart. I believed in our fate wholeheartedly and believed in the Moon Goddess' path for us.

My mother had said to me not that long ago, "Your greatest weakness is your love, but it is also your greatest strength".

We need to find Kellen. I need to find Kellen. I promised him forever. Maybe not the forever we thought we were going to have at one point, but either way, I would always be by his side.

Mathias came into our room with a cold compress, leaned me forward, and pressed it against my back. "How are you doing?" His concern for me was evident in his voice and I could feel his worry through the bond.

"I need to get out there; I need to be with Mike." I stated with a sigh.

"Abso-fucking-lutely NOT!" Was his reply. "You are in no

condition to go anywhere. You will stay here where it is safe." I heard the command in his voice, but I ignored it. His steeled gaze glared at me, daring me to argue with him.

I knew he was right, and I knew I had no business traipsing around all over the kingdoms, but I needed to be there with Mike.

Five days ago, I collapsed when I felt like my back was being ripped open. It wasn't my pain I was feeling - it was Kellen's. Wherever he was, they were torturing him. I couldn't reach his wolf and I had determined that along with whatever was being done to him, they had also suppressed Conri.

Mathias rushed me to the pack doctor. That's when we found out that I was carrying triplets and they were all growing at an exceedingly fast rate.

The doctor explained that it was probably the cause of my larger than usual three-month belly and that the pups or cubs or whatever I was carrying were draining me. Coupled with the stress of Kellen going AWOL and then feeling his pain, I had been put on bed rest.

Of course, Mathias was taking this all a little too seriously and didn't understand mine and my wolf's need to find Kellen.

I felt absolutely useless.

I recalled a memory; the night of our eighteenth birthday, after our wolves rejected each other. He came in, right before the party, to give me my present and I gave him his. The watch he never took off. The inscription on the back of the watch was the reason for the memory.

'Our bond is as timeless as our friendship and love – L'.

I knew then that I would always love him, that he would

always own a piece of me, a piece of my heart.

When I last saw him, it wasn't just a goodbye, he was letting me go. And I was thankful. I loved him, but I was not in love with him.

Kellen had a mate out there somewhere and I wanted him to find her. Yet selfishly, a part of me would be jealous, just the thought made me shift uneasily. I wouldn't be his girl anymore.

What kind of a woman did that make me?

I looked down at my rounded belly. The doctor said I was three months pregnant, and gave a sarcastic laugh.

A wolf shifter's gestation period was six to seven months and a bear shifter's was seven to eight, or maybe even nine months. But who really knew with mine and Mathias' DNA?

So, we were extrememly surprised when we visited the pack doctor and learned that I had *three* little pups growing inside me. The kicker was that they were fraternal triplets. Three separate eggs were fertilized and we had no idea if they would be cubs, pups, humans, or something different.

Mathias had been walking around with his chest puffed out, shoulders back, and head held high proudly since the day we found out.

That was three days ago, two days after Kellen went missing. Those two days I had felt his pain.

"Little Wolf, I need to help Travis with the paperwork..." He looked at me sadly, reluctant to leave me alone. "It should only take a couple of hours," he said, trying to find his own justification for leaving me.

I gave him a small smile and a slight laugh. "Go... and thank you, King, for taking care of our pack. I know you need to go back to the clan soon as well." He was helping Travis and Josiah fill out the paperwork for them to transition to alpha and beta, papers that needed to be sent to the council.

He and Xander also needed to return to the Kodiak Kingdom, to the Clan Mansion. Abner Brooks and Tobias had been running things so far, but now Tobias was with Mike trying to get a lead on Kellen's whereabouts.

"I could always come back home with you," I suggested hopefully.

"Maybe, we will see. Abner said Finnegan had woken up and was well enough for questioning. We can talk about this later, when I am done, yeah?" He said, kissing me sweetly before he headed out the door and left me to my thoughts.

I let the cold compress fall from my back, placed it on the nightstand, and then leaned back against my headboard.

I couldn't go to Mike, but there had to be a way I could help find Kellen.

I sighed and tapped my belly. I couldn't sit here and do nothing, but there was no way Mathias was letting me go to look for Kellen. We already had that argument and I lost when Rhett and Travis both took his side. Hunji stayed out of it as usual.

Hunji, where are you? I opened a mind-link to him and he wasted no time in responding.

On the training fields, Your Majesty.

Meet me in your office, and don't tell anyone where you are going or that you are meeting with me.

Yes ma'am. He replied and I cut the link, getting up from my bed and scurrying out of the room and down to his office.

When Hunji entered his office, he found me sitting at his seat, behind his desk. It was the comfiest chair. His office wasn't like mine; it consisted of a desk, his chair, two other chairs, and a small table.

His office was decorated very much like himself, simple and to the point, which is what I wanted to get to right now.

He took a seat in a chair opposite me, looking a little out of place and unseated.

"Hunji, I won't beat about the bush. We all know King has pretty much grounded me." I laughed a the term I used for Mathias' controlling behavior.

"Yep, but I have to agree with him. You are in a delicate state, even for a shifter. With the rate you are growing, I wouldn't be surprised if you gave birth in two months." Hunji tipped his head at my belly, a grin playing at the corner of his lips.

"Don't even joke about that Hunji." I grumbled, rolling my eyes at him. "Look, I will get straight to the point. I have a job for you."

He cocked one of his eyebrows, his dark eyes held curiosity. He was intrigued and shifted to sit more comfortably in the chair.

"Go on." He spoke.

I sat up straighter, my eyes meeting his and holding his dark gaze. Hunji was different; no one knew much about his past except that he came from Asiarian and that he was a skilled fighter, quick and composed. He was the only wolf who had ever been able to knock me off my feet and for this I held high regard for him. That and he was loyal to me, my protector. He had stood by my side since the first day I had met him. He and his wolf were the first to pledge their allegiance to me.

"As a Knight of the Queen, I am tasking you with your first quest. Find Kellen in my place. Use whatever means necessary. You will have the full support of our kingdom as well as the New Moon's. I want you to meet up with Mike and I want you to bring Kellen home." There was finality and command in my voice. This was not up for negotiation.

I could trust Hunji with this task and knew he could find my best friend. It wasn't that I didn't have confidence in Mike, it was nothing like that at all. Mike was a skilled investigator, but I knew Hunji was one of the best trackers around and Mike needed help. I would never say it out loud, but if Hunji had been allowed to lead the search team for me, I was sure I would have been found sooner.

"Pardon my response, Your Highness, but what makes you think I can find him when there are already numerous parties searching for him? Or what makes you think I can do any better than Tobias or Mike?"

"Because you see things that aren't always apparent, it's like a sixth sense, Hunji's hunch. Your hunches are always spot on and if anyone can track his whereabouts, it's you."

"When would you like me to leave?" He asked, not even batting an eyelash at my request. Another reason why I loved him so much, always the wise, calm, and collected wolf who would follow me to the pits of the underworld.

"As soon as possible. King has to go back to his clan. He wants to take Xander so he can run the territory and I am going with them. Supposedly, Finn woke up."

"And Mathias is letting you travel with him?" He drew the question out, curiously asking but already knowing the answer.

"Well, he hasn't said yes *yet*..." I smiled a cheeky grin and waggled my eyebrows, "but he will. I am sure we will take Birdie so it won't be so taxing on me. Do you want to come with us, and that way you..."

"NO!" He shot out the word, waving his hands in front of him. "Nope, I can leave today, and go by car."

I laughed loudly at him. "What, you don't want to fly in Birdie?" I joked.

His dark eyes narrowed at me and his lips tightened into a thin line. "There is no chance in hell I am getting into that flying death trap. Shifters don't fly!" His one hand cut horizontally through the air as if to say his words were final, not up for discussion.

I couldn't help but chuckle. I was pretty sure that was the same thing I said when I first saw Birdie. I admit though, that it is a much faster way of traveling and wondered why shifters stopped using that mode of transportation over 250 years ago when the shifter wars came about.

It was agreed that Hunji would leave later today, after finishing up some paperwork for the training schedule. Now all I had to do was convince Mathias that he needed to take me with him back to his kingdom.

A little while later, once I had gone back to our chambers, I sent Ria a mind-link asking her to come up to the room. I was grateful that she now had the ability to be linked by me, it came about when her brother Rhett became a knight. Once he had the ability to mind-link, for whatever reason, the same ability was given to Ria. It just took us a little longer to realize it.

I smelt her scent before she had even knocked on the door and called for her to come in.

"Hey what's up Lam's?" She said, coming in and closing the door behind her.

Ria and Xander had been taking things slowly. Although it was killing Xander on a hormonal level, he was patient with her. Something Ria appreciated. She hadn't been very receptive to shifters after she was almost taken when I first met her and Rhett.

I could tell she was in love with Xander, her eyes lit up every time he walked into a room and she would blush at the mention of his name.

"I need to ask, have you made up your mind about whether you will be returning to the Kodiak Kingdom with Xander or not?" I walked back into my closet and took a bag out, putting it on the bed.

"Kind of... Are you going somewhere?" she asked, obviously noticing the bag I had just put on the bed and began stuffing some underwear in it.

"Don't try and change the subject," I paused to look at her as she crossed the room and slumped onto the end of my bed.

"I want to..." She let out a big sigh and flopped backward. "But I'm not sure. It's a really big step, Lamia. We haven't even... umm... you know... mated."

I let out a small laugh as her cheeks became flushed with embarrassment. "Do you want to mate with him?" I looked at her and raised a quizzical brow.

"Well, yah. It's just, I don't know," her blush deepened and spread from her cheeks down to her chest and below the low-cut blouse she was wearing. "I have never done it... What if I'm no good?" She mumbled shyly.

"Lamia, he has so much experience and I don't! Don't laugh at me, what if I... What if I disappoint him?"

"Oh, my goddess girl!" I threw my head back in laughter. "First of all, you don't have to worry about disappointing him, and second of all, he will worship you. That, I can promise." I pointed at her.

I sat down beside her and took her hands in mine, her blue-green eyes peered at me, "I need you to come to the Kodiak Kingdom. I have to go with Mathias and speak with Finn but the only way he will let me go is if you and Xander advocate for me."

She nodded her head. "Basically, if I go and say I want you with me because I am scared... the brothers will cave?"

"Exactly my goal," I said and stood back up to grab more things to pack in my bag. "Ria, a mate bond is hard to look away from, even harder to walk away from. Xander loves you with all his heart and I know you have fallen for him. Once we get to the Clan Mansion, I am sure everything will fall into place for you."

"What about Rhett? And what do I know about being a den mother?" she huffed.

"A den mother is the same role as a Luna, and you have been filling that role here at MacTire for over two years now. I have confidence that you will do just as excellent there and be loved just as much. As for Rhett, he has his own path and that path right now is to serve Alpha Travis as his third in command."

She stood up and headed for the door. "Right, I'm off to go convince my mate to convince his brother that you need to come to the Kodiak Kingdom with us. Did I get that right?" she said, turning around before opening the door.

"Thank you, Ria."

She smiled before slipping through the door and out of sight. I definitely owed that girl a favor.

Chapter 5 – The Babysitter

MIKE
8 DAYS AFTER THE DISAPPEARANCE OF KELLEN

A failure, that's what I was. I had failed my king, my best friend, Lamia, and most of all, our kingdom.

I was meant to be the Royal Beta. Once sworn in, I would become the second most powerful wolf in our kingdom. How was I supposed to be powerful and take charge when I couldn't even keep our king safe?

I had let my guard down. I had let our king disappear.

It had now been just over a week since Kellen had gone missing. Poof! Vanished into thin air! Mathias had sent Tobias to help me look for him that first day and we came up empty-handed. The next day, I had trackers across the continent scouring the kingdoms for him.

Tobias had sent a mass email out to all the clan alphas in their kingdom asking them to search for the missing Wolf King. I had also called Tawny and told her what had happened, although Lamia had beaten me to it, and they already had what little warriors they could spare looking for him in their kingdom.

When I first called my father, I thought for sure he and Uncle Marcus would scold me. At the very least, hold some kind of disappointment in me, however, that wasn't the case. They were more concerned about how he could have gone missing, and how there was no trace of him.

The truth was, we were all on edge, getting the same vibes as when Lamia disappeared. It took us weeks, almost months, when we finally got that break and found a lead as to where Lamia was. By the time we found her, the damage had already been done, and I feared the same for Kellen.

"Hey want to hit the bar with me?" Tobias asked as he stepped out of the bathroom dressed in a pair of dark jeans and a royal blue button-up shirt, his curly brown hair still damp from his shower.

I just shook my head 'no'.

"Come on dude, loosen up, we have been searching for a week straight. Something will turn up." He said as he crossed the hotel room we had been sharing for the past week.

I turned to him, agitated, and the snap in my voice was obvious. "And would *you* be able to go out and party if it was Mathias that was missing? If it was your best friend that... just upped and disappeared, without a trace?" I cocked an eyebrow at him. My wolf was on the surface as he, too, was feeling defeated and miserable.

"Mike, man, we are doing everything we can. We will find him." His voice wasn't harsh, but he was holding back. I could tell he didn't like my tone when I spoke to him.

"Just fuck off and go get high, find some female to fuck." I again snapped at him and turned my back, then carried on reviewing the map I had sitting in front of me at the small table.

I was marking off where we had looked for Kellen and plotting several radiuses around where he went missing. I heard the hotel door open and then slam shut. I slouched over and put my head in my hands, glaring at the map.

"Where the fuck are you, Kellen, where did you go?" I said to nobody as I still studied the map and growled at my frustration.

My phone dinged and I picked it up to see a message from Hunji. 'Your block is up. I will be there by morning.'

Great! Just fucking great! Now Lamia has sent me a babysitter.

I rubbed my tired eyes for the millionth time. The threat of tears was there, but I would not cry. The welling of my eyes was not from sadness, but rather frustration. Once Hunji got here, I was planning on heading east, towards the coast to widen the search.

I didn't hate that Hunji was coming, he was a skilled tracker and I knew he could only help my search. I did resent the fact he would be here though, it just meant I wasn't trusted. It made me feel like Lamia had no confidence in me, that I wasn't a good enough beta to find our king.

Well, why would they think any differently? After all, I was the one who lost him. I just couldn't wrap my head around how he could have disappeared. If he was taken, how could he even let them? I mean come on, it's not like he was some weak omega or human, we are talking about the King of fucking Wolves! He's the most lethal wolf in all the New Moon Kingdom, for goddess's sake.

If he was snatched…

I shook my head at the thought; I just couldn't see how that was possible. How could he have gone to the bathroom and then vanished? He didn't leave through the front door, I would have seen him when I was waiting in the car, so it was obvious he had to have gone out the back.

The lack of cameras in the diner we had eaten at pissed

me off beyond belief. If their cameras had been operational, we would have been able to track him easily or at least know exactly what happened.

I didn't bother replying to Hunji, instead, I lifted my block and my head was almost immediately filled with Lamia's angelic voice.

Hey, how are you holding up? Did Hunji get a hold of you? Her non-condescending voice was music to my ears, all I detected was love, compassion, and a boatload of worry in her tone.

Yah, said he should be here by morning I heard the weariness in my own voice as I linked her back.

Good, I am on my way to the Kodiak Kingdom. Finn woke up. She paused and I waited. *Mike, I sent Hunji because I can't be there, there is no way Mathias is going to let me go search with you.*

Why wouldn't he let you come here? I asked out of true curiosity. I knew she was pregnant, but that shouldn't slow her down. I would never think something like that would slow her down or get in the way of her and Kellen.

Because... Because I'm carrying triplets, I'm lucky he let me fly to his kingdom. The doctor wanted me on bed rest.

Holy shit, triplets! I chuckled through the mind-link, it was the first time I had found anything to make me smile in the last week. *Wow! I'm gonna be an uncle to three. The Moon Goddess really made it up to you.* It was a light-hearted joke, but as soon as I said it I wondered if I had said the wrong thing, thinking of how she had lost her first pup.

She must have felt my worry because she chuckled back at me. *Yeah either that or it's a punishment.*

Her tone turned serious with her next words. *I will keep

you posted on what Finn says, and just let me know if you find anything... And Mike? You will find him, I know you will. I love you.*

I love you too. And I hope so. She cut the link after that and I closed my eyes, leaning back in the rickety chair I sat in, pinching my nose between my thumb and forefinger.

The door to the hotel room opened suddenly and I jumped, looking to see Tobias enter. I hadn't been expecting him until way later.

"Back early, aren't you?" I questioned.

"Yeah. I sat there, had a drink, met a female... but it wasn't the same. I kept thinking about what if it was Mat or Xander? I'm sorry Mike. It's just we have been at this for days now and I don't see a break, my beast was getting strung up. I thought a little relief might help, but he wasn't interested." He sighed and sat on his bed next to mine.

"Hunji will be here in the morning," I told him and watched his face fall. Did he not like Hunji?

"Yeah, that's good. Try and get some sleep, ya?" He said while stripping off his clothes, then climbed under his covers.

I turned the light off and sat on my bed, still fully clothed. I hadn't slept in eight days; I doubted it would claim me tonight. I wanted to run but both Duke and I didn't have it in us to even bother to shift. A pang of heavy guilt was weighing on us, making our guts churn with the thought of: what if we don't find him? What if we don't get him back?

*****

Somehow, I managed to sleep. I hadn't even realized that I drifted off until I was awoken by the loud banging on the other side of our hotel door.

"Tell him to fuck off," Tobias grumbled from the bed beside me. I gave him a quick glance as I hopped up from my still sitting position to open the door for a very annoying Hunji.

I knew it was him just as Tobias did, his scent had hit me as soon as I opened my eyes.

"Coffee," Hunji said, and thrusted a drink holder into my hand. "And you need a shower, you smell like a rogue." He peered at me, scrunching his nose in disgust.

"Well, good morning to you too, sunshine." Tobias yawned and stretched his limbs out, waking up. He stood from the bed naked as the day he was born.

"Go put some clothes on Tobias, no want's that little thing waving in their face." Hunji deadpanned, indicating that Tobias' dick was less than average.

"Excuse me! There is nothing small about my manhood, I'll have you know!" Tobias feigned hurt but grabbed his dick in his hand and started flopping it side to side. "See, nice and big and not even at full attention." He smirked.

"For fuck's sake man, put it away," I grumbled, trying to find the humor in the banter but failing miserably. I could already tell that the three of us traveling together could go one of two ways between Hunji and Tobias.

Either they kill each other, my money was on Hunji, or they become the best of friends.

I went to take a shower as Hunji suggested and when I walked out freshly washed and in clean clothes, Tobias and Hunji were standing over the small table in our room studying the map I had been going over for the past week.

I walked up behind them and pointed to the red circles I

had made on the map. "Here, here, and here are where we have searched. These lines here indicate where trackers and warriors have been sent out to search for him or any clues."

"Mike," Hunji said with a somber tone, "don't let regret and the feeling of defeat determine your path." He placed his hand on my shoulder, lightly squeezing it while turning to face me, those emotionless dark eyes peering right into my soul. "You will find yourself wanting and lacking. Look forward, young wolf. Hope is a path that leads us to clarity."

I should be used to Hunji's cryptic phrases of inspiration by now. He was right, I knew he was right. Duke, my wolf, hummed in agreement with Hunji's words of wisdom. I also knew he could feel my emotions rolling off of me, which was why he tried to offer me words of comfort.

"This is where he disappeared from. These are the areas we have checked, and also any operational business cameras." I carried on after clearing my throat and swallowing down my emotions. "We came up empty-handed. I wanted to move eastwards, towards the coast. My wolf seems to think we should head that way too."

I had been grasping at straws this whole time, but my gut was pushing me this way. Every time I cast my eyes across the map, my eyes found their way to the same place. The Cheregwen Pack. A pack located on the coast with a shipping and receiving port. It was actually a place I had visited before with Kellen, the Alpha of that pack ran an export business that the Royal family owned.

"Trust your wolf. His instincts will give you your gut feelings, so if you both feel drawn to a place, we should go. Chances are there's something there. Let's get a move on." Hunji stood up, looking between Tobias and me.

"I'm going to?" Tobias looked at us in surprise.

"Yes, you are under your king's orders to assist us, are you not?" Hunji scowled at him.

"Well, yah but…"

"Tobias, if you don't want to go, then don't." I was irritable at his attitude and clenched my fists tightly, trying not to let my wolf come to the surface as the irritation turned to a slowly simmering anger.

"It's not that, Mike, I just didn't think you guys wanted my help or wanted me there. I mean, you wolves are pretty tight-knit, ya know?" Tobias palmed the back of his neck sheepishly, obviously embarrassed by his confession.

I dropped my shoulders, my fists unclenched and became loose, and my features softened. I had automatically assumed he wanted nothing to do with the Wolf Kingdom or finding Kellen. I didn't even cross my mind that maybe he felt unwanted or would feel left out.

Now that I knew he wanted to be a part of this and wasn't just here because of King, I felt even more of an ass for being so angry at him.

"Yeah, we want you with us dude," I told him, clapping his shoulders for reassurance. I had no idea he had felt this insecure.

Tobias was a handful, but he was smart and if we got into a fight, his brute strength would come in handy. Plus, his tracking skills were almost on par with Hunji's.

All three of us held a second-in-command position. There was no reason we couldn't find something to trace Kellen if we combined our strengths and skills.

"Then I suggest we get a move on." Hunji declared, rising from the chair again. "We will take my car, my bag's already in there, get your shit together and let's go."

With that, we shoved our shit into our bags, piled into the car, and headed east, coastal bound. I was feeling a little more relaxed and instead of feeling like I was being babysat, I was grateful that Lamia had sent Hunji and I was hopeful that the three of us could figure out what happened to Kellen.

Chapter 6 – My Reality

KELLEN

The morning after they stuck me in the back of the neck with that large needle that made me feel like my brain was an inferno, I found myself being transported again with the same three men, the beta, the omega, and the mute rogue.

They had ushered us into an open-back truck with our little sack of supplies. They had put silver cuffs on us again, but thankfully without the spikes this time.

The truck slowly moved through the town, down the dirt and stony road. The truck bounced and jarred us around and the hot sun beat down upon our bare skin, causing the skin on my still-healing back to be pulled tight. The dried blood and skin pulled tightly and caused me slight discomfort.

I lifted my hand to the back of my neck, feeling the hard, small lump that sat just below the surface of the skin. I wasn't a hundred percent sure what they injected into me, but by the feel of it, it was a kind of chip, maybe?

I could feel Conri stirring in the back of my mind but his communication with me was limited, and I wasn't sure if that was by his choice or not. I was just thankful he was there. If I could feel him then I knew he was still with me.

Ranked wolves had better communication with their animal spirits, unlike omegas or rogues. We were able to have more open communication with them and a closer relationship with our counterparts. So, to feel Conri like this and not have that closeness made me wonder if this was what omegas experienced.

I wiped the sweat from my brow as the truck jerked and I looked around at my surroundings as we passed them by. We were definitely in a wolf pack, I determined as my nose had caught the scent of pack wolves.

One guard sat with us in the open truck bed and two more trailed behind the truck on horses, carrying the dreaded cattle prods as they sat high and mighty on the backs of the beautiful animals.

As a shifter, I never bothered to ride a horse. There was no need, we either took a car or shifted, our animals being able to match the speed of a horse easily. I had seen them used in the human towns in our kingdom, on the fields, but I have never seen a shifter ride one before. I pondered at the thought of why they would be riding the horses, utterly confused. I wanted to ask them, but they didn't seem very friendly and I really didn't want to get shocked again.

We passed several buildings, all built with the same red clay and sandstone as the rest of the places I had seen. The buildings were all single-story and low to the ground with red-tiled roofs. The residents mulled around shopping in the market and the ones that passed by us shrunk towards the wall of the buildings as if in cower. I raised an eyebrow at their odd behavior.

One man dared to look as we rolled by him, he had stopped talking on his phone and stared at us, more particularly at me. His mouth hung open slightly and strained to remember if his face seemed familiar. It did not.

What caught my attention the most was his lavish clothing, not a suit but a thin, silk coat with gold trim and a pair of fine cotton white pants. So different from the clothing we wore in my kingdom. Even the women seemed to wear a strange fashion of long, light-colored dresses with a pinafore of some color over their cotton attire.

I heard a cry from behind me and turned to see what was going on. On the side of the road stood several young women, completely naked. A man was beating one with a stick.

"Good for nothing whore!" he shouted at her while cracking the lithe stick across her legs and ass. "You take it and accept it. Next time you bite you fucking half-breed, you will be sold to the Delta House!" He screamed at the poor girl as she whimpered and cowered from him.

I looked at the guard in the back of the truck with us and raised a brow at him.

"Fuckin' half-breeds need to know their place." He laughed and showed me a smile full of rotten teeth.

Half-breeds, I thought. I tried to catch a scent from the women, but we were now too far. "Half-breeds?" I dared to ask him.

"Yeah, human shifter hybrids, ain't good for nothing but fucking." He laughed again.

"Humans?"

"Quiet Slave! Before I use this on you!" One of the men on the horses came up beside the truck and waved the cattle prod at me.

I bit back the growl that was ready to leave my chest, and I felt my wolf stir at the disrespect this guard had shown us. I would love nothing more than to tear the disgusting prick shreds, yet something in my gut told me to not lash out. I could only assume my gut feeling was Conri.

A few miles after passing through the town, the two trucks holding us and a few females, along with the guards that trailed behind, approached a very large and very tall wall that seemed to span for hundreds of feet. The wall looked to be constructed in the same sandstone as the buildings from the town.

On the far side of the wall, sitting high up with its roof kissing the cloudless blue sky, sat an elaborate building akin to a palace with several spires. The structure looked smaller than the Royal Palace but larger than a pack mansion, yet it was too far away to determine its true size.

I noticed no flags or colors flew from the spires.

It appeared like the palace was inside the walls of this place.

We came to an abrupt stop outside a small door in the wall. This was not the main entrance, that I could tell just by looking at it.

"Out, out!" The guard hustled us.

We were pushed towards the metal door that looked out of place against the plain texture of the wall. The door opened and led to a long dark tunnel. I was thankful for the darkness, as it was much cooler than the harsh rays of the sun, and my body began to cool down instantly, my eyes adjusting to the darkness as we ventured further into the boundary of the imposing wall.

"Keep moving!" A guard bristled, prodding a few of us as we passed by him to make us move a little faster. Either that, or the guy just wanted to be an ass.

At the end of the dark tunnel, I saw a bright light illuminating the entrance, and when I thought about it, it gave me a sense of doom. The stories that people describe about a light at the end of the tunnel before they meet the Moon Goddess seemed a believable notion at this moment.

I took a deep breath, not because I was scared, far from it. It was more the anticipation of what I would find at the end of the tunnel. In truth, I was curious, despite my situation, about where I was and what I was in for.

I kept my eyes wide open and alert as we emerged from the darkness into the bright and heated light of the day. The sun caused my eyes to squint for a few seconds until they once again adjusted to the stark contrast.

"Line up, slaves!" A new guard bellowed at us. "My name is Baron. You will call me Beta or Sir. Is that clear?" No one said anything. "I SAID IS THAT CLEAR, SLAVES!"

A whip cracked behind us, making the omega jump. "Yes Sir," the omega and Ajani said in unison.

"You!" The beta pointed at the rogue. "You will address me as Beta or Sir!" The rogue bowed his head to the beta. "Speak you, idiot!" The beta spat at him and then backhanded the rogue.

The rogue stumbled slightly but squared his shoulders as he stood straight and looked up past the beta, not daring to make eye contact. I saw another guard come up behind the rogue with a whip and lift it - ready to strike.

"Beta Baron, sir!" I called out. The guard paused his action, hand held high, poised, and ready to administer a lashing. The beta turned to me and was in front of my face in two strides. "Beta Baron, the rogue has no tongue. He is mute. His bow was to acknowledge your words." I said in desperation to hopefully stop the rogue from taking an unnecessary beating.

"You dare to look me in the eye, pretty boy?" He sneered.

"I should give you a lashing just for the audacity." His eyes wandered over me and looked me up and down. A look of pure disgust was on his face, and when he began to push his aura out, I stood tall. His rank and aura did not affect me, even in my wolf's weakened state.

I stared into the poor excuse of a beta's eyes, his murky blues glaring at mine. I called on Conri, hoping to exert a little of my power, and luckily for me, he responded. I pushed my aura slightly toward the beta, all the while still holding eye contact.

The beta huffed and dropped his eyes from me, though I didn't fail to see the surprise in them before he averted his gaze back to the rogue. A look of bewilderment sat on his features as he took a step back. I internally smiled, pleased that he now knew my rank was higher than his.

Even though I couldn't do anything about my predicament at that moment, I knew it was just a matter of time. It would be foolish of me to try anything right now; I was outnumbered and still had no idea where I was or what kind of slavery I had been thrown into. Everything about this was so bizarre and I needed all the facts before I could make a move and attempt an escape.

"Slaves, welcome to the Sandstorm Royal Pack. You are now the property of Alpha Vargr! He has purchased each of you. Henceforth this day, you will be a slave to this pack and serve as entertainment. You will be known as Gladiators."

My head snapped up, my eyebrows knitting together. Gladiator? Did he say, gladiator? Surely, I must have misheard?

'We did not.' Conri's voice filled my head, and it was a welcoming sound making me breathe just a little easier.

"Tomorrow, you will face your first challenge. Tomorrow

you will either live or die, but today is the beginning of the rest of your lives. Do well in the games and you will be rewarded. Follow the rules and you will live an easy life as a slave. If you try to deviate from the rules, you will suffer, or you will die." The beta bellowed, his voice droning on.

As he spoke, I looked around and took note of every entrance, exit, guard, and their position. Only then did I noticed that we were standing in a large, open arena. On the north side of the arena were a vast number of stone steps arranged like continuous bleachers or seating for an outdoor auditorium.

The internal walls hosted various entryways, like the one we walked through. I wondered where each of them led to. On the south wall, there were archways like windows with bars across them, either to keep someone out or more likely to keep something in. On the west and east side of the arena, the entryways were either open or had a metal door blocking off the passage behind them.

As I stood there, still in the same pair of black boxers I had been kidnapped in over a week ago, I couldn't help but laugh. This couldn't be real, could it? I felt like I had been transported back in time, to an age that was briefly brought up in history, to a place that was something straight out of a movie.

I knew what a gladiator was, but surely this man who calls himself a beta couldn't mean the same thing?

Still in a daze, my mind not comprehending the rest of Beta Baron's words, I felt Ajani nudge me. I looked at him and then at the guard who was leading us towards another entrance on the south wall, towards the structures with the barred windows.

We took a step or two down into the covered building that

lined this side of the arena. Still holding my sack of supplies, I followed Ajani down and inside.

It was dark, only a limited amount of light reached inside the building, just enough to see and not be shrouded by darkness. It smelt musty and damp, coupled with the scent of old sand and wood shavings. There was the distinct smell of blood, some fresh and some old. The coopery tang to the blood permanently ground into the floors and walls of what looked like they used to be holding cells.

The loud bang and clanking of a barred door brought me out of my observance. I looked behind me to find we had been closed in, the only way out barricaded by a cell door.

"These are your new digs. Find an empty cot or sleep on the floor. You will be given three meals a day, eat or don't eat." One of the guards yelled to use through the bars and then turned away and left the four of us to discover this place for ourselves.

I looked at my three travel buddies. The omega's eyes were wide and I knew he could smell the underlying scent of death that surrounded us. The rogue ventured forward, I assumed to find a cot, and Ajani had a perplexed look on his face, which I was sure mirrored my own.

I walked further into the building and realized we were not alone.

Chapter 7 – His Games, Her Torture

TALA

"I will not marry him, Mother!"

"He has been chosen for you, Tala. You are expected to mate within your rank and that is what you will do!" I groaned loudly in frustration at my mother's words, clenching my fists tightly and trying not to let out the scream that was bubbling at the surface of my mouth.

"Exactly! He has been chosen for me! I didn't choose him, and he certainly didn't choose me! I am twenty-one years old, and I'm still not allowed to make my own decisions!" I was beyond frustrated and rubbed my eyes harshly with my palms, gritting my teeth tightly.

I glared at my mother, shooting daggers at her, willing her to burst into flames. This wasn't the first time we had argued about my arranged mating, and it wouldn't be the last.

"Tala," my mother's grey-blue eyes softened towards me, "I am losing myself. I cannot help you. This pairing of you and Jasper is a good thing. He will become Alpha and you Luna, then, maybe you can live happily. Please, for me." Her eyes and voice begged me, imploring me to see the reasoning behind her words.

Today was a good day for her, but tonight may not be

so good. It was potluck with my mother. Some days, she was the Luna I remembered her being: a powerful she-wolf who would take command, and the kind Luna who would sympathize and held kindness towards all.

That person seemed so long ago, a memory of a distant mother I once loved. I still love her, but years of abuse and torment at the hands of my father had broken not only her spirit but her wolf's spirit too. So much so that she couldn't even shift anymore, and on a full moon she became feral, her twisted and tormented mind winning over the sane and rational side of her.

It wasn't her fault, this I knew. It was his fault; it was his *entire* fault that my mother had lost the plot of life. She no longer lived; she survived. Just like me. We were both surviving this hell.

My cruel father had even turned my older sister, Shayna, against her. When King Orion came to him many moons ago, my sister had foolishly fallen in love with the bear-shifter king. King Orion had taken an interest in her, even though he was quite a few years her senior. It wasn't her he had an interest in, no, it was her inventions. Her ability as a chemist and her very own twisted mind, that's what he wanted from her. Orion sought to use her, and Shayna was more than willing to be used by him. She was blinded by lust.

She had left the Sandstorm Pack to go with King Orion in pursuit of the Throne of Riocht. A fable, or at least I once thought so, that whoever could claim the throne would become the King or Queen of Shifters.

I thought it was a fairytale, something mums would tell their little girls as bedtime stories. Yet a couple of weeks ago, there was a shift in the realm. A shift in power, and like a radio wave that honed in on every shifter, our counterparts recognized a new power, a new leader, one that was above every other shifter.

A King and Queen had risen; they would rule over us all. My wolf, Mora, had felt the power shift and called to her king and queen. I had felt the power wash through me, every ounce of instinct in me telling me they were the supreme rulers.

It wasn't just me who had felt it, every shifter had felt it. My maid, Eloise, had felt it too.

"Tala." My mother's soft voice brought me back to the now, jarring my thoughts from that day. The same day she felt the break of her ties to Shayna. "Please…" Her eyes filled with unshed tears as she regarded me.

"Let's just see what happens, mother. We have time." I said sympathetically, not wanting to argue with her anymore. It was futile anyway. She probably wouldn't even remember these conversations come tomorrow, then we would have the same argument all over again. Maybe.

I turned to walk away from her and leave her room when she suddenly cried out in pain and fell to the floor, clutching her stomach and heart.

"Motherfucker" I gasped. He was at it again! "Eloise!" I shouted. My maid and best friend came hurrying through the door. "Get her strapped down and get her medications." I hastily commanded her, my voice a little panicked. I took my mother over to her bed and began securing her with the leather straps that had been fashioned for her bed while Eloise ran to the bathroom to grab the medication I would inject her with.

We got her strapped down; all the while, her cries rang out and echoed through the room. Her hands grasped at her chest and stomach, trying to claw at them, but her wolf had abandoned her years ago, so now she just felt the immense pain.

Once secure and injected, her body began to relax some, but I could tell she could still feel the burning pain, as she had once described it.

I stomped towards the door. I was a woman on a mission.

"Where are you going, Tala?" Eloise called out behind me as she sat on the side of the bed, nursing my mother.

"To put a stop to this." I spat as I yanked the door open and scented where my father was in the palace.

I ran down the halls towards his bedroom on the east wing. When I reached the large, heavy wooden doors that were painted a hideous blue, I halted with my hands outstretched ready to open the door.

I took a deep breath, not just to calm myself but also my wolf. She was reeling and I felt her boiling anger. I had to keep her in check before she tried to challenge my father. That would not end well for either of us.

I turned the handle and burst in to find my father knelt behind a slave girl, thrusting into her like a madman. I cast my eyes down for a second out of pure disgust. Not because he was fucking a slave, but because the look on the poor girl's face was horrifying. Tears stained her red cheeks, and I could see claw marks across her skin where my father was holding onto her hips so tightly.

I could smell the blood seeping from her, and her whimpers and pleas carried to my ears, making me cringe. She looked at me and held my gaze, her eyes red and puffy, and the tears still streaming down her face. 'Help me' was what she conveyed without saying anything.

"Father enough!" I yelled at him, not moving from my spot. "You are going to kill her!" I hissed at him through my teeth.

"She a fucking rogue hybrid, she will either heal or die." He said between pants, not caring that his own daughter was standing there while he fucked the sense out of some poor girl. He didn't even attempt to slow down or pause.

"I'm not talking about her, I'm talking about your mate, my mother! You are going to kill *her*!" I had to clench my fists and bite my tongue. I so wanted to cross the room and rip him by his hair and punch him until his face was unrecognizable. My wolf hummed with the thought.

He paused mid-thrust, his head snapping to me, his eyes dark with the presence of his wolf. "She made her choice when she chose you." He snarled, his lip twisting up on one side. "Now stand there and watch quietly or GET THE FUCK OUT!" He roared at me, and my wolf whimpered.

I fought the command but backed out of the room, closing the doors behind me in defeat. I leaned against the wall next to the ugly ass doors and waited for him to finish with his slave girl. I mind-linked a guard to bring me a sheet and stood there waiting.

After the guard had brought me the sheet, I made him wait with me. We stood in silence outside my father's room, listening to the screams and painful cries that came from the girl he was violating. I looked up at the guard, who must have felt my stare, as he lifted his eyes to meet mine.

"This is not how you treat a woman," I said pointedly.

"Yes, my lady." He replied with a bow. He looked indifferent to what was happening behind the closed doors, and I couldn't tell if he felt for the girl, didn't care, or relished in the idea that his alpha was abusing a female for his own pleasure.

We stood there for a least another thirty minutes and another ten minutes after the poor girl's screams had ceased.

It was then that the doors finally opened and the slave girl stumbled out naked and bleeding. She fell to her knees as she came through the entrance. The tears still fell, and the blood was still trickling from my father's claw marks and from between her legs.

She had been a virgin. She wasn't anymore.

I felt my heart skip a beat at the thought of what she just went through, she couldn't have been any older than me. I felt ashamed at this moment, ashamed that I carried his last name.

I quickly wrapped the sheet around the girl and helped her stand to her feet. She was a wreck, shaking and trembling uncontrollably.

"I'm so sorry," I tried to soothe her. "You will heal, you are strong." My words fell short, I knew they did. Even I didn't believe my words.

"I want to go home." She sobbed.

I felt my eyes fill with tears for this girl. She would never go home. This was her new reality. I wish I could change it, but I was powerless against my father.

"Take her back to the slave chambers, have the head madam get her cleaned up and give her some healing herbs." I told the guard as I lightly shifted the girl from my arms to his. "And keep your damn hands to yourself," I told him sternly.

He nodded and helped the girl walk, taking her down and out to where the slave whores were kept. I took a big breath and sighed, leaning over to grasp my knees. My nerves were shot and I needed to calm my wolf again. She hated to see a sight like this and wanted to tear my father's head off. We both knew we couldn't though.

It was that defeated feeling that got us every time.

I went back to my mother's room where she now slept, or rather passed out. I tipped my head at Eloise to leave my mother and come with me. I sent a link to my mother's maid and asked her to come and watch over her. I didn't need to explain what was wrong or what had happened. We were all well aware of the cause that had her doubling over and had sent her insane.

Her mind was getting worse day by day, last week she had a breakdown and we had found her in the middle of the arena, stark naked and slashing at her wrists with a knife. The week before that, she had used some arousing herbs and ointment and raped a guard.

She literally tied him down, applied the ointment, and was found riding him with everything she had. She had said the goddess wanted her to get her own back on my father. I had tried to explain that her actions made her no better than her abusive mate, but she didn't understand. Instead, she just gave me a blank look like I was the one who had mental problems.

I had been dealing with this for years, but on days like today, when she having a good day, that's when the situation got the best of me. It just made me so mad that he would purposely ruin her good day.

My father was a selfish, bloodthirsty, egotistical, narcissistic, man. He cared for only a handful of things; money, blood, my sister, his whores, and his games. Probably in that exact order. Although, the slave girls and the fighters did line his pockets very nicely, as he had put it himself on so many occasions.

As soon as Eloise and I stepped into my room and the door was closed, I lost it. The pent-up anger let loose and my hands began to tremble as my wolf's claws extended and tore through the room, tearing the sheets from the bed and swiping at the walls, clearing the shelves of all the trinkets and upturning my mattress.

I let out a scream of frustration in an attempt to get it all out. "WHY?" I shouted at no one in particular, "Why must I endure this hell hole?" I turned to Eloise who stood there pale and frightened at my outburst, her usually small eyes wide with fear.

Looking at her made me and my wolf calm down instantly. "I'm so sorry El," I said, suddenly aware and ashamed of my outburst. "I just can't live like this anymore, this... this place is hell!"

I slumped down in the small wooden chair that sat in front of my vanity that miraculously survived my rampage. Eloise came up behind me and placed her hands on my shoulders. She was the closest thing I had to family, at least family that cared and loved me. My mother loved me, in her own deranged way, when she remembered that I was her daughter.

"I'm so sorry Eloise, I just can't stay here anymore. I can't live like this, I can't watch my father destroy the lives of people anymore." I sighed.

"Hush your mouth, Tala! You can't leave!" Eloise hissed in a whisper. "What would I do if you left? What would happen to Jasper?" Her voice trembled as she mentioned Jasper's name.

I slumped my shoulders and stared back at my reflection in the mirror on my vanity. "Maybe be happy?" I hoped and shrugged my shoulders.

"After the annual games, my father expects me and Jasper to mate and wed." I looked at her through the mirror and instantly saw the tears and the deflated look on her face.

Eloise was my best friend and more of a sister than Shayna had ever been, which was why I was so against this pairing in the first place. When Eloise turned eighteen two years ago, she found her mate. It was during the annual mating ball my father held once a year.

Another excuse for him to find and feast off young, unmated she-wolves.

It was at that event he had announced that Jasper and I would become chosen mates when I turned twenty-one. It was also at that event Eloise and Jasper found out they were mates. However, Eloise was an omega, a 'weak wolf' as mine and Jasper's fathers had declared on many occasions. It was also that night that Jasper and Eloise told me they were mates, and we knew we had to keep it a secret.

If my father and Jasper's father, who was the Royal Beta, found out he was mated to a lowly omega, they would kill her.

"I will find a way out of it by hook or crook, El. I promise." And I meant it.

Even if Jasper and I were against our pairing, our fathers had a way to ensure we mated and marked each other.

Chapter 8 – Teal the Alpha

<u>KELLEN</u>

Our 'digs' were primitive, but I didn't expect much more. We had running water and a toilet, that was good enough for me. Although we are called slaves, I didn't expect the level of treatment to be… well, to be as good as this.

I mean, there was nothing, absolutely nothing *nice* about this place and the people, but the fact that they gave us toothbrushes and toothpaste was a luxury. The food… hmm. It was food. We would get porridge in the morning and a piece of bread and fruit in the evening. The third meal was only when they remembered to bring it.

I had seen humans treated a lot worse than this back home, especially in the boroughs where human slavery was still a problem. A problem we were working on as a kingdom, we wanted equal rights for all races.

I woke when the first rays of light hit my cot. I managed to snag the cot by the open-barred window, a prime view of the compound, where I could watch the comings and goings of people as well as the guards when they changed shifts.

Because I had woken up so early and hadn't noticed any of the other men I was trapped with were up, I began doing pushups and crunches. Working my body up into a sweat as the sun rose higher in the sky and dawn broke. I had no concept of time as I worked my body and only stopped when a deep baritone voice broke my concentration.

"I see you are already preparing for the games... this is good." I hopped up onto my feet to look at the owner of the voice.

The tall, muscular man leaned against the open wall, legs and arms crossed. His red hair was curly and his blue eyes were almost as clear as mine. He looked weathered and had scars littered across his body. He wore a pair of cotton shorts and nothing else.

He stood straight and uncrossed his arms. Standing at his full height, I could tell he was almost as tall as me. He looked to be in his late forties, maybe even pushing fifty, but I saw no grey in his hair.

"You look like him, you know." I furrowed my brows at his remark. "Your father, you look like him." He said, tossing me a pair of cotton shorts, the same as his.

"You knew my father?" I questioned, wanting to know more.

"I met him some time ago when he visited my pack," he paused, his eyes getting a faraway look in them before he shook it off. "That must have been more than twenty-five years ago."

"How long have you been here for?" I asked, dropping the clean pair of shorts onto my cot.

"Too long," he said solemnly, leaning back against the wall. "Twenty-two years they have held me here."

I think I gasped like a little girl because the alpha-male with the red hair let out a deep chuckle. I was lost for words, twenty-two years was a long time. He had been stuck in this shit hole since before I was born! I cocked my head in disbelief and he laughed again.

"Death does not greet us when we ask for it, no matter how many times. My name is Teal, former Alpha of the Seadog Pack. It is a pleasure to meet you, Your Highness." He bowed to me, acknowledging my rank and title.

"Kellen Moon," I reached out and offered him my hand. "Former King of the Royal New Moon Pack." He took my hand, giving it a firm shake.

"Former?" He questioned, raising an eyebrow.

"My father and mother were killed by the same men who sold me to... this," I said waving my other hand around.

"You are no former king, you are still a king. I can feel it. My wolf acknowledges your rank." He told me with a sense of determination in his voice as if to solidify his words and meaning. "Now come, I will show you around our humble abode as well as show you the ropes. As the eldest and longest resident here, I try and help the newcomers."

I had so many questions for this man but stumbled to find my voice. He gathered Ajani, the rogue, and the omega, whose name I finally learned was Aaron.

Teal showed us the rest of our 'abode', which was more like a barracks or one of our warrior wings. It was just a lot... less. I listened and watched as he talked, taking in as much as possible.

"...So yeah, on game days, spectators are free to wander around and visit our small compound. Some will jeer and some will cheer. We are also free to wander around the compound during certain hours, but never on game day."

"Exactly what is 'game day'? And what is our role in 'game day'?" The omega took the words right out of my mouth, asking the question I had been waiting to be answered but Teal had not explained to us.

He had only shown us the weapons room that we would have access to on 'game day', the bathroom that the twenty-six of us men who were here would share, yay, and the common area that we could gather in if allowed.

Teal stopped and turned to look at us all, his head bobbing. "I was getting to it young one." He addressed the omega, Aaron. "You know you are slaves, I assume. But I am sure Baron did not tell you what kind of slaves you are?" He asked us.

"He told us we were entertainment and called us 'gladiators'." I supplied, crossing my arms and waiting for Teal's explanation.

"Aye, that you are. Slaves to his sick mind and games." His eyes shifted over all of us until they settled on me. "Game day is when we are sent into the arena to fight for our lives. We do not know the rules until we enter. Sometimes the only rule is to survive. He can pit us against each other or an outside prizefighter; sometimes he has us fight the guards."

He sat on a rickety wooden bench that was against one of the sandstone walls and leaned his head back. "The crowds will pay money to see a fight, they will cheer for their warrior. Or, if a gladiator captures their interest, they may place a bet on you to win a fight. That's why on game day, spectators can come and view the contenders, the contenders being us, like betting on a race."

"The Alpha wants us to win?" I was a little stunned that we would be given the opportunity or allowed to kill his guards or pack warriors.

"Oh yes, because then it brings in more money." Teal chuckled.

"He does not worry that we would retaliate?" Ajani

queried. I could see where his thoughts were leading.

"If we could, I would have done it twenty-two years ago."

"What about escaping?" I had to ask because I was getting out of here. No ifs, no buts, it was a matter of *when* and figuring out how.

Teal laughed at me, his chuckle just as deep as his voice. "Young king, again, if I could, I would have." He tapped the back of his neck with his finger. "This thing they injected into you, it controls your wolf, or whatever other counterpart a shifter has."

"It does what now?" I asked in horror as I too felt the back of my neck, letting my finger run over the slight bump where they had stuck me with the large needle a few days ago.

"It's a chip, an inhibitor. It restricts your spirit animal so you cannot shift at will. It can also kill you if Vargr decides to push a little button. It will send two shocks through your body, one to your heart and one to your brain. Instantly killing you where you stand. Why do you think I am still here after twenty-two years and haven't made an attempt on his life?"

This was insane. Absolutely, one-hundred percent pure madness. How did they even come up with a piece of technology that could control your animal and restrict them from shifting?

"It was Vargr's daughter and King Orion," Teal said, I must have said it out loud or he read my mind. "His eldest daughter, Shayna, was the brains behind it and Orion supplied the funding and guinea pigs."

"They are dead. Orion and that bitch died." I spat their names out like they were poison because that's what they were: poison to the realm of shifters, sick fuckers, and the monsters they created. "My beta killed Shayna and Orion's other son, Mathias, killed him."

"That is the best news I have heard in over twenty-one years." A small smile played at the corners of Teal's lips. "I felt a shift a couple of weeks ago, but because of this," he tapped the back of his neck, "I didn't know exactly what had transpired. Plus I am sure you have noticed young king, that you are unable to mind-link or connect to another wolf? Again, the inhibitor."

That explained why I couldn't reach Lamia or the other three knights.

Fuck, I thought. I was truly on my own and could only hope they would find me. I was going to need help getting out of here.

Our conversation was interrupted when a guard came into the barracks compound with a rolling cart and bowls full of the nasty slop they call porridge.

"Prince-ee, Braids, mute rogue, and omega scum!" He bellowed out so all the gladiator slaves could hear, "You are up first this afternoon, eat well, this could be your last meal." He chuckled at the end and was still chuckling as he exited the barracks.

I looked at Ajani and then Teal. "When the sun is high and the clock strikes noon, you will be taken to the arena and forced to fight." His deep, rich voice held an undertone of melancholy and was laced with something I couldn't determine, hatred maybe?

"How did they even come up with or make these drugs and this thing… this inhibitor chip?" I questioned Teal, wanting to know everything.

He got up and walked to the rolling cart, taking one of the wooden bowls and sitting back down. "Shayna was a chemist and very smart with technology. She and Orion concocted all kinds of drugs and serums with the help of a witch." He snarled at his last admission. I concluded he had no love for witches, but I thought they had all died out, the last of the line being Finnegan who was only part witch according to Mathias.

"Now eat, you will need your strength," Teal said pointing towards the cart.

I got up and stood in line waiting to get a bowl like the other men. I sat back down to eat and the five of us ate in silence. It was a somber silence as all of us wondered what our first gladiator match would entail.

Before long, the sun had reached its high and the guards came, a dozen of them this time. Each with a cattle prod and called forth the four of us.

"Prince-ee, Braids, Omega scum, and Rogue, let's go! Grab a weapon and make your way to the arena!" Beta Baron came marching into the barracks, yelling and giving out orders as he unlocked the weapons area.

I looked at Teal and he nodded towards where the old and blunt swords stood. I grabbed a blade while inspecting it. It was worthless, with chipped and dull edges, I would be lucky if it could slice or pierce a mouse.

We followed the beta out, stepping into the blazing sun that scorched the ground. I could feel the heat from the dirt and sand burning the bare soles of my feet.

I felt Conri stir, deep in the back of my mind. 'Are you with me wolf?' I asked him with hope.

'I am with you' His reply was quiet and soft, unlike him. I had my reservations about exactly just how much he really was with me after what Teal told us.

The arena was packed full, crowds of spectators lined

the wall, and the stone bleachers were full of jeering and cheering. I could smell the excitement of hundreds of wolves. They enjoyed this, eager to watch whatever and whoever was going to fight.

The guards and Beta Baron escorted us to the center of the arena, surrounding us almost like a shield, but I knew better. They were making sure we were kept in line and didn't try any funny business. The same tactic was used at home.

The sound of drums began to beat, filling the arena with the steady thumping, and the vibrations could be felt beneath my feet. The beat quickened and Beta Baron walked towards the crowd, climbing up the stone steps until he reached a tented section.

He took his place by two large chairs that looked like makeshift wooden thrones. When a large man with wild brown hair stepped out and into the covered tent with a woman who had long blond hair, the penetrating rudiments of the drums sped up faster and then suddenly came to a halt. They were the Alpha and Luna.

The sudden quietness stilled the air and my wolf's fur bristled with the change. Murmurs from the crowd and excited chatter from the young rang out. The voices died down when the Alpha stood.

The guards around us suddenly turned, forming two lines, and then marched from the arena to a wide entrance below, where the Alpha and Luna sat.

"Let the games begin!" He bellowed. The only four words he spoke before he took his seat again.

The four of us stood there looking around, waiting, anticipating.

"Place your bets!" A man's voice rang out and the excited

chatter of the crowd grew once again.

I held the dulled blade in my hand, not having a good feeling, when the sound of multiple heavy feet pounding against the ground reached my ears. I turned towards the sound. From the same entrance that the guards disappeared from, twelve more men were appearing.

They smelt like warrior wolves, strong and trained.

I looked at Ajani and shook my head, this was not good. I then cast my eyes towards the omega, who was shaking, and the rogue, who was breathing deeply.

My instincts took over and I twirled the sword in my hand, getting used to its weight and balance. It was every man for themselves. Twelve trained warriors against four gladiator slaves.

"Back to back, watch each other's six! If we want to survive this, we are going to have to work together!" I began giving out orders; it was second nature to me. Ajani nodded and understood. The omega backed up towards me, shaking more, and the rogue wore a sense of calm as if he had already accepted his death.

"We will not go down without a fight! Grip your weapon tight and do not let go!" I couldn't give them any more instructions as the harsh blare of a horn filled the arena and the twelve men rushed us.

Aaron was shaking more and almost dropped his weapon. I gripped his hand around the hilt tightly "Do *not* drop your weapon." I commanded with grit. His eyes were wide and filled with terror and I turned just in time to block the first of many attacks.

Chapter 9 – First Blood

<u>KELLEN</u>

The warriors descended upon us, thirsty for blood. Hungry for a kill.

Their moves were fast and calculated, reigning down blow after blow with their steel weapons that were sharper and stronger than ours. We were at a disadvantage, but I wouldn't let that stop me from taking down each one.

I thrust my blade into the belly of one and slashed at another, both dropping their weapons as they went down. I scooped them up and turned to meet the next attacker, blocking his slice as I backed up to my comrades.

I thanked the Moon Goddess for all my training and sent a silent 'thank you' to Hunji and my uncles for training me well. My muscle memory began to kick in, and my wolf side began to take over. The primal urge to survive: kill or be killed.

I took down two more and watched Ajani drop one, a look of triumph on his face. The rogue fought with determination and was holding his own until he left his back open and a warrior went in for the kill. I was quick and dodged under Ajani, only just making it as I crossed my swords like scissors, slicing the head off the warrior.

The crowd gasped, and I made a grave mistake by taking my eyes off the fight and glancing at the spectators. One quick second was all it took, and I heard the scream from Aaron and the thud of his knees hitting the ground.

The sword was plunged deep into his chest, and the warrior who speared him grinned, pulling his sword out and then ramming it into his neck.

The scent of his blood reached my senses. I could taste his death, the coppery tones of his blood. My canines elongated and I snarled, showing off my sharp teeth. A grunt from Ajani told me he was injured. From the corner of my eye, I could see a large gash in his forearm.

The warriors began to back up, putting some distance between us and them.

"Regroup!" I called out to my two remaining companions and again stood back to back.

The eight remaining warriors dropped their weapons once they were a good distance away.

"What are they doing?" Ajani asked. Before I could open my mouth to tell him I had no idea, we got our answer as the warriors all shifted into their wolves. They were snarling and snapping their teeth as they began to circle us.

We couldn't shift. We had to face them in our skin. I didn't need to shift to take them down, but it would have been better with teeth meeting teeth.

I watched and waited. "Watch for their move, go for the neck and underbelly," I instructed.

Suddenly, all eight large and menacing wolves leaped at us at once. A frenzy of fur and gnashing teeth flew at us. I slashed one right under his belly as he leaped, spilling his guts and drenching me in his blood. I rolled out the way before his limp body could fall on me.

As I lifted to my feet, I caught another by the scruff of

his neck and threw him as hard as I could across the arena, where he tumbled in the dirt. I turned to my left, my sword meeting the neck of another wolf.

Six left, I counted. Five, Ajani just killed one. Four, the rogue took one wolf out. His weapon cut deep into the wolf's shoulder before he pulled it out and stabbed it in the chest. Ajani went down as the flash of sharp white teeth caught his shoulder. A grunt from the rogue had my eyes watching as claws swiped his chest.

I let out a menacing growl as I flew forward with inhuman speed, my wolf pushing forward but not shifting. Like a rabid wolf, I grabbed the warrior wolf off Ajani's back, one hand holding his scruff and the other plunging my sword deep through his skull. I swiveled to the side just in time as a wolf was going for the killing blow, ready to rip the rogue's neck out. My arm shot out and my hand curled around the large wolf's neck, barely latching on to his windpipe before I ripped it from his neck.

The last two remaining wolves began to cower away, backing up with their tails curled under. I snatched a weapon from the ground, not caring what it was, and hurled it at one wolf while charging at the other. A high-pitched whimper was heard when the blade pierced the first wolf, and the crunch of a neck cracking sounded as I ripped the head off the last warrior wolf.

I stood above the last one, my chest heaving and my body coated in blood as I looked at my victory. My wolf was pacing in my head, ready to spill more blood. He wanted out, but he was trapped. I felt his frustration and I sympathized for him, for myself.

During the fight, I barely noticed the sound of the crowd or that they were even there. I now noticed the eerie silence that had descended upon the arena, the low mumble of the crowd, the gasping whispers full of shock.

Was this not what they wanted? The entertainment of a blood sport? Did they not get what they came for?

I felt a hand touch my shoulder and snarled at the person, ready to take out another wolf. "Easy, Your Highness." Ajani spoke calmly, wary of my wolf and the adrenaline that was still coursing through me, driving me to kill.

I have no idea what I looked like, drenched in blood from head to toe, a monster? A blood-thirsty wolf? Something out of a horror show, maybe? Because that's what this was; a useless, unnecessary horror show.

Whatever I looked like, it gave the crowd a look of shock as they stared at me. Some mouths gaped, some whispered. I took it all in as I tried to calm my beating heart and uncoil my clenched fists. My chest rose and fell heavily with the rage I felt.

I stood facing the spectators and lifted my head, looking straight at the Alpha, who sat there all high and mighty on his false throne. My eyes glared daggers at him, piercing him with my loathing stare.

The same guards that escorted us into the arena came out and surrounded us, the cattle prod's sparking in warning that if I moved, I would feel the bite of them.

The rogue stood to my left and Ajani to my right. Their wounds were open and seeping crimson liquid, they would heal slowly, but they would live. My gaze found Aaron, his body crumpled on the blood-soaked sandy dirt, lifeless and still.

A cruel and shameful death. The kid stood no chance. It was unnecessary, the shame was not his because he fought the best he could. No, the shame belonged to the Alpha who allowed his death, who cheered his death.

My eyes lifted to the Alpha again, ocean blues meeting misty, dull grey. I held his stare, both of us curling our lips, sneering at one another. He stood, watching me as his lips began to curve into a cruel and menacing smile. A smile full of evil.

"Lords, Ladies, and Pack. I present to you our newest gladiators!" He began a slow clap and the crowd, as if coming out of a trance or their stupor, began to clap and cheer.

He addressed them not like an Alpha but like he was some self-proclaimed king. He reveled in the crowds' cheers, thinking they adored him and were thanking him for bringing them this bountiful entertainment.

"You are no king! You are no alpha! You are a coward!" I roared out, pointing my blood-soaked finger at him. "A leader protects the weak in the pack; they don't enslave them and send them to their death. Only a man who is weak and cowardly does that!"

His growl filled the stadium, hushing the onlookers. His teeth snapped at me as his wolf pushed forward, brimming on the surface.

Sometimes I just didn't know when to quit; this was one of those times. "You call yourself an alpha? Then face me man to man, wolf to wolf. I, Kellen Moon, Alpha and King of the New Moon Pack, challenge you to the Alpha title!"

Gasps rang out and the look on the Alpha's face would have sent me six feet under if looks could kill. His face was red with anger, and I could visibly see his body shaking with rage at the challenge. The Luna gave a small smirk, a twinkle in her otherwise lifeless eyes. She was happy I challenged him.

The Alpha stood and began a slow clap once more, this

time the crowd did not react. He stepped down from his chair and pointed at me.

"You are nothing." He declared while taking another step down, his silky red long over-shirt rippling with his movements. He dressed like he was holding court in an age long ago forgotten. "You are nothing but a slave! Here I make the rules, and you will do well to remember that *slave!*"

He waved his hand, and the guards began to corral Ajani and the rogue out of the arena. I stood there, still seething at the thing who called himself an alpha.

"Teach him a lesson." He growled the command at the remaining guards that flanked me.

I felt the first bite zap through my skin, then the next, setting all my nerves on end. The third brought a burn through my muscles, then another prod of the long pole and I hit the ground, blacking out.

*****

I blinked my eyes open, groaning with the stiffness that encased my whole body. I still felt the trembling of my muscles and the hair on my body felt like it was still standing on end.

"You live." I heard Ajani's voice as my blurred vision started to clear. My throat was dry and raspy, my tongue was still swollen, and I tried to lick my lips.

A cup of water was brought to my lips and I drank it greedily. "Fuck, I feel like I went ten rounds with Lamia." I groaned out.

"Who is Lamia?" Ajani asked, "Is she your mate?" Again with the questions.

"You did well young king, but next time you may want

to keep your mouth shut." Teal chuckled as I lifted my tight arms to rub my face. "A lesser wolf would have died, or at least would still be unconscious."

A flash of memory shot through me, reminding me of the cattle prods that kept shocking me over and over again.

"Maybe next time, try not to issue a challenge to Vargr, huh?" I looked a Teal, who wore a frown. His red eyebrows pulled together in concentration as he wiped the blood from my body with a cool cloth.

"He's a fucking coward." I spat.

"That he may be, but right now you are at his mercy. Another stunt like that, and he may just trigger your chip. What good would you be if you were dead?"

"He is right. You are no good to us if you are dead." Ajani agreed.

"What good am I to anyone stuck in here?" I laid my head back down and covered my eyes, willing the burn and stiffness to leave my body.

"You killed nine of his men, five of them with your bare hands and without shifting. I would say you are worth a whole lot. The other men here have been waiting for you to wake up. They want to show you their respect, young king."

I scrunched my eyes closed while listening to his words. I did nothing but survive. Kill or be killed. Today was not my day to die, but lying here, it sure felt like I should have.

Finally feeling like I could move, I sat up, swung my legs off the side of the cot, and leaned my back against the rough and cold wall. "How long have I been out for?" I asked, thinking that they would say a day or more.

"Only a couple hours. The number of times they shocked

you, I am very surprised you are awake," Teal said with pride in his words.

My wolf must have been able to heal me quickly. I was thankful. I looked at Ajani, more specifically at his arm. His wound had been cleaned and was now bandaged. Next, I looked at the rogue. His wounds had also been cleaned, but there was no bandage; instead, some green, goopy compound had been rubbed into his wounds.

"The healers came and took care of them." My unspoken question was answered by Teal once more.

I stood up from my cot on shaky legs, feeling like I hadn't used them in years. I stood by the small, barred window and looked out into the red sky. The sun was setting, and the faint glow of the moon could be seen as the sun ducked down behind the wall and the moon rose to take its place.

I closed my eyes and thought of Lamia and Mike. Were they looking for me? Had they found out where I was yet? Did they know I was a million miles from home on another continent, in a strange kingdom?

I then thought of my parents, something that was hard for me to do. Every time I recalled a memory of them, it was clouded and replaced with the image of their corpses. A lone tear slipped from the corner of my eye as the memory of their deaths haunted me.

I prayed to the Moon Goddess to keep what was left of my loved ones safe, and I prayed for the slaves of the realm, now having a fraction of an idea of what they went through. Lastly, I prayed that she would present me with a solution, a solution that would help me get out of here.

I stood there for a while, long after Teal, Ajani, and the rogue had left my small area. They left me to my thoughts when they realized that I was not going to engage in conversation.

    I watched the red sky turn to a dusky purple as night crept in, the dry air turning cooler as the black skies slunk their way in. It creeped like a menacing shadow that eventually gave way to the vast stars and the glow of the hooked moon.

Chapter 10 – The Brother

<u>LAMIA</u>

Mathias walked into the Clan Mansion, Xander and Abner close behind him. The smell of blood permeated the air and clung to Mathias, covering his scent of aged black rum and vanilla. I crinkled my nose at the offending metallic and stale scent and my stomach churned. Certain smells would set me off, and it was a tossup of whether I would be 'tossing' up my stomach or not.

"Did he say anything?" I asked Mathias as he bent to kiss me.

"No." Was his one-word answer. I looked into his silver eyes, holding them for a moment.

"Did you give him a chance to say anything?" I asked. I then raised my hand to cover my nose, the scent of blood making my insides gurgle and had me gulping the thick saliva that sat at the bottom of my throat.

They were meant to be interrogating Finnegan, who had been sitting in the same cells my father and I had once been housed in. Although, I had a feeling they had just been working him over and not even asking him any questions or giving him a chance to answer anything they asked.

Mathias held a deep-seated hatred for his brother Finnegan, even if he did save my life at the battle of Riocht. I'm not sure where the hatred stemmed from; if it was just because Finnegan had been considered Orion's right-hand man, or because he had put his hands on me the first time that we saw him. Maybe it had something to do with him being Mathias' brother. I didn't know, but if we were going to get anything out of Finnegan, they had to stop beating the shit out of him.

"Where's Ria?" Xander asked. His honey-brown eyes wandered around the large sitting room like he expected her to jump out at any second declaring, 'here I am!'

"You need to mark that girl so you can mind-link her." I said, pointing a knowing finger at him. "Besides, she is with your mother. She took Ria on a tour of the clan territory, hoping she will fall in love with the Kodiak Kingdom and never want to leave." I smiled at the thought. Amitola, Xander and Mathias's mother, was so excited that Ria would be coming here that she made an itinerary of things they could do with each other.

"I want to speak with Finnegan," I stated loudly. If they weren't going to get answers from him, maybe I could.

"Absolutely *not*!" Mathias growled out. "He tried to kill you!"

"He also saved my life, King!" I argued back at him.

"There is no way I am letting my pregnant mate near his sorry ass!" I could see the veins in his neck and forehead pulsing. He was being overprotective and unreasonable.

"I remember you were going to kill me at one point too!" I made him recall my time in the dungeons and the time he had been drinking from a bottle of rum that had been laced, altering his mind. Travis and Rhett were still investigating how that had happened and still trying to find Orion's sleeper cells, spies, whatever you want to call them, not just at MacTire but also at the New Moon Royal Pack.

Rhett had been working closely with Tyron, who would eventually be the new Royal Delta if, no, *when* Kellen was found. Another reason Finnegan needed to be questioned, not beaten. He may know something about Kellen's disappearance.

At this point, Mike and I would take any lead, no matter how small or insignificant. I felt so useless and couldn't help but wonder if this was how they all felt when I had been kidnapped.

I hadn't felt Kellen's pain since those first days he had disappeared, and I wasn't sure if that was a good sign or not. I knew he was alive. I could sense it, rather my wolf could sense it. Every day, several times a day, I would try to reach out to him, but every time I was met with a block like he had put a permanent wall up to block anyone mind-linking him.

It had been almost three weeks now. Mike, Hunji, and Tobias had not found any leads. The trail is as cold as the day he went missing. I felt tears gather in my eyes and I bit them back. I had to be strong for Kellen, yet these damn hormones made it hard to control any emotion.

Where are you, Kellen?

*****

I woke up desperately needing the bathroom and rolled out of bed, trying not to wake Mathias. It wasn't until I was standing that I noticed he wasn't there. His scent was still strong, so he hadn't been out of bed long.

When I came out of the bathroom, instead of going back to bed, I left the room in search of my mate. I followed his scent downstairs and into the kitchen, but he wasn't there. I tried to mind-link him, but his block was up.

He obviously didn't want me to know what he was doing. I chuckled to myself because there was no way he could hide from me. Whatever he was up to, I was about to find out. He had been slightly cold since we had come back to the Clan

Mansion, even toward me. I knew he had a lot on his mind, as we all did, but it was no excuse for him to take out his frustrations on me or ignore me.

My feet led me towards the front door of the building and as I opened it, I got a slight whiff of his rum and vanilla scent. I grabbed my stomach as a small pang of pain shot through it and a slight burning sensation in my chest flared. This had been happening quite often these past few days, and the only way I felt settled was when Mathias was with me.

The night breeze was warm and tickled my bare shoulders, and the grass under my feet felt freeing and soft. I stood for a moment taking in the crisp mountain air. It was beautiful when it had been covered in snow, but now summer was approaching the barren white lands had turned into a whimsical forest of greenery. On a night like tonight, I could almost smell the dirt churning and the new vegetation come to life.

As if on auto-pilot, my feet carried me over the greenway and towards the familiar path that led to their cells. I felt Inanna stir. Her desire to shift and run was strong.

'Soon,' I promised her. Immediately I felt her calm down and her anxiousness ease. We couldn't shift into our wolf, but she had said we could morph into our beast and it would not harm the babies. Like Lycans in their were-form, we could shift while pregnant because our bodies stretched out rather than reshaped like our wolf form.

However, Mathias was still skeptical and had asked me to wait to morph until he had more clarification on whether I or the babies would be harmed or not.

When I reached the door that led down to the cells, I could smell my mate's scent strongly. He was here. I could also smell the decay and rot of the cells, along with fresh blood, before I had even opened the door. I took several gulps of the fresh air before opening the door and descending the dark stairs. The aching burn in my chest, and uncomfortable pain in my stomach, lessened slightly.

My stomach did flip-flops the further I ventured, but I swallowed down the rising nausea with great difficulty.

"You shouldn't be here." Mathias's deep voice startled me, making me jump when he appeared in front of me, seemingly out of nowhere.

I put a hand over my chest, calming my racing heart. "And neither should you, I woke up and you were gone. What was I to think? Especially since you blocked me out." I gave him a pointed look, raising one of my brows, daring him to say anything else.

"The smell of blood makes you sick right now, I don't want you down here." His tone was cold and final, but I wasn't about to listen to him.

I shoved around his thick muscular body, gulping in his scent to override all the others that swarmed around me, and proceeded further into the dank hall to where I could hear Finnegan's heavy breathing.

The cell door was already opened, and one guard stood across from it. I felt Mathias' heat at my back and pleasurable little shocks ignited down my arm as his fingers ran over my bare shoulders. I was only wearing a light camisole top and a pair of loose-fitting shorts. I bit back my moan and shook the feelings of desire from me. It would do no good for me to release my lustful scent down here, it would only agitate my mate more if his brother smelt my arousal.

"Baby, I don't want you down here. I can handle this." His voice was now smooth and caressing. The icy tone he held before melted.

"Without beating the shit out of him?" I skeptically asked.

"I was about to start interrogating him. I haven't touched him... yet."

I turned, looking up at my mate, my hand reaching to cup his handsome face. "Let me talk with him, King" I cooed. "Maybe he will talk if he is treated like a person and not a criminal."

"He is a criminal." He grated between clenched teeth.

"Maybe," I said and turned back to face Finnegan. He was sitting on a cot, his head in his hands, looking deflated.

"Finnegan," I called to him, and he lifted his head towards me. "Can I ask you some questions?" I kept my tone soft and sympathetic to his position. He nodded his head and I pointed to the chair in the cell. "May I sit?" Again, he nodded.

"If you fucking touch her, I will kill you where you stand. Do you understand?" Mathias wasn't warning him, there was no mistake that what he said would happen if his brother put one finger on me.

"Why did you save me, Finnegan?" I thought I would start with what I wanted to know the most.

"I never wanted to hurt you. I didn't want to hurt anyone." I heard him gulp down the lump in his throat. "I-I didn't have a choice, he made me."

I squinted my eyes, narrowing them at him. "What do you mean made you? How did Orion make you hurt people?"

"Does it have something to do with this?" Mathias threw a small metal chip at Finnegan's feet.

Finnegan lifted his hand to the back of his neck, feeling and rubbing it, then bent and picked up the small chip, examining it. His head snapped up to Mathias, then his wide gaze shifted to me. "How, is this from me?"

Finnegan held a look of shock on his face, and I took that moment to really look at him. He was handsome. He looked like Mathias, except where Mathias had naturally tanned skin, dark hair, and grey eyes, Finnegan had pale skin, almost white hair, and the most alluring violet eyes I had ever seen. His build and height were almost as equal to Mathias.

The two brothers were polar opposites. Like Yin and Yang, the dark meets the light. At least in looks, I didn't know Finnegan as a person, so I couldn't compare them in that sense.

"We took out of you when you were unconscious. You almost died," I told him in regard to the chip the clan doctor had found.

Xander was quite sure the little chip had triggered when Finnegan was stabbed by Mike and almost died. It had 'shorted out' and caused an electrical current that shot straight to Finnegan's brain and heart. Of course, this was all speculation; Xander needed time to examine the chip before he could determine its function.

"You should have let me die." His dejected tone made me flinch and I wasn't sure why. My wolf growled in my head at his statement; she wasn't happy that he was so ready to die, so easily ready to give up.

I went to lean forward, my intention to intimidate him, but my larger-than-should-be stomach got in my way. Instead, I leaned back and let out a slow breath.

"Listen to me carefully Finnegan; I don't believe you are a bad person, despite the circumstances. Now, I have a very good friend, as close as a brother and more. He went missing a few weeks ago. When I say I need to find him, what I mean is I will do everything and anything necessary to find him. Do you understand?" My tone was cool as a cucumber, my words slow and calculated so he couldn't miss what I didn't say. "I also want to know about these sleeper spies you and your father had hidden in the packs."

I waited for a beat to see how and if he would respond. Finally, his gaze met mine and I drew in a sharp breath as his violet eyes swirled with flakes of silver and held my stare. I shifted uncomfortably. His eyes bore into mine, creating heat and I felt my face flush. Mesmerizing was the only way I could describe the way they looked into my soul.

A low, threatening growl echoed from behind me, and Finn's eye quickly looked away from mine, a small smirk gracing his lips. I wasn't sure what just happened, but I was glad it was over. He had left me feeling flustered and the heat in my cheeks was still there.

"I will tell you whatever you want to know, but I ask of two things."

"You have no right to ask or demand anything," Mathias spat out. Finnegan ignored Mathias' displeasure and carried on.

"I want to know if Petra is okay, and I want you to find my sister." He glanced at Mathias and scowled at him. "Those are the only two things I ask in return and I will tell you as much as I know. You have my word, my queen." He finished with a small bow of the head and a tilt, baring his neck in a sign of submission to me.

Chapter 11 – A Face from the Past

<u>MIKE</u>

I walked out of the pack house we were staying at. Following my gut and wolf's instincts, we had traveled eat and had ended up at the Cheregwen Pack, located only a few miles from the coast and their packs docks. Cheregwen had one the largest ports for import and export trade and the Alpha, Jonathan Price, had been more than accommodating.

I had been out for an early morning run. Duke needed to expel some energy and I agreed, we both still had so much pent-up adrenaline. I had hoped we would find something once we got here, but there was nothing in the two days the three of us had been here. No gut feeling.

Even though we were still a few miles off from the ocean, I could still detect the salt that hung in the breeze that floated in from the east. The scent carried from the ocean and the smell of seafood could just be noted.

On any other given day as beautiful as today, being this close to the ocean, I would have happily skipped my duties and taken a drive down the beaches and basked in the warmth of the sun, with sand between my toes, and let the sounds of the lapping waves soothe my inner turmoil.

"Mike, Beta Mike?" I opened my eyes, not even realizing I had closed them, when the sound of a feminine and familiar voice filled my ears.

I looked up to where the voice came from and saw a woman around my age, with her arms crossed over her chest, making her way towards me. Her blonde hair was tied neatly in a ponytail and her caramel-brown eyes were trained on me, wide with surprise.

"Ella?" I cocked my head in confusion. What was she doing here? It was a long way from home.

Ella went to the high school in the New Moon Pack, she was Tawny's main tormentor until we came back and Lamia bluntly put a stop to her and her friends' bullying.

From what I knew it, wasn't just Tawny they bullied, but a few other omega wolves and humans. Somehow, Tawny got the worst of it just because she was a werecat. Ella had tried to lie about what happened between her and Lamia, but it didn't work out the way she had hoped. Then everything went down with Silas, and we never saw her again. Maybe her father had shipped her out here.

"What are you doing here Ella?" I asked.

"Wow, it's really good to see a familiar face." She smiled at me, and I was stunned that it was genuine. There was no hidden nastiness and none of her superior attitude that she used to carry, thinking she was hot shit because she was an alpha's daughter.

Just then, a tall male walked up with a little girl in his arms. "Momma!" She wailed, holding her hands out to Ella, grasping for her. Her blonde hair and big round brown eyes were the replicas of Ella. I smiled.

The male was Alpha Price's son, Eric. A tall and lean wolf, also with blond hair. He walked over to Ella, depositing the little girl in her arms and gave them both a kiss on the cheek before turning his attention to me, acknowledging my presence.

"Beta Mike, good to see you again. I hope my father has been welcoming." He said with a knowing smile, his hand stretched out to shake mine.

"Of course, he has been most welcoming," I replied, letting go of his hand. It was no secret that his old man could be a stubborn mule and grumpy at the best of times. "He hasn't given up his title, yet I see." Hinting that even though Eric was our age, his father was still the Alpha.

"No, not yet," he chuckled, placing his arm around Ella. "Soon, I hope."

"So, you guys are mates?" I noted, pointing out their marked necks.

Ella blushed and nodded. "Yes. We met when my father dragged me out here for business two years ago." The smile dropped from her face, and she peered up at me. "I'm not the same person Mike, I grew up. I'm a mommy now; living in the Cheregwen Pack really opened my eyes." She then cleared her throat.

"How is Tawny?" I noted the hesitation in her voice. "What I did to her was wrong, I hope one day I will be given the opportunity to apologize to her in person."

"I think she would appreciate that, Ella. Tawny is a good person and like you, she has changed. She is actually in Cambiador. I regret to say I haven't spoken to her in quite a while."

"So, what bring you out here with the queen's second in command and a bear shifter?" Eric asked while giving his mate a little comforting squeeze.

"We are looking for someone. We were hoping to find a lead out here."

93

"Who are you looking for?" I smiled at Ella's question, not sure if I should give her a straight answer or not.

"King Kellen." I watched both their faces go from placid to shock in one motion, a quizzical expression coming over both of them. "The king disappeared almost three weeks ago. I trust you can keep this to yourselves?"

"Yes of course!" Ella replied instantaneously, shifting her little girl, who was playing with her hair, from one hip to the other. "How can we help?"

I briefly explained to them the situation, and for some reason, both myself and my wolf trusted them. Usually, we wouldn't trust anyone outside the ranked wolves from the palace with this kind of information.

"You need to speak to Jonda," Ella told me after I was done telling them how and when Kellen had disappeared and my gut instinct to head this way. "She is from the Sea Dog Pack but is regularly on this side of the water. If anyone knows anything, it would be her."

"She discovered a trafficking gang not too long ago, they were running boats from our docks. We had no clue they were transporting humans and hybrids" Eric supplied. Hybrids being half shifter, half-human. "We shut that shit down, but I couldn't tell you if they moved to another port once we got them. As Ella said, if anyone knows something, it would be Jonda. She seems to know more of what's going on at those docks than we do."

I gave them my thanks and they gave me Jonda's information before we parted ways. It wouldn't hurt to ask her a few questions. It's not like we had any other leads to go on.

Hunji I opened my mind, establishing a link. *Let's take a drive to the docks. I was given the name of someone to speak to. I was told they know a lot of what goes on down there.*

Heading your way now, Tobias is with me.

We took the thirty minute drive down to Cheregwen's docks, the whole time Tobias was getting on Hunji's last nerve. I couldn't help but laugh, Tobias was brazen and full of jokes and was picking on Hunji's driving, just to rile him up.

"Seriously, King's mother drives faster than you." He goaded Hunji from the back seat.

I could see the vein in Hunji's neck pulse with irritation and his jaw clamped shut tightly. There was nothing wrong with Hunji's driving, Tobias was just being an ass and pushing his buttons.

"And what's with the brooding all the time? That's so last century." I saw the smirk on Tobias' face. "You seriously need to get laid bro. Find yourself a nice female, give her a good pounding, work that scowl off your face…" He started pumping his arms by his waist and flexing his hips, but it was the face and grunts he made that had me in stitches.

"I swear to the Moon Goddess, Tobias, if you don't shut your snout, I will pull this car over and I will be having bear steak tonight!" Clearly annoyed by Tobias, Hunji gripped the steering wheel tight and kept his face forward, eyes on the road.

"Seriously though Hunji, why not? Do you not like women, or do you bat for the home team? I mean there is nothing wrong with that, I occasionally don't mind sharing a bed with a male…" Tobias was just dribbling crap now and flung my head around, giving him a stern look and a shake of my head.

This was a touchy subject for Hunji and Tobias was crossing a line. The last thing I needed was for these two to go all claws and teeth. In all fairness, even though Tobias was a hulking male and a bear shifter, I had seen them both fight and my money would be on Hunji. He was just that much more skilled. Plus, aside from Kellen, he was the only other wolf I had seen put Lamia on her ass.

Thankfully Tobias took the hint and shut his mouth. The rest of the twenty minute drive was quiet.

"Let's grab some lunch first, then we can seek out this Jonda chick," I suggested as we pulled into town and my stomach growled. It was still early, not quite noon yet, but I had skipped breakfast and well, a shifters metabolism was fast, and we could always eat.

We found a small diner that was not far from the main loading dock and overlooked the main strip. The hostess sat us in a booth by the window. The small town was quaint with brick buildings that looked old, yet had a certain charm to them. Newer warehouses had been erected at some point and they were made with a metal covering. The smell of saltwater, fish, and brine assaulted my senses.

I looked at the menu, ready to get some grub in me, but scrunched my face up when all I saw was tuna, shrimp, crab, and some other fish.

"What's wrong pretty boy?" Tobias asked, "You don't like fish?"

"No, not really, I'm more of a meat and potatoes kind of guy." I glanced over the menu again at the breakfast choices that I hoped they were still serving. "What the fuck are grits?"

Tobias laughed at me, a deep chuckle, and then reached across the table and turned my menu over. I smiled when I saw the title 'classic burger'. Thank fuck for that. I guess I could never be a sailor, I just wasn't into fish.

The waitress came and took our drinks and food orders. As

we sat there, my wolf started to stir, pacing in my head like he was waiting for something and the wait was making him anxious.

'What ya got Duke?' I asked my wolf, he didn't pace unless there was a good reason.

'Gut feeling. I think we are in the right place,' he told me. I had the same feeling, like I was meant to be here. Like something drew us here. I remembered Hunji's words: trust your gut, trust your wolf.

Shortly after our food came out, my eyes were wide with greed when the loaded double bacon cheeseburger was placed in front of me. I looked at Tobias' plate that held some kind of fish steak, fries, and some creamy-looking goo, then I looked at Hunji's. His plate was piled with shrimp, muscles, and some green vegetation in a white sauce. It looked gross and slimy.

I must have made a sound, as mid-bite Hunji looked up at me. "What's your problem?"

"That." I pointed to his plate, "It looks... gross." He shrugged his shoulders and shoved the food in his mouth.

"You think this is gross, you should have seen what ate where I grew up." He gave me one of his rare smirks with a twinkle in his eye, "I think you would have thrown up if you had to eat at my mother's table."

I cocked my head, my eyebrows pulling together slightly. It was the first time I had ever heard Hunji mention his mother or even where he came from. It took me by surprise. Kellen and I had always joked that Hunji wasn't born, he didn't have a mother or father, he had just become.

Of course, Tobias hadn't known Hunji long enough, so he didn't realize that Hunji rarely, in fact never talked about his past. He didn't know Hunji had killed his mate. Nobody knew why; it was just something he had come out with when he was talking to Tawny. We had all seen the scars on his chest, but nobody ever brought it up.

I had always wondered why, if his mate had betrayed him, he didn't just reject her. Break the bond instead of killing her. I mean, that's one way to break a bond, but it's almost like suicide if you have marked and mated.

A marked mate's betrayal against the bond would cause your wolf to claw your heart out. If you or your mate were unmarked, the betrayal would be nothing more than a burning sensation in your chest and stomach. I mean, it's no picnic, but distance and time can temper that pain down. So I have heard. But a fully mated pair would definitely feel the effects of their mate cheating, and if you kill your mate, the chances of you surviving are pretty slim. It has always made me curious, what exactly had Hunji been through? He was the big brother of the group, our mentor, and we all looked up to him.

The waitress pulled me from my thoughts. "You boys need anything else?" She asked, playing with her blonde ponytail and smiling sweetly at us, her eyes lingering on Tobias a little longer.

"Actually, yeah," I cleared my throat and wiped my hands on my napkin. "We are looking for a woman named Jonda."

The waitress's smile dropped and her hand stopped fidgeting with her hair, her blue eyes narrowing. "What do you want with her? Is she in trouble?"

"Nope, no trouble. A friend of mine, Ella, said she maybe be able to help us."

"Oh, in that case, you are in luck. She came into town last night, staying over at the B&B, but she is probably holed up in Edgar's office right now." Her whole demeanor changed back to cheery and flirty once she realized this Jonda chick wasn't in trouble.

"And where can we find Edgar?" I asked.

She pointed to one of the metal warehouses, "Round back they have offices, and his is around there."

Hunji stood from the table, thanking the girl and leaving a hefty tip. We made our way out of the diner and headed over to Edgar's office. Edgar was a businessman and controlled most of the trade ships here. I had never met him, but I knew my father had. I had heard his name.

We found Edgar's office easily. The three of us walked in, but came to a stop when we heard the harsh cut of a woman's words.

"I have told you before, if you don't have your paperwork filled out, we aren't delivering... No thank you, your puny dick cannot make a deal... You're a pig, you threaten to put that shriveled limp stick of yours anywhere near me and I will cut it off... Try talking this shit to my brother and see where it gets you!"

The slam of a phone could be heard, followed by a frustrated groan mixed with a growl. I smiled, I didn't know who this chick was, but I liked her already, her harsh, no-bullshit attitude and her confident tone had me and my wolf a little excited. I wondered if her face would excite me just as much.

"Hello," Tobias called out, smirking as he had heard the same thing as me. Was he also thinking the same thing as me?

"Yeah, I'm coming." Her voice rang out with a little less annoyance, but it was still present.

I had to steady myself and take a sharp breath when the

owner of the voice came around the corner into the front entrance of the office.

She was absolutely gorgeous! Her chestnut hair lay in silky layers and my hand itched to reach out and touch it, to feel its smooth texture fall through my fingers. My gaze wandered over her body, from head to toe, taking in the tight ripped jeans that molded to her legs and the red blouse that tucked in at her slim waist, accentuating her breasts that were full and needed my hands to massage them.

Finally, my gaze landed on her eyes, those dark hazel shining orbs that said 'come fuck me'. Her perfect, creamy skin tempted me to lick her - and her pink lips looked soft, their fullness urging me to bite them and stain them red. She was the most beautiful woman I had ever seen and my wolf was instantly attracted to her, as was I.

She was not my mate. Still, the urge to take her in my arms was strong and I glanced at her neck, unmarked.

"We are looking for Jonda," Hunji broke the static silence, but I couldn't take my eyes off her.

"I'm Jonda, what do you want?" She asked. Her deep hazel eyes held mine, it was like we couldn't tear our eyes away from each other.

She licked her lips as she took me in, and I felt like a piece of meat. I smiled because I liked the thought of her wanting to devour me. Did I make her feel like the most delicious dessert? Because that's what she looked like in my eyes. And oh did I want to taste her - to lick her slow from head to toe... like my favorite ice cream.

Chapter 12 – Fake it till you make it

TALA

Initiation week. The week I dreaded every year.

When I was a little girl, I used to dream of finding my mate. He would whisk me away to his kingdom, because of course he was be a prince in my childhood fantasy. He would love and cherish me, give me gifts of jewels, I would wear a crown, and we would live happily ever after.

Unfortunately, as I grew older, that fairytale began to fade. Instead, nightmares of being mated began to override the sweet innocent dreams. The older I got, the more I realized how much my mother hated my father, and the more I realized how fucked up their bond was.

They were true mates, but I always questioned if they ever actually loved each other at one point. And if they did, where did it all go wrong? Oh, that's right, my father's unfaithful ways were where it went wrong. Why would the Moon Goddess pair my mother with a man as hateful and greedy as him? What had my mother done so horribly to deserve him as a mate?

Needless to say, I grew up watching my father screw woman after woman, and I don't mean that as in he brought them home and then took them to bed. I wish. No, he brought these slave women to the dinner table, bent them over in front of my mother, sister, and me, and had his way. He would laugh when the pain would hit my mother and after he had finished with the woman, he would take my mother upstairs, fuck her, and beat her.

It was a wonder she was still alive. Even at the tender age of eleven, I remember him having a string of these slave women come to the palace. He would invite all the rich men, bankers, business owners, and anyone who had their pockets lined. His lords, he would call them, like he was some super important king.

I scoffed at the thought.

It wasn't until a few years after that I realized this was what he called initiation week. All the newly acquired female slaves would be served up as a dish to these men, initiated into their new way of life. They became whores, whether they wanted to be or not. Used and abused however the men who owned them for the night wished to treat them. They would pay my father a great deal of money to possess a slave girl for the night.

The girls were usually shifter/human hybrids because they could take a beating and then some. Plus, they were able to recover, unlike humans. Every now and then, one of the girls would be a full-blooded shifter. The girls came from all over the realm, kidnapped, and shipped to this living hell to serve as nothing but meat. Some were as young as sixteen, never any younger.

It still didn't make it right.

Then there were the male slaves, thrown into the arena barracks, forced to fight as entertainment to this pack and a few others around. My father called them gladiators, and huge wagers would be placed on either them or whoever and whatever they were made to fight against.

They were chipped with an invention my sister and Orion had concocted, an inhibitor that controlled your animal counterpart to some degree, making it impossible for the gladiator slave to shift without killing himself. Slaves to technology and slaves to my father's sick games.

The worst thing was - these gladiator slaves were also stolen from their homes. They came in all ranks from alphas to rogues. If they were no good for fighting, one of two things would happen to them: they would either be fed to my father's pets, alive, or they would become slave whores for those with that particular taste.

I truly hated my father. My wolf, Mora, even refused to acknowledge him as our father and often got us in trouble when she refused to submit to him, resulting in a good beating.

Why hadn't I left and escaped this god-forsaken place? Because I knew I would feel guilty if I just left my mother, and then there was Eloise and Jasper. I couldn't leave, if I did, I knew they would be the ones to suffer the Alpha's wrath.

Jasper's mother, Alice, had been preparing the palace for the past month for initiation week. She was a meek woman with light blond hair and beautiful, honey-colored eyes. If her husband said jump, she wouldn't even ask how high, she would just do it.

I had entered the grand foyer, coming from the kitchen to grab water, when I found her holding a clipboard and looking around.

"Ahh, Tala!" She called out cheerily, always trying to find the bright side of life. "I have your mother's medication. I think it would be best if we just knocked her out for the week, what do you think?"

I had to take a moment to still my tongue. It completely stunned me how she could act so casual about having to sedate my mother because my father would be having the orgy of his life this whole week. I rolled my eyes at her, not even sure what to say. I should be used to this at twenty-one years old, but I'm not sure I ever could. Nor did I want to.

"Don't worry, I have some for myself. Baron said he would only participate on one night and would let me know what night that was." Her smug grin was way too pleasing to herself. Like she had the best mate in the realm because he would only betray her one night and he was letting her know ahead of time.

This was so wrong. Is this how every pack functioned? I didn't ever want to find my mate and I never wanted to be marked. To hell with that if this is how it goes.

"Yeah, just give the medication to me, I will be staying with her. I can take care of her." I managed to give her a very small fake smile.

"Oh no, Tala! You have to be present, both you and Jasper. Alpha will be announcing your mating on the opening day of the games." She clasped her hands together, a dreamy look on her face. "All the surrounding alpha's will be there for the opening day, and all the richest families will be attending. It's going to be the best opening day in a long time. Then in the evening, we have the ball, and the slave girls will be presented. This will be Jasper's first year he gets to attend the slave girl auction."

I had to swallow down the bile that rose in my throat. I had never attended the gladiator games, not even on opening day, and I didn't want to start now. I didn't agree with any of it, forcing men to fight in a barbaric and inhumane way. More so, I didn't want to show support or encouragement for my father.

I hated him. And as for the slave girls being initiated... well, it is a wonder that at twenty-one, I was still a virgin after growing up in this hell hole.

We need to talk, meet me in my room. Jasper's voice filled my head. I told him I would be there shortly before I cut the link and excused myself from his mother, making my way to his room on the second floor.

I knocked softly and looked left and right down the hallway, making sure no one was watching. The door opened and Jasper grabbed my arm, yanking me into his room and closing the door behind him quickly.

He pushed me up against the wall and began rubbing his body all over me and licking my neck. Covering me in his scent.

"Jasper! What the fuck are you doing?" I gasped at him while shoving him away, horrified at what he was doing, it was so unlike him.

He ran a hand through his blonde hair and blew out a breath. "My father caught me in here with Eloise," he admitted with a tremble in his voice.

I opened my mouth, forming an 'O'. "Did... did you guys, um... you know. Did you mate?"

"No, but we were fooling around when he walked in. I managed to hide her head, but he will be wondering who was in here. If he finds out it was her... Fuck if he finds out Eloise is my mate, he will kill her." Jasper started to rub his eyes and forehead aggressively. "I didn't know what to do, so I thought if you had my scent all over you... He would just assume..." He gave me a pleading look.

I leaned my head back against the wall, tucking my hands behind my back and closing my eyes. "This is so fucked up," I sighed.

"You're telling me? I can't even mate and mark the one

person the Moon Goddess gifted me! It's been two years Tala! Two years! I don't know how much longer I can keep my wolf at bay, he wants his mate." The sadness in his voice jarred me.

I knew how difficult it was for him and El, but I hadn't met my mate, so I couldn't fully understand the pull of the bond. I never expected it to be so strong after watching how my parents treated theirs. So, to see Jasper and Eloise fight it day in and day out, the bond wearing them down, calling to them, it was breaking my heart. I just wanted them to have a happy ending.

"What the fuck are we going to do Tala? Opening day is in two days, your father is going to announce our pairing, then I am expected to participate in initiation day! How do I explain that to Eloise?" He slumped down the wall. "How did we get such fucked up lives? How can our parents do this to us?"

I slid down, leaning against the wall beside him and taking his hand in mine. His hands were huge compared to my tiny ones, but I tried to offer him some comfort and patted his calloused hand.

"Jasper, what if we could change things?" I said after a few moments of silence. He turned his head to look at me with a questioning look on his face.

"How so?"

"I don't know, but what if we could? What if somehow, instead of fighting our parents, we could pretend? Wouldn't you want to change this pack if given the choice,?" I was thinking out loud, not really thinking of the words, just processing random thoughts.

"Worst-case scenario, I could mark you, but we wouldn't have to mate. Then, once I was Alpha, we could reject each other?" He, too, was now processing.

I lifted my hand to smooth out the deep lines on his forehead. He was too young to have those types of creases, deep worry lines from constantly frowning, furrowing, and worrying.

"It would kill Eloise," I whispered, thinking how it would never work. Him marking me could kill Eloise's wolf, and in turn, she would suffer heartbreak and die. "Besides, they have 'a way' to make us mate, remember."

"Tala, I don't know how to protect El from any of this." His voice broke, and his audible gulp echoed in my ears. I leaned my head on his shoulder, one hand still holding his, and let a lone tear slide down my cheek.

I hated this for both my best friends. I hated my father so, so much.

I left Jasper's room. His scent stuck to me like glue so if anyone came across me, they would think we had been rolling around in bed together, except the scent of arousal and sex were absent. Hopefully, they would just assume we had been together.

Everything about my life was shit. Secrets and lies.

I made my way up to my mother's room, opening the door quietly in case she was sleeping. I found her sitting in a chair by the window, looking out. Her maid was laying out some food and tea on the little table that stood by her side.

She gave me a look, shaking her head, lips pressed tightly together. My mother was having a bad day. I sat in the chair next to her, took her hand, and stared out the window with her. The barren land of Bhakhil was dry and depressing. Not a tree or bush in sight, just sandy dirt for miles upon miles.

"Your father will save you. He will come for you. He loves you." Whispered words passed my mother's lips and I looked up at her. Tears graced her eyes.

She was having one of her delusional days. I know this because my father would never save me from anything, and love me? Ha! I didn't think he even knew what the word meant.

She said nothing else as we sat there in silence and watched the light breeze dance across the desert earth, lifting particles of loose dirt and scattering them across the plains. I gave her a kiss when I had sat there long enough and left her in peace.

Maybe tomorrow would be a better day.

I decided to take a walk around the palace grounds, not knowing what else to do with myself. Six guards entered through the main door with Teal, one of the gladiator slaves.

Teal was an older man, around my father's age. Late forties, maybe? He had been here over half his life, since before I was born. He was handsome, with bright red hair like mine and eyes as cerulean blue. Tall and muscular. They had him cuffed in silver as they ushered him toward my father's office.

Every year, just before the games began, my father would summon him. I always felt a soft comfort coming from him whenever I saw him.

He smiled at me as he passed by, and an emotion I couldn't decipher shone in his eyes. Funnily enough, my wolf, Mora, would always preen when he was around. Like she was happy to see him and wanted him to notice her.

He was the longest gladiator resident in history, and I could never figure out why my father had not granted him his freedom yet. Or, if he wasn't going to release him, why he hadn't killed him off. Realistically, he would never let anyone go, never mind grant them their freedom. So how had Teal survived all these years?

Chapter 13 – Respect

KELLEN

The days had passed by slowly, and I understood why prisoners would make tally marks in the cells to count the days. I had no idea how long I had been here, three, maybe four weeks?

It was two days until the opening day when the gladiator games would begin. That much I knew. Twenty-eight days of challenges, twenty-eight days of fighting to survive.

When Teal explained the specifics of the month-long games, he told us how we wouldn't just be fighting each other. We would also be fighting slaves or volunteers from surrounding packs, their champions.

Teal was considered the Alpha's champion, but we would be facing other challenges. He gave examples of past competitions, but he couldn't say for sure what we were to expect as it was different every year.

Our slave barracks were large and could house around twenty-five to thrity men; there were around twenty-six holed up in here with me. Over the past week, the guards had allowed us to exercise and train in the common area.

Each day I had woke before sunrise and began a round of exercises, pushups, crunches, squats, and even jumping jacks. There was nowhere to really run, so I had to stick to the basics. I was also teaching Ajani and Rogue better sword skills, passing on all the training I received from The Alpha Academy.

I had bulked up despite the lack of food and nutrition. I thought of King Mathias as I finished my last pushup and wiped the sweat from my brow.

The dude was huge. I didn't think any amount of exercise, training or even weight-lifting would bring me to his level of bulk. The man was a sheer beast. I bet he would never have found himself in this position, a fighting slave.

I grabbed a clean pair of cotton shorts the guards had provided yesterday and headed towards the communal shower. Still grateful that we had running water and a toilet, no matter how disgusting they were.

When I was toweling off, I heard a commotion from the other end of the barracks. Usually, I would mind my own business; however, curiosity got the best of me, and my wolf stirred.

That was another strange thing. My wolf was getting stronger each day and if I didn't know I couldn't shift, I would think there was nothing wrong - that everything was as it should be.

I hadn't really spoken to the other residents of the barracks since I had been here, except for our small group of five, or four now that Aaron had died.

When I rounded the corner where other small cell-like rooms were located, I heard the laughing and jeering from other slaves. They were encouraging someone to do something.

"That's right, little bitch. That's what you are now, the slave bitch!" I heard one man laugh out.

"Fuck him good!" Another called.

The smell of male arousal was strong, the offending scent assaulting my nose. Ten other slaves stood around, crowding in a circle. I heard a slap and someone making a panicked noise. Some of the men had their cocks in their hands watching whatever was in the middle of the circle.

Just beneath the scent of their desires, I could get a distinct whiff of fear and realized exactly what was happening. I pushed through the circle to find a large male bent over Rogue, and another holding him down over a short partition wall. They had pulled his pants down, and the large man had smacked his ass. I could see the red print of his hand. He was spreading Rogue's ass cheeks apart, his cock by his back door. His feet kicked Rogue's legs further apart.

I let out a growl and ripped the man away from Rogue, throwing him into the wall. The other man let go of Rogue's arms and lunged at me. Suddenly, the sounds of growls and snarls filled the small space as the other slaves lunged at me all at once.

There was a flurry of fists and feet coming at me, but I did not falter. Using the back wall as leverage, I sprung off of it and hurled myself at the ten or so slaves, taking out three of them at once. I caught a fist to the face and my nose split open, gushing blood.

I grabbed the assailant and snapped his arm that had caused me to bleed. His scream bounced off the walls and echoed through the barracks. With each slave that attacked, I put them down. Breaking an arm or a leg, and knocking them out until none stood before me.

I huffed as my adrenaline spiked, my chest heaving with rage. When I was sure no one was left or going to attack, I looked at Rogue. He stood there shaking, his legs trembling, barely holding him up. He looked at me with fear in his eyes.

I just saved him from being raped, why would he fear me? I walked out of there, stepping over the knocked-out and crying men.

I held my hand out to Rogue, and he cowered back against the corner tighter. Fuck this shit, I thought and stomped away.

I was still reeling from the fight, and now I was annoyed that he was acting like this. I didn't expect him to hug or kiss me, but a little gratitude would have been nice. I made it back to my little area... I couldn't call it a room, it was a doorless cell.

Rogue followed me in and I gave him a snarl at his ungratefulness. He shook his head, then pointed to his eye then with the same finger pointed to mine and shook his head again.

I cocked my head. "Is there something wrong with my eyes?" I asked, trying to figure out what his problem was.

Rogue bent down and drew a cross in the dirt then pointed at my eyes again, then at the mark he had made in the dirt.

I was a little slow on the uptake and lifted my hands, palms up. "I have no idea what you are trying to say," I said agitatedly. I was about to shoo him away so I could put my nose back in place when he grabbed my arm. His finger pointed at the mark over my chest and again at my eyes.

"Oh!" I said, and dumbly lifted my hands to feel my eyes and dropped them quickly. "Did my eyes go dark, like the pupils widened?" Rogue nodded his head vigorously. "Was there a white mark in the middle of them?" Again, he nodded and took a step back.

I pursed my lips, wondering how the power of a knight could come forth if I couldn't shift and I couldn't contact the other knights or Lamia. I had tried to establish a mind-link with them every day, and so far, nothing.

I pointed to my chest, "This is a mark of a knight, I am one of the Queen's Knights." His eyes widened in shock and his mouth parted, jaw slack, just showing the stump of his tongue. He took a knee and bowed down to me, then crossed his arm over his chest.

"Get up Rogue," I hissed, looking around hoping no one would see. "This is not the time to pledge your loyalty, I am not a king or knight here." I bent and lifted him by his elbow. "I am nothing here, I can't even shift. A true king would never have been caught; a true king would have found a way out of this mess by now." I wasn't sure why I was voicing my thoughts out loud to him, but I knew he wouldn't tell anyone. Probably because he, well... he couldn't.

"A knight is meant to protect his queen, not get abducted and sold." I sat on my cot, feeling sorry for myself for the first time since I woke up on that goddess-awful boat.

"A knight has their own path, not just to protect his queen. A knight must go through their own trials. I believe you came here for a reason. I believe you are here to help us. I believe the Moon Goddess set you on this path for a reason."

I looked up to see Teal standing in the doorway, his arms crossed, leaning against the red stone frame. He was standing in the same position as when I first met him.

"Well, I wish she would show me what that path is, so I can get on with it," I grumbled.

"The gods and goddesses work in mysterious ways. I'm sure in time, all will be revealed." I was sure his words were trying to encourage me not to give up hope and to keep faith.

No matter how low I felt, or how useless I saw myself, I

would never give up hope. I would find a way out of here and I would find a way to bring this Alpha Vargr down.

Just then, the guards entered the barracks with the rolling tray, the scent of charred meat wafting from the cart.

A few men lined up at the cart to grab their portions, but none would look me in the eye. I noticed the line was much smaller than usual; the absent men were probably still licking their wounds. It could take up to two days for a shifter to heal from a break depending on the strength of their animal.

'Don't eat the meat.' I heard Conri's voice fill my head.

Once I got my portion, I sniffed the meat and dropped my plate in horror. Underneath the charred burnt outside, I could smell the type of animal it had come from.

Human.

Rogue was just about to take a bite from it and I quickly raised my hand, smacking it out of his. He gave me a look like, 'what the fuck'.

"Human," I said, and he began to gag and dry heave.

"For fucks sake, the first time we are given meat and it's human!" Ajani was also making a face like he was ready to empty his stomach.

"So... they are also cannibals?" I asked Teal, who came in with his own portion, minus the meat.

"No." He let out a hearty laugh. "They just try to feed it to us, thinking it's protein before the games. A few of the guys will eat it, but they are the worst. Eat enough of it, and it will send you crazy.

At least they weren't cannibals, but still, that's fucking sick to try and feed us humans.

*****

The next day was much of the same. I exercised and then trained with Ajani, Teal, and Rogue. While training with the swords and going over basic movements, two more gladiator slaves came up to us, making us halt our practice.

"We would like to join you if you will let us?" One of them asked. I looked at Teal, and he grinned. I nodded my head at the two men and told them to fall in. They grabbed a weapon each and paired up.

Ten minutes later, we had an additional four men come to join us. By the end of the afternoon, all but five of the men were lined up and training with us. We moved from weapons to sparing and general defensive moves.

"You did good, young king." Teal patted me on the back as the group broke up.

"Thank you, I felt like a leader again today." I smirked because I truly did. For a while, I forgot where I was, and it felt like I was back home leading one of our mandatory training exercises with the elite warriors.

"You are a born leader, Kellen. I see it, these men see it. Soon they will all see it." He said, motioning to the arena that lay outside the barrack walls.

After showering, I took time to lie on my cot before the guards rolled in dinner. Thankfully there was no 'surprise meat' this time. Instead, they gave us a baked potato, fruit, bread, water, and... chocolate? I picked up the brown square and sniffed it. Warily, I licked it. Yep definitely chocolate.

Teal, Ajani, and Rogue came into my area, sat on the floor, and began eating. We ate in silence until I looked and saw one of the slaves who joined in our training session today standing at the entrance.

"Can I help you?" I asked arching my brows at his fidgeting stance.

"No alpha," he said before taking a step in and placing his square of chocolate on my dish, bowing at me, and then leaving quickly.

That was weird.

Another gladiator slave came in and did the same thing, dropped his square of chocolate on my dish, bowed, and left. This carried on until my dish was piled with the squares. All but three of the other slaves came in and gave me their square.

"They see you as their leader now. It is their way of showing you respect and telling you that you are of a higher rank than they are. They are paying you tribute." Teal smiled at me and then added his piece of chocolate to my pile. Ajani did the same. Rogue just looked at me and held his hands up in a sorry gesture, then pointed to his mouth.

I laughed, he had eaten it, and I didn't care. I felt guilty that they had all given me their portions, but I also understood the meaning and sentiment behind it. They respected me. They had all seen my display of power when I stopped the assault on Rogue.

In their own way, they had all just pledged their loyalty to me.

I laughed loud and fully at Rogue's expense, his gesture and expression was comical. I felt an ease in my soul as the four of us sat there and conversed. Of course, poor Rogue did more listening than trying to join in.

'Give Rogue our blood,' Conri whispered. I didn't know why he was whispering, it was only me that could hear him.

'Why?' I asked, super curious.

'Because then he can mind-link with you.' He said like I should have known.

'How can I do that when you have been restrained?' I was confused at Conri's request; I couldn't establish a link with Lamia or the other knights, so how would I establish a pack link with Rogue?

'Just try it,' he pushed. I pushed him to the back of my mind, not something I wanted to do after fearing that he could never return, but he was talking crap.

Tomorrow, the games began.

Chapter 14 – Game Day

TALA

I stood outside my father's office, pushing myself against the wall as tight as possible, listening to the conversation that was taking place inside.

"I brought the fucking King of Wolves, show me some respect Vargr!" A familiar voice hissed and bit out at my father. "Show me some respect, because all this... can be taken away."

"You dare to threaten me, you disgrace of a bear!" My father shouted back at the man. I could only think of one werebear that would talk to my father like that, aside from Orion. Jack.

"Since Orion's death, a power struggle has emerged. You do not want to find yourself on the opposite side to me." Jack spat back - the tension in his voice was strained and vicious.

"I will take back my rightful title as King of Bhakhil, it is my birthright!" Along with the anger, there was also desperation in my father's voice.

So, he truly was born a royal. He always said he was a king, but I could never believe him.

"I want what's owed to me Vargr... Where is the witch? I know Orion had you hide her."

"I don't know where she is Jack... As you said yourself, the continent is in an uproar, kingdoms are at war!"

"I want one-thousand chips and the witch..." I heard jack begin, then there was a beat of silence before a third man spoke. It was a voice I had never heard before - it was smooth and calm.

"We have ears listening to us." His smooth voice carried to my ears. He sounded friendly enough, but I knew better than to trust a wolf that walked with a bear.

Before I could move and make a run for it, the door to my father's office opened and a large hand snagged my hair. I yelped from the sting of having my hair pulled. I was yanked backward and dragged into the room. The door closed behind me.

"And who might we have here?" Jack fisted my hair tight, pulling my head back so I had nowhere else to look but at him.

He ran his nose along my neck, inhaling my scent, then let the tip of his tongue taste the flesh just below my ear. I cringed and tried to pull away, but his grip fastened tighter around my red hair. I let out a whimper, but that only seemed to spur him on.

"She smells delicious." Jack purred. He pulled his head back and looked at me. He was tall and bulky, his dirty blond hair cut to a neat length. His blue eyes looked so kind and full of life, like a deep blue sea, yet his body language told a different story.

"Tala." My father spoke my name through clenched jaws.

"Tala? So grown up since the last time I saw her, and much prettier than her dead sister." I was shocked to hear him say that my sister was dead, although I already knew it. Maybe because I hadn't seen her die or her body, I don't know, but the way he said it had my eyes staring wide at his and my mouth parting.

"Maybe I could just take her until you give me what I want." Jack chuckled. He finally let go of my hair, only to push me into the grasp of the unknown wolf.

"She has been promised to Beta Baron's son. You can't..."

Jack whipped his head towards my father and let out a menacing growl that had me shaking. The wolf holding me chuckled, and my father took a step back. "And you promised me a thousand chips and a witch, yet I have none."

"What Jack is trying to say, Alpha Vargr – is that we know how these chips work. Give him what he is owed, or we can take the Wolf King from you. Not only that..." The wolf looked down at me. His hands that were securely fastened around my shoulder and waist, now began to roam. One was palming a breast, the other gliding down my stomach while still pressing my back flush against his front. "...We could also take away everything, including this little princess."

I felt his hot breath at my ear. "Would you like that, little red?" His smooth and even voice calmly taunted me, sending a shiver of fear down my spine. "In fact, I have decided, she shall be escorted to the games by myself and Jack today. What do you say, Jack?" He looked up at Jack, his hand groping my breast harder. His other hand found the waistband of my long skirt and pushed his fingers just under it, but not any further.

My father's face was beet red and his fists were coiled tightly, arms ramrod straight as he tried to compose himself. I thought he would argue, at least for Jasper's sake, as he was meant to announce our pairing at the games today.

Of course, I shouldn't have expected anything remotely heroic from my father.

"Fine," he said with a cold breath, "but you cannot fuck her, do I make myself clear? You can have your pick of any slave girl, shit I will even give you my Luna, but *she* must not be touched. I want her intact when she mates with the beta's son."

"Oh, we don't have to deflower her to have our fun. You know that, Vargr." Jack winked at me, and the twinkle in his eye as he said that scared the shit out of me. It looked so... innocent, yet I knew he meant every word. My legs shook, barely holding me up, and there was no doubt in my mind that they could smell my fear. Especially when the unknown wolf took another sniff at me, and I felt the low vibration of his growl vibrate against the pulse in my neck.

"Now about these chips... Oliver let her go, we will have her later," Jack said with an icy tone. His eyes wandered over my body, settling longer on my chest.

Before the conversation went any further, the wolf, who Jack had just called Oliver, reluctantly let go of me. My father sent me out of the room, telling me to get ready and dress up now that I had two new escorts.

Leaning against the wall, I put one hand over my heart and one over my mouth, trying to calm my shaking body down. He wouldn't just pimp me out like the slave girls, would he? As I thought this, I internally laughed at myself. Of course, he would. If it meant him getting what he wants or staying out of Jack's wrath, then I was as good as sold. He wouldn't blink an eye at handing me over.

There was no hope of getting out of going to the games now. That was why I was originally standing outside his office door, in hopes of persuading him to let me stay home, in the palace. It was a slim chance to begin with, but I was going to give it a shot and plead my case. Now, however, I realized my mistake.

My mistake was thinking that somewhere deep in his cold heart, he actually gave a shit about me. How stupid of me.

I walked away from his office and made my way up to my room, looking for Eloise and Jasper now that my heart had calmed down a little and my legs seemed to start functioning again.

What I really needed to do was let my wolf out. It had been so long since I had last shifted and let Mora run. Once a month, I was allowed to shift and run in the palace gardens, always under guard. I was sure it wasn't for my safety, but rather to make sure I didn't make a run for it.

My wolf was quick and slick. She was big, even for a female alpha, and her red fur danced like flames of fire when she ran. The first time I shifted was when I was sixteen. I was so happy that my wolf was so beautiful and I wanted to run, just like the other pups who had shifted that night, but my father commanded me to shift back again.

When I shifted, I was met with an angry glare. "You will not shift again unless I say so." He had spat the words at me, so much hatred in that one sentence. That night seemed to be the icing on the cake and just fueled his loathing of me. I couldn't do anything right. His detest for my mere presence was made known when he banned me from the table.

He had always treated my mother horribly, calling her names, hitting her, and cheating on the mate bond. The night of my shift, I could hear them arguing. As a newly shifted wolf, my hearing could pick up little bits. Like when my father called me a good-for-nothing carrot whore, or when he told my mother he should just feed me to his pets.

I don't know what she said to him after that because I ran from the palace, tears streaming down my eyes, not knowing what I did to make him hate me so much.

I was so wrapped up in my thoughts that I wasn't paying attention to my surroundings. I opened the door to my room to find Jasper in my bed, his face in between Eloise's legs. "Oh, my goddess!" I cried out, clamping a hand over my mouth, not being able to look away. Then, realizing I was staring, I clamped a hand over my eyes, backed out slowly, and closed the door.

Why the heck were they in my room? That is so gross!

You better change my fucking sheets I said, pissed when I established a link with El and Jasper, cutting it off before either could reply.

I was a stranger in my own home. At least that's what it felt like.

I found myself standing on the terrace that overlooked the arena, leaning over and resting my head in my hands, elbows braced on the stone ledge. It was game day and pack members and visitors were mulling around down below. On game days, we allowed spectators to come and walk around while the arena hosted various stalls and carnival games. They could even walk around the slave barracks and see the gladiators in their element; however, only people with a certain size bank account were able to view the female slaves.

It was like taking the family to the horse tracks. You could get a first look at who you wanted to bet on, or with the women, a first look at who you wanted to pay for.

How I wish I could escape this place.

'And where would we go?' Mora's voice echoed in my head.

'Somewhere, with lots of water like the ocean. Or maybe somewhere with lots of green trees?' I sighed, thinking how I had never seen the sea or how my wolf had never felt the soft black dirt under her paws, like in the green and enchanted forests we read about in books.

My wolf hummed in my mind, liking that idea.

I had never been allowed to leave the compound of the palace, never been outside the wall that surrounded the grounds. I didn't have a phone like other wolves I have seen using them, and I had never seen a movie. I was homeschooled and led a pretty sheltered life.

I wasn't even meant to train like the other wolves my age, but Archie, my father's delta, had trained me and taught me a lot in secret. That was until my father found out and had his head removed in front of the pack. He said: "This is what happens when you disobey your alpha. Let this example be a lesson." And then he stuck Archie's head on a spike and left him there for three days until his pets were let out to eat him.

I shuddered at the memory. That was only three years ago, another reason for me to detest coming to the arena or watching the gladiator matches. Death was a form of entertainment in our kingdom.

It was just a reminder of what my father would, could, and has taken from me. Now he had just offered me up to Jack and his wolf, Oliver. I frowned when I thought of Jack's words, "We don't have to deflower her to have our fun." I wasn't oblivious to what sex was just because I had never done it, but I had no idea what he meant and shuddered at the possibilities of what he could have meant.

I took in a deep breath, finding my resolve to go back in and begin dressing for the opening of the games.

A light breeze picked up and I closed my eyes, relishing the feel of it across my cheeks. The scent of spice and another smell that I thought could be what I imagined as some tree, floated with the tail end of the slight breeze. It was the most alluring scent I had ever smelt. Causing a sensation, like the flutter of a flurry butterflies in my stomach.

All too quickly, the scent evaporated, leaving the dry and dusty scent of the barren land that surrounded us in its absence.

My wolf perked up, pushing to the forefront of my mind, trying to pick up that scent again. I could feel her excitement at the unusual smells and I smiled. 'You like that too huh?'

She mentally wagged her tail. I wished a simple scent could make me as happy as she seemed when she caught a whiff of it. I had to admit, it was pretty tantalizing as far as fragrances went.

Chapter 15 – Let the Games Begin

<u>KELLEN</u>
GLADIATOR GAMES DAY 1

Earlier in the morning, we had been given another new pair of shorts. They were the same off-white cotton as the other pairs. Thin and lightweight, and barely came down to the top of my thigh. I looked down at them, they reminded me of an adult diaper, yet these were almost see-through and held nothing in place.

I found out that we would not be fighting today. Instead, we would be presented to the crowd and brought before the Alpha. After that, they had a small show, and then the Alpha's and surrounding pack's champions would put on a fight to showcase their strength.

I wasn't nervous, more like anxious. Conri had been bouncing around in my head all morning, eager to get into the arena. I had to tell him several times to calm down, and when I asked him what his problem was, he just got more excited and paced. At this point, he was giving me a headache and I had to block him out.

I wanted to stay alert, and he was breaking my concentration. It was unlike my wolf to act this way. Maybe he was eager to spill blood, maybe he just wanted to show off his power? I had felt him getting stronger in the past weeks, and I was sure we were at full strength, despite not being able to shift.

As the sun rose to a high position and the heat of the day became stifling, the sound of the crowd grew. Their excited chatter reached my ears. Patrons began to walk around the arena and by our barracks, peering in with curiosity and pointing at some of us.

I slipped on the new shorts, went to the common area of the barracks, and sat down by Teal.

"I feel like a fuckin clown," I mumbled to Teal,.

"Get used to it. That's what we are, expendable entertainment." His voice lacked his usual charm. His deep baritone voice was filled with melancholy, and his usual blue eyes lacked a spark.

"Are you okay, Teal?" I asked in true concern. I knew he had been summoned to the Alpha's home yesterday, but he had never mentioned what happened or what was said.

"When we go out there today, keep your wits about you. The Alpha already has his radar on you. Don't give him a reason to end your life. No matter how much he paid for you, his wolf craves the scent of blood and Vargr has a quick temper. He will act without thinking." He kept his voice low so no one else could hear him, just me.

I mulled over his words. The last time I had encountered Vargr, I had royal pissed him off by calling him a coward and a false king. I said nothing that wasn't true, and he would be sorely mistaken if he thought I would bow down to him. I would rather die than show him submission.

"What's bothering you, Teal?" I tried again. He only shook his head and offered me a weak smile. I nudged him, pressing him to tell me what had him looking so defeated. In all my time here, I had never seen Teal look as... sad, as he did now.

"It is nothing for you to worry about, young king. I feel

this may be my last year here." His head bobbed down, and his red hair fell over his eyes. "I fear my time is up, I am old by gladiator standards, and I have championed the games for many years. This year Vargr told me I would be fighting the final battle. Only the winner will live. It is a fight to the death."

My breath caught in my throat, and I swallowed down the lump it left. He had been here for twenty-two years, and now he had been told when he was going to die. "If that is the case, Teal, then I have no doubt the Moon Goddess will meet you with open arms, but who is he to say you will not win?"

"My fate has already been chosen, young king. As have all our fates." Teal stood up and moved over by the wall where a section had been barred off. Spectators were currently walking by and assessing the gladiator slaves they could see.

"Mama, mama, look it's him, the Wolf Prince!" I turned to see where the familiar little voice was coming from and spotted him jumping up and down by the barred wall Teal stood by. His mother, the woman who had handed us our sacks, stood next to him, gripping his arm in a bid to halt his excited jumping.

I got up and walked over to where they were and smiled at the young pup.

"I knew you were going to fight!" He shouted with enthusiasm. "You look like the strongest wolf here, even stronger than the Alpha!" The young pup claimed, his eyes bright with excitement. "I made this for you. Mama said I could give it to you if you were here, and I just knew you would be."

The boy, who was maybe around ten, shoved his hands through the bars at me, opening his closed fist. "I made it myself," he said, holding out a small carved piece of wood in the shape of a wolf.

"You made this... for me?" I gave him a genuine smile, awed by his gift and the gesture it represented. "I will treasure it, young pup. What is your name?" I asked, bending down so I could look at him properly.

"Augustus." He smiled back.

"Auggie, time to go," his mother told him. Her lips were pressed tight and her gaze would not meet mine.

"It was nice to meet you, Augustus. I will treasure my gift," I told him, closing the tiny wolf in my hand.

"I will cheer for you, Wolf Prince. I hope I get to see you fight!" He said over his shoulder as his mother dragged him away.

I walked back to my area, placed the wooden wolf on the ledge of the barred window above my cot, and stood there for a moment looking at it. The child's kindness reminded me of Lamia when she was that age, full of love and innocence, a kindness that knew no discrimination.

The sound of trumpets rang out across the arena, and the chatter of spectators died down. The guards came to the main entrance and called out for us to line up. Once lined up, we were led out into the arena. The stadium was almost overflowing with hundreds, maybe thousands of shifters.

"Lords, Gentlemen, and Ladies. Welcome to the Bhakhil Annual Gladiator Games opening day! Please stand for Alpha Vargr and Luna Mila!" The trumpets rang out again as the announcer finished, and all eyes turned to the main tent where the Alpha had sat last time.

Vargr and his Luna entered the tent, coming to the front and giving the crowd a wave. The crowd met him with cheers and when Vargr lifted his hand, the crowd quieted down and tilted their necks in submission. It was not an act of pride for their alpha, it was an act of fear. It would have shown respect if they had bowed, but to tilt your neck at a gathering like this showed that his pack feared him.

Teal stood next to me, his eyes not once leaving the tent where the Alpha stood, staring at the Luna with an obvious grievance. Did they have a history? I wondered to myself.

My eyes were drawn back to the Alpha as he began to speak. His rough and vile voice carried throughout the arena without the need for a microphone. "Loyal subjects, this year is not just any year. The beginning of the games this year will mark the announcement that my daughter will be taking a chosen mate. I am pleased to announce that the pairing of Lord Beta Baron's son, Jasper, and my youngest daughter, Tala, has been approved." There was a slight hesitation in his voice when he said 'my youngest daughter'.

"On the full moon at the end of the games, they will mate and mark each other. And in true tradition, the coupling of this chosen pair will be overseen by the ranked members and elders. I present to you the beta's son… Jasper." Vargr held his hand out towards the side of the tent where a young man who looked my age stepped out and made his way towards the Alpha.

"I now present my youngest daughter, Tala!" Again his words fumbled, ever so slightly, when he said 'daughter'.

I looked towards the tent, expecting to see another version of Orion's bitch, Shayna, who was Vargr's eldest daughter. Instead, my sight was drawn to the woman who entered the tent like a moth to a flame, her red hair catching all of my attention.

My heart stopped. I swear it did. My breath caught in my throat and my body tingled all over, sending a wave of goosebumps across my skin despite the raging heat and causing me to shiver.

I was a good distance away, but the scent of sea salt and oranges drifted to me like tendrils reaching out and searching for a host to latch onto.

Teal stiffened beside me. A look of anguish crossed his features, and he held a longing as he watched the red-headed girl be escorted into the tent by two men and came to stand next to her father.

"May this year's gladiators be presented to the Alpha!" The announcer called out. I barely heard him and barely acknowledged walking forward. My eyes did not leave the flaming redhead that I walked towards.

We were being presented in groups of four. Myself, Teal, and two others walked towards the Alpha who we were meant to greet. I had already told Teal that I would not show any kind of submission to the piece of shit who called himself an alpha.

Like I said, I would rather die.

As we walked the length of the arena, the announcer began to present us. "I present our Champion Gladiator, our longest and most formidable competitor, the strongest and meanest... Teal!" The crowd broke out into a chorus of shouting. Some cheered while others booed. "Next, we have our newest and biggest gladiator, coming from a land far away. He thinks he is a king with the mouth to back it up, but can he fight like one? Prince-ee!!" He yelled.

Again, the sounds of the crowd erupted. This time, there was more booing, but the sounds of the chanting were drowned out and the realm stood still as I took in the sight of the redheaded beauty. I was closer now and could see her features more clearly.

Her flaming hair was woven into a braided crown framing her tiny face. Big, round, and bright blue eyes stared back at me, capturing my breath and making my heart pound faster. I felt my cock jolt in response and willed it to go down. This was not the time or the place for my desires to take over.

I let my eyes roam over her perfectly shaped body, the blue tunic dress hugging her curves tight, the color illuminating her eyes. Her rose buds lips were parted and her tongue came out and licked them. I copied the action, feeling parched from her beauty.

'Mate!' Conri cried out over and over again in my head.

My lips parted as the word wanted to tumble out. I wanted to take her in my arms and make those perfectly pink lips red with my bite. My eyes met hers once more and I saw her give a small shake of her head, her eyes holding a look of fear, pleading with me not to call her out.

Was this a rejection? Was she ashamed of me because I stood here as a gladiator slave and not the king I truly was? The slight stab of pain that flitted through my heart had my jaw clenching at the thought of my mate rejecting me.

It was over before I even had a chance.

No, this couldn't be. The Moon Goddess was not that cruel, was she? I had already lost one girl. Would she grant me another that I could not have?

I furrowed my brows and saw her eyes shift to the man beside her. I had been so enamored by the tiny pale-skinned beauty and the need to claim her that I hadn't even noticed the two men who stood beside her. When my eyes finally recognized them, I couldn't help the low growl that resonated from my chest.

My mate was flanked by none other than Oliver and Jack.

The rage built inside me, crawling through my skin like a parasite. I bit the inside of my cheek, my wolf wanting to shift and kill the two men who stood way too close to my little flame.

'*She is mine,*' my wolf growled, his hackles raised and ready to fight for what was his.

My mate's face flushed, and she looked around nervously when she heard my growl. I pinned my sights on Oliver, who began to tremble slightly when he noticed me. Then I watched as a smug grin came over him and he looked from me to my little flame and back again.

The fucker knew she was my mate, and he bent down low to whisper something in her ear. I would kill the fucking prick.

"Get a hold of yourself, Kellen." Teal whisper yelled at me, bringing me back to the now.

He nudged my arm, our group had been presented and we were to return to the slave barracks. I gave the beauty one last look before turning my back and following Teal. My head was a mess of thoughts, and Conri was howling, urging me to go back and claim our mate.

'She is his daughter. She doesn't want us.' I spat at him in my mind. 'We are not good enough for her.' My wolf went quiet and crawled to the back of my mind with his tail tucked. A whimper of sadness filled my head.

When we reached the barracks, I went straight to my area and sat on my cot with my head in my hands. I just wanted to touch her. Her flushed and rosy-cheeked face filled my thoughts, and her blue eyes were bright and mesmerizing. I groaned when I thought of how those soft lips would feel against mine.

"She is your mate." I heard Teal, only to look up and find him standing with Ajani and Rogue.

I cocked my head at him. Was it that obvious? His bright blue eyes stared at me, and his arms crossed tightly against his broad chest. I took him in, not letting his gaze go. I could see him shift, he was starting to feel uncomfortable at my staring. He finally averted his eyes, not being able to hold mine any longer.

It was that small movement, when he cast his eyes to the side and then down, that I realized who he was. My jaw slacked and hung open. "And she is your daughter," I said with a catch in my breath as I voiced the truth.

My little flame's eyes were a copy of his, her red hair a little brighter, but there was no mistaking it. My mate was Teal's daughter.

Chapter 16 – Let the Games Begin Part 2

<u>TALA</u>

Eloise helped me put on the thin blue tunic dress and then braided my long red hair, wrapping it around my head like a crown. I applied a coat of mascara and clear lip gloss to give my lips a shine.

I stared at my reflection in the mirror of my vanity. "You look beautiful Tala," Eloise praised.

"El, won't you be coming too? A lady always needs her maid." I asked my best friend.

She smiled, her lips pulling into a tight line. Her smile was not of happiness, it was fake and forced. "I have been told I am not needed. You will be escorted by Jack and the wolf," she spoke.

I could tell she was upset and holding back, but I didn't need to ask her what was wrong. I already knew. Today, my father would be announcing my pairing with Jasper, her mate, and there was nothing we could do about it. I felt guilty. Even though I didn't want to, I was stealing her future, her happiness. Her mate.

"We have twenty-eight days until the full moon. Jasper and I will find a way out of this, I promise." Her hands rested on my shoulders. I brought one hand up and laid it on one of hers, squeezing it gently, trying to reassure her that this was not what Jasper or I wanted.

Jasper was in love with her, and she was head over heels for him. I was the obstacle in the way of true love, a fated pair being held apart because of rank and greed. Eloise didn't deserve to be tossed to the side. She didn't deserve to have her fate ripped away from her. She didn't deserve to be treated as less, because she wasn't. She was so much more than a maid, so much more than my best friend. She was strong, and not once did she scream or yell at me in anger, not once did she blame me or Jasper for our fathers' decisions.

A knock came at the door and Jasper entered, his gaze immediately falling on El. The look of love poured out from his light green eyes as they cast a wanting look over Eloise. I blinked for a long second, trying not to cry for my two best friends and their tragic love story.

I could not let my father win. I would find a way out of this pairing for them, for Jasper and El, I thought to myself. I just didn't know how yet.

"Jack and Oliver are waiting for you in the hall. Father said they will be escorting you to the opening ceremony instead of me." I gulped and shivered.

"Yes, that's right. Jack has decided to be my companion until my father gives him what he is owed. If my father doesn't, then Jack said he will take me as payment instead." My voice trembled as I relayed what transpired in my father's office.

Jasper shook with anger. "You are not a fucking bargaining chip." He gritted out "How can a father do this to his only living daughter? It's sick. What he is making us do is sick. What he will put El through is sick and my father is no better." I could see his skin become red, the color creeping up and over his face.

"Tonight, after the opening of the games, when they introduce the slave girls, the three of us will form a plan. A good plan, one that will get you two out of this... this... pairing!" I nodded my head, agreeing with Eloise.

Jasper crossed the room and took her in his arms, smoothing down her black hair as he administered kisses on the crown of her head. "You are right little mate; we need to form a solid plan."

Eloise was smart, smarter than me, just a little sheltered from the day-to-day life. I was well educated, but Eloise had a natural talent for math and science. Like my sister Shayna, El was a whiz when it came to electronics. Of course, she wasn't a chemist or alchemist like Shayna had been, that had been a gift from the goddess - a gift Shayna had abused.

Eloise, though could build a radio from scraps and could calculate time, distance, and speed in her head with the click of a finger. Between the three of us, we should be able to come up with a solid plan and be able to stop the forced mating and marking that was meant to take place in twenty-eight days.

If it meant me taking my life, then I would gladly do it if it meant Jasper and Eloise could live happily ever after.

I straightened my shoulders, lifted my chin, and took several calming breaths before I opened my door and was met by Jack the bear and his wolf, Oliver.

I would not let them intimidate me this time.

Jack was big and scary, the epitome of evil, with a viciousness that rivaled even my father's cruelty. Oliver had a look that was sly and cunning, he was calculating. I thought that if the Moon Goddess had given evil shifters mates, these two would be a match made in heaven.

"Why, don't you look gentle to the eyes." Oliver's slimy

voice cooed at me as I emerged from my room and took steps towards them.

"Very pleasing to the eye," Jack complimented.

"Gentlemen, shall we?" I said, ignoring their looks of lust as their eyes roamed my body.

I would not let them intimidate me today, I said to myself again. My wolf growled in my head, she did not like these two being so close to us and neither did I. However, for the sake of getting through today and my sanity, I pushed the nauseous feeling of being so near to these two shifters to the back of my mind and chided my wolf to behave herself.

I plastered on the best smile I could fake and held my arms out for the two sacks of skins to take. I tried not to gag when they both took an arm each, oblivious of my aversion to them, then led me down and out to the arena.

The arena was packed with spectators. Shifters from all ranks crowded on the stadium's stone seating. Neighboring alphas and higher-ranked wolves were seated in private tents, with slaves serving cool drinks as the sun beat down heavily. The air, thick with humidity, made it hard to breathe.

I stood behind our tent while my father addressed the pack and visiting shifters. I stole a glance at Jasper, who looked nervous as shit, and hoped I didn't convey the same unease as he did.

Jack and Oliver conversed over my head as I waited to be announced. They were muttering something about a prince, but I couldn't concentrate on listening to them. My wolf was bouncing around in my head like a jackrabbit, excited about something, and I was having a hard time reining her in.

I saw Jasper round the tent and heard the clapping and cheering of the crowd. Then I heard my name, and my legs went stiff. I couldn't move, but Oliver's large hand took my elbow and pulled me forward and out of my stationary state.

I was oblivious to what my father said and gave the crowd a small toothy smile and a slight wave.

"May this year's gladiators be presented to the Alpha!" The announcer called out, and I shifted my gaze to the approaching gladiator slaves. I had only ever seen Teal, so I was curious as to what the rest looked like – if they would be as big and strong as him.

Four gladiators approached our tent, walking swiftly as they crossed the arena to us.

My skin heated up as the wolf gladiator next to Teal walked forward; my heart was fluttering, and my breath was caught in a stutter. The closer he got, the more my body trembled.

Holy mother of the moon, take me now, I thought.

He was so... strong looking. His body was sculpted to perfection, each dip and cut of his muscular chest and ripped abs were pure perfection.

Each muscle flexed as he strode toward me. I couldn't pull my eyes from him. I just wanted to touch him, to reach out and feel him, just one touch.

When his head lifted, our eyes met, and I shuddered with desire. I was lost in the depths of his deep blue eyes. The warm sensation building up in my abdomen had me clenching my thighs.

My breath stuttered at those blue eyes, so bright against his tanned skin and light brown hair. Take me now, my body hummed.

From my side, I felt Oliver shift his stance. His head craned around and he looked at me knowingly. He looked at the gladiator, then back at me.

A smug grin crept up from the corners of his mouth, and he bounced on the balls of his feet. Just once. I shuddered at his posture and that menacing look he now held on his face.

He knew.

He knew the gladiator wolf was my mate.

I glanced at Jack who was talking with a man next to him. He hadn't noticed a thing. Thank goddess.

Mora was screaming 'MATE' over and over in my head, desperately wanting to claim her mate. I clamped my lips together. The word was at the tip of my tongue, the need to say it out loud was overwhelming.

I felt Oliver shudder next to me before he went rigged. I looked up, his eyes were wide and mouth in a tight line, lips pressed firmly together.

Was that fear? The emotion in his eyes was gone before I could be sure.

I looked into the gladiator's godly eyes again, wanting nothing more than to feel his breath on my skin, for those large hands to hold me and envelope me in his exotic scent of spice. I didn't know what the other masculine scent was, but it was divinely calming.

I gave a slight shake of my head. Please don't say it, I silently urged him.

My father would kill him on sight. Especially as he had just announced my pairing and my mate was a slave.

I saw his face fall when I shook my head, the look of rejection in his eyes. Teal nudged him and he turned his back on me, walking away back to the gladiator barracks.

My heart pounded furiously at his retreating figure, and Mora cried out for her mate. He thought I was rejecting him.

A tear slid from my eye. I would never reject my mate, but I couldn't let anyone know that I had found my fated mate.

The need to find a way out of my pairing with Jasper had suddenly become more prominent than it was an hour ago. Now I needed to figure out how free my mate also. A sense of hopelessness came across me, and my chest fluttered for a different reason. The heat of the sun and the force of the bond made me light-headed, a dizzy spell taking over me. Before I could brace myself, my legs gave out and my body crumpled.

It was too much.

I braced for impact, but a pair of strong hands grasped me under my arms and hauled me up before I could hit the stone steps. I looked at my savior, Oliver. He had a concerned look on his face and gently brought me to my feet.

His actions were unexpected, but even more unexpected was the worried and troubled look he gave me.

"Hold yourself up princess; do not let them see your weakness." Oliver's harshly whispered words filtered into my ear. My eyes were still on the retreating figure of my mate. He turned around, giving me one last glance before he disappeared back into the gladiator barracks.

I wanted to cry out, but Oliver pinched the sensitive skin under my arm. There was a hard look on his face when I turned to him, his stern eyes imploring what he just said. 'Do not let them see your weakness' I repeated to myself.

The rest of the events that took place for the opening of the games were a blur, my mind on one thing only. The gladiator wolf.

I was so relieved when my father excused me and told me to take my mother back to her room as the celebration was ending.

The visiting alphas and higher ranks would be moving to the main palace hall where a banquet was set up. After the banquet, the induction of the female slaves would begin. I wanted to get my mother settled and drugged up before the events began.

I prayed that Jasper would not have to take part in the slave induction. I also knew he may not have a choice, and I was thankful that he and El had not marked each other. Otherwise, the pain she would feel could be so much worse.

Another drug my sister had concocted, at the request of our father, was an herbal concoction that made a male lustful, driving his wolf with the urge to mate. I had seen it used. The male would grow hard, even without the owner being aroused. His dick would stand to attention, and his wolf would want to mate.

This is what they planned to use on Jasper when they wanted us to couple. I would be given a dose of belladonna and a little wolfsbane to make my wolf compliant. Therefore, allowing me to be receptive to Jasper and him forced to mate with me whether he wanted to or not.

I hated my sister for being a smarty-pants and hated her even more for being given the gift of an alchemist. Her death was of no consequence to me. I thought I would shed a tear, but in the past few years, she had become a bitch. Selfish and power-hungry, just like my father. She deserved to die after the monstrosities she and Orion had created.

I took my mother to her room. Her maid had left her some food, and she nibbled at it before lying down on her bed. She hadn't said a word to me. Today was a great day as she knew what her mate would be doing tonight, and I think she welcomed the meds. She knew that if she didn't have them, she could very well die tonight.

I strapped her down on the bed because even though the medication would subdue her and leave her unconscious, her wolf could still wake and claw her own heart out. She laid down, her head tilted towards the window and her eyes glazed.

I took the first needle and injected her. Once the liquid had been pushed into her, she turned to me. The effects of the drug began taking hold immediately.

"Tala, my beautiful girl," she whispered, her eyes becoming heavy, and her body relaxing. She would be out in mere seconds. "Vargr is not your father." She again whispered, and her eyes closed.

"Mum!" I said, shaking her lightly. "What do you mean he isn't my father?" I tried again, but she was out, the drugs did what they were designed to do.

Was she confused? What did she mean he isn't my father?

Chapter 17 – The Horrifying Truth

LAMIA

"Can we trust what he has told us?" Abner asked as we sat in Mathias's office.

"I trust him," I said. "So far, Finn has not shown any signs of lying and he has been more than cooperative."

"Yet he still had the balls to make demands," Mathias grunted from his chair. He was sitting behind his desk, I was pacing back and forth.

We had questioned Finnegan, and true to himself, he had told us everything. His mother had not died when Orion claimed - but many years later, after she birthed another child from Orion. A daughter who was five years younger than Finnegan and had been locked away since she was fifteen years old. He explained how when Orion did kill Finn's mother, he left her corpse to rot in the cell with her daughter.

He told us about the inhibitor chips Orion's bitch, Shayna, had invented. He knew how they worked, but he didn't know how they were made or how to deactivate them. This was why we sent for Damon, who was currently with Xander trying to figure the thing out.

We showed Finnegan pictures of Petra that Travis had sent us, and also admitted that she had been worried about him. His features softened when he saw that she was okay.

"He only demanded to know about Petra and for us to find his sister." I chided my mate. "If it was Xander, you would want him to be okay, right?" I think I was a little more sensitive to the matter seeing as we still had no leads on Kellen.

"It still doesn't sit right with me. He spent his whole life serving Orion, who's to say he isn't as sick-minded as that fuck?" Mathias leaned back in his chair, sweeping a hand through his now longer black hair. I loved the length, more to grab on to. "I just don't trust him, and I don't trust him around you," he said, giving me a pointed look.

"He saved my life, King. He also sent us warnings about the attack on MacTire. For a man who was controlled by his father mentally and electronically, he risked his own life trying to do the right thing. And as far as Petra is concerned, she told us how protective he was of her. That Finn did everything to keep her away from harm." I tried explaining.

I trusted Finn. I didn't know why, maybe because he saved my life, maybe because he was so concerned about Petra, maybe because I could see his heartbreak when he talked about his sister. Or maybe it was because of my hormones.

I rubbed my belly, I was close to four months pregnant and I looked like I was ready to give birth. Fucking triplets. I stopped my pacing and Mathias quickly jumped up, taking me in his arms.

"You need to stop stressing little wolf, this is not good for the cubs." He soothed.

"Pups." I countered.

"Babies." He said, chuckling. We were still not sure what the babies would come out as. As they grew, their scents became stronger, but the three scents were so mixed that I couldn't pinpoint and separate just one of the babies' scents. I was sure at least one was a cub, but I wasn't going to tell King that and give him the satisfaction to gloat.

Mathias had urged me to get a scan done, not something wolves generally did because our wolf could tell us when the baby was due or alert us if there was a problem. They would even know the sex of the pups. However, Inanna was just as baffled as we were, so I would be going to a hospital in Lonely City tomorrow for a scan so we could get a better look at the little sprouts inside me.

I was both excited and nervous, and so was Mathias.

Xander and Damon came bursting into the office just then, wide and cheesy grins on their faces.

"We got it!" Xander exclaimed. "Your boy Damon here is a fucking genius! Even I'm impressed." True, Damon was a genius, but Xander was not without skills either. They were two of the smartest people I knew.

"Ria is going to be jealous of your bromance," Mathias chuckled at his brother. "With how close you two have been working together, it's a wonder you haven't completed your mating bond yet."

"Fuck off. That's none of your business, brother!" Xander said, clenching his teeth and giving King an angry glare.

Xander stepped over to the mini bar and poured himself and Damon a drink, handing the third glass to Mathias, who shook his head and pushed the glass away. Ever since he had been drugged, he hadn't touched a drop of liquor. He used me and my pregnancy as an excuse, but I knew better. He hated the way he treated me, what he did and said to me.

I had to give him props for his restraint, but it also showed just how much he loved me.

"So, what do you guys have?" Abner asked, taking Mathias's drink instead and sipping it.

"Well," Damon scratched his head, searching for the right words. "Okay, so, what separates shifters from humans?" He asked us, looking around the room.

"Umm, the fact that we have a counterpart, a spirit animal." Mathias said, looking at Damon as if to say 'where is this going?'.

"Okay, yeah, I'll give you that. But the other thing that makes us different is our abilities; it is widely known that shifters have larger access to their brain capacity, thus allowing us to communicate with our wolves as well as mind-linking." He shifted from foot to foot, "Now bear with me, this thing is exactly what Finnegan said it was, an inhibitor. However, this little piece of genius work doesn't work on humans or anyone who doesn't have a counterpart." He smiled at the tiny metal object he was holding between his fingers, and I couldn't have missed his excitement over this piece of advanced technology.

"What Xander and I found out was that once it has been inserted, four tiny prongs latch on to the base of the neck and send out a frequency that disrupts the shifters counterpart," Damon waved his hands around animatedly, the more he explained, the louder and more excited he became.

"Like a radio wave." Xander supplied.

Mathias scrunched his eyebrows together. "You mean like ghosts and white noise?"

"BINGO!" Damon pointed at King, showing a wide, toothy grin. "The center of the chip is infused with blood, so whoever made these, or whoever's blood is infused in it, can control whoever has been injected with it. Do you see where

I am going with this? It's very complex and quite genius." His smile faded, and a frown replaced it.

"But it's also very dangerous and immoral. The chip isn't just designed to control, it is also designed to kill. It can give out two short bursts of voltage, one directed at your heart, the other directed at your brain, effectively killing you where you stand. There are only a few ways to deactivate it. You either die by natural causes, it kills you, or a high voltage of electricity can spark it out. But again, the amount of voltage it would take to do that would kill you. Like being struck by lightning."

"Basically, if you try to shift, the chip reacts to the frequency of your spirit animal, trigging the mechanism. It sends out its own frequency in the form of a shock. Like a defense mechanism." Xander put it in Layman's terms for us, and a collective 'oh' came from me, Mathias, and Abner.

"So how did it deactivate in Finn?" I asked curiously, wanting to start pacing again as I processed the information. "He didn't die. Almost, but I stopped Mike before he delivered the final blow."

I cast my mind back to that day, replaying the scene at Riocht over and over again in my head, but could remember nothing out of the ordinary. Or at least nothing that would have caused the chip in Finnegan to deactivate.

I closed my eyes, slowing down the scene, taking even breaths, and asking Inanna for help to recall every detail. I watched as I was stabbed with a silver knife, Shayna blew silver dust in my face, Finn killed the man who stabbed me, Mike killed Shayna, then threw his sword at Finn.

I screamed *'no'* when he leaned over Finn, ready to drive his sword into Finn's neck. Mike looked at me, his eyes almost black with white symbols in them. I replayed it again, Inanna helping me slow down the memory.

'There,' Inanna said, showing a piece of the memory again.

Right as Mike pulled his sword from Finn, a small current traveled from his hand to the blade. As the tip left Finn, an arc of blue light sparked from the blade into Finn, like the little jolts of lightning I share with Mathias.

I gasped out loud at the realization, opening my eyes wide with disbelief, and looking at my mate. "I-I think I know h-how, where the volt of electricity came from!" I stammered. Mathias wound his arms around me and led me to the couch. My breathing was labored as I tried to process what this could actually mean and how it was possible for Mike to produce that much electricity from his body in such a small spark.

"That's not all," Xander addressed us and handed King a piece of paper with a printed photo. "Under closer examination, we found it had been stamped with this symbol. I don't know what it has to do with Orion."

The printed photo held the image of a blown-up stamp mark - a triangle with the initials SRP in the middle and the tiniest head of a wolf etched under it.

Suddenly my heart began to flutter, and my wolf began pacing in my head giddily. From out of nowhere, a feeling of arousal and unrequited love passed through me. The emotion was so strong that I began to pant and squirm, tingles erupting all over my body, and then I smelt him. The familiar scent of spice and pine invaded my senses.

Kellen!

I got up and tried to establish a link with him. Nothing. But his scent was strong. I began to walk towards the door, ready to search him out.

"Little wolf, are you okay?" Strong hands wound around me, and I looked up into Mathias' beautiful silver eyes. I was getting lost just for a moment when I noticed the feelings had subsided, and Kellen's scent had vanished just as quickly as it had manifested.

"I-I," I rubbed my temples, "I thought I smelt Kellen, I thought I could feel him." I was confused, had I just made it up? "I was going to go look for him" I confessed, not even sure why I thought he would be here.

"Maybe you need to rest, are the cubs, okay?" His worried gaze roamed my face, down my body, and back up again, meeting my eyes with concern.

"Pups," I countered again and giggled at him. It was a habit to correct him on this - an inside joke.

"I'm okay. It was just really strange, it felt... It felt like I had sensed a mate. His scent was so strong, and this feeling of love and lust... they weren't my feelings, they were his." I hesitated to tell him, not knowing how he would react, but I wanted to be honest with him. "It was consuming me, my wolf was acting strange."

I saw his jaw muscles flex and his lips press together harshly. I could feel his annoyance through the bond and I rubbed his arm, hoping to soothe him. The last thing I needed was for Arcas and him to become jealous. That wouldn't end well for anyone.

I explained to the four men in the room what I remembered and how Inanna was able to help slow down the memory. Each of their faces mirrored the confusion and bewilderment I felt.

"What else was Finnegan able to give us?" Abner asked, his pale blue eyes looking at me for an answer.

"Well, he told us how they were able to move the Crawlers around undetected and how they were controlled. He also told us how their army came from the other continent, and about the ports they would use to traffic people in and out of our lands," I told them.

I pursed my lips, "He also told us his sister, Morgan, had been hidden away on the other continent too. He said her last known location was in Andora, but he couldn't say where exactly. Orion kept her hidden since she was a child, using her powers to his own advantage."

"And what powers might they be?" Narrowing his eyes, Abner pressed his question with much hesitance. I could tell he wasn't sure if he wanted to know or not.

"Sight," Mathias provided. "He said she has the gift of sight and is not a shifter. We made no promises that we would find her, but..."

"But... Once we find Kellen, I see no reason not to send a team out there to find her. She is your sister too." I directed the last part toward my mate, who gave a grunt and a shrug. He didn't care much for his other half-brother and sister.

As far as Mathias was concerned, they meant nothing to him. He didn't have a relationship with them like he had with Xander. They were Orion's children, and he loathed the thought of his real father and cared nothing for anything that had to do with him, including the fact that he had another brother and younger sister.

"I think we can all agree that Orion and his woman Shayna were a hell of a lot more sinister than we originally thought," Abner said.

"Definitely, and I think the information of these chips should be kept secret. Technology like this in the wrong hands... is dangerous." I agreed with Damon, and I could see Mathias did also.

It was unanimously agreed upon that Damon and Xander would write up a report of their finds on the inhibitor chip, but those finds would only be shared with our most trusted and our inner circle.

My thoughts went to Tawny, I would need to tell her. But right now, she wasn't sure who she trusted, not even her own mate. I sighed as I thought of what she was going through right now. I had tried to ask her to come back to MacTire or even to New Moon, but she had turned down my offer, promising she would see me before the babies' were due to be born.

I didn't like her out in Cambiador on her own, but I realized this was her path to walk, and she was no longer the weak little kitty I had first met. She was a fierce leader, strong, and was putting the people of the Werecat Kingdom first. I couldn't be any prouder of her.

I was thankful Mason had decided to stay with her; he was loyal and would protect and watch out for her. I knew he would make sure no one took her for granted, but I also knew it would be a cold day in the pits of hell before Tawny let anyone bully her again.

That thought brought a small smile to my face. However, the confusing feelings I felt earlier were still playing on my mind. I was sure they came from Kellen, but how could I feel him when I couldn't even mind-link him or establish a connection with our wolves?

The emotions I felt were so strong; as I said to Mathias, it was as if I had discovered a mate. Was that what happened to Kellen? Had he found his mate, or was I just so emotional from the pregnancy that I was manifesting these things?

'He is getting stronger, soon.' Inanna whispered into my mind before she went silent.

Where are you, Kellen? I asked silently. I promise we will find you.

Chapter 18 – A Beautiful Truth

KELLEN
DAY 4 OF THE GLADIATOR GAMES

Three days had gone by since I first laid my eyes on my mate. I hadn't slept because each night, when I closed my heavy lids, her striking blue eyes with just that hint of green invaded the dark corners of my mind, keeping sleep at bay.

I needed to see her again.

What were the chances of me being sold into slavery, coming here, and then meeting my mate?

Fate. My own conscious whispered to me.

I didn't even know her name. I wasn't even sure if I had truly let go of Lamia, but I wanted my mate; to touch her, to feel her, to whisper her name on my lips as I looked into her eyes. I wanted to unpin her flaming hair and let my fingers run through its length.

I laid on my cot, my cock hardening for the first time in over a month at the thought of her porcelain skin pressed against mine, pretending I knew what It felt like. Heaven is what I imagined, soft and smooth. Without thinking, I found my hand dipping down into my shorts, wrapping around the length of my cock, and began stroking myself as the vision of her angelic face filled the black void behind my eyes.

My movements became faster as I tugged on my erection,

imagining pushing past her rosebud lips and filling her mouth with my length. I groaned at the thought and stroked myself harder and faster. So close, I could feel my release building up.

"Kellen, are you training us... Holy mother of the moon, I did not need to see this!" Ajani came in and interrupted my fantasies.

My eyes flew open, my cock immediately becoming flaccid, and I was sure my face had turned a crimson red. Conri let a growl resonate from my chest, pissed at the interruption. I tucked myself back into my shorts and sat up. Ajani had his back to me and his hands over his eyes.

"What do you want Ajani?" I said, irritated, and threw him an icy glare whether he could see it or not. I had been disturbed and hadn't gotten to finish, I was also a little embarrassed that he had caught me pleasuring myself. I didn't know why, it's not like guys didn't do that all the time. However, I felt it was wrong in a place like this.

Especially when only a few days ago, Rogue was almost raped by a few of the other gladiator slaves in here.

Yet my body still hummed with the thought of my little flame. I had to get her out of my head, she was sure to reject me. Who wants a slave as a mate?

'We are no slaves.' Conri gnashed angry words at me.

'What good are we if we cannot shift, our title is nothing here!' I bit back at him.

'Soon. Each day I grow stronger, but we are a king, and don't you forget it!' I had never felt Conri so angry and irritated at me as he was right now.

Ajani peeked from behind his eyes. Once he saw I was no longer pleasuring myself and had tucked my cock away, he turned to me. His brown eyes were holding amusement. "I came to ask if we would be training today." He pursed his lips, trying to hide his smile.

"Yeah sure," I replied, getting up and motioning for him to lead the way to the common area.

When we arrived, all but three of the gladiator slaves were lined up and waiting for me to start training. My eyebrows met as I looked at the men, furrowing in confusion as they stood there in formation, patiently waiting for instructions and making me think of the new and ready-to-train Elite warriors back home. The thought made me miss home.

I briefly wondered if Mike had taken control of the kingdom or if he was looking for me. What if he never found me? How long until they gave up?

I pushed those thoughts aside. I knew Mike and Lamia would never give up on me. Washing away the nostalgic thoughts and feelings, I gained a little confidence in my own mind. I had no doubt that they would leave no stone unturned to bring me home.

I knew I would have to hold up on my end and survive this living hell. I would need to take control and figure out how to get out of here. I couldn't wallow in self-pity and wait for a rescue that may never come, I had to take matters into my own hands.

That began today.

I looked around the open area of the gladiator barracks. I was a bloody mess mentally, in the past few months I had lost so much. A hole in my heart from the loss of my parents sat open and gaping. I had opened my heart to love, only to have it crushed, not once, but twice the Moon Goddess had overlooked me and given Lamia to another.

Now there I was with a tainted soul and weakened heart,

and it was only now that the Moon Goddess had decided to give me another chance. Another chance to open my heart, another chance to become stronger, another chance to look forward to life. The irony of that chance did not escape me.

I was done being a fool. I was no one's bitch. I deserved my mate, I deserved some sort of happiness, and the only way I was going to have that was to make it happen myself.

I was the King of fucking Werewolves, and it was high time I started acting like it!

Something snapped in me.

I don't know if it was my self-pep talk, the thought of spending twenty-two years here like Teal, or the thought that my mate may reject me because I was sitting here in slave barracks. I was pathetically whacking off to her image instead of getting my ass in gear and going to claim what is mine.

Whatever is was that had my resolve strengthened, it had my wolf cheering on the inside.

I squared my shoulders and held my head high, puffed my chest out, and addressed the desperate men who stood in front of me, ready to give them a reason to fight.

"Gladiators!" I bellowed. "We are four days into the games and twenty-four more to go! We have already lost two comrades, let's not lose anymore! Today you become warriors, gladiators no one has ever seen the likes of, gladiator warriors that will go down in history!" All eyes were on me as I began my speech.

If these men saw me as a leader, if they wanted to follow me, then I would give them a leader. I would give them the courage to survive, the skills to fight, not just for themselves but as a pack, a team, to fight for each other. A chance to take our freedom back.

I would do this for me, for these men sold into slavery, for the women stolen from their homes, and for my mate. She would not see me as a weak slave. She would see me as the man I was, the king I was meant to be. I would do this for my queen, for the other three knights.

I will not cower, I will not submit, I will not go down without a fight. I vowed right there and then; Vargr, Jack, and Oliver would wish they had never set eyes on me. Their deaths will be a service to the realm.

"Today we learn to fight! Tomorrow, we survive! The days after that, we conquer and become gladiators of legend! ARE YOU WITH ME?"

"ARGHOOH, ARGHOOH, ARGHOOH. LIVE OR DIE WE FIGHT!" They chorused, chanting the warrior code from my kingdom.

I could see the smile on Teal's face, pleased with the turn in my approach and pride shining in his eyes. I knew he had a hand in this.

"Will you fight for the man who stands next to you?! Will you fight alongside me? Will you take back your freedom?! Again, ARE YOU WITH ME?"

"ARGHOOH, ARGHOOH, ARGHOOH. LIVE OR DIE WE FIGHT!" They recited again, louder and clearer.

"Now pair up and begin defense!" They turned, finding the first person, and began to spar; starting with the basic movements Teal and I had been teaching them.

I felt evocative, lifted.

I felt Conri surge through me, his honor, his virtue, and his nobility shining like a beacon inside me. "Yes," I whispered as my mind came to terms with my decision. By the end of these games, Oliver and Jack would meet my wrath and I would have Vargr's head.

For the rest of the day, we trained and trained hard, going over defensive moves and hand-to-hand combat. Half of these men had never held a weapon before, and those who had been here longer had never been taught. Ajani and Teal began teaching them the basics of weapon handling, where I worked with those who demonstrated some skill.

We were not required to enter the arena every day, only when our name was called. Teal explained that in the first week of the games, each visiting pack would demonstrate their fighters and then, depending on their level of fighting skill, the gladiator slaves would be selected for each fight. The crowd would decide whether we lived or died by cheering or booing.

Ultimately, the Alpha had the last say, using the age-old technique of thumbs up or thumbs down. However, not many of the slaves were expected to make it out of the arena alive. The visiting pack fighters would crush the opponents the first chance they got, not hesitating to deliver the final blow, no matter what the spectators chanted.

*****

DAY 7 OF THE GAMES

It was much of the same for the next three days, up before the sun rose, training the other gladiator slaves. They were becoming stronger, and I couldn't be more proud of them. Even the weakest of the bunch had shown a vast improvement.

Before my father handed the Alpha title to me for the New Moon pack, Mike and I oversaw training the warriors. The Academy had taught us how to lead, how to train, and how to command. Those skills became fundamental as we built trust and relationships with not just our warriors, but other pack members too.

This is what I had begun to implement with the gladiator slaves.

Each day I stood by the barred wall, watching the fights. And each day, I couldn't see her, but I knew she was there, in the stands, under the tent. Watching.

Every now and then, I would get a whiff of her scent carried across a slight and rare breeze. I would close my eyes and imagine she was in front of me.

It was night, the moon was high, and the vast amount of stars that sprinkled the never-ending black sky shone down, casting a soft light across the barracks. I was lying on one of the stone benches with no thoughts, no fantasies, just conversing with my wolf. Conri was adamant that we were getting stronger, and he felt like he would soon be able to shift.

It was wishful thinking on his part. After Teal had explained the chip and its function, I had no doubt that if we tried to shift, it could be the death of us.

'Give him your blood,' Conri had said about Rogue. The same argument we had been having since the first time he suggested it.

'There is no point. We cannot open a link with Lamia and Inanna or the other knights. Why do you think it would work with him?' I was starting to get a little agitated with his incisive pestering at trying to make Rogue a pack member.

He thought if we did that, we would be able to establish a mind-link with him.

'If it does not work, then no harm done.' He huffed before mentally turning his back on me.

I closed my eyes, enjoying the cool night air, so different from the hot and humid sun that beat down in the day. I heard the shuffle of feet and peeked one eye open, turning my head to where the sound came from. When I saw it was Teal, I closed my eye again, just enjoying the quiet, until Teal sat down by my feet and leaned against the gritty sandstone wall.

"Orion ripped me from my home over twenty-two years ago, almost twenty-three. He invaded our island, him and his witch." He snarled the last word. I could tell he had no love for either, but his distaste for the witch far outweighed his hate for Orion.

I now opened both eyes to watch him as he told me his story.

"He and his rogues came in the dead of night, their boats silently slipped into our port. They killed everyone they came across before they could alert me. I was alpha then. I have a son, John, who is thirty years old now. He would be alpha if he is still alive. My Luna was heavily pregnant with our little girl, due to give birth any day. She would be twenty-three now." Teal's head hung low as he talked, and his hands shook. I felt the bout of sadness that came off him in waves as he spoke about the family he had been ripped away from.

"I have never met my eldest daughter." He took a pause and I remained silent, wanting to hear the rest of his story. "That night, Orion forced me to my knees; he killed my beta, the gamma, and the delta's mate. My delta only survived because he was in your kingdom, visiting your father on business.

Orion was too strong, and his rogues had already swarmed the pack house. They dragged my Luna and son out to the front of the pack house and made them watch while he ordered my warrior's executions. Then his witch forced my Luna to drink an herbal tonic and cursed the child she was carrying.

"She said the child would never shift. Her wolf would be locked away inside forever until a wolf-less mate came to claim her. Only then would her wolf be able to emerge, and she could shift." Teal gave a half-hearted, sarcastic chuckle. "She cursed my unborn child, then Orion told me that if I did not comply and pledge myself to him right there and then, he would slaughter my son and Luna. I had no choice. I was brought here and sold to Vargr.

"I don't know what happened to his witch. I never saw her again and as the years went by, Shayna took a liking to Orion and Orion took a liking to her mind, and Vargr's mines. Vargr was all too eager for his daughter to be Orion's chosen mate, Bear King or not. It only strengthened Vargr, but it also protected him from Orion's wrath.

"Orion had already claimed half the kingdoms on this continent, but it was never enough for him, he wanted more. He wanted to rule the whole realm; to be the King of Shifters."

Teal paused to clear his throat and I took this as an opportunity to ask the question that had been burning in my mind since I had realized. "My mate is your daughter, how?"

He looked at me, an impassive look on his face, then he said her name. The smallest of smiles played on his lips, and just for a moment a light shone in his eyes, but it was gone all too quickly. "Tala." He said her name, and my wolf hummed.

"I had only been here a few weeks and was wallowing in self pity, much like you have been doing, when the Luna,

Mila, came to visit the slave barracks. Even then Vargr abused her. His thirst for blood and women was growing, the power he held was going to his head. Mila fell in love with me, but I did not feel the same. I had a mate, a Luna, a wife who I loved very much and despite the little chip they put in me, I would never willingly betray the mate bond. I felt pity for her and refused her advances.

"One night she came to me, giving me a canteen of liquor. I stupidly drank from it, not realizing it had been laced with herbs that could make any wolf aroused and lustful. She had several guards tie me down to the stone bench in the weapons area and she rode me until my seed spilled inside her. Not just once either. Tala is my daughter, not Vargr's. The only reason I am alive is because he wants me to suffer, to watch my daughter grow up under his command, to watch Mila be abused. Tala is the only reason I endure.

"Young king, I fear that he is planning something. He announced her pairing with the beta's son on opening day. By the full moon, they will mate and mark each other with the ranked members watching. Now that you are here, if he finds out you are her mate, he will kill you. Slowly. Or he may make you watch your mate be claimed by another, without a rejection."

I let out a growl, deep and warning. "She is *mine*." The words echoed through the small space. Standing to my feet, I began pacing, the turmoil of the situation making my hackles rise.

"I need an inside man. The situation is worse than we thought. The two men who flanked her on opening day were Jack, a werebear, and Oliver, a wolf." I said with slight panic. "They were the ones who duped and sold me. They are also the ones who kidnapped the Queen of Shifters, Lamia Langley. We have been after them for three years now. With them in the picture, I don't want to imagine what roles they would be playing in all this." I pinched the bridge of my nose as I paced back and forth in short bursts.

"Teal, will you help me? I promise I will protect your daughter with every fiber of my being. I will not let her be claimed by another and I swear I will kill Vargr. I need three things: to get this fucking chip out the back of my neck, the other gladiator slaves to fight with me, and a man on the inside. Only then can we take back our freedom and the freedom of this kingdom. The people deserve to be free from his rule. Not just us."

He stood and stopped my pacing by putting both of his hands on my shoulders, leveling his gaze at me. "Spoken like a true king. I am with you, Kellen. Live or die we fight."

"Live or die we fight." I heard Ajani's voice as he came into view. Rogue was standing beside him, put his fisted hand over his heart, and gave me a small bow. He may not be able to talk, but his actions echoed Ajani and Teal's words.

Chapter 19 – A Deal with the Devil

<u>TALA</u>
DAY 7 OF THE GAMES

It had been a week since I last laid eyes on my mate. I hated the games, but each day I went in hopes of catching a glimpse of him. Each day I watched as men fought and men died to entertain the higher ranks.

All of our gladiators were slaves, whereas the visiting packs' gladiators were volunteers or criminals who were condemned to the games. Only a few other alphas had slaves in their packs, and they were the ones who were closely allied with my father.

Each day I had been escorted by Jack the bear and Oliver the wolf. I was told they would be staying by my side until my father paid them what was owed to them for delivering the Wolf Prince.

It made my skin crawl whenever Jack and Oliver were near me. The way they looked at me like I was their next meal, a platter of meat ready to be feasted on, had my stomach in knots. I put on a brave face, not letting them see how badly they affected and scared me.

Today, I wore a simple light blue summer dress that hung just above my knees, void of a tunic or petticoat. It was too hot today and I hoped my father would not give me grief about what I chose to wear to the games today.

I knocked on my father's bedroom door, the ugly as shit blue doors making me cringe. I held my breath, waiting for him to respond. After a few moments, I knocked again and heard a mumbled sound.

I pushed the door open, hoping to the moon that he wasn't fucking some poor slave girl again. The only reason I came here was because I thought he might be alone as my mother was having a good day.

"Father," I called out, seeing that his bed was messy still. I walked further into the room and heard a mumble from the bathroom. "Father," I called out louder this time and watched the bathroom door swing open.

Luckily, he was wearing his robe. He was towel drying his semi-short brown hair and he stopped mid-step when he noticed me. "What do you want Tala?" He narrowed his eyes at me, his lip curling in disgust as he regarded me.

"I came to ask, when will Jack and Oliver stop escorting me? I don't like them." I was blunt. Although my father was a scary man and powerful, I refused to back down from him. He often told me that my boldness would get me killed. What he meant was that one day, he would kill me if I crossed the line.

I wasn't sure what that line was, but I was sure that I was teetering on the edge of it just by being here.

"They will escort you for as long as they see fit until I have paid them what I owe them. Not that I owe you any explanation." He huffed, his eyes scanning me like I was a putrid bug.

"Father, how can you let me be paraded around with two rogues when you have just announced that I will be paired with Jasper? I think it is sending out mixed messages to your people." I said honestly and with confidence, hoping he would see the logic.

Without warning and quicker than a flash, he had his hands around my neck and slammed me up against the wall. My feet were lifted from the ground. I refused to cry and show weakness to him; instead, I grasped his hand with mine, trying to give myself some stability as my legs dangled beneath me. I met his hardened gaze, his eyes darkening as he looked into mine. There was so much hate there, so much loathing. His hand squeezed tighter, cutting off my air supply and my throat began to burn.

"How fucking dare you tell me what my pack thinks." He hissed with venom. I could feel his anger building up, the heat from it spreading out like a blanket of poisonous fumes. His hand squeezed around my throat tighter, and my eyes began to bulge.

"Maybe I should make you the payment, you good for nothing wolf!" He spat out - his saliva spraying my face. I shook my head in fear, I actually feared Jack more than I did him. "Here I was thinking you would make a good and obedient Luna for Jasper, but maybe I was wrong. Maybe what you need is to be broken in first." His words were cruel, and I didn't want to cry. I knew exactly what he meant by 'breaking me in'.

I had heard him use that term in regard to slave girls plenty of times. I blinked back my tears as much as I could, unable to swallow them down.

His face twitched and he slowly blinked. When he opened them again, I could see his wolf coming through his eyes. They were so dark and glaring, like a demon. "Make no mistake, Tala, you are a piece of shit wolf. The only reason you are alive is to make your mother suffer and for me to use you as I fucking please. If that means selling you off or making you a slave, then that is what I will do. You exist to benefit me!" His hand tightened even more, and his palm began to crush my windpipe. I gasped for air, clawing at his hand, but he would not let up. "Maybe, I should just kill you." He pondered like he was choosing linens. The darkness of his stare bored me like hot needles.

This is it, I thought. Today will be the day he kills me. Why did I ever think he would listen or show mercy? He has never liked me.

As soon as I thought it, he let me go.

I choked, gasping for air as he released my neck, and falling to the floor when my legs neglected to hold me up. I scrambled to stand, rubbing my neck. Before I could even get my bearings, I felt the hard hit of the back of his hand sting my face, sending me stumbling again.

Still, I refused to cry out, even though I could feel the swelling of a bruise immediately. I stood to my feet again. "I apologize father." I tried to sound sincere when really, I was seething inside and my wolf was encouraging me to lash out and take a bite out of him. I pushed her down as that would not do us any good. We were not strong enough.

"You are a pathetic waste of skin." He sneered, advancing on me. "You are useless, like your mother. If you had any smarts like Shayna, maybe I would have accepted you." He raised his hand again and I flinched, but the hit never came. "Get out of here! You're a slut like your mother and I can hardly stand the sight of you! I raised you and all you are is a great disappointment. I should have made your mother abort you the day I found out she was carrying you!"

I wanted to scoff. That was rich coming from the man who destroyed my mother and sent her insane. How could he call her a slut when he was the one who raped and bedded all kinds of women? I scowled and moved around him quickly in a bid to leave his room, having no desire to stay there any longer than necessary.

I turned before I slipped out the door, and like a child, I stuck my tongue out at his back. I fucking hated him, but his words were embedded in me. It hurt to hear him say he should have had me terminated.

I had no idea what I had ever done to him for him to hate me so much.

I ran down the hall, making my way back to my room when I slammed into a hard wall. I stumbled back, bracing myself to fall on my ass, but a pair of hands held me up. I looked up at the person who had my arms in their hands.

I sneered when I realized it was Oliver.

"What has you in such a rush little princess?" He asked with amusement, his eyes twinkling with a mischievous glint.

I was about to reply that it was none of his business when his hand lifted towards my face. I flinched as he touched the swelling bruise on my cheek. A deep scowl took form on his face as his thumb gently caressed my cheek.

"Who did this?" He asked sternly.

I huffed. "That is none of your concern Oliver. Sir." I said, turning my face from him.

He grunted and pulled me by my arm towards my room, opening the door and pulling me inside with him before closing and locking the door behind him.

I began to shake. Had my father already given him the okay to use me as payment? Seeing my turmoil, Oliver's face softened slightly. "I won't hurt you Tala, I promise."

I again scoffed, not meaning to. I highly doubted that he wouldn't hurt me. He was Jack's friend. I had seen how Jack treated women and what he was capable of, and I knew Oliver was no better.

Oliver sat down on my bed, looking comfortable as he looked around my bedroom. I wrapped my arms around myself, still standing in the middle of the room.

"Why do you guys insist on escorting me? What does my father owe you?" I spoke up confidently, even though I didn't feel it after a few moments of silence between us. The silence was what provoked me to speak.

"Do you know what... *who* we sold to your father?" He asked, his hazel eyes trained on me.

I shook my head. I expected it must have been slave girls since that's what Jack did. Sold slaves. He had known my father and Orion since he was a boy and had grown up in the realm of trafficking.

I had once overheard my father talking about Jack. How he had been born a rogue, and when his father died, he had taken over the business at the young age of fifteen. So yeah, anyone who associated with Jack was just as vile in my eyes.

"I know the gladiator slave is your mate." Oliver declared and then sat and stretched out across my bed, folding his hands under his head, looking like he had no care in the realm.

I gasped, afraid he would tell my father, and I began to fidget, trying to think of what to say. I knew he knew, but I didn't think he would be so bold about his knowledge.

"Don't worry little one, I won't be telling your father. Or Jack for that matter. At least not today." He casually said, still lying on the bed like it was the most natural thing ever, making himself comfy.

"Why?" I whispered. Not understanding why he would keep my secret.

He raised his head to look at me and cocked an eyebrow. "Maybe you can help me if I keep your little secret. Maybe by keeping your secret, it will benefit me." He smirked and then laid his head back down.

"Again, why would you keep my secret, and how could I help you?" I unfolded my arms. At this point, I was more curious about him than I was afraid.

"Come sit next to me. Let us... chat before the games." He patted the space on the bed next to him.

I cautiously moved towards my bed, hesitating when I got to the edge. "I won't bite," he chuckled, "Unless you want me to?"

I took a step back, the fear coming back of what he may do to me.

"Tala, sweet Tala. I promise I will not touch you like that. I just want to talk, nothing more." He sounded sincere, but I couldn't trust him. Even so, I stepped up to my bed and sat down next to him.

My hands were slightly shaking and clammy. Why couldn't he just leave me alone?

"Your mate," Oliver started. "He's what your father owes Jack for. The payment was meant to be a life for a life. He gets the King of the Wolves, Jack gets the witch,"

"What???" I asked, not sure if I heard him right or not. My mouth hung open and my eyes were wide with shock.

Oliver chuckled again and then turned on his side, propping his head up in his hand. "Oh, you didn't know your mate was the King of Wolves? Kellen Moon. I helped kill his parents, and when Jack and I ran from the battle of Riocht, Jack just happened to come upon him and kidnapped him. Very clever is Jack, even if he doesn't seem it." I saw his eyebrows pinch together, seemingly thinking about something or someone.

"See, aside from chips and money, the one thing Jack wanted in exchange for King Kellen was Orion's daughter, the witch."

I looked at him, confused. Everyone knew about Finn, his son, but his daughter? This was news to me.

"The problem is, this witch was hidden away, and no one knows where except for your father, and he refuses to tell us. Or he really doesn't know where she is." He leaned over and took my hand in his. "Tala, if you can find out where the witch is, then Jack will go away. If Jack doesn't get his witch, then he will set his sights on you."

"Why are you telling me all of this, Oliver? Sir." I asked, sounding respectful as I did not need another confrontation today and I certainly didn't want to anger this wolf. I wasn't sure if I really wanted to know, but now I needed to. The last thing I wanted was for Jack to set his sights on me. A little shudder went through my body at the thought, a cold sensation creeping up my spine.

However, with the way Oliver was looking at me, with a slightly menacing smirk on his face, I knew there was more. His thumb began caressing the back of my hand, making little circles, and I gulped down my nerves.

"Because, my dear little princess," his eyes were now trained on me, and I met his gaze without hesitation this time, hoping I looked stronger than I felt. He wanted something else from me and depending on what he wanted, it would either put me in a very good position or an even worse one.

"I have lived this life for far too long. I am afraid if I stay in this… environment, my time will be up." He paused and took a breath. The menacing look in his eyes faded to a more sorrowful one.

"I have lived as a rogue my whole life, serving one pretentious monster after another. Now that is not to say that I am not a monster myself. Like Jack, I have done unspeakable things, things that would give you nightmares, young princess. I am tired of this life, and it is time for me to disappear. I think I can do that in this continent."

I furrowed my brow. So he wanted out? Oliver didn't want to live the life of a rogue or trafficker anymore. "…but why?" I asked, truly wondering, not prepared for his answer.

"Your mate, he will have me killed on sight. I am not ready to depart from this realm and would actually like to enjoy what the other side has to offer for once. Now, I propose a deal." His sinister smirk was back on his face, and it had me huffing out a little breath that was full of tension.

"I know what is beyond that wall," he pointed towards the westerly wall. "And what is in those mines can help me disappear and live very comfortably for a very long time. Give me access to those mines and I will help you keep your mate a secret."

What little hope I had deflated. It wasn't a secret that my father's money came from the mines. That's how he was in a position of power. His mines produced the largest and most abundant diamonds. The walls down there were covered in rough and uncut stones from top to bottom. To add to that, the river that crossed our lands produced more gold than most had ever seen.

My father was not poor by far, which is why so many turned a blind eye to his misdoings. The slaves, the gladiators, the cheating, no one cared so long as they were getting a cut or were in good graces with my father. The sad thing was, those mines had belonged to my mother's family until they were paired and married. And because he was an alpha that came from a noble family, he instantly became the successor. The mines were signed over to him through the marriage.

Now I understood. In order for Oliver to disappear, he would need the funds. Especially if he wanted to live comfortably as he had said.

"I don't know how to get you access to those mines," I said truthfully because I honestly didn't care about the money, gold, or precious stones. My father had the mines locked up tight; no one got in or out without being thoroughly checked and weighed.

I would happily help Oliver if it meant he left me alone.

"You have a week to figure out where the witch is and to get me access to the mines. I can keep Jack away from you for now, but after that..." His hand let go of mine and reached up to tuck a strand of my hair behind my ear, his eyes roaming my face in a caressing manner. "...After that, I wonder what your father would say if he found out your mate was none other than his prized gladiator, the King of Wolves?"

He would kill him on sight! That's what he would do! I jerked back from Oliver's touch, the lump in my throat hard and thick. The cunning bastard was blackmailing me. I narrowed my eyes at him, determined to not back down.

"Oliver, sir, it sounds like you have everything to gain from this... deal. Yet the only thing you have offered me is to not tell my father that my mate is a slave?" Oh yes, I could be cunning too. I may not be the bravest, but if he wanted something from me, two could play at that game. There was one thing my father loved more than bloodshed: money, and his mines were his money.

"That hardly seems like a deal to me. What would my father say if I was to tell him that you were here sitting on my bed, asking for access to the mines and the witch girl, blackmailing me? I am already promised to someone, so whether the gladiator wolf is my mate or not, it really doesn't matter, does it?" I internally praised myself for my fast thinking.

Oliver stopped and glared at me. I could see his eye twitching, visibly showing a crack in his plan. "Now if you want me to help you obtain your fortune and the information about something I have no clue about, I suggest you bargain better with me instead of throwing idle threats. Because let's be honest, all I have to do is mention your interest in my father's little jewel mine and he will have your head cut off where you stand."

I tilted my head up in defiance, still feeling quite smug with myself, proud that I had turned his bullying conversation back on him. My wolf gave me more confidence when the feeling of her pride rushed through me.

"I had no idea you were this sly, young princess. What is it you want?" Oliver gritted out through his teeth. I had made him mad and by the way his jaw pulsed, I knew I had backed him into a corner. At least, I hoped I had.

"I don't know; let's wait until the end of the week. It will depend on what information I can find on the witch. I'm sure I can come up with something, but I need something from you in exchange for a large fortune of diamonds. Until then, let's hope I don't let it slip to Alpha Vargr that you were oh so very interested in his operation." I raised an eyebrow at him and cocked my head. "Do we have a deal, Oliver? Sir?"

I had used Oliver's own method against him, and I felt like I looked and sounded confident; however, I was shaking like a leaf on the inside. Alone with this wolf in my room, he could do anything to me, and I would be powerless to stop him. By the time I had linked a guard, I could already be dead. Worse, if he decided to rape me, my father would probably turn a blind eye to it.

Oliver didn't know that though.

"We have a deal, Tala." Standing from the bed, Oliver agreed to my terms. Now I just had to think of something he could do for me. As he got to the door, his hand on the knob, he turned to me. "Oh, by the way, your precious mate will be the main fight today." With that, he left, leaving me to replay our conversation over and over in my head, wondering if I had missed anything.

Surely it wasn't that easy to get Oliver in my pocket, was it? I was sure he could be most useful to me, somehow, in some way. I just needed to think about what he could do for me. What he could offer me.

Chapter 20 – Fear not, the Despair

<u>TALA</u>
DAY 8 OF THE GLADIATOR GAMES

Initiation week had ended, thank the gods. And even though Jasper had to attend the slave girls' initiations, he wasn't made to partake, just observe.

I was so relieved because even though my mother was pretty much knocked out for the whole week, I sat by her bed every evening after the games anyway, with Eloise by my side.

El and Jasper may not have marked each other, but if he had had sex with anyone, Eloise still would have felt something. Not the shredding burn that makes you want to rip your heart out like I have heard my mother describe, but something more akin to an ashy taste in your mouth and a really bad stomach ache.

Since Eloise hadn't felt any discomfort over the last week, I knew Jasper had remained faithful, and I had a much deeper respect for him for not following in our fathers' footsteps. His respect for the bond gave me hope for my two best friends.

I looked at Jasper, who was sitting on the lounge chaise in my room with Eloise curled into his side. If the gods truly had a heart, I hoped they would side with my friends and allow them to be together in happiness.

Jasper had a hard look on his face while El sat there, mouth gaping as I finished telling them I had found my mate and then my encounter with Oliver, also telling them who my mate was.

"Holy stars and moons, Tala!" Eloise exclaimed, her hands slapping either side of her cheeks as the shock sunk in. "So, you are saying your mate is a gladiator slave, and none other than the King of Wolves? What are you going to do?"

I rolled my eyes at her and shook my head. "If I knew that, then I wouldn't be asking you guys what I should do." I looked back at Jasper, who hadn't said a word, the same vexing look on his face as he just stared into space.

"Jasper?" I tried to call out for his attention.

Finally, Jasper came out of whatever trap his mind was in and met my gaze, his face still holding a complex emotion. "Are you going to reject him?" He asked with a monotone voice.

"Ummm," was all I could reply. Was I going to reject my mate? I didn't know. I had never wanted a mate, not after what I witnessed growing up and still witness to this day. Once upon a time, I thought the idea of mates was the best thing in the realm. That was until I was old enough to understand what went on under our roof. After that, I dreaded being mated.

"You can't reject him, Tala!" Eloise whisper yelled, her big doe eyes looking at me pleadingly. "If he truly is a King of Wolves, he could help us!" Sometimes I loved that Eloise was so innocent, but not today.

"Exactly how is he supposed to help us El? He has been enslaved by my father. Enslaved like those poor girls. Enslaved like those poor rogues and bastards who are dragged down into the mines every day. So, tell me El, how is he supposed to help us?"

Tears welled up in her eyes, and I immediately felt bad for talking to her so harshly. I closed my eyes and took a deep breath, "I haven't even spoken to him. I have only seen him in the arena. How can he help us if I can't even talk to him?" My tone was much softer this time.

Eloise wasn't an idiot, not at all. She tried to see the good in everything and everyone, and her innocent features gave a soft look. She was an omega she-wolf, softer by nature, more caring and nurturing. She just didn't have a bad bone in her body, unlike me and Jasper.

"Do you trust Oliver?" Jasper suddenly asked. I immediately shook my head.

"Not as far as I can throw him. He is a friend of Jack, and any friend of his is just as dark and dangerous.

Jasper stood up, leaving Eloise to sit on her own, and went to stand by my window, looking out over the barren land beyond the palace walls. After a few moments, he spoke, still not facing us. "We have twenty days until Tala and I are expected to mate and wed. Our fathers are pushing this because King Panja has begun to move his troops. Your father..." Jasper now turned and looked at me. "Your father seems to think that since Orion is gone, Panja will make a play for the mines."

I threw my hands up in the air, completely exasperated with everything. King Panja of Asiarian had been after the diamond mine for years. The only reason he hadn't declared war over them was because of Orion, and my father had a large and loyal army that he paid well for.

However, with Orion out of the way, King Panja was free to make a move with his army that was as large as ours and just as funded. It is said that Asiarian is just as rich as us, with their own mines of rubies and emeralds. Of course, these were just stories I heard, but I also knew that with the gap Orion and my sister left, the shifter wars would start again. Each kingdom would rally their alleys in a bid to take over and become the king of their race.

"So, within twenty days, we need to figure out what to do about Oliver's demands, avoid getting mated, and what to do about my mate?" I sighed, "Anything else we need to figure out while we are at it? Because I am sure that adding one more thing to our plates is not going to make a difference."

"Oooh! You have to find out about the witch!" Eloise chimed in, missing the sarcastic tone in my voice.

"Thank you, El, I knew we were missing something," I grumbled at her, annoyed that she had reminded me about the other thing we really did have to do.

"Tala, I can get you in to see your mate if that's what you want." Jasper told me with a look of compassion.

My wolf immediately perked up at his idea. I nodded, feeling a small blush creep on my face. "I think I need to see him in person. Not from afar." I agreed.

"I have a friend who is one of the night shift guards, I will take you there tonight." He said, smiling at me.

"Thank you, Jasper." I wasn't sure if I was ready to meet my mate face to face. My wolf was ready, but I was nervous. I hadn't even thought about rejection until El had said something. I had no intentions of rejecting him, but that didn't mean I wasn't scared to meet him. We were in some very strange circumstances.

I think I was more scared of his reaction than anything else. What if he didn't want me? After all, when he fought yesterday and I secretly cheered for *him* over his victory, I was standing with Oliver. Knowing what I know now, he must be livid to see me being escorted by the rogue wolf. I had no idea how he would react to me or what he would say.

*****

KELLEN
DAY 8 OF THE GLADIATOR GAMES

I sat on the floor next to Ajani's cot as he slept soundly, still recovering from yesterday's fight. Although there were no deaths, Ajani had been severely wounded. A blade from an opponent had dug itself deep into his side.

A guard had given us some fishing wire and a dull needle to patch him up with. While Rogue and I had held him down, Teal stitched him up. His wolf's healing was slow, and it would take several days before he was up and about. We had been taking turns sitting with him as he developed a fever in the middle of the night, and we had no medication to give him.

"No gladiator slave is allowed to receive herbs." The guards had told us as we pleaded for them to give us anything, even alcohol so that we could at least sterilize the wound.

"He will either survive or die," is what they said before turning their backs on us.

Teal had led the gladiators in training today, and I lifted my head to him as he walked over to Ajani's cot and bent over to check his wound.

Ajani made a pained grumbling sound and Teal clicked his tongue before sighing. "I think he will make it, but he is scheduled to fight tomorrow." Teal grimaced, his eyes trailing over Ajani.

He was thinking the same as me, that there was no way Ajani would be able to fight tomorrow. "I will take his place," I said while standing up. My mind was made up. I was still perplexed about my mate being so close to Oliver yesterday; he held her by the elbow tightly, smiling down at her like she was his prized doll. I could see the uncomfortable look on her face, so I was sure she wasn't enjoying being in his company, but jealousy still reared its ugly head every time I glanced to towards the Alpha's tent.

"If they let you," Teal sighed before straightening up and looking at me. "I'm not sure they will, but it is worth a try. I think you pissed Vargr off by eliminating the visiting alpha's gladiators and their horses." A ghost of a smile played at the corner of his lips as he said this.

Yes, it was true. Me, Ajani, and one of the other gladiators were put into the arena to fight yesterday. We were pitted against five opponents, all on horseback and wielding various weapons. When Ajani got injured, I felt a fit of protective anger rise within me and my wolf. The results were me slicing the legs of each horse, bringing the rider down to my level, and seriously injuring the five men. Two of which were left with life-threatening wounds, and I doubted they survived through the night. The fight was stopped before I could carry out my revenge on the other three.

As the fight was called to a stop and Vargr's warriors came marching in and circling me, I caught a glimpse of my mate from under his tent. Her eyes were wide with worry, but the inconspicuous smile on her face told me she was proud of me. Conri had relished in the idea that he had impressed his mate.

The day moved slowly, and I kept within the shadows

of the barracks, keeping out of the sun's hot rays. Summer would be just beginning in our continent, and my and Lamia's birthdays were just around the corner. Here it seemed like summer had already grasped the hardened land, and only when night fell did it cool down significantly to give us a break from the scorching heat.

When dusk began to settle, I left Ajani's aide and went to my own cot. Rogue was now looking over him. I laid down, closed my eyes, and hoped that sleep would find me.

When it did, I dreamt of Lamia. Her green eyes pierced through the blackness that I fell into until I found myself in that all too familiar library Lamia would dream of, rows upon rows of shelves lined with books that looked older than time.

From the darkness, I could see her glowing emerald orbs and chased them. I finally caught up to her, but she was different. Gone was her streaked hair; in place of the golden and black streaks, she had cropped short and completely black hair. Three glowing orbs surrounded her, circling her like the hands of a clock. The orbs of light were warm and welcoming and beckoned for me to touch them.

As I reached my hand out to touch one, they dropped to the ground, their light diminishing quickly. Lamia fell to the ground along with them; her face looked pained, her eyes had lost their glow. She cried out soundlessly and I tried to reach for her, tried to comfort her. She doubled over, again crying out with a silent scream.

"Lamia!" I called to her, but she just kept crying out, holding her stomach on her knees as her face crumpled in despair. My words were soundless as I tried to reach her. Suddenly, she began to fade. In her place, the soft glow of light began to take form, brightening as the minutes ticked by.

The glow became brighter, and my surroundings became focused again. I was still in the library, but there sat a fireplace with two high-back leather chairs facing it. I could see a figure sitting in one of the chairs, but as I approached the person, I heard my name being called from a far-off distance.

The voice calling my name sounded so familiar, pulling me towards them. I tried to ignore the voice, but it was too strong and pulled me back into the darkness. The library and the person sitting in the chair faded away, sending me back into the black abyss.

"Kellen. Kellen." The deep voice and the shaking feeling startled me from my sleep, and I found I had woken up in a cold sweat.

"Kellen," Teal said again as I came too. "Are you ok?" He asked.

I nodded, trying to collect my thoughts. The feeling of despair still sat with me, the image of Lamia's pained face not fading anytime soon. A feeling of panic had come over me in my unconscious state from being unable to communicate with Lamia in the library. The vision of the three orbs falling to the ground and Lamia falling after them gave me a tight pinch in my chest.

A worrying feeling for my best friend seated itself in the pit of my stomach.

"What is it, Teal?" I asked hoarsely, rubbing my eyes while regaining my composure and trying to shake off the feeling that something was wrong, that Lamia could be in trouble.

"Someone is here to see you. Come quickly, young king." He said, nudging me to stand.

Dazed and confused, I stood to my feet, wondering who

would want to see me and why? I followed Teal through the barracks quietly so as not to disturb anyone. When we reached the common grounds, he told me, "They are waiting for you in the weapons room."

I gave him a puzzled look. Usually, the weapons room was locked up by this time of night; it was only opened during the day when they had more guards and allowed us to train.

Chapter 21 – Beauty Under the Moon

KELLEN

Teal left me, turning and leaving the common area without another word after telling me the person was waiting for me in the armory.

I couldn't figure out for the life of me who would risk visiting me in the barracks at this time of night. As I made my way closer to the weapons rooms, I caught the scent of oranges and sea salt. Conri was mentally whipping his tail around in my head, the scent of our mate driving his senses and hormones into a frenzy.

My heartbeat picked up as I drew nearer to the entrance, realization dawning on me that my mate was here. Then came the worry. This was no place for a woman. I noticed two guards standing outside the room and as I approached, they nodded their heads and stepped to the side, allowing me entrance.

As soon as I entered, a figure in a black cloak turned to me, and my eyes met her cerulean blues. My heart beat furiously and my body began to tremble as I tracked the parting of her mouth, a barely whispered gasp leaving her perfectly shaped rosebud lips. It took everything in me not to rush to her.

"Mate." She whispered.

"Mate," I repeated just as low, still not believing that this little flame now stood in front of me... finally.

She lifted her hands and removed the hood of her cloak, revealing her long, silky red hair that was pinned up. I took slow steps toward her, not wanting to scare her. I could feel her nerves rolling off of her in large waves. I was sure she could feel my apprehension just as much.

She was so beautiful, like a beacon of light, emanating warmth that was everything good and pure. Like the goddess of hope. I was lost for words, just staring at my little flame, not knowing what to say and lost in the depth of her eyes. My eyes caressed every line of her dainty face, committing each soft and feminine, perfectly structured line to memory.

While I tried to find words, it was she who spoke first. "I'm sorry it took so long for me to come to see you. It was not easy." She said and looked down to the ground. The harsh accent of this kingdom sounded soft and melodic coming from her.

"Thank you for coming," I said. I didn't know what else to say. All I could think about was capturing her lips with mine. Taking her in my arms and breathing her in. I wanted to know what it was like to hold her, to feel her creamy skin under my fingertips, to let my hand tangle in her silky red hair.

I took in a deep breath and took a step closer to her, wanting to touch her.

"You're even more beautiful in person," she said breathily.

I groaned, knowing I affected her just as much as she was affecting me. I felt myself blush at her words, I had never been called beautiful, and I wasn't sure I would have ever associated that word with myself.

I was only wearing the standard thin pair of white shorts the guards gave us, and as she cast her eyes down my body with an appreciative look, I felt a hunger rise within. She licked her lips, and I felt a stirring below.

I had no idea it was possible to want someone this much without knowing them and without ever touching them.

"Tala," I called her name, and she pulled her wandering gaze from my body and met my eyes, showing her surprise that I knew her name and not even trying to conceal her lust for me.

"Kellen," she breathed out, and I groaned again. My name on her lips was like the sound of an angel, but with her fiery red hair, she looked more like a she-devil.

"You know my name?" I asked.

She gulped and nodded, "Oliver told me who you are."

An involuntary low growl crawled up and out of my chest at the very sound of that piece of shit's name. I had not forgotten how he held her arm yesterday, how he looked so comfortable standing with her.

"What is your relationship with… him?" I growled out, not even able to say his name. "He is not a good person."

"I have no relationship with him, and never will if I can help it. He is Jack's friend. He is no friend of mine." I detected hostility in her voice when she spoke of Oliver, and it lessened the building inferno of rage that had begun coursing through my veins.

I was also relieved to know that she had no relationship with him and seemed to detest him. I let out a breath of relief at the admission. I couldn't guarantee my reaction if she had said anything other than what she did. She also spoke with confidence and truth.

"You have been promised to another. Will you reject me?" I know it didn't come out right, but I had to ask. I needed to know; I didn't think I would be able to handle another rejection, I still hadn't moved past Lamia. But with Tala standing in front of me, I was beginning to realize that the bond Lamia and I had felt was so minimal compared to the pull I was feeling now.

This was so awkward. If I wasn't a slave and trapped in her so-called 'father's' pack, I would have already broken the barrier between us and kissed her, accepted her, buried myself deep inside her, marked her, and claimed her as mine.

However, I didn't know what her intentions were. Why she was here? Was it because she didn't want me? Or was it because she wanted me? This situation was so fucked up and I was acting like a love-sick fool, like a kid who had his first crush, flustered and unconfident.

She sighed and shook her head, a deep longing setting in her features, her crystal eyes softening as they held mine. "I don't want to reject you, Jasper and I do not want to be paired. In twenty days, my father and Jasper's will forcefully make us mate." I saw her eyes fill with tears and I moved forward, not liking to see her upset, and I tried not to get angry at the thought of someone else claiming what was mine.

My hand came up to cup her cheek, and when I made contact with her soft, smooth ivory skin, my hand jumped back as I felt the warming sparks dance across my palm. She gasped and placed her hand where mine touched, looking just as shocked as I felt.

Lamia and I had felt the bond, and we still do, but those tingles were nowhere close to the feeling of when I touched Tala. The sparks were strong, warm, sensual, calming, and arousing, causing so many emotions and irrational feelings. I wanted to feel them again. Such a strong reaction compared to what I had experienced with Lamia.

I stepped closer to her, leaving but an inch of a gap between us. I couldn't say it didn't hurt when she stepped back out of my reach. My wolf growled in my head, urging me to be closer to her.

Every step I took, she took one back until she was between me and the stone table behind her. My hands came up on both sides of her, caging her in. The moon from above shone down through the opening in the roof, casting its glow across her.

Beauty in its purest form was all I could think of as I looked down on her. If there was ever a woman who could rule my heart, it was this fiery little goddess that I stood before. I hadn't even kissed her, but already I knew she had the power to bring me to my knees.

I leaned in so I could breathe in her scent, barely touching her with my nose.

*****

TALA

He pressed me against the stone table, pushing me out of the shadows and into the glow that the moonlight cast over the table... His arms caged me in, a hand resting on the hard surface on either side of me.

His body almost pinned me. The tip of his nose trailed up and down my neck, barely making contact, but just enough to send my wolf wild, wanting to claim him.

The pull to this gladiator wolf was strong.

My body trembled and shivers ran across my skin. A heating pulse began to beat between my thighs. He had nothing covering him but a thin pair of cotton shorts. My hands braced behind my back shook. I wanted to touch him, to feel his strong body beneath my fingers as they glided across the planes of his hard chest.

He was magnificent, his chest wide and structured, his cut like marble, and his arms... so muscular, so strong. My heart raced at the thought of them holding me tightly against him. With every small movement, each muscle on his body rippled, and with each ripple, a building swell of need and want began to surge through my body.

"Touch me." The thought slipped past my lips, wispy and breathy, my chest rising as I anticipated his touch. Those two words were full of need and want. I should feel ashamed, I was behaving like a hussy, but I wasn't ashamed.

I could see that I affected him just as much by the way his body trembled as he restrained himself. The need to touch and claim me was as plain as day.

"I'm afraid, Tala. I'm afraid that if I touch you, I won't want to stop." His voice was raspy as he breathed out his confession. I almost moaned as the heat of his breath danced across my skin.

I turned my head slightly, baring more of my neck to him, my wolf mentally rolling over in submission. I felt him shudder, and the vibrations from his sultry growl made my knees buckle.

The pull was so strong!

He held me up, his hot breath fanned over my neck. Again, my knees gave away when I felt his lips lightly kiss the skin.

I moaned at the contact, not being able to hold it back. The pulsing sensation from his touch had my skin igniting in heated sparks, erupting across every nerve. He pecked his way up to my jaw line, slowly and tenderly.

I was aching for more. My eyelids fluttered closed, and my breath hitched as I anticipated his lips finally reaching mine. He stopped and my heart skipped a beat, wondering why he hadn't kissed me yet. I began to panic, thinking he didn't want me.

"You are so beautiful, my little flame." He raised his head, and his eyes found mine; I gasped when I looked back into his. They were brighter, illuminated, and it was no trick of the moonlight. I had read that only those of a royal bloodline had wolves whose eyes glowed the way his did.

He reached up and unpinned my hair, "I have dreamt about running my hands through your hair while I kiss you." He said while doing just that, giving my hair a sweep with his fingers as the long strands cascaded down, falling freely.

He gave my hair one more sweep, abruptly stopping at my nape, grabbing a fist full of my hair, and tipping my head back. "Look at me, my little flame." He commanded, and I did. I looked at him and I was lost in the clear lust and want his deep ocean blue orbs held for me.

I melted into him, wanting everything he would give me.

"No man has ever touched me before." I didn't know why I said that or what I was expecting; I just felt the need to tell him.

"*Mine.*" He growled deeply, his chest rumbling, making my panties soaked at the pure power that one word held.

I think I whimpered as he growled out his claim on me. "Yours," I barely whispered, licking my dry lips. The air was palpable, thick with our arousals, his eyes tracking the movement of my tongue before crashing his lips on mine.

My hands came up from behind my back to rest on his wide chest. I let my fingers dance across his hard, sculpted body, the tips of my fingers brushing the light smattering of hair on his bronzed pectorals. His lips pressed against mine and began moving, slowly parting over mine. I felt the tip of his tongue lick across the seam of my lips, and they opened like it was a magic trick to allow him entrance.

I moaned into the kiss. His hot breath and warm tongue caressed the inside of my mouth. He angled his head and tipped mine back further, deepening the kiss and becoming more possessive. I felt his other hand come around to the small of my back, and he pressed me against him.

Holy mother of the moon! This wasn't my first kiss, but the way he moved against me had me gasping for breath. My head felt light and dizzy, he was that intoxicating. My hands had thoroughly explored his muscular chest and ripped stomach, now they were circling his neck and tangling in his longer-length light brown hair, pulling myself as close to him as possible.

It still wasn't close enough.

All too soon, the mind-blowing kiss ended as he pulled away, but still held me flush against him. I could feel his rather large erection pushing against my abdomen, both of us breathing heavily. I stood on my tippy toes and brought his face back down to mine, determined to lengthen the pleasurable feeling of him being so close. My fingers slid out of his hair and came to rest on his face, the scruff tickling my palms, and I brought his lips back down to mine.

This time his hands moved down the sides of my body over the thin black cloak, and cupped my ass cheeks.

Suddenly, he lifted me up, placing me on the stone table and stepping in between my legs.

Moon Goddess, why did I wear this darn cloak. Just as I thought that, he found the opening and pulled it wide apart, exposing the light blue sundress I had on underneath. His engorged cock rubbed against the inside of my thigh, so close to where I was throbbing.

The heated kiss ended again, and Kellen leaned his forehead against mine, eyes closed. "Tala." He rasped, accompanied by a painful moan. "Goddess, you are already everything to me."

"I want you, Kellen, please." I begged as I shifted and rubbed my core against his covered cock. My eyes were closed, relishing the sensation.

He chuckled and stepped back, the distance leaving me cold and frustrated. "There is nothing that I want more than you, but not here. Not in slave barracks. I will not disrespect my queen like she is some floozy."

I opened my eyes to see the tender look on his face. I glanced down to see he was still hard as a rock, knowing I wasn't the only one who was sexually frustrated.

"I want to make love to you, to worship you, to cherish you; I cannot treat you the way you should be treated in here." He said, casting his eyes around the room that was full of various weapons. "I would love nothing more than to spread you out on this table and ravish your beauty under the moonlight, but I will not disrespect you, Tala."

I felt disappointed but also relieved. As much as I wanted him, to give in to the mate bond, to let those invisible tethers tie us together... he was right. This is no place to lose my virginity, no matter how much my body and wolf said otherwise.

"I had to see you, but I don't know when I can come again," I said sadly. "I will try my best. Jasper and I have some friends who will help us, but right now we don't know who we can trust, we don't know who is still loyal to my father."

I told him about my conversation with Oliver. There were a lot of growls and glares as I recounted the conversation verbatim, but all those grunts and growls did was turn me on more.

"Tala," I heard Jasper's voice from the entrance to the room, "it's time to go, I'm sorry."

I huffed, knowing Jasper was right. The last thing I wanted was to be caught here. It would not go over well with my father.

"I will get out of here, Tala, and I will kill Vargr, Jack, and Oliver. Tell me now if you have a problem with this, my little flame." I looked at Kellen, my eyes wide as I saw the truth in his. I believed every word he just said, and the thought of my mate killing not only my father, but Jack and Oliver, too, only warmed my heart in a sadistic yet justified way.

I smiled and shook my head, "How can I help?" My all-too-eager tone made his chest vibrate under my hands from the lulling sound he emitted. He kissed me again, this time short and sweet.

"Fucking perfect," he said as he lifted me down from the table. I walked away from him, pulling the hood of my cloak back over my head. I didn't want to leave, but I knew I would be back. Soon.

I walked on cloud nine the whole way back to the palace, Jasper keeping quiet next to me until we were outside my door. "My little flame?" he teased, and I smacked his arm hard. I happened to like the cute little nickname Kellen had given me.

Dear Goddess, I had already fallen hard for him.

"Seriously, what do you plan on doing, Tala? I know you; you are going to end up doing something irrational and completely insane." Jasper asked with a serious look.

"Help my mate, of course," I replied with a wry smile.

The cogs in my head were already turning, trying to figure out a plan of action. It wasn't just Jasper and Eloise's mate bond that was on the line now. It was mine and Kellen's. Not just that, but I was sure he could help save the people from my father's enslavement and bring balance back to our kingdom.

Chapter 22 – Time to Watch

<u>MIKE</u>

For the past couple of days, we had been working with Jonda, who was able to get us access to the cameras that were active on the docks. We went back to the day Kellen had disappeared, but we found nothing of use. It was like looking for a needle in a haystack.

I had to admit, I did enjoy my brief time around Jonda and if the circumstances were different, I may have actually tried to hook up with her. The timing was wrong, but I would take the little looks we would exchange with each other. The little lustful glances we shared would always leave me wanting more. Maybe after we found Kellen, I could pursue this profound obsession I was developing for her.

If I was completely honest with myself, the more time we searched, the more it seemed he had truly disappeared. I feared that one day his body would turn up and we would never know what really happened to him.

I knew he was still alive, neither I nor Duke had felt a disconnection from our king, but it still didn't lessen the feeling of hopelessness. For the umpteenth time, I was starting to lose faith again.

We were still staying at the Cheregwen Pack House; Alpha Price welcomed us and allowed us to use his facilities as needed. His son, Eric, had accompanied us to the docks a few times and helped us question some of the regulars and the more frequent captains whose boats shipped cargo to and from different ports and kingdoms.

It was strange to think Ella would become a Luna one day, and it was stranger to see her have an active role in the pack. Even stranger was noting how much she had changed; she was kind and supportive of all pack members and showed compassion to the omega wolves and servants of the pack house. So different from when she was in school, the bully had become someone the humans and lesser wolves admired and looked up to.

It just goes to show that people could change, that people could become a better version of themselves. I liked to think Lamia had something to do with Ella changing, and I hoped she had. Or maybe it was because she was no longer under her father's thumb?

I was packing my stuff away, haphazardly stuffing clothes into my bag. We had exhausted our resources here, and the three of us decided it was time to move on. We were going to head north to a smaller coastal town where boats would dock with shipments sometimes.

Hunji and Travis were both doing the same as me in their rooms. We figured that we would head out this afternoon since there was nothing more to find here. My wolf had not said a peep, nor was I getting any kind of vibe from him, so I figured he also thought this town was a lost cause.

I checked the room one more time, making sure I hadn't left anything behind before I walked out and headed down to the main foyer. Tobias and Hunji were already waiting for me and talking to Alpha Price.

"It was a pleasure to finally meet you, Hunji. I have heard many things about you, your reputation precedes you. Please give my good wishes to the young queen." Alpha Price said and shook Hunji's hand.

The older alpha turned to me as I walked up to them. "Ahh Beta Mike, please come back and visit us! I will soon be handing the reins over to Eric and Ella, and I hope you will come to celebrate the passing of the title." He said, smiling.

"If you send the invite, I certainly hope we can make it," I said sincerely. "I thank you for your kindness and hospitality, Alpha Price. Please let me know if you find anything that might be helpful while searching for... the king." I said, letting my words trail off. If we didn't find Kellen soon, I would have to be named successor, and truth be told, I did not want to be king. I just wanted my friend back to take his rightful place.

My phone began to ring as I shook the Alpha's hand. I pulled it out of my back pocket and saw Jonda's name come up. I smiled, thinking she was probably calling to say goodbye. I had kept it professional with her, with minimal flirting. I was here on a mission, and even though my desires were to take her to bed and have her screaming my name, I refrained. Another time, another place, I thought as I answered my phone.

"Jonda..." I said, answering with a wide grin. "No, we are still here... Yah, of course, we will make our way there now... Okay, see you soon." I hung up and looked at Hunji and Tobias.

"Change of plans. Jonda said she had something she wanted us to come see, and to head down to the docs before we left," I told them, watching Hunji's eyebrows pull in tight and Tobias raise an eyebrow.

"She didn't say what it was?" Tobias inquired.

"Nope. She just said, 'I've got something I want you to take a look at' and to head by her office." Tobias started laughing at me, and both Hunji and I gave him a puzzled look, wondering what he found funny.

"She wants you to take a look at something?" Tobias waggled his eyebrows at me.

"Grow the fuck up, Tobias!" Hunji scolded him. I think after the last two weeks, Hunji had really had enough of Tobias and his jokes or innuendos. He was losing patience with the bear shifter fast.

"You know, you two are going to have to figure out how to get along, seeing as you will both be serving the King and Queen of Shifters and living in the same palace," I said, half teasing, half serious. They would truly need to find some common ground, or I could see Hunji killing Tobias and then King killing Hunji. I grimaced because if King killed Hunji, then Lamia would kill King....

I gave up on my train of thought. "Come on you two. I swear I feel like the parent sometimes with the way you two bicker."

We finished saying goodbye to Alpha Price, then climbed in the car and made our thirty-minute journey to the docks to meet up with Jonda. I had to admit, I was glad to see her one last time. I don't know what it was about that girl, but she had me in knots every time I saw her.

*****

We pulled up outside the warehouse where Jonda's temporary office was located. She was standing outside waiting for us: her arms crossed over her chest, her auburn hair loose and flowing. I smiled as we got out of the car and approached her. My eyes skimmed over her again, wishing I could peel the tight jeans from her legs and run my tongue over her flesh.

Our eyes locked and the corners of her mouth turned upwards. "Beta," she greeted me, her look softening and eyes brightening. I noticed a slight blush creeping up on her face.

Oh yeah, she wanted me too. I internally smirked.

"Jonda, Mike said you wanted to show us something?" Hunji's voice interrupted our obvious ogling. She cleared her throat, pulling her eyes from me and redirecting her attention to Hunji.

"Yes sir, come with me." She motioned with her head and turned to go back inside, and we followed.

"I hope you don't mind, but I spoke to my brother the first day you came to me and explained what was going on." She talked as she walked, taking a seat behind her desk and doing something on her computer. "He called me not too long ago and sent over some video feed from our cameras on one of the lesser-used docks on the other side of the island." She explained.

Her brother was the Alpha of the Sea Dog pack, an island situated between the two continents that gave way to most trading routes around the realm. The Sea Dogs were a pack of water dweller shifters and pretty much dominated the import/export trade of the realm. The Sea Dogs Island was located in a perfect position for receiving and shipping for both continents and acted as a mediator.

"I'm not sure how helpful this is to you guys, but my brother caught the culprit smuggling a couple of girls two days ago as well as other contraband. I thought if anything, you would like to take a look at the footage," Jonda said, turning her monitor around so the three of us could see it as she hit play on the video.

Three of us stood there in silence while watching the video feed. We watched as a van pulled up by a small cargo ship and a rough-looking man climbed out. He opened the side door, dragging out a large object that looked like it was wrapped in a sheet of sorts. He passed the object to another guy who was waiting and then repeated his steps, bringing out another large, wrapped-up object. "Are they bodies?" Tobias asked while squatting down and placing his face closer to the monitor.

The feed ended, and then another one came up as the same man ushered two women on a cargo ship, delivering them to another man who roughly prodded them with a long metallic stick.

"There!" Hunji blurted out, pointing to the screen. "Go back two screenshots and replay it." He commanded with a dark expression on his face as he concentrated on the feed. I watched the video closely, looking for what Hunji spotted and what I might have missed, but I didn't see anything.

"Play it again," I said to Jonda, concentrating again.

She played it again. "Freeze!" Hunji's voice demanded, and Jonda froze the video frame. "Do you see it?" Hunji asked me.

I shook my head. "I'm not sure what I'm looking for," I admitted, scanning the paused video. It was grainy, but I could tell I was looking at the exact moment the man from the van handed over the two girls, his arm extended as he shoved them towards the man that was ready to take them on the ship.

I shook my head, giving Hunji a confused look, "I'm not sure what I'm supposed to be seeing." I was confused as to what he saw that I hadn't. I raised my eyebrows, gesturing for him to enlighten me.

"Here," Hunji pointed to the screen, tapping on the monitor. I looked where his finger rested, pointing at the man's outstretched arm. Once he pulled his finger away, I saw what he was clearly pointing to.

"Good fucking catch, Hunji!" I exclaimed in pure surprise and astonishment as I looked at the man's wrist and saw the obviously expensive as shit watch he had dangling around his wrist: a watch he couldn't afford, a watch that had been commissioned and was one of a kind. Kellen's watch Lamia had gifted him on their eighteenth birthday.

"I can't believe I missed that." I sighed, rubbing the back of my neck in embarrassment.

"You two mind letting me in on the secret?" Tobias grumbled.

"That man is wearing Kellen's watch. Lamia had the face custom made and there is an inscription on the back of it," I said, pointing at the screen and the man's wrist. It was such a small visual, but Hunji had been able to spot it. There was so much I could learn from him, his eyes were like a hawk. The guy really didn't miss much.

"Well, I'll be fucked!" Exclaimed Tobias in shock.

"Please tell me your brother didn't kill this piece of shit?" I asked Jonda, who had remained quiet this whole time.

She shook her head, a broad smile creeping across her face and she wiggled her eyebrows. "Nope, got him sitting in our cells on the island," she said smugly, looking very pleased with herself.

"Shit, I could kiss you right now." I was only half-joking because I really would have liked to lock lips with the beauty. I watched her slightly blush again before she clicked her tongue and huffed out in amusement. Our eyes stayed locked for longer than necessary.

"I will talk to Lamia. Jonda, call your brother; if that is Kellen's watch, there will be an inscription on the back of it. If it is, I guess we are taking a boat to the Sea Dog Pack," Hunji said. Even he had a slight look of relief and triumph on his face.

He walked out of the office, leaving Tobias and me with Jonda, who also was sporting a smile as she had helped us and realized the impact this discovery had on our investigation.

This was the first break we had gotten since the day Kellen had gone missing, and that was two months ago. This was a *huge* breakthrough. Thank the gods that Jonda's brother, Alpha John, had not killed the fucker because he might just be able to tell us where Kellen was, at the very least give us some valuable intel. I didn't want to get my hopes up, but I had to admit, I was excited because this was the first tangible evidence that could lead us to our king and my best friend.

Two hours later, after speaking with Lamia and sending her a copy of the footage, the three of us found ourselves stepping onto a boat Jonda had managed to charter for us. One of her pack captains was more than happy to assist us.

Alpha John had confirmed the inscription on the back of the watch that the shifter from the video footage was wearing. He had assured us he would keep him alive so we could question him ourselves.

I just finished up a call to my father, explaining the new development, and instructed him to send a unit of Elites to the docks. He and Uncle Marcus were handling the kingdom while we still searched for our new and missing king. The Elite warriors would follow us to the Sea Dog Pack's island. Just in case this lead turned into something more, I wanted to make sure we had backup. We were still as blind as the day Kellen had disappeared.

I was thankful that Hunji had also backed up my idea and had requested Lamia to send her own unit to the island as well. In addition to that, Mathias had Tobias pull a unit from their southern border to assist. In total, if we needed a small number of troops, we would have thirty-six highly trained warriors at our disposal.

Moon Goddess, please let us find him soon. I sent out a silent prayer as the three of us, along with Jonda, boarded the boat. The trip across the ocean would only take two days, but I was anxious for answers, just hoping this would lead somewhere and we weren't wasting our time.

I stood at the back of the boat, watching the dock we pulled away from getting smaller and smaller. The sun had begun to lower, and the horizon held a strange glow of deep reds and purples. I was so engrossed in the scenery that I didn't sense the presence that had snuck up behind me.

"For someone who has never been on anything bigger than a canoe, you sure seem to be handling it okay." I smiled at Hunji's observation. True, I had never been on anything bigger than a small skiff out on the lake, and it was nothing compared to the choppy waters of the wide-open ocean.

There was a little unsettling in my stomach, but I had put that down to my anxiousness to get to the island as it did not feel like sea sickness.

"I could say the same about you, but I am guessing you have traveled by sea many times?" I asked, turning around to meet Hunji head-on.

He nodded, with a complex look as he said, "Yes many, many times. Where I am from, my family once owned a whole fleet of naval vessels. I am no stranger to the ocean."

Offering me a weak smile, he folded his hands behind his back and stood next to me, watching the sun disappear as we left the western side of the realm behind.

We were leaving my home behind and venturing into the unknown. I relished the idea of an adventure, I just wished it was under different circumstances.

I wanted to push and ask Hunji more questions about his family and past, but Hunji's silence and distant look made it quite clear that he would not open up to me any more than he already had. I took the little crumbs he had offered about his life and said no more. Enjoying the silence and the serenity together, thinking about what tomorrow could bring us.

Chapter 23 – Jonda

MIKE

Neither Hunji nor I slept as we crossed the ocean. Tobias didn't sleep either, but that was due to him throwing up throughout the journey.

"Fuck, I am so happy to be on dry land again!" Tobias grumbled once we had made it to the Sea Dogs Island. He did look a little green and pasty.

I chuckled at his complaining. It seemed there was something after all that could bring down the mighty beta bear. "I guess you can't stomach as much as me. Tell me again how tough you are, big guy?" I mocked him, as he still clutched his stomach and stumbled slightly as he got his bearings.

"Fuck you." was all he replied.

Alpha John was waiting for us once the boat had docked and greeted us as soon as we stepped off the gangway. He had the same deep auburn hair as Jonda's, but his eyes were crystal blue with a hint of green. Like most alphas, he was tall and built, not quite my height and not as bulky as me, but he was a pretty good-sized alpha.

"Alpha John," I greeted him with a nod. "Thank you for not executing the criminal before we had a chance to question him and, of course, for your hospitality."

"The pleasure is all mine Royal Beta." He was very formal and even bared his neck to me slightly as a sign of respect and recognition of my rank and title. "It is unfortunate that we are meeting under these circumstances, nevertheless, I am loyal to the kingdom and hope to be of service to you and the queen's men." He said, acknowledging Hunji and Tobias as well.

"Please come, I have prepared rooms for you in one of the Inns. I figured you would be hungry and tired." He then looked at Tobias, "And I assume one of you don't have sea legs?" He chuckled at Tobias, and I joined in when I also looked at poor Tobias. There was no way I was ever letting this one go.

"Thank you, alpha..."

"Please call me John, Beta..."

"In that case, please call me Mike. This is Hunji - Queen Lamia's second in command, and this poor fellow is Tobias - King Mathias' second in command. And yes, I think it would be best if we rested for now and then question the man." I agreed.

Alpha John and Jonda took us to a quaint little Inn not too far from the docks. Although he took us by car, it was only a ten-minute walk from where they were holding the man in question, whose name I came to learn was Darrius.

"Dinner will be served downstairs at seven," Jonda told me when they left us to our rooms.

"Will you be joining us?" I asked with a hopeful smile.

"Would you like me to join you, Beta Mike?" Jonda countered, pursing her lips and arching a brow.

Moons, she was feisty and drop-dead gorgeous. "Yes." I told

her straight. "I would be offended if you didn't." I finished, giving her a wink.

"In that case, see you boys downstairs at seven." She replied, giving me a sly smile over her shoulder as she walked away. I, of course, kept my eye on her perfectly round ass as she retreated.

"Are you going to tap that?" Tobias asked, coming up behind me and whispering in my ear.

I scowled, not liking the way he referred to Jonda. "Hands off, Tobias!" I warned with a low growl.

"What?" He feigned innocence, "I was just asking. She is all yours man, but in the event that you don't want it, I wouldn't say no. Just saying, man."

At seven o'clock, I made my way downstairs of the Inn, taking my time to look at the various photos that hung on the wall. Most of them were old black-and-white historical photos of the various buildings that were on the Island, some of the docks, and some had people in them.

I double-glanced at one, seeing a familiar face. King Alexander, Kellen's father. He was standing with what I assumed was the Alpha at that time, a heavily pregnant woman, and a little boy no older than five.

I stood there for a moment taking in the photo and the happy smiles on everyone's faces. I noticed how the pregnant woman looked a lot like Jonda and was probably around the same age as her when this photo was taken. I made a mental note to ask about this picture. Then I looked at the smiling eyes of the late king and whispered a promise to him, "I will find him, Uncle, I promise." The feeling of failure began creeping back in.

I found the will to move a few seconds later and walked

into the dining room, where I found Jonda already seated with Tobias and Hunji. The smile on her face was like a beacon of light, warm and welcoming, and I couldn't help but be drawn to her. As soon as my eyes landed on her, the sorrow I had been feeling just minutes ago as I looked at the photo of Kellen's father dissipated.

"Hi," I said, greeting everyone with a wide smile that was mostly aimed at Jonda. I took a seat and grabbed the small one-sided menu.

Hunji chuckled. "I don't think you are going to like anything on that menu," he said, shoving some kind of fried seafood into his mouth as he watched my face for a reaction. He had a playful smirk on his face as he chewed.

I grumbled as I cast my eyes over the menu. No red meat whatsoever. I was going to die from lack of protein before we ever found Kellen at this rate.

"You don't like seafood?" Jonda asked with a concerned look.

"If it's not red meat, he is scared of it," laughed Tobias, obviously amused at my discomfort of eating something that didn't have four legs and didn't come from the land.

"Oh!" Jonda sat up surprised and waved her hand at an older lady to come over. "Willa, would you please make an exception and prepare the Royal Beta a steak, he is not a fan of seafood." She chuckled with the last words. The older lady, Willa, gave me a disappointed scowl and shook her head like I had offended her.

"Of course, Jonda, anything you request." Her scowl quickly disappeared when she addressed Jonda.

Jonda chuckled as the woman walked away, muttering something about foreigners under her breath. "She is very passionate about traditional foods, and she will never understand how people can't like seafood." She watched the woman disappear behind a swinging door to what I assumed was the kitchen.

"Thank you for the company," Hunji said as he stood up, "I am going to go talk with Alpha John. I figured we could question Darrius later this evening? Lamia asked me to set up some provisions with the Alpha for when the Elites arrive."

"Very well," I nodded, "I will link you when we are ready." With that, he bowed out and left.

Tobias then stood up, clutching his stomach. "I think I am going to lay down for a bit. I really don't have sea legs," he said sadly, obviously feeling pity for himself, and his stomach still hadn't settled from the two-day boat ride.

"Yeah, you kinda look like shit. Your face is still green and pale." I laughed.

"Ha ha, fuck off." He groaned but managed to give Jonda a charming smile and bid her goodnight. "Let me know when you are questioning the dude. Not sure if King mentioned my excellent interrogating skills?" He threw over his shoulder as he headed back up to his room.

Now that the baby and the babysitter were out of the way, I turned all my attention to Jonda. "Alone at last," I said with a sly smile.

"Should I be scared?" She laughed.

"No," I shook my head, still smiling like an idiot, "but I was hoping to get to know you a little better on my own."

"Did you plan on your friends leaving so we could eat alone?" She asked with a skeptical look.

"I didn't plan it, but it definitely worked out in my favor.

Dinner with a beautiful woman, a woman I would like to get to know much better." I winked at her.

Jonda opened her mouth, ready to say something, but Willa came back and set the food down in front of us, putting a stop to whatever Jonda was going to say. That's okay, we had all night to get to know each other better.

Jonda and I conversed easily while we ate, and after we had finished our food, neither of us was ready to get up from the table. Jonda had Willa, who I found out was the owner of this little Inn, bring us over a couple of bottles of rum and some tumblers.

"So... Tell me, Royal Beta Mike, what wind of fortune blew your little ship into my harbor?" Jonda said to me after a few drinks in. Oh, this girl was playing with fire and stoking it too.

I watched with want as she leaned closer, resting her chin in her palm and leaning on the table with her elbow, biting her bottom lip. She may not have realized she was doing it, or maybe she did, but it was a huge turn-on for me. I wanted to be the one to bite her lip and make it red.

"I think you are flirting with me, Jonda?" I had to make sure because if I acted on it and it wasn't what she wanted, I would feel embarrassed.

I already determined that Jonda wasn't like other she-wolves. She guarded, feisty, and had no problem getting what she wanted when she wanted it. Yet on the other side, she was quick to blush, or maybe I just made her blush. She was twenty-three years old, and her brother Alpha John had turned twenty-six not too long ago.

"Maybe... but I am also curious about what's going on. I know you are looking for... the king." She whispered the last part making sure it was just me and her who heard, "But I feel like there is more to it, isn't there?"

"Not much more, to be honest." I took a sip of my drink. "Changing the subject, I saw an interesting picture on the wall in the hallway," I described the picture to her, and her eyes lit up for a brief second before they revealed a sadness.

Her usual sexy stern look was gone, now replaced with a withdrawn look. "The picture with the late king. That was my father and mother, and my brother when he was younger. My mother was pregnant with me in that picture." With a sad smile, she told me.

"What happened to your father and mother?" I thought maybe they died in battle or were retired and on their permanent vacation. Maybe they were still here in the pack just hanging out with family.

By the way the light faded from Jonda's hazel eyes, I could tell that was not the case and I wished I hadn't asked her. "I'm sorry," I began but was cut off.

"It's okay, it's not really a secret, just a sad story." She picked up her drink and knocked it back, then poured herself another, twirling the glass in her hands. We sat in silence for a few minutes until she began to speak.

"John was too young to remember what happened, and of course, I hadn't been born. Willa and the delta, later turned beta, family pretty much raised the two of us." She gulped down her drink again and I followed her action, downing mine and then pouring us both another glass.

"It was my birthday the day you three goons showed up at the office," Jonda began, "It was also the anniversary of when my father disappeared."

"You don't have to tell me if you don't want to…" I offered her a way out.

"No, it's okay, I want to," she said, offering a weak grin. "Supposedly, twenty-three years ago, a bear shifter named Orion showed up on our island with his witch mate and their son. They came in the dead of night with an army. Their boats landed on our docks, on the easternmost southerly border, and they snuck through the land killing citizens until they reached the pack house. They killed everyone they came across, dragging my mother and brother from their beds. My father, at the time, had been questioning a rogue in the cells. They had been having rogue problems for a few months back then.

"Anyway, he held my mother at knifepoint, and when my father came upon the scene, Orion made my father bow down and pledge his life. If he didn't, then Orion was going to kill my mother, the Luna, and her son. They took my father as a hostage, but before they left, I was told that Orion gave his witch instructions to poison my mother. Instead, she made my mother swallow a binding potion." Jonda gulped and then took another swig of her drink, a faraway look in her eyes as she told me her story.

"What happened to your mother?" I asked, not knowing what she would say.

"After Orion left with my father, my mother went into labor that very night, and I was born. Unfortunately, the binding spell was for me, not my mother. The herbs she forced my mother to drink caused me to never be able to shift. She cursed a werewolf with the inability to ever shift." Her hazel eyes held a glazed and sad look. I saw the tears gather, but she blinked away the drops that threatened to fall. This girl was one tough cookie.

"So, you can't shift? Or you don't have a wolf?" I wasn't sure what she meant, and l looked for clarification.

"I have a wolf, but I can't shift. And supposedly, I will never be able to until I find a mate who is a wolf-less shifter. On the day of my first birthday, my mother tried to claw her heart out. That was the day she almost died of a broken heart. No one knows what happened, but many have said my father betrayed the bond and took another into his bed, but it only ever happened once in almost twenty-three years."

"Wow, I'm really sorry your family has had to endure all this. Is your mother… still alive?" I asked curiously, thinking about what Zane, Lamia's first-ish, mate went through when she had been kidnapped. Knowing the feeling of a mate's betrayal, whether forced or not, could do some serious damage. It was another reason why I was in no hurry to find my mate, among many other reasons. I felt for Jonda and her family, and my compassion for her troubles was sincere.

"My mother never held it against him, she still loves him to this very day, and I think the only reason she is still with us is out of hope that one day he will return."

"So, you think he is still alive?" I was surprised by this.

"Probably," Jonda mused. "My mother's mark never faded, and the bond never broke. She sent men out to look for him and Orion for years, but nothing ever turned up. I guess this is why I'm so invested in helping you find the king. He is your best friend, yes?"

I nodded. Indeed, Kellen wasn't just a best friend, he was more than that. He was my brother, and I would do anything for him. I wanted to press on the fact that she couldn't shift into her wolf form, but I thought better of it, no matter how curious I was. She would tell me more when she was ready.

"So, how do you feel about interrogating this Darrius your brother has holed up?" I asked, watching for her reaction and changing the subject.

"Let's go cut a bitch," she said a little too excitedly, and

I noted the twinkle in her eye. Just like that, she had shifted from the melancholy somberness to the feisty and intimidating woman I met last week.

Goddess, she was all that and more. It took a strong person to shove their feeling deep down and flip the switch from personal to business as she just did, hiding all her sorrows and focusing on the now.

Chapter 24 - Darrius

MIKE

The Sea Dogs' cells were nothing more than a warehouse with a hidden basement. They were dark, damp, dank, and held the scent of the ocean. Darrius, the wolf shifter, had been tied to a metal chair that was coated in a thin layer of silver. They had stripped him of all his clothing and left him there. The silver was enough to irritate the skin and slowly burn the back of his legs, ass, and balls, but not enough to do any real damage. It was a slow but constant form of torture.

He lifted his head with a whimper when we walked into the large, cold, and barely lit room. His eyes were red and slightly swollen. Alpha John's men had worked him over a little. It had already been decided that I, as Kellen's beta, would question the man, whereas Tobias would be the one inflicting the pain if need be. There would definitely be a need.

Jonda took a seat at the side of the room and Hunji stood next to her, ready to intervene if and when needed. He looked like her personal bodyguard in the way he stood there with his arms stiff by his sides and his feet set apart a little. There was a stern and intimidating look on his face, and as usual, his eyes were dark, almost black, and showed no emotion in them.

"Hello," I said with a false kindness. "Darrius, is it?" I asked the pathetic wolf shifter who sat in the chair, shaking from the slight burn from the chair. He nodded, his eyes wide and fearful.

"Well, Darrius, I am here to ask you a few questions. How well your night goes will depend on how your answer. You are in a lot of trouble as it is, but you could make this easier on yourself. Are you following me so far?" Again, he nodded. I kept my tone light, maybe a little too friendly.

I gestured at Tobias, who picked up a small table and brought it over in front of Darrius. He laid out a few tools on the table, ensuring Darrius saw exactly what was on that table. He definitely noticed when he started squirming in his seat.

"First question; where did you get the watch?" I asked, holding up Kellen's watch which had the inscription Lamia had engraved on it.

He shook his head. "It was a gift," he lied.

I gave a curt nod to Tobias, who picked a small scalpel and brought it to the man's chest, cutting around his nipple and removing it. Darrius screamed in pain, tears streaming down his eyes as blood pooled from the fresh wound.

"Now, Darrius, I will ask you again. Where did you get the watch?"

"I-it w-was given t-to me." He blubbered. I nodded again, and Tobias removed his other nipple. His pained screams rang out through the empty room. I felt nothing for what we were about to do to him if he didn't give us answers.

I cast a quick look at Jonda to see how she was handling this. I internally smiled as I saw her sitting with her legs crossed, watching, not affected at all. An alpha's daughter, I thought. She and Lamia would get on very well.

"I want to ask who gave it to you again, but to be honest,

I don't feel like taking the long way around. So... tell me exactly where you got this watch, who from, and where the owner of it is. Or I will let my friend here carve you up like a fucking turkey."

"Please, please," he stammered, "I can't..."

I nodded at Tobias once more. He put the scalpel down and picked up a pair of pliers and some long, thick needles. Tobias proceeded to pull a nail from the man's finger, and followed up by shoving the silver needle down into the length of his finger.

The man wailed and cried, begging for mercy. I stood and watched patiently until Tobias had successfully removed every fingernail from one hand and shoved a needle down into each digit. I wondered if I was going too far for a moment, but when I looked at Hunji, he gave me a look of approval.

"Darrius, Darrius, are you ready for the next hand?" I asked, still keeping a cool and calm tone in my voice. Darrius shook his head from side to side violently. Snot and slobber drooled from his face. The man was pathetic and weak. "Are you ready to talk then?" I was hoping he would talk before he passed out on us.

He hesitated, and I gave Tobias the go-ahead. This time instead of pulling out fingernails, he picked up a sharp sliver knife and slowly carved his left ear off. The screams pierced my ears, and I just wanted him to shut up. I sent Hunji a quick mind-link and watched him bend to whisper in Jonda's ear.

Jonda jumped up from her seat and walked out of the room. A few seconds later, she came back in holding a bottle of water and went over to Darrius. She bent down in front of him and opened the water bottle, offering him some and holding the bottle to his lips. He drank gingerly.

"Please Darrius, tell them what they want to know and this will be over quick." She pleaded to him, her fingers stroking his cheek.

"They will kill me." He whispered out through his whimpers.

"You will die for your crimes anyway. Would you rather be tortured for days or have an honorable death?" She gave him the choice, but he snubbed her by turning his head.

Jonda got up and went back to her seat, giving me a look as in 'I tried'. I nodded at Tobias once again. I thought this man was weak, but either he didn't fear us, or he feared someone else more.

Tobias began slicing the flesh by his rib cage, filleting the flesh like he was removing the skin of a fish. The agonizing, pain-filled screams echoed throughout the basement, and the smell of his blood permeated the air.

I was about to call for a break to regroup once Tobias had finished taking off a good six-square-inch piece of flesh, but Darrius began spluttering a string of words in between his pained whimpers and sobbing.

"Please, please, no more. It was Jack. He and the rogue wolf, Oliver, they brought him on the boat. They sold him. I swear I didn't know. I swear!" He cried out.

"Who? Who did Oliver bring on the boat? Who did they sell?" As soon as I heard the name, Oliver, I knew. I fucking knew it was him who took Kellen.

"They, they made a deal with Pete. He wasn't meant to be on the boat, but they brought him last minute." He cried, blubbering out his words, and began sobbing uncontrollably.

I was getting impatient and crossed the room with

inhuman speed. My claws extended, and my canines were already elongated as I grabbed him by the throat - piercing the skin in his neck with my wolf's claws. "WHERE THE FUCK IS HE?" I roared out with a growl, my voice mixed with Duke's.

"Where the fuck is he?" I asked again, not much calmer.

"I don't know," he cried. "They sold him into slavery; we are just paid to keep them knocked out and transport them. After that, we have no idea." He cried when I released his neck, shoving him in the process. He was a fucking trafficker, the piece of shit deserved to die.

"I have no more use for you if that is all you can give me." I turned around, ready to walk out, but the man had one last thing to say.

"Vargr, Jack mentioned Vargr. I swear I know nothing else. I swear." He cried like a three-year-old who had been scolded for hiding.

"I have heard of Alpha Vargr." Jonda piped up, and that was all I needed.

I turned on my heel, now facing Darrius again. He sat there slumped, bloody, and half alive. I couldn't care less though. I had no sympathy for a man like him. I picked up the watch, thumbed the face, and took a deep breath. I walked up to Darrius as I extended the claw from my index finger, and pierced it right through the side of his head, through his temple.

Immediately his body slumped. I had ended his life, and I felt nothing of it. I put Kellen's watch in my pocket and walked out.

Once I reached outside, I took several deep breaths and blew them out harshly while bent over and grabbing my knees, trying to regain my composure. Duke was kicking up a fuss, pushing to come out, wanting to destroy everyone and everything after finding out what had happened to our best friend and king. He was out for more blood, Darrius' death didn't satisfy him in the least.

I heard the door open and slam shut behind me; light steps and a sweet smell reached my nose before she had even spoken. "Are you alright Mike?" I heard Jonda ask as she timidly approached me.

"I need a drink," I stated as I righted myself and turned to face her. She nodded her head in understanding.

"Come on," she said gently, taking my arm and pulling me back in the direction of the little inn. "Hunji said they would clean up."

We walked in silence back to the inn. Once we reached it and went inside, she pulled me back to the dining room and went behind the little wet bar and grabbed a bottle of liquor. She opened it and took a pull before handing it to me.

"I have never seen anyone kill someone the way you did." She admitted with a little admiration in her voice. "It was... very... interesting, clean." That was one way to describe it.

"I need as much info on this Vargr as possible. I want to know who he is and where he is." I said, taking a few big gulps of the alcohol and then handing it back to Jonda.

She led me to a chair, shoving me into it and taking a seat herself. "I told Hunji to talk to my brother. He will know more."

"Thank you," I said as I felt my heightened emotions begin to calm and my wolf begin to simmer down.

We sat there, taking turns swigging the bottle down like a pair of teens. I finally had the courage to look at her, her hazel eyes met mine, and the judgment I expected to see in her eyes was not there, only compassion and concern. "Do you think I'm a monster?" I asked her, wanting to honestly know if she saw me as one because I felt it was important that she didn't see me in that light. I didn't want her to know that side of me.

"No, not all." She smiled and brought one of her dainty hands up to my cheek and caressed it. "I think you're a very powerful man, compassionate and honorable. That man was going to die for his crimes anyway. I'm very impressed by you, Mike. I think…"

She paused, not only her words, but her fingers stopped caressing my jaw as our eyes locked and held. "…I think I like you."

It was fast, it was sudden, it was unexpected, but it was welcomed. Our lips crashed together. I didn't even know who made the first move, but we had suddenly come together across the table in a heated passion, and my mouth began devouring hers.

I broke this kiss, pulling back from her reluctantly. "I want you." I told her with a growl in my throat. She pulled me back to her, grabbed my shirt in her fists, and brought our mouths back together as her answer. She wanted me, too, I could feel it in the way her soft lips moved against mine.

The burning desire shifted to my manhood and my cock began to swell, straining against the lining of my pants when the scent of her arousal reached my senses. I stood up, taking her with me, our lips still locked in a race for dominance when I pulled her up. I cupped her ass and her legs wrapped around my waist, and I wasted no time heading towards my room.

After bouncing off several walls, I finally found the door and shoved it open, kicking it closed behind me once we had made it inside. I threw her on the bed, watching her curvy body bounce on the mattress, and I groaned just thinking about peeling her clothes off.

No words were exchanged, none were needed. We were both eager and ready, wanting what the other wanted. I fell over her and captured her in a wild and heated kiss again. I was no stranger to a woman's body, but I was shaking with the need for this woman.

"Mike," she moaned as my hands slid under her silky black blouse. I had no patience and instead of removing her clothes, I began to tear at them, shredding her blouse and bra and using a claw to tear her tight jeans from her body.

"Fuck, you're the most beautiful woman I have ever laid eyes on," I said once I removed every stitch of fabric. Her porcelain skin was soft, and I bent down to take one of her nipples in my mouth and palmed the other large breast. She moaned and arched her back, so I sucked on her more.

"Take your clothes off," she moaned a command to me, and I obliged. I ripped my shirt over my head and unfastened my pants in record time, letting them drop to the floor.

Once we were both naked, I fell over her again, parting her legs and nestling between them. I could feel the heat from her throbbing pussy and wanted to pound into her immediately, but I held back and slowed things down even though my wolf and cock were protesting - wanting to sink into her.

"Fuck you're so beautiful, Jonda," I rasped as I left a trail of kisses down her body, sucking and biting when I reached her large full mounds. She gasped and moaned under my administration and the sounds of her lust drove me wild.

While one hand palmed her large breast and my mouth devoured the other, my other hand found its way inbetween her legs and parted her lower lips, stroking her seam and coating my fingers in with her hot wetness. She gasped and squirmed with delight when two of my thick digits entered her. Her walls closed around them as they thrust in and out slowly.

"Please, Mike... Please, I want you now," she begged. I wanted to take my time with her, but her breathy words appealed to my senses. "Damn it," she moaned. "Sex now, foreplay later."

"Is that what you want, because..."

"Fuck me now. I beg you, beta!" She almost screamed as I felt her orgasm rip through her and her pussy clench my fingers. I couldn't help the chuckle; she was so responsive to my touch, so sensitive.

I removed my fingers and lined up my cock. Lifting my eyes to watch her face, I found her eyes already on me. I pushed into her, not slowly but not fast either, and I almost unloaded right there and then when her lips parted, and her keen whimper of bliss gently released from her pink lips.

I sunk in into her deeply, her eyes not leaving mine. I stilled, thinking she needed a minute. I was a beta, I was not small, and her body was tiny, but when she lifted her hips and rotated them slightly, I pulled back and slammed back into her.

"Yes!" she cried out on the second thrust.

She fit me like a glove, and I began moving in and out of her at a medium pace, holding back from pounding her. Fuck, this woman was perfect. Her sultry groans and breathy wisps of whimpers each time I pushed into her drove me on. I couldn't get enough.

I picked up my pace, feeling her walls tighten around my

shaft. Beads of sweat coated both of us, and she let out the most sexual wail I had ever heard as she exploded around me. Her nails dug into my back, clawing me as she peaked and her orgasm shattered around me, bringing me to my own release.

I don't know how long we made love or how many times, but as I laid there with this sleeping beauty in my arms, her breath even, her body relaxed, I knew I never wanted to let her go.

I kissed her head and pulled her tighter to my chest, inhaling her natural scent and feeling at peace for the first time in a few months. She was not my mate, but I knew right there that I would have a hard time letting this woman go.

Chapter 25 – We meet Again

<u>KELLEN</u>
DAY 12 OF THE GAMES

Ajani finally healed and was able to join us for training in the common area this morning. Although he was still recovering and a little on the stiff side, he was still one the best fighters here. Aside from myself and Teal, Ajani was only second to Rogue.

I had often found myself wondering who Rogue really was or where he came from. Once he had been taught to hold a sword properly and trained in fighting techniques, he embraced the role of a gladiator with the heart of a warrior. He was a quick study and picked things up easily, a natural like he was born to fight. I was sure that if he had a voice, he would be a great commander, his loyalty to me was sincere.

Rogue had shadowed my every move, listening, learning, and watching my back, and had I watched him strengthen and gain the respect of each gladiator in the Barracks. He was becoming a force to reckoned with, and I appreciated him. I trusted Rogue.

After the incident I saved him from, Rogue needed to show his strength and he knew it. His dignity and pride had been bruised. Rogue wanted to redeem himself, take back that self-respect he had lost. He had been made vulnerable, almost violated in the worst way. I had saved his ass, literally, but it was up to him to gain back the respect he deserved. He could only do that by becoming the strongest. And he had.

I had no doubt in my mind that Rogue would never betray me. We had a friendship that I would even dare to compare to mine and Mike's.

I was finding it hard to concentrate, still thinking about my little flame and the taste of her lips from four days ago. She didn't just smell like oranges and sea salt, she tasted like it too. I could still taste her; the salty fruit mix was akin to a cocktail of juice, tequila, and salt. It was the first and only time I had been able to hold her in my arms. It wasn't enough. I wanted and needed to see her again. The primal desire to claim her was great and the bond was burning through me, forcing my wolf to want to search her out and mate with her.

I picked up the carving of the wolf that sat on the ledge of the barred window, remembering the little boy who had given it to me. Each night I held it like a talisman, as if it was an idol used to pray to the gods, and I prayed to the Moon Goddess.

A guard stood in front of the bars, his back turned to me. "Wolf King" he whispered, looking around to make sure no one was listening. "Be ready an hour after nightfall. Someone will collect you to meet with the princess."

Before I could even part my lips and reply, he walked off, leaving me with that message and nothing more. My heart sped up, beating wildly at the thought of seeing my little flame again. The anticipation would stay with me all day, and now I would count down the seconds until the sun dipped and the moon rose.

*****

Two gladiators went into the arena today and did not return. By the smell of the blood and chaos from the crowd,

I had determined that they had died. I asked what happened to the bodies of the fallen and Teal told me two things: either they dumped them in a pit, or they were fed to Vargr's pets.

I still had yet to learn what his pets were. If they belonged to Vargr, I could assume they were nothing good. And after encountering the crawlers created by Orion and Shayna, I dreaded to think what kind of pets they were.

The gladiators housed in the barracks with me had begun to improve vastly, learning how to work together, learning to trust each other. There were still three who had kept themselves separated from the rest of us, and we were now down to a group of nineteen, the others had died in one fashion or another.

If I was going to get out of here, I would need as many men by my side to stand with me as possible, and that was hard to do when you were thrown into an arena where you were expected to die. In the span of a week, five gladiators had already lost their lives before the two today. So far, more than half of these fights hadn't been fair. It was a massacre. Most of the time it would be two gladiators against four men, four trained men, where some rode horses or threw nets over the gladiators and then dishonorably stabbed and sliced them until they had bled out.

I have no idea why I ever expected anything less. I did come to realize that, to Vargr, some of these gladiator slaves were expendable, but he had spent a lot of money on people like me. I knew he was saving me for something special.

Teal was an alpha, and Vargr had kept him alive so he could witness another wolf raising his daughter. By abusing the Luna, Vargr thought he was punishing Teal by causing her pain. However, Teal felt nothing for the Luna; she raped him using witches' herbs. Teal only cared for the daughter that was created that night and still held so much guilt for betraying the mate bond, for causing pain to the one he truly loved, whether it was his fault or not.

I had grown close not only to Teal, but also to Rogue and Ajani. I didn't talk about my encounter with Tala too much to Teal, as he wanted to maintain a safe distance, but I did talk to Rogue. He was a very good listener.

Tala had no idea that Teal was her real father and he did not want her to know. He said it could cause more problems for her and her not knowing would keep her safer. It was for the same reason that we did not want Vargr to find out we were mates. Vargr was too unpredictable; he would either execute me or do something to hurt Tala. I didn't care what happened to me; I just needed her to be safe and I was not in a position to protect my queen.

I would need to meet with this Jasper. I wasn't in a position to start gaining trust and grow a rebellion, but Jasper was, and I was sure I could be of some guidance.

When an alpha wolf meets his mate, their heightened emotions and primal instincts push them to protect, mate, and worship their Luna. It drives them towards an almost frenzy with a crazed need to protect what is his. So, Conri was extremely riled up from wanting to be close to his mate and her wolf. Not being able to see, feel, or smell her for four days drove him insane. His constant need to shift and seek out his other half was becoming unbearable, not just for me but also for him.

*****

TALA

Jasper, Eloise, and I had accomplished a lot during the past four days. After my meeting with Kellen and the intimidating talk with Oliver, I was even more determined than ever to help free my mate and get out from under the clutches of my father.

My mother had become violent in the past few days, another type of episode we had seen her have. This time it was triggered because my father had strapped her to her bed, raped her, and then allowed Jack to have his turn while he watched them and fucked a slave girl right next to her on her bed.

His loyal guard dogs had held me back from the door while I kicked and screamed against them. Her pained screams and cries for help would haunt me for life. I tried to shift, but my father's command had prevented me from doing that.

I could do nothing but cry for her, knowing she had been given nothing to fight off the pain, whereas my father had already taken herbs so he could betray her. His wolf would not feel the pain.

He made me sick. If my father's goal was to make me loath him more than Aodh, our god of the underworld, then he had succeeded.

My mother was strapped down, unable to claw at her chest, but she could certainly feel the pain burning her from the inside out. Even without her wolf, she would hurt and want to attack herself. She once described it as her blood boiling so hot that it felt like her insides were liquefying. I shuddered at the thought and could only imagine how much agony she would be in.

The whole palace heard her screams. Everyone knew what was going on, yet no one dared to help. They were too afraid of the repercussions. I fought to get her, wanting nothing more than to kill him, but all I could do was cry for her as I collapsed to the ground calling to her, pleading to my father behind the closed door to stop, and begging him to show her mercy.

But my pleas were ignored, and my screams got stuck in my throat, choking the strength from me.

When the doors finally opened, Jack and my father came out acting as if they had just finished a movie. Not like they had just raped the Luna. A poor slave girl was dragged behind them.

"You mother fucker!" I shouted and spat at both of them.

"Vargr, it seems your daughter needs to be taught a lesson on how to behave. I would be more than happy to tame her." I almost threw up from what Jack insinuated.

I looked my father in the eye, my eyes spearing daggers at him. My only thought was to kill him, and Mora was still trying to fight the command. She wanted to shift and tear him apart. "You're a piece of shit!" I spat at him again, showing my disgust.

He had me against the wall in an instant. "Your mother is a whore, and she will be treated like one. She deserves nothing less. She chose this. She chose you!" He growled at me. "One last chance. The next time you speak out of line, I will take your virginity myself! Then I will let my whole army fuck you right in the middle of the arena for everyone to watch."

I began trembling; the bravery I had just moments ago was slipping away. His hand cut off my airway, but I daren't move. I saw the truth in his eyes. He meant every word of it.

I felt sick; bile rose up and caught in my throat, causing my eyes to swell with tears. How could a father threaten his daughter like that? He hated me so much, he thought so little of me that he would even go to those lengths to prove it.

He let go and I stayed stuck to the wall while he turned his back and walked away. Jack looked back at me over his shoulder, throwing me a wink, making me cringe and bringing back the feeling of wanting to puke.

After checking on my mother and calling for her maid to tend to her wounds where Jack had got 'handsy' and left his claw marks on her, I met up with Jasper and Eloise in the south wing library. It was a place no one ever went, except for the three of us when we didn't want nosy maids or guards listening in on us.

After recanting the incident with my father and Jack, and finally calming down from the confrontation, we put into motion the beginning of our plan. I hoped like hell that we could acquire enough allies within our own pack and that enough guards would go against their alpha and switch to our side.

It wasn't that pack members wouldn't want to. They would love to see Vargr fall and have their loved ones set free from working in the mines. Alas, they held that fear of what he might or could do to their families.

It was decided - Jasper would work on gaining the trust of guards and warriors we knew, targeting friends and those who had family that was enslaved to work in the mines. Eloise would begin spreading the word to the omegas and humans that worked in the palace, and I was tasked with finding a map of the mines and trying to find out who the witch Oliver and Jack were after was.

Jasper had tried to ask his father, but either Beta Baron didn't know, or he was tight-lipped with it. We had to be careful not to ask too many questions, or they would start wondering why.

The night after I broke into my father's office, lady luck was on my side. I didn't have to look very hard because the blueprints to the mine were sitting there, rolled out, on the table. Lady luck blessed me twice. I didn't have a phone and my father hated technology, but the one thing he did have was a copy machine. I copied the map and was able to put the original back on the table. Hopefully, nobody would be any the wiser.

While I was in there, I looked around for any information on this witch, but lady luck was not able to provide me with a charm for the third time.

Yesterday my mother had been feeling better; either that or the drugs had numbed her body. As she left her room and had gotten down to the dining room, a guard had asked if she needed assistance. Whatever was going through her mind at the time, she decided to attack him, producing a silver knife. The end result was that she managed to kill him and had to be subdued yet again. This was no life for her. She was constantly under the influence of drugs, and it was no wonder her wolf had left her - her mind was in a constant state of flux.

She had no idea what was real and what wasn't.

Jasper, Eloise, and I were back in the library. Jasper and I were going to meet with Kellen again tonight and I couldn't wait. It had been four long days since I had set eyes upon him. My heart fluttered when I recalled our kiss. Kissing him wasn't enough, and I had found myself masturbating to the image of my mate more than once in the past few days.

Finally, nightfall had come. I donned my long cape again, tucking my noticeable bright red hair away, and slipped out my bedroom window. I met Jasper along the way toward the guard's lounge on the other side of the arena.

When we arrived, Jasper's trusted guards already had Kellen there waiting for us. As soon as I saw him, I leaped into his arms. He welcomed me, enveloping me in his big secure arms. We stood there inhaling each other's scents, gulping each other in like it was our last breath.

He pulled back, his hands cupping my face as his eyes wandered over me, scanning me from head to toe like he was assessing me, making sure I was still in one piece. His eyes were pained when they landed on the now-fading bruise around my neck.

Due to not being able to shift unless my father allowed it and exerting so much energy these past few days, my wolf had a hard time healing me, and because this injury was not life-threatening, she let it heal as a human's injury would. I think she was really letting our mate see what was going on because she knew I would never tell him.

"I'm okay," I whispered when he brought his lips to my forehead, planting a gentle kiss there. I wrapped my arms around his waist and buried my head in his chest. I could hear the erratic beat of his heart and knew he was mad as hell seeing the hand mark around my neck, but holding back because there was nothing that he could do at this moment.

"You need to be careful, little flame. I don't want you putting yourself in a position where you can get hurt. Please, Tala, don't give him and Jack any reason to hurt you." The worry in his voice stuck with me and I squeezed him tighter.

"I'll try," I told him, and heard Jasper scoff behind me.

"She has never been able to keep herself out of trouble," he laughed. "That's like asking a fish not to swim," he carried on.

"Jasper, shut up!" I scolded him before he could embarrass me or himself anymore.

Chapter 26 – An unexpected Bite

KELLEN

I was pacing the small room waiting, somewhat patiently, for Tala and Jasper. The guards brought me to a small structure that only housed a bathroom and living room. The guard said they called it their lounge, where they could grab a coffee or a few hours of kip inbetween making the rounds.

The small building was at the far end of the south wall, just after the female slave quarters. There were two desks on either side of the room, and a couch sat in the middle, accompanied by one leather chair and a small table facing the window. The room was well lit by lamps, and the only other door led to the bathroom.

The main door opened and as soon as it did, my breath hitched when my eyes met with Tala's. Pulling back her hood, she then flung herself into my waiting arms and I breathed her in, instantly feeling a calming warmth wash over me, settling my wolf. Goddess, I had missed her presence already.

Her little arms wrapped around my waist, holding on like I was her lifeline.

I pulled back after having my fill, my eyes scanning her, making sure she was okay. I was ready to breathe a sigh of relief until my eyes landed on the faded bruise around her neck. The handmark was obviously a man's by the size of it.

"I'm okay," she whispered, her voice full of guilt because I had seen it. Conri began growling in my head and I had to shove him back as he shook with rage within me. My heart began to race with anger.

'Calm down, Conri!' I chastised my wolf. He didn't like that he couldn't protect his mate, and neither did I, but we were not in a position to do anything about it right now. Hopefully, that would change soon.

I placed a kiss on her head, tasting the sweet saltiness of her skin.

"You need to be careful little flame; I don't want you putting yourself in a position where you can get hurt. Please, Tala, don't give him and Jack any reason to hurt you." I was worried about her safety and didn't want her putting herself in a vulnerable position - it was too dangerous. I couldn't take it if something happened to her, especially as I couldn't protect my woman.

"I'll try." She said, squeezing her arms around me tighter. I heard the young Beta make a scoffing sound behind her.

"She has never been able to keep herself out of trouble," Jasper laughed. "That's like asking a fish not to swim," he said while plopping down onto the chair.

I led Tala to the couch where I sat, pulling her onto my lap so I could hold her. I was going to keep her as close to me as possible for as long as I could.

"Jasper, shut up!" She groaned at him, throwing him a glare.

For the next forty-five minutes, we discussed their plan and what they had already put in place. I was impressed that they had already gotten the ball rolling and had put a lot of effort into the initial planning and outline. We went over some more details, Jasper had provided a map of the palace grounds, and Tala had already been able to obtain a map of the mines.

But no one knew the whereabouts of the witch Jack was after. Or even who she was.

Jasper explained that I would know which guards were allies as they would discretely make a symbol of a cross with their pinkies when they came across me. This way, they would identify themselves to me. Their plan to include the maids of the palace was a good idea. This way, when the time came, they could help us get in and out of the castle undetected. And Tala was going to target families who had been victims of Vargr and who had family members enslaved to work the mines.

As they told me this, I couldn't help but think how bad off this kingdom was under his rule. He didn't just kidnap and enslave hybrids and shifters, but he enslaved his own people. The word tyrant was too soft, no, he was a dictator with an authoritarian attitude that fed his overdeveloped ego.

The alpha wolf was a piece of shit. In my kingdom, he would have been tried for his crimes long ago and executed for crimes against humanity, a law we upheld to the last letter, not just to protect humans but to protect shifters against leaders like Vargr.

"How do I, or one of you, get in contact with either Queen Lamia or the Royal Moon Pack?" I asked when they finished telling me about the plan they already set in motion. It was a waiting game, but if I could get a hold of Lamia or one of the other three knights, I knew they would be here as fast as possible, and this nightmare would be over.

They would bring an army with them and Vargr would be eliminated. His army was large, but it didn't stand a chance against my Elite warriors. Or Lamia's for that matter. I had full confidence in our armies. If I could get this dang chip out of the back of my neck, that would be even better; then I could use my power and command his army to stand down by letting my wolf out.

"Do either of you have one of these inhibitor chips?" I asked while I was thinking about it, interrupting their discussion on how best to contact my friends.

"You're what?" Jasper asked, seeming confused by my question.

Tala, on the other hand, had a look of hopelessness while she wrung her hands tightly. "No, we don't. He is our alpha so there is no need to chip us." She sighed, "The only way I know of to deactivate those chips is if my father dies and his link to the chips dies along with him. However, that does not guarantee that if he dies you won't. Or, you take a huge electrical shock to your system and it shorts the chip out. That is also assuming that you and your wolf could survive the amount of electrical current you would need to fry it."

Jasper gave a low whistle. "Fuck that's brutal!" He exclaimed. "And you have one of those in you?" He asked me, pointing to my neck.

I nodded. Yep, I sure did. And I didn't like my choices of how I could deactivate it.

"How do you know about this Tala?" Jasper asked her.

She squirmed on my lap, turning to face Jasper, and the friction of her ass rubbing against my cock through the thin material instantly caused a reaction.

"Shayna explained to me once, said I might need to know how they work one day. We weren't best friends, and most of the time we didn't like each other, but she did try to protect me in some ways." She explained.

"As far as contacting your friends, let me see what we can do. Very few people here have phones, they mostly rely on landlines or mind-linking. It is another way for Vargr to control us. He doesn't want the rest of the continent knowing what he gets up to and is paranoid about spies and his mines." Jasper talked through his thoughts, his eyes still on my neck after learning what had been attached to me.

He seemed like a loyal person to Tala, and I assumed they had grown up together. I was thankful to learn he had already found his mate, otherwise I would have surely been jealous of this beta wolf, and that would have put another kink in the plan.

"What about Oliver?" I asked, gritting my teeth. The very idea that he had tried to blackmail Tala grated every single one of my nerves. The only thing I wanted from Oliver was his blood on my hands as I tore his heart from his chest. "He cannot be trusted; he will turn on you at the first opportunity. Do not underestimate him."

"Jack has my father's trust at the moment." Tala's eyes went to Jasper, they shared a harrowing look. "If Jack has my father's trust, I am hoping Oliver does as well. I think I have a way to make him help us without compromising our plans."

"Care to share that plan?" Jasper skeptically asked, and Tala shook her head at him.

"No, not yet. You both just have to trust me for now." Jasper rolled his eyes at her and opened his mouth in protest. "I am not an idiot Jasper. I am fully aware of what Oliver is, and don't trust him as far as I can throw him." She reprimanded him. "Right now, though, he could very well be a key to helping us."

I loved that my little flame was as fiery as the nickname I had given her, yet I didn't like the idea of her working with

Oliver. They didn't know him; they didn't know what he was capable of. What a sick and twisted mind he had. The things he had done to Lamia, Travis, and countless other shifters that had been under Silas and his control.

We talked for a few more minutes when Jasper suddenly stood up. "I know what it is like to want to steal minutes with your mate," he said looking at Tala sadly, "so I will give you some privacy, but we will have to leave soon." He bowed his head to me and stepped out of the little building.

No sooner had he closed the door than Tala pounced on my lips and began ravishing them. I, of course, met her lips with just as much enthusiasm.

"I missed you," I rasped between our heated kisses.

"I couldn't wait to see you again," she said, planting small kisses over my jaw and gripping my hair. "The ache to feel you touch me again is so strong, Kellen." She cooed.

I gave her a growling groan as I lifted her and made her straddle my lap. She sat back and removed her cloak, revealing a sheer white dress. It was so thin that I could see she was wearing nothing underneath. She had no idea how much I wanted to bury myself inside her, just how much I, too, had missed feeling her delicate body under my hands. How much my wolf whined to meet hers and complete the bond.

Fuck, I took a deep breath as she moved herself to straddle me better, and I knew she could feel my cock straining against my own thin cotton shorts. My hands moved up her pale thighs, under the sundress she was wearing, and cupped her ass. "What are you doing to me, coming here dressed like this?" I asked, looking into her eyes. It would take nothing for me to sink into her depths right now.

"I didn't think. I just want you, Kellen. I don't care where,

I don't care how. My body and wolf call out for you day and night. I never realized the mate bond could be this intense. So strong. The pull is unbearable." She groaned and rubbed her bare pussy over my covered cock.

Fuck, I didn't know how I was going to resist her; she certainly wasn't making it easier on me. Her lips crashed against mine, heated and frenzied, our tongues at war as we tasted and licked the crevices of each other's mouths. It was like she wanted me to take her. I needed to resist for both of our sakes, especially hers.

"Kellen, please," she begged between kisses. How could I deny her sweet, sultry pleas? I held her tighter, cupping the nape of her neck with one hand while the other traveled down over her mounds. I stopped to take the time to let my hands explore her body before reaching between her legs, the heat of her arousal drawing me in.

Finding her warm center, I let my fingers explore as she gasped and quickened her breath in anticipation of what my finger would do.

"Touch me Kellen. I'm so ready for you."

I groaned again against her lips, my fingers stroking through her folds, instantly coated in her wet heat.

Tala's hips lifted in an effort for my fingers to sink into her. I gave her what she wanted and plunged two of my thick digits inside her, careful not to push them in too far. If anything was going to break her barrier, it was going to be my cock when I buried myself to the hilt inside her.

She let out a moan and the walls of her vagina clenched my fingers. Moons, I wanted to taste her. Instead, I began pumping my fingers, finding that soft spot, crooking them, and letting them rub the tender flesh inside her.

"Fucking beautiful. So pure." I whispered, watching her face contort in pleasure as my fingers fucked her. I bent my head as she arched back, sucking an erected nipple through the thin fabric of her dress. Moons, she was perfect.

The faster my fingers moved, delving in and out of her wetness, the more labored her breathing became. My thumb found her clit and pressed against it, moving it in circles for that added pleasure, and I watched the buildup of her orgasm as she squirmed and panted. It was like waiting for a volcano to erupt. I was so tense with excitement, Conri wanting to mate with her, and her throaty moans of pleasure were outweighing the rational side of me.

I felt my gums tingle, the beginning of my canines extending, but that was as far as it went. The chip stopped the process, and my wolf was fighting against it. I had to push him down and remind him this was not the right time.

Tala threw her head forward, burying her face in my neck. She suddenly erupted, screaming her orgasm out, her tight channel clenching around my digits as her release ran down my hand and her thighs. Fuck she was breathtaking.

I was so lost in the sounds of her that it took me a moment to realize that she had buried her canines deep into my skin. Marking me. Holy shit! I almost came from the sheer pleasure my mate's bite had brought.

My little flame marked me!

I let out a vibrating, deep growl at the shooting spark of pleasure that wracked through my whole body. She rode out her orgasm, rubbing her pussy on my palm as I slowed down my thrusting, needing that extra friction. She kept her teeth buried deep, only letting go when her walls relaxed and unclenched my fingers.

"Holy fuck, that was the hottest thing I have ever seen! Watching you come undone in my arms." I told her as I brushed the strands of hair from her flushed face. Never had I seen anything as sensual and beautiful in my life until I watched my little flame peak and explode around my fingers.

My cock was rock hard, wanting in on the action and ready to explode. I knew just as soon as I connected with her, I would not be able to resist marking her. She had marked me and left her scent buried deep within my blood. I couldn't say I didn't want it, but now we had a matter of weeks before she went into heat.

Our timeline had just been moved up.

I said nothing about it to Tala. She was spent at this moment, and the glassy-eyed look she was giving me told me she had been satisfied.

"I didn't mean to mark you," she quietly spoke, "I'm so sorry."

"Shhh, it's okay. I proudly wear your mark, my queen." I already adored this woman, she held my heart and she could do no wrong in my eyes. I didn't want her to worry over marking me; it just meant she had a strong wolf. I pulled her into me more and let her bury her head in my chest.

"Not quite the right timing," I chuckled, pecking her cheek. "I was hoping for a more romantic place before my mate marked me."

She slapped the side of my arm hard and blushed from my teasing. "You are never going to let this go are you?" Tala said, pouting her lips and glaring at me.

"Nope." I smiled back at her, "Never. Years from now, when our pups ask about how we met, I will be sure to include telling them that their mother found me so irresistible she marked me while we were in the middle of planning a takeover."

I laughed when her eyes widened. "You wouldn't dare! And besides, who said I want pups?" She almost had me until she could no longer keep a straight face. I pecked her lips and went to deepen the kiss when we were interrupted.

There was an upside to her marking me so soon, I had now become her alpha, and Tala's wolf would not have to obey Vargr's commands anymore. She would be able to shift, and her wolf could protect her better.

"Tala, you have to go. Now! Your block is down." Jasper's voice carried through the closed door.

Tala's eyes glazed over for a minute. "I have to go, my mother is having an episode. She killed a guard the other day and she isn't calming down," she said once she had finished whoever she mind-linked with.

"Soon, Kellen, I will get word to you when we can meet again. Until then, watch for the allies, they will be able to pass messages and keep you informed." She kissed me once more, this time lingering a little longer before she slipped her black cape on and then slipped out the door, but not without giving me a look of longing. I could see she hated to leave me just as much as I hated her to leave.

"Let's go, Casanova," the guard chuckled at me.

There was no way he didn't hear Tala orgasm, despite having her teeth buried in my neck.

There was a little extra pep in my step as he led me back to the gladiator barracks. At the same time, my head was full of worry about what was about to come. I reached up and touched where her mark had been placed, wondering if it would form like Lamia's, a symbol, or if I would have an omega mark that was just the bite itself.

Chapter 27 – A Vile Wolf & A Red Wolf

<u>TALA</u>

I couldn't believe I marked him, I didn't regret it, but I was definitely mad at my wolf. Mora had seen her opportunity to push through and take over, and she took it. Lost in bliss when my orgasm started to rip through me, she took advantage of my vulnerable state, coming to the forefront and marking her mate.

I didn't even know Kellen, only what Oliver had told me. Yet I had all these feelings for him, feelings that I didn't understand, or at least understand where they were coming from.

'The mate bond,' Mora's voice filled my head for the first time in a long time. After marking Kellen, I felt her presence more than ever.

'How can I feel so strongly about someone I don't know? I don't even know his age, if he has siblings, what his favorite food is, or color," I began ranting to her.

'All in due time, we can get to know these things. Our mate was made for us. We will love everything about him.' My wolf spoke, her words having a calming effect on me. Telling me there was time.

"Jasper," I called out to him just as we had reached the

back of the palace. I was still feeling guilty about what I had done, knowing this could be a huge hindrance. "I marked Kellen," I admitted to him, feeling my cheeks heat with embarrassment.

"You did what?" He whisper-yelled at me. "Please tell me you didn't?" He gave me a pleading look and brushed his hand through his hair with frustration.

"I wish I could, but I did." His attitude made me feel uncomfortable.

"For fucks sake, Tala, not only did you mark a slave, but now you are going to go into heat!" He was pacing back and forth, and I began wringing my hands together.

"I didn't mean to! My wolf... I understand how you and El feel. I didn't know the pull of the bond could be this... potent." I tried to defend myself.

"Fuck, Tala." Jasper groaned. "You could go into heat at any time between now and the full moon. Every unmated male will smell you, and your mate is not free to protect you." He stopped pacing and turned to face me, giving me a look of pity. "Tala, it's okay, we will work with it. We just have to move faster, and if we can't, then we will have to hide you. I'm not even sure if your masking spray will cover the scent of a she-wolf in heat." He explained, seeming a little calmer but still agitated.

I had really messed shit up. And it was only dawning on me now how badly things could go. If I went into heat without my mate... It was open season on me if I couldn't find a secure location to hide myself and my scent.

"It's okay, Tala, we will figure it out." Jasper tried to reassure me, embracing me in a comforting hug. "It's late. Get inside before someone sees you." He hooked his finger under my chin, forcing me to look up at him. "Everything will work out, don't fret. You are stronger than this. Now go." He said and released me.

We went our separate ways and I snuck in through kitchens. I was just about to open the door to head up the back stairs when a voice in the dark startled me.

"A little late for a stroll don't you think, princess?" I whirled around to where the voice came from, and Oliver stepped out from the shadows.

"Are you spying on me now, Oliver?" I accused him, and he just chuckled.

"Do you have what I want?" He asked, crossing the room with his arms crossed. His light brown hazel eyes held a slight orange glow to them. His predatory gaze made me feel uncomfortable.

"I have a map of the mines," I stated.
"And the other thing?" He cocked his head, waiting for an answer.

"I don't have information on that. Not yet. But you won't be getting the map until I get what I need from you. Do I have to remind you that it isn't the end of the week yet?" I bravely spoke, holding myself as tall as I could.

Oliver took steps towards me and I stood proud, refusing to back down or away. Looming over me and invading my personal space, he scented my neck in an intimate way, making me shiver with disgust at how close he was.

"I won't hurt you," he whispered next to my ear, "I promise."

I didn't dare move, but when I felt his tongue gently lick my neck, my hand came up ready to lay a hard slap on his face. Oliver caught my hand and chuckled. "Now, now princess, I just wanted to know how close you and the prince had gotten. Not as close as I was thinking but still, too close."

He let go of my hand and took a step back. "Princess, I want out of here and fast. Are you aware there is a power struggle going on in this continent? Your father has declared war on several other packs. Each kingdom has internal wars. All I wanted to do was get away from the fighting, yet Jack seems to have dragged me into another war that I want no part of."

"So, you will abandon your friend?" I asked, a little confused.

"Yes. I told you I want out. I have lived as a rogue far too long, and I am done with taking orders. The diamonds from the mine will set me up nicely as I have told you. That's all I want, to be able to disappear and live out the rest of my life in luxury. No wars, no rogue kings, no Orions, and no King of the Wolves." He said, backing up a little more.

"Did you know I was the one who gave the order for Kellen's parents to be killed?" I looked at him in shock. No wonder Kellen loathed him, his hate was deeper than just Jack and Oliver selling him into slavery. "I bet he didn't tell you I was also the one to orchestrate the kidnapping of his little queen? Held her for weeks, months, watched Jack and his friends violate her over and over again."

"You are a vile wolf, Oliver!" I spat at him.

He clicked his tongue at me, "Tsk, tsk, little princess. Now, do you see why I need to disappear? If Kellen gets free, he will kill me. If I stay by Jack's side, he will drag me through another war and it is not always third times the charm, especially for a wolf like me."

"Why are you telling me this, Oliver?" I narrowed my eyes at him, watching his face closely, trying to determine his angle.

He scrunched his face up before he relaxed his posture and his eyes softened. "For many years I have lived with hate. It was all I was taught. I was taught to hate the royal family; I was groomed to exact my revenge. I helped Silas, a rogue king, my father, capture the Dire Wolf. Not only did it hurt your prince immensely, but it gave me great satisfaction that I could hurt him the same way I had been hurt my whole life. Growing up without my mother, I felt like I had been cheated.

"After Riocht and seeing that there were worse things than my father, like Orion, I couldn't say I wanted that life anymore. However, Jack was a means to escape the current situation. Then Jack, who I swear was born with a four-leaf clover up his ass, runs into King Kellen in a bathroom of all places, and decides your father will give him a pretty penny for him. Trafficking him was not part of my plan. At one point, yes, I wanted to kill him. Now I just want out."

Oliver paused and hung his head. "I didn't want this, not this time. I wanted to start again, and you will help me, Tala. I am not a good man, but I promise if you help me, I will not hurt you and I will keep Jack away from you." He lifted his head and peered straight into my eyes, baring his emotions to me. I saw the look of failure cross his face; and his eyes, although icy, held a saddened and regretful look.

I couldn't detect a lie, but I still wouldn't trust him. As I held Oliver's gaze, I realized that if I eliminated his personality, Oliver was a handsome wolf; tall, built, with eyes that were intimidating yet alluring. His blond hair was kept neat and moderately short. I wondered just what had happened to him. Was he born into the slave-trading business as Jack was?

In another lifetime, he could have been a good person, someone I could have been friends with. Alas, he was not a good person, he was a monster, and I was sure this was all some kind of façade. No matter how much he would try to appeal to my better nature, I would not fall for his lies.

"We are running out of time, princess. War will be upon this kingdom soon and by the smell of it, you will be going into heat even sooner." I gasped in shock, my eyes bugging out.

"H-how, how did you know?" Shit, if he knew, that meant my father would easily figure it out.

"I smell him all over you. You have no mark on your shoulder, yet you smell like a marked female. I am assuming you marked him?" He had a smug smirk on his face. He wasn't really asking me because he already knew, he just wanted to hear me say it out loud and confirm it. Oliver was smart, sly, and a slime-ball bastard, that was for sure.

"Well, at least your wolf doesn't have to take commands from your father anymore. She has a new alpha, whether he is enslaved or not." He shrugged his shoulder nonchalantly.

"What? Vargr can't control me anymore?" I was shocked. This was not something I had thought about and only realized when Oliver told me plain as day. I suddenly felt like leaping, which meant I could shift whenever I wanted. I held my smile to myself, but the comprehension of his words and realization had both me and my wolf silently shouting with glee.

"I see that look on your face, princess, but I wouldn't rush into anything. You need to play the game first, like a fox, cunning and sly."

"You mean like you?" I tilted my head towards him.

"Exactly," Oliver smiled. "Goodnight princess, let's speak soon. I quite look forward to our little chats." He winked at me before leaving the kitchen area, leaving me to ponder everything that had happened tonight. As soon as I thought of Kellen, the achy neediness set in between my thighs with lustful wanting.

I ran upstairs to my mother's room; her maid and Eloise were already there, along with Jasper's mother, Alice. The three of them were trying to calm her down as she held a large men's shaving blade in her hand. Blood trickled to the floor from her wrist, soaking her long white nightgown in deep crimson that almost looked black where the blood had gathered on the material.

I stopped, taking in the scene, trying to determine if my mother was having an episode of crazy or had remembered what my father and Jack had done to her. Her sky-colored eyes met mine and we held our eyes locked. I watched as the tears gathered and began to fall down her pale cheeks.

"Leave us," I ordered, hearing a collective grumble. "It's okay," I looked at Alice and my mother's maid, "I can take it from here."

I had already assessed the damage, and it didn't seem like she had really harmed herself too much; the cut was too far up her arm and too far around. She had done this for attention, I concluded. Alice and the maid looked at me like I was nuts.

"It has taken us over an hour to calm her this much! Where were you, Tala?" Alice hissed at me. I turned and scowled at her, giving her a death glare for taking that tone with me.

Instead of replying to her, I gritted my teeth and tightened my jaw. "I said you can leave." I didn't shout, but the fury was evident in my voice. Alice clicked her tongue and left the room, stomping as she went. The maid gave me a sympathetic smile and I nodded to her that I would be fine.

Eloise stayed behind and approached my mother. "Luna Mila, it's okay, they are gone now," she gently spoke, which had me questioning why she would say that. I raised my brow tilting my head until El turned and saw the look on my face. "Let's get your mum cleaned up, then maybe the Luna can tell us all about what happened."

I arrived just before you did. She was screaming at Lady Alice to get out and that it was her fault. Her maid told me they had been arguing earlier, and Lady Alice had followed her in and said some pretty nasty and weird stuff to your mum. I heard El's voice fill my head, not wanting to talk out loud.

Eloise not only looked, but also sounded frazzled. No doubt my mother's actions scared her, especially after her last episode where she managed to kill a guard. We got my mum into the bath after taping her wound and gently washing her down, then drying her off and changing her clothes. The whole time my mother remained silent as I spoke soft words to her.

"I need you to hang on for me, mum," I said while seating her in bed, Eloise cleaning up the blood as best as she could. The rug that covered the floor would need to be thrown out. "I will get us out of this. I don't know how yet, but I will. You don't deserve this life." I said, shaking my head in pity not just for her but for all of us: me, Eloise, Jasper, and the members of this pack that were enslaved to my father's commands.

It was that last sentence that had my mother's head snapping up to look at me head-on. A sudden fire burned within her eyes, where they were void of any emotion only moments ago. "That's where you're wrong," she suddenly burst out. This time she was shaking her head at me.

I looked at her, not being able to determine how she could even think that.

"I deserve it all. He hates you because of me." Her words drifted off into a whisper as her head turned towards the window. "Run, Tala, run far away and never look back." Her voice broke. I ran a hand down her blond hair in an effort to soothe her.

"Mum," I called out, not knowing if this was the right time or not, "You said Vargr is not my father?"

"Shhh," she put a finger to her lips and laid her head down against her pillow. "The three sister fates will make everything just fine. My beautiful daughter, you were never a mistake." She reached up as I sat by her, one hand cupped my face as she looked into my eyes tenderly. "None of this is your fault. He is angry with me. Always angry at me, but stay away from him."

"Who is my father?" I asked, ignoring her confusing words. Her lips parted, but she said nothing before closing her mouth again.

I looked at Eloise, who looked as equally confused by my mother's riddles as I was. "Mum," I tried again, but I was cut off.

"You are a red wolf, Tala. Beautiful and rare, I have been commanded to never speak his name. I cannot tell you, but find the wolf that smells of the ocean. You know him, you have his eyes. He will save you." She got that far away look in her eyes again and turned her head from me.

I let out a heavy sigh, knowing that I wouldn't get anything else out of her. She had recessed back into her own mind, her prison of thoughts. She could be like this for days or hours; I could never tell.

"What was that about?" Eloise asked as we left my mother's room and closed the door behind us. I shrugged, not knowing what to say, but her words played over in my mind. My wolf was silent but present, and I knew she was trying to figure it out too.

"I have no idea," I said truthfully, still trying to make sense of what my mother had said. I linked for her maid to go back to her room and watch over her again, not trusting my mother on her own. She was becoming too unstable with each passing day.

Chapter 28 – The First Gift

<u>KELLEN</u>
DAY 13 OF THE GAMES

Today was my day to fight. I had woken just before sunrise, watching the sun's peak rise over the horizon. Its orange glow of the breaking dawn reminded me of the hot flames of a fire, distorting the air around it as the heat rose with a golden orb, creating a mirage.

I walked out into the open common area, where it was still deadly silent. I had noticed the lack of vegetation and animals in my first few days. Not a single bird called out in the morning, and not a single cricket chirped when night fell.

I walked the common area for a couple of hours, not really thinking of anything in particular except for my upcoming gladiator match today. My thoughts drifted to home, they were mostly of Mike and Lamia. I also couldn't help but wonder if Uncle Michael and Uncle Marcus were still running the kingdom or if Mike had taken over. I wondered if they were still searching for me or if they had given up.

I had been here for how long? Two months? I couldn't remember, as the days all rolled into one. I watched the guards change shifts and the new ones who came to stand around the barracks, wondering if any of them were allies.

I didn't have to wait long to get my answer. As I made a lap around the open area again, passing guards, I took note of a few of them giving me the signal that they were indeed in league with Tala and Jasper. Their discrete movements, making a cross with their pinkies as I walked by them, were the sign that they were against Vargr.

The other gladiators woke and joined me in the common area and stood in formation, ready to begin training. We worked hard until we heard the clanking of metal, and one of the gates opened.

"Breakfast!" The guard shouted and tilted his head to me to come forward. I obliged, and he handed me a separate plate that was piled up with not the usual oatmeal and fruit. I took the plate, and he made the symbol with his fingers. I gave him a curt nod back of acknowledgment.

Soon the arena began to fill up with onlookers and the usual traders who were allowed to come in and sell various goods. I saw a familiar face in the crowd making his way up to the barred wall.

"Hey, Auggie." I smiled when the little boy stuck his face against the bars, his mother close behind him, looking everywhere but at me.

"Hi!" He smiled brightly. "Your name is on the posters for today's fight! That's why mum let me come today."

"It is, is it?" I asked, smiling back at his excited grin. "And what name have they given me?"

"They call you prince-ee, but that's not what we call you." The young boy's smile did not fade from his face. "The crowd is starting to call you the Wolf King." He said with admiration.

His name for me startled me a little. "Wolf King, huh?" I pondered out loud, wondering how that name had gotten started.

"Yeah, when me and my friends play, I am always the Gladiator Wolf King." The kid was beaming, and I had to admit, it felt good to have a fan.

"Auggie." His mother called and looked up, directing my attention to her. I noticed a large purple bruise around her neck, not hidden enough from the collar of her dress. I grimaced, not liking to see females hurt. I could never understand how a mate could hurt his female, unless that bruise came from another.

"I hope you win today, Wolf King. I will cheer for you!" Auggie said as he turned back to his mother, taking her hand. They both gave me a glance over their shoulders as they hurried away.

"So do I kid, so do I," I mumbled, watching their retreating figures. My hands were still wrapped around a bar each, and I looked down at the dry sandy dirt. The kid loved the gladiator fights, but I wondered if he knew we had been kidnapped and sold. That being behind these bars and fighting in the games was not our decision.

I suddenly felt a sting on my knuckles as something rapped against them, something hard. "Ow!" I grunted, scowling as I looked up at who hit my hands. An old woman stood infront of me in a brown tunic-like cloak, her white hair scraggly and sticking out from under the hood, and holding a cane in her hand. "What the fuck?" I scolded the old woman.

She narrowed her eyes at me, sneering with a look of disgust. "Humph," she shrugged, "some gladiator you are if a little stick hurts you." I could tell by her tone she was trying to get a rise out of me. She almost did, but I bit my tongue, figuring it wasn't worth arguing with an old woman who just wanted to poke fun at me.

"Wolf King," she whispered, leaning in closer to the bars. "Ashe sends her regards."

I was momentarily taken aback by her words, not even sure if I heard her right. I looked at her, puzzled, this time really looking at her. "How do you know that name?" I asked.

Ashe was the oracle that had visited Lamia in her dreams. The firstborn werewolf, and first and only daughter to Lycaon. When Lamia and Mathias had traveled to Avalon, Mathias had known Ashe as Odeia. How did this strange woman know Ashe? And how did Ashe know where I was?

Did that mean Lamia and Mathias also knew where I was?

"That's for me to know, young king. But she has sent us here with a gift. Not sure why she wants you to have it." She lifted her eyes to mine, peering up at me. Her wrinkled face was in contrast with her eyes that looked too young.

I sniffed, trying to scent what she was, but I only smelled the slight hint of a sickly sweet honey smell. So light it could be easily missed. "Who and what are you?" I asked, suspiciously letting my eyes roam over her, still trying to figure the woman out. I wasn't even sure if she was actually old now, despite her appearance.

"You don't look like a king," she carried on. "Now, Mathias, that's a king." She cooed with a lustful look in her eyes, and I shuddered, sarcastically thinking how Mathias would just love to be fawned over by this wrinkly female.

She looked around at the receding crowd. The fight would be announced shortly and the patrons were making their way to the arena. "I hope you enjoy the show," I told her before I went to turn away from her.

Just as my back was turned and before I could take my first step, she called out to me. "King Kellen," she hissed in a low voice. "You will receive three gifts; the first I bestow upon you is strength." The old woman rushed out her words and produced a sword from under her dirt brown cloak. She shoved it through the bars, her eyes darting around looking to see if anyone had seen.

The sword landed by my feet. I peered down at it, just staring, debating whether or not I should pick it up. I looked up at her when she spoke. "My name is Nandie. I wish you luck, Your Highness." She gave a curt bow of her head and swiftly walked away, pulling the hood over her head to shield her face.

I noticed she didn't use her cane, and she walked with speed. There was no way she was as old as her wrinkly face led me to believe. Her hands were smooth and soft looking, free of age spots.

*****

I walked into the arena, flourishing my sword, getting used to the weight and loosening up. Ajani had been picked along with me for today's fight. We had no idea what to expect.

I wasn't scared, per se, but I was apprehensive. I kept my guard up and my wits about me. Focusing my mind on the battle I was about to enter. Any day could be my last day, and I hoped today was not it.

I looked at the sword I held; it was sharp, strong, and shiny. Much better quality than what was available in the gladiator barracks. The inscription on the bade glistened under the sun; I had no idea what it said, but the style of the scripture reminded me of Lamia's own swords. The ones she used to channel her power, making them glow an ethereal green or golden color. The ones that I had watched her use to slice through hordes of enemies.

I briefly wondered about her and what she was going through, if she was having just as hard of a time as I did when she went missing. She would be five months pregnant now, and I was determined to get back before those pups were born.

The crowd's cheering and booing made me come to my senses and leave every thought or worry back in the barracks as I stepped forward and looked up at the mass of spectators. Resolving to get in the right frame of mind, I didn't want to make a mistake and die today. My eyes instantly pulled to the far end of the arena, where I knew my little flame would be standing under the shade of the tent.

Ajani stood tall and proud next to me as we listened to the announcer introduce us. Guards flanked us on either side as we walked toward the center of the arena. Our opponents had already been announced and were taken off to the side. When we reached the middle, the noise of the crowd was almost deafening. The stadium was more full than I had ever seen it.

"Somebody is making a name for himself." Ajani chuckled nervously. He still hadn't fully recovered from his last fight. The wound had closed, but his wolf was healing him slowly, making me think the weapon that stabbed him was probably laced with wolfsbane. That would explain why he hadn't healed any faster and why we found no evidence of silver in the wound when we patched him up. As a beta werewolf, he should have healed in a matter of two days.

Ajani also looked around at the masses, and I took note of his shaky breath when he inhaled deeply. He was nervous. He had a right be. "Live or die we fight," I said with a matter-of-fact tone.

"Live or die we fight." He repeated, nodding his agreement as he resolved himself. Shaking off his nerves.

We were meant to turn and bow to the three sides of crowd, then our fourth bow was for Alpha Vargr. The traditional gladiator slave would bow and put his hand over his heart in a pledge to the Alpha that they were fighting for. It would be disrespectful if you didn't, a direct insult to the Alpha and the host.

However, I was not going to do that. Fuck no I would not bow to him! Today I would make a stance. I glanced over at Ajani. "You ready, brother?" I asked, and I meant it. He had become a brother to me, we had fought together, and we had each other's back. More than that, I respected his strength and values. I would be proud to run alongside this man in battle. And that is exactly what we were doing.

"I am with you. Although, we could be dead before we even get to fight." He cringed.

Yep, we could very well die without fighting. I thought.

The announcer finished his introductions and speech, indicating it was now our time to bow before the crowd and the Alpha. I sucked in a huge amount of air and puffed my chest out as I turned to the crowd, raising my arms wide. Ajani copied my movement. Moving from left to right, but always keeping my back to Vargr's tent.

The crowd simmered down, and we turned to face Vargr. He stood from his wooden throne, also outstretching his hands, and the crowd began to cheer. This was when we were meant to bow down with our fists over our hearts. Instead, Ajani and I gave each other a quick nod. Simultaneously, we turned our back on him and instead took a knee and bowed before the crowd.

The stadium went deathly quiet. The people were shocked that we would blatantly defy the Alpha, the King of Bhakhil.

"Live or die we fight." I heard Ajani mumble to himself.

Suddenly, 'live or die we fight' was yelled out from somewhere in the stadium. I could hear gasps and chattering, then I smirked as I heard the first call of our chant. I threw my head over my shoulder and trained my eyes on Vargr as the gladiator slaves began chanting. "ARGHOOH, ARGHOOH, ARGHOOH." The sound of them knocking their metal cups against the bars of the barracks could be heard loudly and clearly like a warrior's melody.

The boys were making noise.

Even from this distance, I could see Vargr's face contort with anger, twisting and growing redder by the second. The man was not just fuming, he was flustered. I kept my eyes trained on him and my smirk sly, almost laughing in his face.

The gladiators continued their chant and when we stood up, they abruptly stopped. The silence continued for a moment, and then to our surprise, the crowd went wild! They weren't just cheering, they were repeating our chant.

"ARGHOOH, ARGHOOH, ARGHOOH."

This was very unexpected. I shared a look of 'wow' with Ajani, and we turned to face Vargr's tent. I couldn't wipe the smirk off, not even if I wanted to.

I let my eyes roam to where Tala stood, like a beautiful summer day. Her beauty made my heart beat a little stronger and a little faster. My wolf whined for his mate; he scented the air, gulping in her delicious fruity flavor that was stronger now she had marked me. I couldn't let my eyes linger on her too long, not wanting people to figure it out just yet. That did not mean I didn't want to shout it from the rooftop, but for us to get out of this place unscathed, we would have to be smart.

Tala's eyes were looking at my neck and I wondered if she could see her mark from there, how visible it was. I also wondered if, or I guess when, Vargr would notice.

Vargr lifted his hand to the announcer, clearly irritable with not only the crowd's reaction but also, he was still seething from our public display of 'fuck you'. I couldn't be more pleased with the result so far. I did have to hand it to Vargr, though. He had not lost his shit like I had assumed he would. He was in it for the long game.

A horn blew, the crass sound filling the stadium, and the guards that were flanking us began to retreat, revealing our opponents. Six men; two were on horses, each holding a flail with spiked ends. The other four men were large and built, some donning large visible scars.

They were all wolves except the two largest men, that stood a foot taller than the others, and they were holding large battle axes. They were bear shifters. Bear shifters were naturally strong, not as quick as us wolves, but they had brute strength and when you got hit by one, you definitely felt it.

This was an unfair fight, two against six. But could we expect any less from a coward like Vargr.

The horn blew again to signal the beginning of the fight.

Chapter 29 – The Roar of a King

KELLEN

The opposing contenders began yelling something in a foreign language at each other. However, I didn't need to understand their words. Their dark and malevolent eyes said it all, and the vicious and barbarous smirks they each wore told me they were going to go for the kill.

"This is it," I heard Ajani say, and I turned my head to look at him.

Without the need for words, we turned our backs on each other taking a fighting stance, weapons in hand at the ready. Standing back to back, we had a better chance of fending off the opponents. They would not be able to come at us all at once, otherwise they would end up striking each other.

I watched them as they circled us, waiting for them to make their move, the two on horses cantering in a wider circle. We didn't have to wait long as the other four advanced, twirling or swinging their weapons.

The first clank of metal on metal came from behind me when Ajani blocked an attack. I had no time to look as two of the barbarians leaped towards me, one swinging an ax, the other a sword. I ducked and rolled out of the way of the heavy descending ax, only to meet the swing of a blade and manage to block it.

I was quick to my feet and managed to kick the legs from

under one, only to meet the bear shifter's heavy ax again as it came swinging towards my head. I swiveled to the side, avoiding the bite of the cold metal yet again. This time I was able to turn and stick my sword deep into the side of the wolf attacking Ajani. I pulled it out quickly and turned back to my own two challengers.

The sound of hooves beating on the dry dirt signaled that the animals moved swiftly towards us. The shifters riding them were swinging their flails, the spiked black ball on the ends were circling in the air faster and faster as they approached. Our challengers backed off as the two on horses advanced.

"Jump them!" I yelled quick instructions to Ajani, and right as they swung, both of their attempted blows missed us as we launched ourselves onto the back of the horses as they passed. I brought my sword to the rider's neck and sliced it quickly. The rider fell to the ground, clutching his open wound.

I hopped off the horse looking for Ajani and spotted him also dismounting the horse after killing the rider. We were on opposite sides of the arena; we began to move toward each other as the four remaining opponents closed in on us. The one I had stabbed moved slower than the others.

I picked up the flail the rider had dropped and rushed forward, meeting the sword of a wolf. I was quicker and trained better. I blocked his attacks and, when the opportunity presented itself, I let the sword pierce through his leather attire, twisting my blade until he fell to the ground. I pulled my sword from his body and met one of the bear shifters. The heavy ax slowed down his movements, yet I didn't see the kick that came from behind me. I landed in the dirt face down. Rolling onto my back, I cringed when the glint of a sword came hurtling towards my face.

I thought I was a goner until I saw Ajani, whose blade had intercepted the bear's, stop the life-ending blow from connecting with my head.

"Thanks," I said and quickly went to get to my feet when Ajani's body stiffened over me. His deep brown eyes were wide with shock. He coughed once, and the blood trickled from his mouth. "Ajani..." I went to call his name.

It was quick, with only the slightest sound of a whoosh as the blade cut through the air. A sickening sound of flesh separating pierced my ears, and Ajani's head fell from his neck, his body following and slumping to the ground as dead weight. The smell of his blood quickly reached my nose, the crimson liquid gushing from the stump on his shoulders as his head rolled between my legs.

Conri began to stir, pushing forward.

For a split second, shock overtook my senses as I started at my friend's head in utter denial until Conri surged forward again, breaking me of my stupor.

There were still three of these barbarians ready to take another life. Two bear shifters and the lone wolf. I had no time to mourn my friend, no time to wallow in his death or even spare a second to think about him.

I regained my composure and quickly got to my feet. The three of them weresurrounding me, each wearing a sinister smile. The bear shifters tapped the large axes in their palm and the wolf twirled his blade. I took a deep breath and felt the burning rage gather throughout my muscles, glancing briefly at Ajani's dismembered head that lay only feet away from me.

I felt Conri's presence and knew he wanted to shift but couldn't, his own temper flaring at the loss of our comrade. I felt my eyes come to life, their blue color glowing and narrowing. A primal growl left my throat and my wolf's instincts began to take over, hungry for vengeance and for the taste of blood. Ajani was not pack, but he was a brother and a friend. Someone who had been with me from the beginning, and I felt his loss deeply.

That loss is what drove me. *'Kill, kill,'* my wolf's voice sounded repeatedly.

"ARGHOOH, ARGHOOH, ARGHOOH LIVE OR DIE WE FIGHT!" The chant began. "ARGHOOH, ARGHOOH, ARGHOOH LIVE OR DIE WE FIGHT!" Their cups hit the bars in a steady tempo with the words. "ARGHOOH, ARGHOOH, ARGHOOH LIVE OR DIE WE FIGHT!" The beat of my heart slowed to match the rhythm as the crowd began to chant after them.

Like a war cry, I screamed out my frustration and made quick work of my steps. The attackers swung their weapons and I ducked, weaved, dodged, and blocked. Sliding under their attacks, my sword met with a bear shifter's legs cutting them off, the steel of my blade easily and effortlessly slicing through the bone and dismembering him. I turned to the wolf shifter, who looked scared now that there were only two left.

I advanced and swung, my sword chopping at him. He blocked each thrust, but the power behind my hits was too much and he stumbled backward, falling on his ass. I stomped forward, my foot meeting his face, and drove my sword deep into his chest. Blood squirted, large splashes hitting my naked chest and face. I twisted the blade and pulled it from his chest aggressively, a heavy spray of the red liquid coating my arms.

I turned just in time as the swoosh of the ax came down above me. I caught it just under the head. The bear shifter exerted his strength as he leaned over me, trying to push me down.

Not today, I thought. This was not my first fight with a bear shifter and today would not be the last. I twisted my body, one hand holding the top of the ax handle, the other gripping my sword. I pushed up, drawing strength from my wolf until I was standing level with the bear. His eyes were wide, not believing I could overpower him, in such shock that he didn't see my attack as I thrust my blade into his side.

The look that came across his face made me smile in a sadistic way, the pure look of not understanding what had just happened. I pulled the blade from him just to thrust and dig it back in. Not once, not twice, but three times until his ax fell from his grasp and into my hand.

I drove my sword back down one more time, delivering the final blow.

Around the arena, I heard the muffled mumbles and whispers as they looked in shock at my blood-drenched body. I was soaked in the rich red of their essence.

The warrior cry from the gladiators came to an abrupt stop. The crowd gawked at the pure display of power they had witnessed.

I lifted my arms, the ax in one hand and the sword from the old woman in the other. I tilted my head back and let out a full, deep, prolonged roar like a wild animal. It was full of pain and anger and silenced those mumbles. It echoed, and the tremor of its power was felt by everyone.

Finally, I turned towards the head of the arena and walked slowly towards the main tent where Vargr and my mate stood. I stood below them, glaring at the shit alpha who called himself a king. I flung the ax to the floor, turned my back, and began walking back to the gladiator barracks. Guards flanked me, but they kept their distance.

*****

TALA

Oliver stiffened beside me, his hand gripping my elbow bruisingly tight. Jasper had a look of awe plastered on his face as the fight began and astonishment as it ended. Everyone under the tent could not only see my father's fury, but felt it too.

His outrage trembled from him, his fisted hands shook, and I heard him mumble, "That fucking gladiator will wish he was never born."

Jack chuckled next to him, "But what a show Vargr, what a show. I am curious what else you can throw at him. I wonder how many men he could handle on his own, ten, maybe twenty?" I glared at Jack, willing him to shut his mouth as he fed my father idea after idea.

I hate the violence of the games, but I couldn't take my eyes off the match, keeping them trained on Kellen the whole time. Even when his friend's head was severed, I couldn't look away. I wasn't afraid of missing anything, I was just afraid for my mate.

Your mate is a freaking badass Jasper linked me. I think this was the beginning of a man-crush.

I let Oliver hold onto me, not because I liked it, but because he kept me steady as I thought my heart would stop several times throughout the fight. I gasped with each attack on Kellen and cried out loud when the ax almost connected with his head. Oliver growled lowly at me, reminding me to keep my emotions in check.

The steady and strong chorus of the gladiator slaves had my heart pounding, and when Kellen overpowered the bear shifter and ended his life, I felt my legs give out and exhaled a breath of relief that he was still standing. The abrupt halt of the methodic warrior chant caused silence throughout the arena. When Kellen lifted his head and roared out, I felt the power resonate from him and engulf the arena like a tidal wave drowning out any other voice - causing a rippled tremor to echo through the masses.

He shook us all to the core with his display of power, leaving everyone in awe. That is, everyone except my father and Jack - who both stood with stoic expressions on their faces.

"You fucking idiot, Jack." My father had hissed at him with a red face full of vexation. That's when Jack began to give him ideas again and ask him how many men he thought Kellen could take on at once.

My mother sat beside my father, and I noticed a small smile appear on her lips as my father cast worried glances toward Beta Baron and angry ones toward Jack. He was not expecting the match to have this outcome.

As Kellen left the stadium, he did not turn to look at me; in fact, he did not spare me a glance throughout the whole fight. I wanted nothing more than to lock eyes with him, but I also knew he was fighting for his life and I was a distraction. That was why he spared looking at me, I told myself.

"Come on princess," Oliver said, pulling me with him out of the tent. Now that the match was over there was no reason for me to stick around, and I got the feeling that Oliver didn't want to stick around any longer either. I sensed his fear, and I knew it was because of my mate.

"Fuck." He cursed when we reached the palace and it was just me and him. "I need to get out of here," he worried, running a hand through his hair, messing up his short blond locks that were neatly styled but now stuck up in all directions.

He turned to me, eyes blazing. "Chip or not he is strong, stronger than I remember." His eyes searched mine. "What do you want from me, Tala?" His question took me by surprise. Oliver's lips were pressed in a thin line, and he stared into my eyes, causing me to flinch slightly with the dangerous look he was giving me.

I opened my mouth and closed it again, several times like a fish out of water. I hadn't decided how he could benefit me in our little deal yet, so I was at a loss for words. Before I could think of an answer or he could press me for one, I was saved by the yelling of my father as he came stomping in through the main door of the palace.

Oliver and I stood there as he passed on the way to his office. Beta Baron and Jack walked either side of him and Jasper followed behind, giving me a quick glance as he passed, looking at me and rolling his eyes as my father ranted on about the 'fucking disrespectful gladiator'.

"You coming?" Jack threw over his shoulder to Oliver.

"Later, princess," he mumbled to me before he, too, traipsed towards my father's office. The sound of the door slamming shut echoed throughout the lower floor of the palace.

"What was that about?" Eloise came up behind me, laying a hand on my shoulder.

"I don't know," I shook my head, "he is mad because Kellen

disrespected him in the arena, then he shook everyone up." My voice was quiet, and my gaze was still lingering on the corridor to my father's office.

"Was that your mate who roared? We could hear it from the kitchen, it stopped us all in our tracks." Eloise exclaimed, flabbergasted.

I finally turned around to look at her, her hand falling from my shoulder. "Yes, it was."

Just then, the palace doors opened and a dozen guards came marching in with Teal. His hands were bound with silver cuffs. He looked like a giant, as tall as Kellen and almost as robust. His bright eyes met mine, and we stared at each other as he passed us by.

My wolf repeated my mother's words: 'You are a red wolf, Tala. Beautiful and rare, I have been commanded to never speak his name. I cannot tell you, but find the wolf that smells of the ocean. You know him, you have his eyes. He will save you'.

"Wait!" I shouted as the guards and Teal passed us. They halted in their tracks at my command, and I stepped between them, standing in front of Teal. I raised my head to look up at him, our eyes locking; his bright blues mirrored my own and his red hair was just a shade darker than mine. I tilted my head and leaned in and scented him. He smelt like salty water, the ocean.

My heart raced, beating thunderously, and Mora began to yelp with excitement in my mind. How had I not noticed it before? I stared at him, my mouth gaping. His eyes softened as he regarded my observation and let the recognition sink in.

Teal was my father.

All these years and I never had a clue. All these years and he was so close, yet so far. All these years I thought Vargr was my father and I had anguished over his loathing for me. All these years all I ever wanted was for my father to accept me. Now I knew why he couldn't. Now I knew why he hated my mother. Now I knew why he kept Teal, and now I understood how Vargr could easily hurt me and have such a high disregard that he would threaten to ruin me.

My eyes glazed over with unshed tears. I gave Teal a look, hoping he could read what I wanted to say but couldn't. "You can go." I reluctantly dismissed the guards and Teal, watching his retreating figure round the corner.

"What was that?" I heard Eloise.

"My father," I whispered, still in a daze.

"What?" Eloise hissed, dumbfounded.

Chapter 30 – Closer

<u>KELLEN</u>
DAY 14 OF THE GLADIATOR GAMES

The atmosphere amongst the gladiators in the barracks was somber, to say the least. Not that any of us were ever really charismatic being enslaved. Ajani's death had hit our hearts, and the reality of our situation was once again shoved in our faces.

We had lost gladiators previously, and we all acknowledged each of their deaths. No death was good and each man we lost to the games sat heavy in our hearts and minds. We had become an unaffiliated pack of sorts.

However, Ajani had been a strong fighter. The gladiators looked up to him and they all knew he was not in top shape when he went out to fight. That was one reason why I was taking his death harder than the others. The other reason kept playing in my head over and over like a film being rewound. He had saved my life in the arena. We both could have been dead if it wasn't for him.

Rogue sat by me. He had been by my side since I walked off the arena floor, patting my shoulder as I passed through the other gladiators who gave me words of encouragement and praise for my display of power. Though their words were encouraging, they were also earnest given that Ajani's body had still lain there for a few hours, even after they had taken the visiting gladiator's bodies away, until guards had been ordered to clean him up.

"What will they do with his body?" I asked a guard who was part of our growing coup.

"He will be taken underground and fed to Vargr's pets," the guard told me. All I could do was nod, knowing already that would be his answer. I asked about the other Gladiators, and he told me they would be sent back to the visiting alpha's packs to be buried. They were going to receive a warrior's burial.

Ajani would be tossed into... wherever and fed to some beasts that nobody could tell me what they were. He would not be received by the Moon Goddess. He deserved better than to be treated like nothing.

Rogue tapped my shoulder and made hand gestures to me, using his fingers to spell out 'TEAL' and then bumping his fists together. "Teal... meeting?" I said, finally getting what he was trying to say after he repeated the motion a few times. He nodded his head.

I hadn't seen Teal since yesterday. He had already been called to the palace by the time I had washed all the blood from me. One of the Gladiators told me he had been escorted by a dozen guards on Vargr's command.

I frowned realizing he still hadn't come back when it was the early hours of the morning. I got up walking from the little area, Rogue following me as we crossed the barracks to where Teal usually slept. He wasn't there either.

"Corey," I yelled to one of the gladiators. He came walking through the barracks, "Did Teal come back?"

"No, he didn't." His face creased with worried lines as he realized Teal was not amongst us.

I was ready to walk to the common area to see if I could

ask a guard when the gate to the arena opened and Teal was dragged in by two guards and unceremoniously dropped into the dirt.

Rogue, Corey, and I hurried over to him. His body was black and blue; his face was swollen so badly that I couldn't see his eyes. I took note of the lacerated burns that sporadically marked his skin. I could hear a faint heartbeat, but he was severely damaged.

Rogue nudged me and made a sniffing motion. I leaned close to Teal and smelled him. A trace of silver came from his wounds, but more prominent was the whiff of wolfsbane that covered every open wound.

"Help me get him up Rogue. Corey, go get a bucket of water and any clean shorts you can find. We need to clean and dress his wounds," I instructed. Corey hurried away while Rogue and I picked Teal up off the floor and carried him to his cot.

"Fuck Teal, what the hell happened to you?" I mumbled to him as we got him situated and began cleaning him up as soon as Corey returned with a bucket of water and some clean-ish rags.

Later on that evening, Rogue and I made ourselves comfortable in Teal's quarters, not wanting to leave him alone in his vulnerable state. I felt Conri, who had been abnormally quiet since yesterday, stir.

'Give Rogue your blood,' he said. This wasn't the first time he had suggested this, but I couldn't figure out why he wanted me to.

'What is the point, Conri?' I replied as he paced in my mind. *'It's not as if we can establish a pack link with him. So why are you being so persistent with this?'*

I felt his agitation and growled at me, causing a

thrumming buzz in my head. *'Just do it,'* he snarled, very unlike him.

"Hey Rogue," I said, looking at him. He lifted his head; his deep dark brown eyes held no emotion as he waited for what I was going to say. At that moment, I was reminded of Hunji and how he rarely showed emotion, how Hunji's eyes always looked so dark, like his wolf was just sitting on the surface. Rogue had that same wild look in his eyes.

"My wolf wants me to give you… my blood." I watched for his reaction. He gave me a confused look, pursing his lips and then raising his palms and asking me why, or the gesture meant 'AND'. "I don't know why, but he is insisting. It's not like the mind-linking would work if I became your alpha." I told him my honest thoughts.

Rogue stood up and left the room, coming back a few seconds later with the sword the old woman, Nandie, had given me. He shoved it towards me and nodded his head.

"You want to do it?" I asked him; again, he nodded his head and narrowed his eyes with a determined look. "Okay." I stood up, still unsure about this, but what did we have to lose? Worst case, nothing happened.

I slit my palm and then slit his. "I, Kellen Moon, Alpha of the New Moon pack, King of the New Moon Kingdom, accept you into my pack. Do you pledge to honor and uphold our laws, to remain loyal to not only your king but also members of the pack and kingdom?"

He nodded yes and we held our palms together, letting the blood mix. Surprisingly, I felt a link form, like a rush of adrenaline pulsing through my veins. It was brief, but a pack bond had been formed.

I immediately tried to connect a mind-link to Rogue, but just as I thought, there was still a block from the inhibitor chip. I sighed, feeling disappointed, when a stronger feeling of disappointment started to creep across me accompanied by the feeling of what I could only describe as admiration.

I looked at Rogue with wide eyes. Those were not my feelings. To be sure, I decided to do something mean and raised my hand, slapping him hard across his face. I felt his anger and confusion, and I began laughing.

'Told you,' Conri said smugly. I brushed my wolf off.

"I'm sorry," I told Rogue, who was holding the side of his face. "I felt your anger. We may not be able to communicate by mind link, but I can feel some of your emotions." I was still slightly chuckling at the outcome. We may not be able to communicate, but if he could channel his thoughts into emotions, I would be able to read him and understand him better.

It actually felt good to have some kind of connection with another wolf. Tala had marked me, and she should be able to feel me, but I could not feel her yet. Not until I marked her.

*****

TALA

During the day I tried to stay out of my father's way, but with the new revelation that Vargr wasn't actually my father and my wolf no longer had to submit to his commands after marking Kellen, I became a little braver. I was as determined as ever, and more so now, to bring my father down.

Jasper was currently running a training session for our warriors, and Eloise and I had been pacing the palace ever since yesterday when Teal was brought into my father's office along with Jasper, Oliver, and Jack. We had been patiently waiting to talk with him, but now it was the next day, and our curiosity and patience were wearing thin.

Something happened yesterday behind those closed doors, and Jasper hadn't had the chance to converse with us yet. I had mind-linked him last night and this morning, but he told me he couldn't talk. He even brushed off Eloise, which was rare as he took every opportunity to be close to her. So, we knew it was serious and a conversation that he needed to have face-to-face.

We were sitting in the library in our favorite nook discussing how many people were joining our coup. Eloise had every single omega that worked in the palace backing any play we came up with. A few of the head maids had even told her that members from outside the palace were rallying to go against Vargr. The main thing they worried about was his army.

"We need an outside voice," I said, thinking about how the omega members of the kingdom could be heard. "Someone who can bring them all together, someone who can... be their voice and organize a meeting amongst them," I said, milling my thoughts over possibilities.

"What about Mildred?" El contemplated.

Mildred was not only one of my mother's personal maids but also the head maid for the palace. She had a lot of pull in the palace as well as outside the compound. Her husband was a warrior, on the verge of retiring.

"Possibly," I replied as I thought more about the idea. "What about her husband? He is a respected warrior, do you think he would be on board?"

"There is a good possibility he might. We know Mildred is with us, we can ask her about her husband." I smiled at my friend's response, happy she was thinking along the same lines as me.

"What can we do about Kellen's chip?" I asked her.

"It would help if I had more information on the device so that I would know more about it, not just what it does." She paused, scrunching her face into her familiar 'thinking' look. We had not had a chance to try and reach out to anyone by means of telephone, plus we really didn't know who we were calling. I would need more information from Kellen before I even attempted that. We could use a radio, but again, who were we contacting? We needed a signal to connect to another party, as Eloise had explained.

"Come on!" I suddenly exclaimed, jumping to my feet as a thought occurred to me while thinking of the chips, which led me to think of my sister Shayna.

Eloise looked taken aback by my sudden movements and over-excited voice. Like the best friend she is, she took the cue and stood up too. "Where are we going?" She asked as we exited the library.

"To the cellar" I smiled at her and waggled my eyebrows.

She gave me a groan and an eye roll; she hated the cellars. "Why? You know that place creeps me out, it's scary." She complained, her body giving a slight quiver as she thought of the cold and unfriendly space below.

"You want answers about the chip? The only place we are going to find them is in Shayna's lab." My father had built her lab in the old wine cellar beneath the palace floors when he became aware of her gift and potential. As far as I knew, everything should still be there.

"We aren't allowed in there, alpha forbid it." She protested while biting her bottom lips out of nervousness.

"Yah well, I don't have to listen to him anymore," I

chuckled. "Besides, he didn't command you personally, did he? Just the staff I thought."

"Well, no, but..."

"Stop trying to get out of it, El, we're going down," I said with finality in my voice.

She gave a loud huff. "Fine, but if there's weird shit and dead bodies in there, I'm out." She was absolutely serious and all I could do was laugh at her childish fear. A fear my sister had put in her head when we were much younger.

Shayna had convinced Eloise that the cellar was full of ghosts and that dead bodies had been buried under there. Ever since, El had been too scared to find out for herself if my sister's words were true or not, despite how many times Jasper and I had told her Shayna was pulling her leg.

The cellar was cold, damp-smelling, and uninviting. There were several corridors down here that led to various rooms nestled under the palace's foundation. Eloise stuck to my side like glue, jumping every now and then at the sound of nothing. Her werewolf senses were not as astute as mine, her being an omega.

Finally reaching the end of one of the corridors, we found the door to my late sister's lab. I found it a little odd that none of the doors were locked like I had assumed they would be. Seeing as my father had forbidden people from entering down here, I would have figured that he would have everything shut up tight. I guess he thought more highly of his commands than I gave him credit for.

Entering, I closed the door behind us and fumbled on the walls to find a light switch, finally finding one and flipping it. The room came to life as ugly, bright fluorescent lights flickered on.

"Mother mercy, Tala! This is something straight out of a horror book!" I chuckled at Eloise's discomfort and looked around.

It was not as bad as she was making out. Sure, there were a few glass cases with questionable things in them, some burners and a small forge in the corner, a few filing cabinets, and locked shelving. Otherwise, the lab housed several metal tables that held various items such as tongs and prongs and other equipment you would generally see in a school science lab. On the far wall was another door and my feet automatically took me there.

"Don't open it" El gasped, grasping my elbow.

"Shut up, you wimp." I laughed at her and pulled the stiff metal door open; lights automatically flickered on this time. This seemed to be a small office with two desks, a bookshelf, and a small make-shift bed. "Let's see what we can find. You take that side." I pointed to the left side of the room, and I moved to start searching the right side.

We began carefully sifting through draws, cupboards, and shelves. I didn't want to disturb too much as I had no idea if Vargr came down here anymore. After an hour of looking in the room, back to the lab, and then back in the room, Eloise and I had found nothing of consequence and were ready to give up.

We sat on the floor by the makeshift cot in silence, both of us wondering if there was an area we had missed. I began to think maybe we should see what was behind some of the other doors when Eloise broke the silence.

"So... you marked your mate. What is he like?" I smiled at how casually she could ask me. My best friend may be ranked under me, but our friendship superseded the expectant way my father thought we should associate with omega wolves.

I felt a little flutter throughout my body, primarily in the heart and my lower stomach when I thought of Kellen, and a coy smile graced my lips. "He's wonderful," I blushed my confession. "I had no idea the pull of a mate bond could be this strong, the way you and Jasper have described it... it doesn't compare." El giggled at my sheepish words. "How have you guys not marked and mated?" I asked, truly curious because when I was close to Kellen, that's all I could think about. My wolf would send me mental images of him and me in throws of passion and I wanted that. So badly.

"I think the pull is stronger for you being an alpha, and your mate is very powerful from what Jasper has told me." After a beat of silence, Eloise spoke up again; her words now holding a sense of sorrow. "Besides, Jasper can't claim me. We both know your father and his would probably kill me."

I swallowed the hard lump in my throat and felt tears brim my eyes for their situation "I'm sorry El," I said quietly, feeling ashamed that this was partly my fault. "This is why it is important to get my mate out of here and overthrow my father. All I want is for things to work out for you two." I threw my arm around her shoulders and brought her against me, hoping my hug was a least a little comforting to her.

"I know, it's just... hard." I understood her position more than I did two weeks ago. This had to work out, it just had to, and we were running out of time. There were only fourteen days of the Gladiator Games left.

"Hey, what's that?" Eloise asked, pointing to the vent on the lower half of the wall under Shayna's desk. She scooted forward closer to the vent, her finger running over the screws that held it in place. "The screws are stripped like it had been open and closed frequently."

I shuffled up next to her, seeing what she meant. "Get the

scissors off the desk," I instructed.

Using the scissors, we managed to remove the vent cover, and of course, I had to put my hand in there. El was too chicken shit, thinking something would grab her or there would be spiders. I felt around and stopped when my hand landed on fabric.

I pulled at the fabric that had some weight behind it, dragging it out of the opening. It was a knapsack, and when we opened it, it contained five leather books and some drawings in a clear plastic folder.

"It's her diary!" Eloise exclaimed upon closer inspection.

"Yeah, and the blueprints for the chips," I whispered, still unbelieving that we had actually found something that could prove to be useful.

Chapter 31 – Lies upon Lies

TALA
DAY 15 OF THE GLADIATOR GAMES

"Eloise! Tala!" Jasper's frantic voice could be heard along with his hurried footsteps.

We didn't get a chance to see him yesterday and he had put a block up to us. So, when he sent us a mind link early in the morning to meet him at our usual nook in the library, Eloise and I rushed here.

"Jasper, what's wrong?" My friend rushed to his side quickly, seeing the panic in his eyes and the distress that his whole posture held. His light green eyes were rimmed red from exhaustion, and his brown hair was ruffled like he had been grabbing it all night.

"Jasper…" The state of his discountenance caused my own heart to flutter with anxiety. Something had really unsettled him.

He shook his head, seeming perplexed. "He is going to kill him,"

"Who?" Both Eloise and I said before Jasper could even utter another word.

"He knows, fuck, he knows he is your mate, Tala! He is going to kill him today if he survives the arena. He is making him fight again, changed the whole schedule."

I felt my chest constrict with burning pain, and panic began to rise. I looked from Jasper to Eloise and again back to Jasper, the words sinking in. "How does he know? Was it Oliver?"

He shook his head again. "No, it wasn't Oliver. They brought Teal in because of your mate's actions. Questioned him, and when he wouldn't give him answers about the Wolf King, they beat him, gave him a high dose of wolfsbane and... and they almost killed him." Jasper ran a hand down his face then squared his eyes at mine. "Tala, I have to tell you something. I swear I only found out last night," Jasper took a deep breath, closing his eyes for a second as he prepared to tell me something I knew was going to be life-altering.

"Vargr is not your father..."

"I know," I cut him off, "Teal is." My shoulders slumped, all these years Vargr had hated me and I could never understand why I wasn't good enough for him, but now I did. "I realized yesterday. My mother gave me a hint and when he was brought into the palace, it finally dawned on me."

A look of relief briefly passed through Jasper's eyes and he pulled El into his arms, inhaling her scent. Instantly he calmed down, his body relaxing, his posture seeming to ease. Eloise melted into him. I felt jealous that I couldn't do that with my mate, which brought me back to the point of Jasper declaring that Vargr knew he was my mate and was going to kill him.

"Jasper, how does he know Kellen is my mate?" I got a sympathetic look from both of my friends.

"He guessed when he was questioning Teal about him; someone said they saw him leave the guard's lounge right after you. I don't know who the spy is, but if I am correct, it was Jack." He blew out an exaggerated breath, "I can't think of anyone who would betray us, they would have nothing to gain from it. One of our friends had reported seeing Jack wandering around the compound that night; he is the only person I can think of. Plus, Vargr saw your mark on Kellen, Tala..."

"And... Teal?" I asked, the words catching in my throat. I had really fucked up by marking Kellen. If he died, this would be my entire fault. I would be the cause of my mate dying.

"He is alive, barley. He refused to say anything, but his silence just confirmed your father's paranoia." Shit, this was so not good. "He is throwing Kellen into the ring this afternoon to fight, but if he lives, he is going to kill him anyway. Vargr said the trouble he was causing was not worth the money."

Despite my turmoil and fear, I couldn't help but scoff. Since when did my father brush money aside? Kellen must have really rattled his cage yesterday for him to discard a moneymaker.

"I have to go." I suddenly said out loud, thinking of the one person who could possibly help us out of this mess. Oliver.

I picked up my sister's diaries that Eloise and I had been reading through, handing four of them to Jasper and keeping one tightly wrapped in my fingers. The blueprints for the chips had told us nothing we didn't already know. You either died or killed whoever was controlling the chips.

"El, show him the diaries, I have to go see someone." I was only half there, my mind someplace else, so my words were mumbled and strained. I couldn't let Kellen die. No, the Moon Goddess could not be that cruel.

I ran out of the library, rushing through the corridors so fast that my hair had come unpinned and was flying wildly behind me. The book was grasped in one hand while the other lifted my long lemon tunic dress so I wouldn't trip on it while I ran.

I knocked on the guest suite with heavy and rapid knuckles. Please be there, I thought. The door opened and I barged in, noticing Oliver was only covered in a low-lying towel. His appearance frazzled me for a second. I took note of the scars on his body from past fights or battles.

My eyes roamed over him. Another place, another time, and if he had been any kind of a decent wolf, his lean and toned frame may have had me licking my lips. I shook the sight of Oliver in a towel with his blond hair still wet from my head and turned my back on him. "Please get dressed," I sighed.

"Why, princess? Afraid you might want me? That you might like what I have to offer you?" I could hear the smirk in his voice and the rustle of him putting clothes on.

I huffed in annoyance. "You wish." Suddenly I felt his body press against my back.

"Yes, I think I would quite like you wanting me. I wouldn't turn you down." I cringed at the creepy way he flirted with me and then shuddered at how close he was to me. I took a step forward, away from him.

"I know you know what happened yesterday; you were in there with them. You are going to help me save Kellen." I turned around, thankful he had a shirt and a pair of pants on now, looking him dead in the eyes. I wasn't asking for him to help, I was telling him he was going to.

He took a step back from me, scrutinizing me with a cold and beady look. A ring of orange gleamed in his otherwise hazel eyes, flashing his wolf. "Why would I help you save him?" He glared at me.

"Because I have what you and Jack want," I said with confidence, holding up one of my sister's diaries. I gave him a smug look, now was no time to show this sly wolf weakness. He had to help me, he just had to.

"Oh?" He raised his eyebrows, losing the cold glare and replacing it with one of interest. His personality shift was so fast it made me hesitate.

"Yes, and per our deal, you will help me save Kellen for the map of the mines and the location of your witch." I tapped my finger on my lips, pursing them, and paced the room slightly. "If you help me save Kellen, I won't just hand you the map to the mines, I will sweeten the deal." I let my words trail and stopped my pacing to observe his reaction.

"Go on, I'm listening," he growled.

"In fact, you won't even have to get in the mines, I will personally deliver two sacks full of diamonds to you, and I'm not talking about small pouches. You won't have to lift a finger to get a whole shit load of diamonds. But you won't get them until Kellen is out of the compound." I finished, hoping to the moon that he would accept the deal and not screw me over.

"And the location of the witch?" He asked, and I threw the diary at him. He caught it and examined it.

"It's all in there. It seems my sister knew more than anyone thought, and true to her nature, she recorded it all down in her diary. The last known location of the witch is amongst those pages."

"You have a deal, princess. I warn you though, if I don't get my payment, I will come back for you." He promised while thumbing through the pages of Shayna's leather book.

"And if you don't help secure Kellen, you won't get your

jewels, Oliver," I promised back to him.

I exhaled a long breath once I was out of Oliver's suite. It was only then my hands and legs began to shake. Oliver was going to try and save Kellen from being killed by my father, but he couldn't stop him from sending Kellen into the arena later today. I prayed to the gods that he would survive the fight, not knowing what my father had planned for him.

If Kellen survived, which he had to, Oliver was going to try and help get him out of here. It would take a little planning, but with more people backing us, we had a solid chance. Oliver wasn't as watched as me, Vargr didn't trust him or Jack, but he sure liked them a whole lot more than he did me. I was counting on it.

Now I had to figure out how to obtain two sacks of jewels. I hadn't figured that part out when I offered Oliver the deal. I was just desperate to help my mate.

I met back up with Jasper and El, and for the rest of the afternoon, we snuck around the compound discretely, getting word to all our supporters of what Vargr had planned for the games.

Hopefully, the people's word could change his mind if it came down to it. The timing was too short to come up with any viable plan of action, but planting the seed in minds of supporters was easier than we thought. Kellen had more people on his side than we could have hoped for.

*****

JASPER

"Cameron," I greeted my future beta and one of my other best friends. "What are our numbers looking like?" I asked him in regard to the task I had given him; to find warriors and pack members that would be loyal to me and Tala once I took over as alpha.

"Good, but not as good as they could be." Cameron was my trusted man here in the palace compounds. Unlike Tala, he and I were able to attend a school. That was where we had met and bonded through the years.

Now that we were older, both twenty-three and the majority of our peers were the future of the pack, Cameron and I had begun to suss out who was loyal to me as the future Alpha of Bhakhil and him as my future beta. Over the last week, we had secured the loyalty of over 100 warriors and guards. That seems like a big number, but it was a far cry from the 1,500 other warriors Vargr had in his army. Aside from that, Eloise and the palace maids had been gathering the omegas.

Each loyalist to us hated Vargr and his rule. Most had a family member that had been enslaved to work the mines, and some knew whole families who were stuck down there day in and day out.

If it wasn't for the fear the kingdom had of their ruler, I was sure we would have a lot more people ready to stand against Vargr and my father. My wolf growled at the mention of the word father.

I had always wondered why Vargr treated Tala so awfully, why he loathed her. Tala was a kind-spirited soul whom he locked away in the confines of the palace walls. Instead of attending school, she was given tutors. She wasn't allowed to shift and run freely like us; instead, Vargr had commanded her to never shift unless he gave her permission. I could only guess how weak her wolf was. Well up until she marked her mate.

I shook my head when I thought about what she did, this could seriously screw all our plans up. I was also a little jealous that she had marked her mate, a slave, and I couldn't even touch Eloise in fear that if Vargr and my father found out, they would make me reject her, or worse, end her.

"Some shit went down last night," I told Cameron as I began walking the perimeter with him.

"Oh?" His footsteps faltered.

"Yeah, our timeline has moved up. Tala marked the Wolf King." I sighed out, and then lifted my head to see his reaction.

As expected, Cameron let out a groan and threw his head back. "Fuck, so all this work has been for nothing? If Vargr finds out, he will kill him. What kind of time frame are we looking at now? Because we need to start getting people and things in place. It wasn't going to be easy before, but now it's going to be near impossible."

I nodded, agreeing that it was going to be damn hard now. "We need to figure out how to get him and Tala out." Tala was my main priority, especially with everything that came to light last night. I hadn't even told Tala the whole story. I was still trying to come to terms with it myself and was debating on how much I should tell Cameron. What I now know could put me in a very bad light.

FLASHBACK TO YESTERDAY

I walked into Alpha Vargr's office, following him, my father, Jack, and Oliver. Vargr was fuming after the Wolf King's display of power in the arena. I could tell by the way he was pacing and his eyes were going from his usual hazel to dark, almost black, as his wolf made himself present.

"Have the guards bring Teal in." He hissed the command to my father, whose eyes immediately glazed over, mind-linking the slave barrack guards. A few minutes later Teal, Vargr's champion gladiator, was escorted in wearing a pair of silver cuffs.

"KNEEL!" Vargr commanded, and Teal sunk down to his knees, head lowered in both submission and embarrassment.

I watched as Vargr threw punch after punch at him. Once he stopped, he grabbed Teal's hair, yanking his head back so he could look him in the eye. And with a growl, he revealed something that shocked me to the core, "Twenty-one years I have fed and clothed your little whore. Twenty-one years I looked the other way, only to find out she is mated to one of you!"

"I believe, Alpha, she marked the slave too. He wore a mark today in the ring." I looked at Jack, only now realizing it was Tala they were speaking about. How did he know?

"She did what!" Vargr cried out, this time delivering a kick to Teal's face, who slumped sideways down on the floor. "Is this true? Did your little bitch mark that fucking wolf?" He screamed while kicking him in the ribs. Teal said nothing.

"I did not raise her to be mated with my son, just for her to spread her legs for her mate!" He screamed. "Baron, show this piece of shit alpha slave how to talk!"

I watched my father pull out a silver-bladed knife and begin to cut the gladiator in various places on his body. Teal stayed silent but I could see he was in agony. I was still replaying Vargr's words, his son?

I stayed silent as my father worked Teal over until hundreds of cuts were spread across his body and his face was unrecognizable. "Looks like he could do with some wolfsbane in those cuts of his," Jack said with a sadistic smile curling upon his lips, his eyes dark with his beast.

Vargr called the guards in and had them take him below the palace, where there were a few holding rooms he used to extract information from various people.

Who is Vargr's son? I asked my father through the mind link. I was meant to take over as alpha, but Vargr had just said 'his son'. I could tell I was not going to like the answer, whatever it was.

Not now, son He hissed back at me, still walking.

I stopped mid-step and halted my father by grabbing his elbow. "Who is Vargr's son?" I asked, letting my wolf come forward.

"Jasper, not now." He bit back.

"No, now would be a really fucking good time, father, because after what Vargr said, I don't think I am going to like the answer." I stood firm, not letting him go, staring him down, and daring my father to tell me the truth.

"You are not a beta, you are an alpha. And that is all I can say." I saw the look of betrayal flash in my father's eyes and an emotion that reflected regret. His eyes began to soften, begging me to let it go.

I dropped my grip on him, momentarily stunned. Lies. It had all been lies. Mine and Tala's life had been one big fucking lie. As the truth of who mine and Tala's real fathers were settled itself in my mind, so much began to make sense. The veil of ignorance had been lifted, showing me the clarity I had yearned for all these years. I felt nothing but sick.

"Do not show him weakness. No matter what, you are still my son, and you will mate with Tala." He took this opportunity to walk away from me, following the Alpha underground.

His words left me broken and humiliated. He hadn't outright confirmed it, but I had just found out Vargr was my father. Above all, I felt like an imposter. I didn't know who I was anymore.

END FLASHBACK

"Vargr needs to be taken out. He can no longer hold power, and the sooner we kill him the better," I said to Cameron, deciding not to disclose everything. The fact that Vargr was my real father was a secret I was willing to take to the grave. I had no intention of letting anyone know that truth.

Chapter 32 – The Second Gift

KELLEN

I felt Rogue's worry and deep concern as Teal dropped the bomb on me. "He knows she is your mate," he coughed up when he came too. "He will fight you, he will kill you." Teal's pained-filled words had sat heavily on my mind since he uttered them this morning.

Rogue was clearly upset, and I wished we could somehow converse. I may understand him better now, but I needed words. It was important to me that I had his opinion, not just give him commands or tell him what to do. I was definitely missing my beta at this moment.

Everything I did, every decision I made, was with Mike's input. We were a team and I valued his advice. I valued Rogue's too, more so now that Ajani was no longer with us, but the communication barrier with Rogue hindered me: us.

I found myself wandering the common area, gathering my thoughts, twirling the sharp and shiny sword the old woman had bestowed upon me in my hand. My mind was on the fight that I was being thrown into this afternoon. There was no way to determine what Vargr had in mind as he had deviated from the schedule just to make me fight. There was no way of knowing what was coming my way.

I was trying to mentally prepare myself for anything when I heard, "Psst, psst." I looked around, my eyes landing on a woman who was in the same fashion cloak as the old lady. This woman was younger, with medium brown hair, and she waved me over.

I cautiously and curiously sidled up to where she stood on the other side of the bars. I frowned at her obvious paranoid and jerky movements, she looked around like she didn't want to be caught. Although younger looking, the woman's eyes resembled the old lady from two days ago.

"How can I..." I went to ask how I could help her, but I was cut off by her hushing me.

"Shh, Shh!" She gestured, pressing her finger to her lip, looking around again. She pushed a small container of water through the bars toward me. "Drink this," she said with a hurried tone. "Quickly"

I took the container from her and opened the lid, giving it a quick sniff. "Water?" I was bemused why she would insist on me drinking the container that only held what smelled like water.

"My sister Nandie gave you the gift of strength." She pointed to the sword in my hand. "I am Tandie; I give you your second gift: the gift of life." She wore a proud smile on her face as she said the latter part.

I was confused; she had given me a container of water. Noticing my confusion, she sighed. "Just drink it, water is life, life needs water. Ashe said you could be a little on the slow side," she chuckled.

I frowned at her, feeling a little insulted that she and Ashe would think of me as... slow. "Just drink it," she hissed. With hesitation, flicking a glance at her momentarily, I lifted the open container to my mouth and drank it all down.

"Good boy," she praised. I had just determined that I

didn't like this woman when she said something to change my mind again. "Nandie said Mathias was better looking. Personally, you are much more pleasing to the eye, young king." She chuckled and then walked away, throwing a little finger wave over her shoulder at me and pulling her hood over her head before joining the crowd of people who were starting to enter the arena.

"Kellen," Corey, another gladiator, called my name as he wandered into the common area. It was only then I realized that I had been the only one out here. "It's time," he said, meaning it was time for me to step into the arena.

Maybe for the last time.

'We are stronger,' Conri said, filling my mind with hope. *'We can draw from the power of the Knights, from the Queen, even if we can't shift.'* His words held aspiration and a feeling of trust.

Goddess, I prayed my wolf was right and that the confidence he felt would start seeping into my own determination right about now.

When I stepped into the arena, the place was packed. I was on my own, no other gladiators. I was escorted by the usual unit of guards, twelve just for me. There was no cheering, no booing from the spectators, just the hum of their mumbles and whispers as I confidently walked to the center.

The air was stagnant, not just from the source of heat that beat down on us, but from the anticipation I felt from all the shifters seated around the stadium. There was a clear sense of apprehension and unease.

I heard my name announced. "Your favorite gladiator – Prince-ee," he bellowed out. The crowd was quiet for a few minutes until I turned to them and held my arms out wide.

"I fight for the people!" I roared. "Not for your false king!" Fuck it, it was too late to turn back and deviate from my intentions now, so I went with it. I stood there like the king I was meant to be, greeting my people and bowing to them.

The uproar from the crowd was in favor of me and I knelt on one knee, placing my hand over my heart. A king is fierce and strong, he isn't meant to just lead his people, he serves his people, and I will fight in their name.

"WOLF KING, WOLF KING, WOLF KING!" The crowd began to chant. The gladiators began taping their cups against the bars and crying out their melody.

The guards filed out of the arena and made way for my opponents.

Only three, I chuckled as the large men stomped closer to me. They were huge, and I compared them to Tobias' height and frame. All three were bear shifters.

By the look in their eyes, they weren't here to have a good time. They had come with a purpose, a purpose to kill. To kill me.

The three bear shifters stopped several yards from me. They shared a look as the horn blew for the fight to begin, a sardonic smile lifting from each of their mouths.

Then, to my horror, they began to shift. Their clothes tore and then shredded as dark fur began to sprout from each of their extremities. A thick coat of hair quickly covered their bodies, their faces began to reshape into their beasts.

The two smaller ones shifted into a brown and black bear, standing at equal heights of around seven and a half feet tall. The third was a darker brown color, bigger and taller at almost ten feet high. Their weapons were still branded in their now paws. Long claws curled around the handles of the various weapons.

It was easy to gauge their strengths by looking at them: the smaller of the brown bears was the quick one, the black bear was the one with skills as he swung his weapon, and the largest one was the brute force I had to look out for.

The small brown bear held two swords, the black bear a morning star, the heavy ball and spikes intimidating, and the gigantic bear that had me swallowing the dry sandpaper feeling of my saliva held an axe.

I had faced bear shifters before in battle, but never without the use of my wolf form.

'Goddess, I hope you are right.' I groaned internally to Conri.

My wolf huffed. *'We are a king and a knight of the queen,'* was all he had the chance to reply before the smaller of the bears growled out and rushed forward. I had never wanted to go up against Mathias and his spirit animal, but at this moment, that was exactly what I felt like I was doing. I was no match for Mathias, I would never kid myself. But hopefully, I could take down these three and come out still breathing.

"Here we go," I grumbled out loud to myself as the first bear descended upon me.

I would like to say it was an easy fight, but it wasn't.

I blocked the brown bear's attack, our swords meeting with a clash, the metal scraping as I pushed back against him. He was intense. I managed to lift my leg, kicking him in the stomach and sending him back a few feet. The black bear descended upon me, swinging his morning star. I dodged and ducked each swing that aimed for my head and managed to maneuver behind him by twisting my body, driving my sword right into his back, withdrawing it and dropping to my knees, and slicing the back of his joints.

The black bear dropped to the ground, his wounds keeping him down for now. I was sure he would heal quickly. A kick came to my back, flinging me forward, tasting the dirt as I hit the ground. I rolled to the side, narrowly missing the axe that landed right beside my face.

I jumped up to face the two bears that were still standing. I could see the black bear beginning to stir from my peripheral vision. The two bears charged at me, and I took fast steps forward, sliding to my knees at the last minute and catching the small brown bear right in the groin. My sword sliced upwards, severing his manhood and going to his stomach, slicing it open. The brown bear let out a painful roar as his body slumped and his intestines began to seep from the open wound.

The larger bear came at me like the force of a hurricane, swinging his axe in a fury of fur, dodging each blow he attempted. The air left my lungs when he took a page out of my book, and his large clawed back paw connected with my chest. I flew back and hit the ground with a thud, unable to move as I tried to breathe and regain myself. I rolled over and pushed up on my hands and knees, constantly checking to see where the large bear was and if the black bear had recovered.

The larger bear had taken the opportunity to show his dominance to the crowd by beating his chest and roaring out. I was too focused on myself and recovering to notice if they favored him or not. I did not care. This was a game of survival, and if I didn't get my shit together, I was going to lose.

I saw the black bear shake out his fur as he came to stand on all four paws, still slightly stunned and injured.

I mustered up all the strength I could and flew towards him with as much inhuman speed as Conri allowed me. I flew through the air, jumping high, sword raised, and came down upon him like the fire of the gods, growling out my strength as I did. My sword sliced through his thick neck, the blood gushed, his head rolled, and his body shifted upon the severing of his head. Gone was the mass of black fur; instead lay the headless body of a tattooed man. Every inch of him was covered in ink.

I turned to face my last opponent. I was a little too late in turning to face him and felt his claws rip down my arm as I moved away from the swipe. "Fuck!" I cried out as the wounds gaped open. It was only then I remembered the spectators and registered their presence as their loud gasps of astonishment met my ears.

The last standing bear shifter swiped at me again, this time catching my leg. Again, I hissed at the pain. The third time I was ready, and when his paw came up, spread out with his claws glistening in the sun, I raised my sword. And with a swift, quick, and precise swing, I sliced his hand clean off. The bear stumbled back and whimpered. I saw the snarl and his roar of adrenaline as he ran towards me, standing on his two back paws. His axe was raised, his vision so full of rage that he failed to realize I was waiting, sword poised and feet planted. I would not die today.

As the large, one-handed bear came upon me, all teeth and fur, I twisted my hips and sliced right, immediately followed by a twist of the wrist and swiping left. The bear stopped and looked down at his torso, then his dark gaze met mine. In his moment of being stunned, I saw my opening and drove my sword straight through his heart.

When the bear shifter fell backward, the sound of his body thudding against the ground echoed into the silent arena. I stood above him and ripped my sword from his chest as I heard the beat of his heart slowly thump to a stop.

The crowd went wild and began to chant, "Wolf King, Wolf King,"

I paid them no mind as I walked towards Vargr's tent, picking up one of the small brown bear's swords on the way. I could feel my skin stitching itself back together with each step I took. Healing faster than I had in the past couple of months. Suddenly the gates opened, and warriors piled in, surrounding me.

"Is this the best you can do!" I yelled towards the tent. My eyes fell on Tala, who stood between Oliver and Jack. Even from this distance, I could see the sheen of tears in her eyes. "You are a coward that will not accept the challenge of a gladiator, you have shamed the goddess! You call yourself an alpha, a self-proclaimed king, but all I see is a tyrant. A wolf who condemns his own people! A greedy and murderous man!"

I twisted the bear's sword in my hand, ready to lob it at the vile alpha. He was fuming, his face red with anger, his mouth curled into a snarl showing his fangs. Then he began to laugh, loudly and fully. Although it was fake, he was trying to look undisturbed by my win; trying to remain in control. He steadied his gaze on mine, his eyes dark with his counterpart. Even though he looked poised and stoic on the outsight, the bead of sweat that slid down his face said otherwise. He was scared. Scared of what I could do.

He tore his stare from me and looked around at the packed arena before he narrowed those eyes on me again, trying to look intimidating and in control. "We are what the goddess meant us to be. We are animals, top of the food chain!" He growled viciously, and suddenly. "Your fancy words and attitude mean nothing here. Here you have no title. Here you are nothing but a *slave*! Here I make the rules. You are nothing but a slave. A gladiator, Wolf King." He half turned from me and whispered in the ear of one of his men.

"YOU ARE NOTHING!" He declared. He then stood from his 'throne' and clapped his hands.

"LET THE REAL FIGHT BEGIN!" He roared while addressing the crowd, but his eyes never left mine. Like he already knew he had won.

The sound of metal against metal grinding together stabbed my ear drums. He turned back to me, his eyes ablaze with fire and fury. "A slave cannot challenge their master, the penalty is death, but I have paid a pretty penny for you, so you will do what I bought you for... gladiator."

I looked around to see several entryways had opened through the walls, metal doors that had remained closed since I had been here. I couldn't believe my eyes when I saw what came walking out of those four entryways.

I didn't know which emotion or reaction came first. Was it the shock of seeing something I thought I never would in my lifetime, the fear of the reality I was living, or amusement because the Moon Goddess seemed like she really had it in for me?

If the gods were testing me, then I was over it. I no longer wanted to play the game.

Lions? Fucking Lions?

This had to be a joke.

'We can take them, we are the Queen's Knight.' Conri's confident thoughts filled my head once more. I kept hearing these same words from him, but they were empty. I was already drained from the first fight. Now, I had to defend myself again. Conri pushed as much of his strength onto me

as he could, and I exhaled hard, trying to shake off the burn in my mauled cuts which were healing fast, but not quite fast enough.

Indeed, I had gotten stronger. If only we could shift.

'And this sorry son of a bitch has no idea what he bought,' I replied, equally as confident. Finding that resolve of strength to carry on and fight my way through this living hell. If this is what Vargr wanted, then so be it. I would not go down easy.

One by one, the lions stalked into the arena growling and snarling as their noses scented the air. Their manes were thick and full, like a crown that covered their heads. I can do this; I gave myself a pep talk. These were animals, not shifters.

A high pitch whistle sounded from behind me, under the tent, and I briefly heard Tala cry out my name. I didn't turn around. I needed to concentrate, even if I only wanted to turn and take a long look at my mate and think about holding her in my arms. I will live through this for her. I fight for her, for my queen.

The high pitch whistle sounded once again, piercing my eardrums and sending a grating vibration through my head. I shook it off and watched the lions shake their heads too.

All of the sudden, the lion's bones began to crack, the golden fur they wore like a king's robe began to shed, leaving a strange ashy pink skin in its wake. Their skeletal structure became larger, bones shifting into something unreal, something larger.

'What fuck is this?' I said to Conri as I watched a beast of an animal begin to shift into something unholy that defied the very laws of nature. The golden manes were now shredded, and in place stood a furless pale creature with red eyes and jagged teeth.

Crawlers? That is what they reminded me of. A more animalistic version of Orion's Crawlers.

The creatures attempted to growl at me, but instead of something deep and menacing, it was a screech that sent a shiver down my spine, piercing every single nerve ending and shaking my very core.

Chapter 33 – The Death of Kellen

KELLEN

The creatures stalked towards me. I cast my eyes to the sky, sending out a prayer that I hoped would reach the ears of the gods and they would favor me.

In the distance, I saw a mass of darkness, a shelf cloud that was rolling in from the north and heading our way. My shallow breaths halted as I registered the ominous doomsday storm approaching. The screech of the creatures brought me tumbling back to the now, and for the umpteenth time, I raised my sword and planted my feet, readying for the attack.

My mind went a mile a minute as I tried to gauge the movements of the monstrosities I faced.

The first one leaped in the air, snapping its jaws as his body flung itself in my direction. As the creature came down to pounce, I swung my sword, wounding the thing and twisting as it landed beside me on all fours. Its paw reached out, swiping my stomach, and it felt like a billion hot needles poking into my skin at once. I didn't look down. Instead, I attacked the creature at full force. I had no time to stumble, no time to second guess, and no time to assess my injuries. I needed to survive.

A rage built inside me as Conri came forward. The mark on my chest began to burn, but the slight heat was nothing like what was coming from my abdomen. "Arrghhh!" I screamed while plunging the sword into the creature as deep as I could, then drawing my sword from his body and stepping back, bracing for the next attack.

I was caught off guard when the creature began to turn to ash and evaporate, just like the Crawlers. The sharp sting of pointed nails dug into my back. My legs gave out as the burn intensified. Large and knife-like teeth dug into my shoulder, and my sword fell from my hand as I wailed in agony on my knees.

'Draw on the power of the knights!' Conri yelled at me from within, wanting to shift. I didn't know how. I didn't know how to do what he was telling me.

I closed my eyes for a brief moment as the creature's teeth dug in further. I envisioned the rest of the knights, I envisioned Lamia, my mind pleading for strength. All at once, I felt the surge of something ancient, something magical come to life from deep within me.

My eyes opened, and I could tell I was looking through the eyes of my wolf. I reached behind me and grabbed the animal that was gnawing on my bone, gripping his head and pulling his teeth out from deep into my flesh. I flung it over my shoulder with a loud growl, watching him land on his back.

My chest was heaving, not from exhaustion but from a newfound magnetism of strength that was coursing through my veins. I picked up the sword which sent a zinging sensation through me. The electrical force powering through me and the inscriptions on the blade seemed to come to life. The feeling was surreal; I had never felt this strong before. It was as if my wolf and I were connected on a much deeper and cosmic scale. His power radiated through and out of me, and the feeling was addictive. I liked how I felt; powerful, destructive, almost as if my body was as free and unhinged as I was in my wolf form.

With a new determination, I attacked the creatures one by one, avoiding each swipe and snap. My movements were frenzied, so full of determination, anger, and power that it didn't take long before the remaining three monsters had been eliminated.

There were no corpses, no blood soaking into the sandy dirt, only those of the three werebears I had defeated, and my own blood stained my naked chest. I stood there seething, waiting for the next challenge, my eyes darting left and right as my body circled, poised for whatever Vargr threw at me next. It would take more than that to put me down.

I met my mate's eyes, who looked relieved but still trembled with worry. I gave her a smile. Goddess, she was beautiful. I couldn't wait to mark and mate her. Make her mine.

Soon, I thought. Soon this would all be over, and I would be free to take her in my arms and make her mine in every sense of the word. She had been given to me, a beautiful gift. One that I would receive graciously and take my time with, cherish for all of time. I would take her far away to the New Moon kingdom, and this hell hole would never darken her beautiful mind again. I had been in love with Lamia for so long that I had no idea how strong the pull of a mate bond could be. I hated that she had been mated to Mathias and another before him. I could never understand why she was so willing to give in to fate, especially when both of her mates were arrogant assholes.

Now, after meeting Tala, I understood. Each day away from my little flame was a challenge. The aching, the wanting, the craving to inhale her sweet scent of oranges and sea salt, it was almost a blessing to have this inhibitor chip implanted into me. If Conri was able to shift, there would be no stopping us from claiming Tala.

I would sink my teeth into her marking spot as I was buried deep inside her. I was in love, and I hardly knew her. I would do anything for her and that included getting the fuck out of here. I wished there was a way I could mind-link her. I would tell her how much I adored her, how much she meant to me, that I loved her. That I wanted her.

Instead, all I could do was hold her gaze. Even from this distance, her striking eyes were a prominent blue.

Just as I finally understood that there were no more left, my body and wolf began to calm, and my eyes returned to their normal blue instead of the black of the knights. The gates opened and in no time, I was surrounded by a wall of warriors.

I felt the sting from my wounds, like acid burning through my skin or the vile venom of wolfsbane. "Arggh," I growled out when I felt the bite of a shock on my back. Only to turn and feel it again, and again, and again until the cattle prods had me wavering on my feet.

"One hundred lashes, then leave him to die!" I heard Vargr's foul mouth command the warriors.

"No!... Please!" My mate's panicked voice rang, out and I lifted my head to look at her. "Please no!" She begged, throwing herself at Vargr's feet.

He kicked her away. My wolf started growling, and the sting of the prod was felt in my ribs.

"I denounce you as my daughter and rescind your pairing with Jasper. Henceforth you will be nothing but a slave girl and treated like the whore you are!" Vargr snapped at Tala and motioned to Jack. "Have her put in the box!" He spat out with disgust.

"ONE HUNDRED LASHES!" He roared, and the warriors

began to drag me away, the shock of a prod stinging my flesh further with each restrained jerk I gave them.

I wanted to fight back, I wanted to defend my mate, I wanted to rip Vargr and Jack's heads off, but I had no energy. The fights had weakened me, and the voltage from the prods had my body unresponsive. All I could do while they dragged me backward was watch Jack grab Tala's hair and rip her away from the tent. My mate was screaming and kicking. Jasper tried to reach for her but was stopped by the beta, who shook his head. Oliver watched, and I saw a shadowed look come across his face, one of harrowing and perplexity. He watched my mate being dragged away from the tent by his accomplice, and he didn't like it.

Jasper was just as helpless as his hands furled and face reddened in anger. I felt the silver of the cuffs sting my wrist, my arms were hoisted upwards, and I was turned to face the wall. The cuffs connected to a hook as they suspended my limp frame - my toes barely touching the ground.

In the distance, the rumbling of the storm could be heard. The sky became darker, and the air chilled for the first time in almost three months. The light breeze that rolled in was heaven. I liked to think the gods were angry, and if it rained - it would be their tears shedding for me.

"KELLEN!" I heard the last call of my mate; her painful and wallowing cry pinched my heart. "I love you." I thought I heard her whisper, the wisping breeze carrying the faint words to my ears. Maybe it was just what I wanted and needed to hear as I felt the first bite of the silver-tipped and dipped whip as it lashed against my back.

I refused to cry out at each excruciating thrash that flicked and flayed my skin. I couldn't help the grunts, but that was all they would get from me. I held on to the image of Tala when she came undone in my arms. I desperately wished to see that look on her face again.

Tap, tap, tap, came the clang of the cups against the metal bars. How many lashes I had received? I did not know. "ARGHOOH, ARGHOOH, ARGHOOH. LIVE OR DIE WE FIGHT!" Came the voices of the gladiators as the punisher handed the whip to another.

The cups clanging echoed the beat of my heart, keeping me steady as I received ten more lashes. How many was that, twenty, thirty? I was focusing on staying conscious and alive.

When the whip switched hands again, the gladiators chanted our melody like it was our creed. I focused on that beat and not the anticipation of the next lash. Their steady beat, my life. Tempered and strong. The breeze took some of the heat from my back as it brushed against my flailed skin and softly curled away back into the darker growing sky. The clouds cast shadows against the high sandstone wall as the storm moved closer.

I thought of Teal and how I would have liked to reunite him with his family. I was sure they would accept Tala; did they even know they had another sister?

Then I thought of Rogue. What would happen to him? He would either die here, or if he ever got out, would he become a rogue again? I didn't want him to. Rogue had become important to me; I would give him a place by my side.

"HARDER!" Vargr commanded. I had no idea he was still watching. I couldn't turn my head to look at him, but I could feel his vengeful eyes on me.

Thunder clapped loud, reverberating through the arena, its powerful tremor shaking the stone walls. The sky darkened, casting a false and moonless night over the arena.

"DON'T STOP!" Again, Vargr commanded.

The steady beat of the cups did not let up, and again they chanted when the punisher changed. My body was slumping, and I didn't know how long I could retain consciousness.

The crimson coppery scent pooled under my feet, and the smell of the metallic fluid reached my nose along with the scent of silver and the poison of wolfsbane. My legs were weak, and my arms were strained. My head fell back - and my eyes rolled into the back of my head.

It was then I felt the fresh and first drop of rain splash on my cheek. My eyes fluttered open and gazed above. The gods were weeping for my death. Weeping for the end of a tragic love story that never began.

Thunder boomed, a flash of lightning lit up the sky, and the rain began to fall faster and heavier. Each fat drop that graced my face and bare torn back was welcomed.

I could hold on no longer. I could feel my wolf slipping away, taking the essence of my life with him. Images of each person I hold dear to me flashed before my eyes. First came Lamia; I would never meet my niece or nephew. How would Lamia cope with my death? My heart constricted, knowing the grief and loss of me would almost kill her. She was strong, she would survive, and Mathias would make sure of that.

And Mike, he would make a fine alpha and king. I knew it wasn't what he ever wanted, but he would make me proud and take his responsibilities seriously. I had full confidence the kingdom would be left in good hands.

I thought of Hunji and Rhett. Not much would change for them, they would be losing a brother, but Hunji would carry on protecting Lamia. My only regret was not getting to know his secrets. And Rhett was still finding out who he was. He would make a hell of a leader once they had the Enforcers established throughout the continent. In my head, I wished them all the best, I wished them long and prosperous lives.

I wished for them all to find happiness.

The last person whose face filled my vision was my mate, my little flame. The goddess had blessed me with someone special. It wasn't fair to my mate that I should be taken away so quickly. I believed in second chances and hoped my mate would be happy, even if that happiness wasn't with me.

"Tala," I whispered her name as I felt the tip of the whip dig so deep it licked my bone. My sight began to wane, and I let my lids close. Fat drops of rain splashing into my dry mouth.

'Water is life, life needs water.' The woman's voice echoed through me, and from the blackness behind my lids, Lamia's green eyes fill my vision. *'I call on the Knights to lessen your brother's pain, share it and give back your strength'.*

I was delirious, and my subconscious was conjuring the faces of my friends. Hearing the echoes of Lamia's voice gave me hope that I would descend to the afterlife, where the Moon Goddess would be waiting to receive me and my wolf.

I stilled in the thought and felt at peace with my death. I would meet my parents again, and they would embrace me and welcome me home.

My heart slowed, and the noises of the gladiators became a distant sound. The claps of thunder, though loud, were now dull.

So far away as I felt myself receding further into the darkness of my own consciousness.

I called out to my wolf, but he had already left me.

The only thing holding me up were the cuffs that cut into my wrists as my body gave out, followed by my mind.

I took one last breath and thought of my little flame, who

I craved time with. One last time - until I succumbed to the desolate void. The stilling of my heart was the last thing I felt as I left the planes of this realm.

Chapter 34 – The Queen and the fourth Knight

MATHIAS

Things had not been going according to plan. I thought things would get easier after Riocht, or at least Lamia and I would find some normalcy in life. How wrong I was. The life of a king and queen would always be anything but normal.

We had been crowned the King and Queen of Shifters, and the work began to pile up. That wouldn't have been so bad, but Lamia was heavily pregnant with triplets, who according to the doctor, had grown at an exceedingly faster-than-normal rate and seemed convinced that she was further along than we originally thought.

We thought she had conceived when we were at MacTire before the battle. However, if we put the timeline back to the first time we mated, it was in January. We were now in June. A few days later, we completed the bonding in Avalon, her heat never fully surfacing because our souls bonded. Maybe that's when she fell pregnant?

She was almost at full term if she was carrying pups, and another month or two if she was carrying cubs. I had the doctor perform a scan on her, and he put her on bed rest. Two of the babies were large, yet the third was small. Smaller than a shifter baby should be, causing the doctor to worry that the smaller child may not survive. Or if it did, they would be severely underdeveloped - if she went into labor, he couldn't guarantee its life.

I picked up a bottle of rum and poured myself a glass. We were still at the Clan Mansion. The original idea was to have a crowning ceremony for Lamia as the Queen of Bears.

However, since Kellen had gone missing - that was put on the back burner. We began to focus on transferring the Alpha title to Xander. I would remain king, keeping my title - but he would oversee our kingdom. As the days went by and we were still upgrading Riocht, I began to think maybe I should step down and hand the crown to the Kodiak Kingdom to the next in line.

The next in line would not be Xander though; it would actually fall to my half-brother Finnegan. After many discussions, we released Finnegan from the dungeons and had given him a room here in the mansion. There was no fucking way I would make him king.

I still didn't trust him. Not one bit. But Lamia had faith in him, she saw something I didn't. Or maybe I just didn't want to see it. I told her she was too soft and that we should have taken his head as soon as we had answers. Yet, the more he was around, the more I began to appreciate his presence.

I took a deep gulp of the rum, sighing in satisfaction. This was my first drink since I had been spiked and attacked Lamia. I had missed the rich and heavy taste. Arcas had been on edge since visiting the doctor, concerned for his cubs. The fact that one was too small had him constantly pacing. His drive to be near his mate made it almost impossible to get anything done, and there was still so much to do.

Lamia had already handed MacTire to Travis, who was allowed to keep some businesses that Lamia said belonged to the people and that's what MacTire survived on. Those businesses were what built the kingdom to what it is now.

Rhett had become Travis' Gamma, a respected advisor and enforcer. Travis was still looking for his delta after Josiah was named his beta. I smirked at the thought of Travis having a bear shifter as a beta. When I first met him, he hated me because of my race. I thought he hated all bears, but it was only because I was mated to my little wolf and he had firsthand experience of what she went through at the hands of rogue werebears.

I felt the void of Tobias; his presence was greatly missed. It had always been the three of us since I could remember. My thoughts went back to Finnegan, I refused to call him my brother, and I did hate to admit that he had been doing a good job of filling in and helping Xander. He was no Tobias, that was for sure, but he had some strengths, and even though he was under house arrest, he was still proving to be valuable.

Abner had gone back to the council. We could no longer cover for Kellen's disappearance and decisions had to be made. We had a call from Hunji, and thank the gods, they had a lead to his whereabouts. In two days, they would set sail from the Sea Dogs Island to the second continent in search of an alpha named Vargr, in the faraway Kingdom of Bhakhil.

As soon as we asked Finnegan if he had ever heard of Vargr, he didn't hesitate to supply us with the information and his kingdom. Telling us that Orion's bitch was the first daughter of this Alpha Vargr, and he was just as murderous as Orion. He also said if that's where Kellen was, then he would pray he was still alive and Vargr hadn't ended his life - or that he wouldn't lose his life to the gladiator games. Kellen meant so much to my little wolf that I had begun to worry for the Wolf King too. I was not a fan of him at first, but knowing what I know now and how close the Wolf King and my mate were - I knew if anything happened to him, she would suffer severely. She did not need the stress, and I hoped our men would find him and bring him home soon.

I just wanted to take care of my mate and the babies, and the faster we could get the kingdoms organized, the sooner we could take the much-needed time for us. Things were moving so fast, and Lamia wanted to deliver back in MacTire as Riocht wasn't even close to being ready to move into.

We had left Lucien, the leader of the Lycans and Guardians of Riocht, in charge. Although they had lived in a place where time had stood still for so long, I was told that Lucien and the other Lycans had welcomed the Elite guard and were doing their best to accommodate the troops we had sent from each kingdom. Construction was going well on the palace, slow, but it was getting there. However, Lamia didn't want to move in until we had power, running water, and communication towers erected.

MATHIAS! "MATHIAS!" Lamia's agonizing cry through my head and out loud jarred me from my internal turmoil. I sprang up from my chair, clearing the desk as I bolted out of the office and towards our room.

"Mathias!" She cried out again, this time with more discomfort laced in her voice. "There's something wrong!" She said, looking into my eyes when I burst through our bedroom door.

Her eyes were full of tears and her voice was shaky. "I'm bleeding." She pulled back the sheet from the bed and a small pool of blood was gathering between her legs.

She suddenly groaned in pain, and her hand reached behind her back. "Fuck," I grumbled, beginning to panic. We couldn't lose the babies, we just couldn't.

I rushed over to her, fling the sheet off the bed, and lifted the hem of her nightgown carefully and hesitantly. Afraid of what I was going to find. I furrowed my brows when her lower region was exposed.

The blood was not coming from her vagina but from the scars on her upper thigh. "Lamia, your scars have opened," I scowled at the sight and ran a palm down my face. She tried to look down, but her massive belly didn't allow it.

"Arggh," she said, reaching around to grab her back again. "Get me up." She moaned, shifting her feet.

I gladly helped her out of bed, still concerned about her scars reopening and why, but very relieved that the blood was not coming from between her thighs. The babies were okay. "Are you in labor?" I asked, pulling her to her feet.

"No, I don't think so, but I feel like my back is being whipped..." she started, and then looked at me with horror in her eyes. "Kellen," she breathed out and went to take a step forward.

"Arggghhhh!" She let out a shrill wail, almost falling to her knees, but I caught her, holding her by her arms.

"Fuck, Lamia, what's going on?" I didn't know how to help her. I was trying to mind-link my mother and Ria, but I was failing because all my attention was on my mate. I halted any action when her eyes began to glow that brilliant emerald color when her wolf came forward. She threw her head back, making a weird breathing noise - when her body jerked. Her arms spread out wide, and her marks began to illuminate in a blue hue like they did when we bonded.

"Lamia, baby, speak to me. What's going on?" My voice was shaking. Her body began to lift from the floor, suspended in midair. Her emerald eyes glowed like the flames of the underworld. I had no idea what to do and managed to link my mother and Ria.

"I call upon the power of the Knights, your brother needs you. Take his pain and lessen the burden, share it and give back your strength. Your Queen commands this of you."

It was not Lamia's voice, but Inanna's, that was speaking through her.

I raised my hand, still in awe of what was happening. Lamia being suspended in the air was scaring the shit out of me. I had never seen anything like it. It was demonic and eerie, as if her body and mind had been taken over. I wrapped my hand around hers and gave her a tug, trying to bring her back down. As soon as our skin touched, she gripped me, and I felt the heat begin to rise inside of me. A burning warmth traveled throughout my body straight to the hand that held hers; I felt my energy being drained.

'One, two, three, four, five, six, seven...' I listened to her count. When she reached fifteen, Ria, Xander, my mother, and Finnegan came into the room. They all stopped dead in their tracks as they saw Lamia hanging in thin air. Her eyes were ablaze, and Inanna's voice emanated from her, counting. To what... I had no idea!

They stood in momentary shock and bewilderment until Ria stepped forward and grabbed her other hand. The contact had Lamia's body lowering, then Xander touched her shoulder, and she lowered more until we all had a hand on her. I took her in my arms and placed her back on the bed, the whole time she kept counting. 'Twenty-four, twenty-five, twenty-six...'

"What is she counting up to?" Xander asked, standing over the bed. I had lain down next to her, trying to ease her stiffness and give her some comfort, but my touch had no effect, only that she seemed to be drawing energy from me.

"I don't know, she just... her wounds reopened and her wolf pushed forward... she said something about calling on the Knights to help their brother and began counting."

Ria gasped, "Rhett!" and ran out the door, Xander close behind her.

Inanna kept counting until she reached one hundred, and that's when Lamia cried out, screaming and pleading. She wasn't coherent. She was in her own mind. Eventually, she collapsed and fell into a fitful sleep leaving me confused and worried even more. The way she cried out was agonizing to hear, like she was witnessing death. Her pleading held devastation, and I watched the roots of her hair begin to darken, and another strand turned black.

While she was in a self-induced deep sleep, I had the doctor come to check on her. "Keep an eye on her," he grimaced. "She could go into premature labor any day and stress will help induce that labor," he warned, leaving me to worry even more about my little wolf and what had happened to her.

I would not get my answers until she woke up.

*****

TRAVIS

Rhett, bring me the proposals for the new Enforcers buildings in Myrtle Cove I opened up a link to my gamma. He replied immediately, and I turned back to Josiah, my beta.

"He is on his way," I informed him while shuffling some papers and stacking them to the side of me. "So, what choices do we have left for the delta position?" I asked Josiah. I had already turned down the last five candidates. None of them were what I wanted or what I thought MacTire needed.

MacTire was a kingdom, and while regular packs had an alpha, beta, and gamma, Royal packs had a different hierarchy. It went alpha, beta, delta, and then gamma.

Gamma's were more of an adviser role, while strong and could lead a team of warriors. A delta's job: they were third in command and led our armies. They were our generals. It's what I was to Lamia, even though I never dropped the Alpha title. Rhett's position of gamma was still highly praised, but he was a hybrid, and Lamia had already tasked him with setting up a new council of sorts; enforcers, shifters, hybrids, and humans who would enforce the Queen and King of Shifters' laws. They were not much different from the laws we had now, but Rhett would put together special teams around the continent and place them in each kingdom. Working closely with the council, they would investigate any crimes and bring those responsible to trial.

The door opened and Rhett walked in, dropping the files on my desk before taking a seat next to Josiah. "No luck with a delta yet?" Rhett asked, pulling a smoke from his pocket.

"Don't smoke that in here!" Josiah groaned, scowling.

"I wasn't about to, I just wanted to get on your nerves," Rhett laughed at his best friend.

"Dude you are half-human. That shit will kill you eventually you know." Josiah pointed at the rolled-up tobacco Rhett was twiddling through his fingers.

"We all gotta die at some point, my friend," he laughed. "Besides, every one of us is born with an expiration date the day we are born, it just wasn't filled in."

"So morbid," Josiah complained, rolling his eyes.

"Could we get on with shit?" I asked annoyed with the banter between them. "I have shit to do and would like to leave this office at a decent time for once."

"Does alpha have a date?" Josiah jested.

The truth was, no, I did not have a date, and I didn't want

one. Recently my wolf had been complacent, constantly in a state of restlessness, and the only way to calm him down was to run for hours. If I didn't let him out, he would become irate and foul. A few times, he had gone as far as to take over when I was sleeping, causing an uproar around the castle or finding a shifter to have his fun with. His sex drive was higher than it had ever been, and it was not what I wanted.

After Lamia, I had no desire to seek out any females. I didn't want them touching me. It felt wrong. I still had nightmares, and she had been the only one to soothe them back into the darkness from whence they came. Like tendrils of evil seeping from my aura, she would push them back. Locking them away until they managed to find a crack and slither through again.

Rhett's phone rang, pulling my attention back to the room. He stood up, taking it out of his back pocket, ready to answer it, when the phone fell from his hands and he dropped to the floor. Josiah quickly went to him, concerned for his best friend.

Rhett's body began to shake, and a warning growl rumbled from him. He snapped his eyes up. That's when I saw that they were black, and the barely visible white mark of a cross settled in his eyes.

"Don't touch him!" I ordered Josiah, and he stepped back immediately, his beast trying to fight the command as he worried for his friend. All I thought about was the last time I had seen this, the night Hunji attacked me and Petra. "He may be going feral," I offered a reason for my command.

Rhett's body began to shake and he clambered to his knees, throwing his head back. His eyes were open and trained on the ceiling. Stretching his arms out wide, he began speaking in a voice that was foreign to my ears.

"I call upon the power of the Knights, your brother needs

you. Take his pain and lessen the burden, share it and give back your strength. My Queen commands this of you."

Then he began to count 'One, two, three, four, five, six, seven...'

I looked at Josiah, then back to Rhett. "What is happening?" Josiah asked. I could hear the unease in his voice as he swept his hands through his hair, he was scared. I could tell he wanted to go to his friend, but because of my command, he couldn't.

I scratched my beard, then smoothed it down as I looked at my gamma in a state of distress, observing the scene in front of me. Rhett's phone rang again. "Answer it," I told Josiah.

"Hello.... Ria, umm he can't come to the phone. He is, ugh... busy." I listened to him converse and snapped my eyes to him. "What! The same thing is happening to Rhett right this very instance!" Josiah's eyes met mine and he swallowed loudly. "Yes, okay." He hung up.

"Lamia was suspended in mid-air, her wolf talking through her, saying the same thing as Rhett," Josiah told me, biting his bottom lip and shifting uncomfortably where he stood.

Rhett didn't have a wolf, so who's voice was he speaking with? I cast my eyes back to my gamma, who hadn't moved from his position and was still counting.

'Twenty-nine, thirty, thirty-one...'

"Ria said to let him finish whatever he is doing." I nodded my head and kept observing Rhett.

I saw claws extend from his hands, and his teeth poked out over his bottom lip. When he reached one hundred, his body collapsed, and his eyes rolled into the back of his head.

Rhett was still a mystery. He had no wolf, yet when the

powers from the mark of the knight pushed through, he grew claws and canines. He was an anomaly, a wolf-less shifter. He was interesting, and my wolf had been studying him for some time now.

"Take him down to the cells until he cools off and wakes up, we don't want a repeat of Hunji" I commanded my beta. My hand found my beard and rubbed my chin through the thick hair again as I contemplated this new development.

Chapter 35 – The Bond of the Knights

TOBIAS

Hunji and I were walking behind Mike and Jonda on our way back to the Inn. We had just come from a meeting with Alpha John, Jonda's brother, where we had been discussing where the three units of warriors would stay when they arrived tomorrow.

After learning that Vargr was an alpha to a kingdom in Bhakhil, the information supplied by Finnegan and related to us by Mathias, Mike didn't want to wait another minute to head out and find King Kellen. Every second was a delay in bringing his friend home, so Jonda secured a charter boat for us and we were to leave first thing in the morning.

Hunji and I were not keen on the idea that Jonda would be accompanying us. She couldn't shift, and her werewolf abilities were barely there, making her more human than shifter. It was too dangerous for her, and we did not want to have to worry about another body.

Mike, on the other hand, was so besotted with her that he overruled us and was excited that his little love interest would be joining us on the journey. They had been joined at the hip since he took her to bed. I didn't care so much, but Hunji had shaken his head and said that he and Jonda were a bad idea. That the Moon Goddess had not paired them, and it would only end in tragedy. Luckily, the idiot had enough sense to demand that once we arrived at the port, she was to stay there and wait for our troops. Who would follow behind us and arrive two days later.

It was smart to not all travel together. It would draw a lot less attention to us. If Kellen was where Finnegan had told us, the last thing we wanted was for this Vargr to get wind that we were on our way to rescue the Wolf King. No, it was better to be inconspicuous. Though the three of us butted heads more often than not, we worked well together, the three of us being a small unit of our own. Of course, I was the biggest and baddest, being the only bear shifter in our threesome.

"When we get back to the room, you better make good on your promises Beta," Jonda giggled playfully, whispering to Mike, unaware that we could hear her and the sly seductiveness of her voice.

I looked at Hunji, who shrugged his shoulders, and I rolled my eyes at his none reactive demeanor. The dude was way too laid back in some instances and way too tense in others. There was no in-between with Hunji. What annoyed me the most was how I could never tell what he was thinking. He was so closed off that I didn't think he even knew what emotion was.

I couldn't count how many times I have tried to rile him up, purposely trying to get on his last nerve and poking fun at him. Still, he would look at me with those dark and ominous eyes. They were like pieces of onyx, so dark they looked permanently black, like his wolf was just hovering below the surface, ready to take control at any second.

"Get a room, you two," Hunji yelled at Mike and Jonda, his face blank and tone even. Yet again, he lacked any trace of emotion. The most I had ever seen him show that he had any kind of personality was when he spoke to Lamia or on the rare occasion he would joke with Mike.

Maybe he just didn't like me. Maybe it was because he was older? Only four years older than me, but his soul cried out that he was ancient and had the knowledge of a priest. Not that I cared, well, maybe just a little. "Why don't you like me?" My thoughts spilled out like diarrhea. I hadn't meant to say it out loud, but I guess I was a little insecure and wanted to know.

"I don't dislike you." He deadpanned. I waited for more. But that was it.

"You never try to hang out with me or start up a conversation unless it is business!" I shot back at him, determined to get the truth from him.

"Tobias, you're reading too much into it. Don't take it personally." He stopped walking and turned to face me. I also halted in my tracks - Mike and Jonda unaware that we had stopped. "I don't dislike you, I just don't get you. You squander your life partying like there's no tomorrow. Not caring who it affects or how your poor choices reflect on your King and Queen. When Riocht is finished, we will all be living there and you cannot bring your playboy, fuckboy attitude with you." Once he finished reaming my ass out, leaving me there to stand stunned at his honesty - he began walking again.

I wish I had never asked.

"You are such a hypocrite!" I rebuked him. "You think you are all high and mighty like you are some powerful wolf when really, you are nothing but a sheep. A follower. You let your queen think for you and blindly follow her instructions. Just because I like to have a good time doesn't mean I am not loyal. I am not hurting anyone! Yet you - a wolf who can't even look a woman in the eye - dare to judge me?" I was angry now. If he wanted to get my beast in a tizzy, well, he had succeeded.

"I don't care what you do, Tobias! I just wish you would be a little more responsible about it." Hunji bit back with a strained voice. Now I was getting a reaction. Exactly what I was looking for.

"What and be boring like you? I mean really, Hunji, who are you? No one knows anything about your past. Is your name even Hunji? Is there a last name to go with that?" I spat, letting my beast show in my eyes, pushing the queen's second just that little more.

A growl ripped from Hunji, and so quick, he had me by the neck and dropped my ass to the floor. I was a good few inches taller than him and had a lot more meat on me, but the dark wolf loomed over me, his eyes fully black. He bared his canines at me, and I saw the dark and dangerous wolf I had heard whispers about.

"What the fuck is going on with you two? Hunji, let him go!" I heard Mike shouting, but Hunji's grip tightened on me, crushing my windpipe - stopping my lungs from filling with much-needed air. Not soon enough, Hunji's grip finally loosened, and his hand was removed from my neck along with the force of his weight. I coughed while gasping for air.

"Fuck." I finally let out. "Your fucking unhinged." I thought out loud, thinking this was how King would have reacted before he found Lamia. Completely out of control. Hunji had a long fuse, but I had lit the end and found out just how explosive he could be. It must have killed him to lose his cool and show me his not-so-tempered side.

When I looked into his eyes as his fingers had tightened around my thick neck, I saw the look of murder. A man so broken - that he would not have cared if he had taken my life. A man who is said to have only killed while defending his queen. I was told he doesn't like to take a life.

I scoffed to myself. That was not what I had just witnessed. More like he is afraid of losing that precious control he holds onto so dearly. Hunji was so intent on not letting people see what he is truly capable of, that he forgets we are all beholden to our own dark skeletons. Maintaining the level of control he seems to have will be his undoing one of these days.

I didn't like boats to begin with, but now I really didn't want to have to spend other two-plus days on a charter with Hunji.

Hunji stormed off towards the Inn, and Mike offered me a hand and pulled me up from the ground. "Dude," he said, scratching his neck and looking a little embarrassed. "I guess no one ever told you Hunji is the only one to go toe to toe with Lamia and knock her off her feet?" He gave a small chuckle and wrapped his arm around Jonda when she came to stand next to him. Their level of infatuation was sickening, and the smell of their arousals was making me crave my own pussy to devour. I wondered if Mike would share his little bit.

I had heard that Hunji was a force to be reckoned with, but now that I have experienced it for myself, I would not repeat the mistake of trying to rile him up. That was enough of a response for me. If I was a werewolf, my tail would surely be tucked between my legs.

I moved around Mike and Jonda, the young couple in love holding hands. Hunji was several yards in front, walking at a quick pace towards the Inn. I, too, just wanted to retreat to my room after embarrassing myself like that.

'He put you in your place,' my beast, Eyota, made fun of me. I told him to shut up and groaned internally at his mocking.

"Oh, my moons! Shit! Mike!" Jonda cried out in a desperate

voice. I turned to see what was wrong and saw Mike bent over on the ground, on his hands and knees, and breathing heavily. His body was shaking like he was hurt.

"Hunji!" I shouted, seeing Mike in agony and a worried Jonda bent over him. I heard Hunji's hurried footsteps before they abruptly stopped. I turned back in his direction. "Shit." Hunji was now in the same position as Mike, on all fours. Were they going to shift?

"Tobias, what's wrong with them?" Jonda was freaking out, and she wasn't the only one. Her hazel eyes blinked away frightened tears. Gone was the sassy bitch we saw in the room when Darrius was tortured. Gone were the googly eyes of love. Instead, her face was full of alarm and distress as she bit the bottom of those full lips.

I shook my head, I had no idea what was happening. I looked from Mike to Hunji as they both came up on their knees and stretched their arms out. Mike's eyes had turned black like Hunji's, and they both donned the mark of the knights in their irises. "Don't touch him," I said slowly to Jonda. Afraid they may wolf out, I had heard what Hunji did the night he received his 'knighthood'.

"What...?" She looked at me like I had three heads, her hands still on Mike trying to get his attention. Her worry seeped out and showed her vulnerability.

"Back away." This time I was more forceful with my words, and she hesitantly removed her hands from his face and shoulder and stood up, taking steps back toward me. No sooner than she had - they both cried out and the voice of their wolves growled out.

"I call upon the power of the Knights, your brother needs you. Take his pain and lessen the burden and share it and give back your strength. My Queen commands this of me." They said in unison, their claws extending and teeth elongating.

Then they began to count. 'One, two, three, four, five, six, seven...'

"Tobias," Jonda worried, taking my hand. "I don't understand..."

"Neither do I," I admitted. This was odd and scary, but my beast told me to leave them and let whatever was happening play out.

'Forty-seven, forty-eight, forty-nine, fifty...' They continued to count, and all we could do was watch.

The higher they counted, the more Hunji's veins began to pop, his muscles contorting like he was holding back something. I worried for Jonda. If either of them wolfed out, they could attack her and I couldn't fight off both, but I would do my damned best if it came down to it. I was no slouch, but these were high-ranking and skilled wolves.

Jonda pulled on my arm. "Oh my goddess, what is happening to him?" She gasped and turned my attention to Mike. Small arcs of blue electricity began sparking across his skin. He shredded his shirt, still counting, eyes wide and towards the sky and spaced out. The small currents licked his skin like a high voltage coursed through him.

'One hundred.' They both said at the same time, and as if on a queue, a huge clap of thunder resonated through the clear sky and a bolt of lightning came down, striking Mike in the chest. I wasn't sure who screamed louder, me or Jonda.

Hunji's body had slumped to the floor and Mike dropped just after him. Both lay unconscious in the middle of the street. The hum of the thunder and the strike of lightning left a buzz in the air. An eerie quiet engulfed our surroundings.

I didn't realize that Jonda and I had jumped into each

other's arms, gripping the other tightly in fright, until we came to our senses and pushed away from each other. I scrubbed a hand over my face, and Jonda gnawed at her lip nervously and kept giving me side glances.

"Help me move them," I told her with a hushed voice. She couldn't lift either one of them on their own, so we would have to move one and come back for the other. Luckily, we had almost reached the Inn and it was mere steps away. "Pick up his other arm." I pointed to Mike as he was closer to us.

Jonda stepped forward and poked one of her dainty nail-clad fingers on his arms, jumping back. I couldn't help but chuckle at her reaction. "Shut up. I thought he might... you know, still be... I thought he might electrocute me. This isn't funny Tobias." The woman was feisty, but she was right, he may very well have been still 'active'.

She bent her head down to his chest, pulling her auburn hair to the side. "What are you doing, woman?" I asked with confusion.

"What does it look like? Listening for a heartbeat, idiot." I again chuckled at her frustration, forgetting she did not have the advanced hearing of a shifter due to her wolf being dormant.

"He is good. I can hear it from here, or I would be in a total state of panic. Lamia would have my balls if I let either of them die. Besides, I'm pretty sure this had something to do with her seeing as their mark heated up and their eyes held the mark of a knight."

"The mark of... what?" She looked at me, scowling. Oh yeah, she had no idea.

"Let's get them indoors, and I will explain all this weird shit to you," I said, grabbing Mike's arm and gesturing for her to grab the other.

"Creepy shit." She grumbled as we hoisted him from the ground and began dragging him back to the Inn.

We left Mike just inside the door and went back for Hunji. After getting back with Hunji, I carried them one at a time into my room. Jonda and I took a seat at the small table provided and she opened up a bottle of whisky she had stolen from the bar downstairs, not even bothering with glasses she took a long pull and then offered the bottle to me.

"So, what is the mark of a knight?" Jonda asked as she leaned back in the rickety wooden chair, taking another swig from the bottle, then running her perfectly manicured red nails through her hair and ruffling it up a bit.

I began to tell her from the beginning what I knew, which wasn't much of everything. I personally didn't understand it either, only knowing what I did from what Lamia and King had told me. By the end of my tale, Jonda sat there with an expression of pure disbelief, and for a few minutes just sat and stared at me.

"You're telling me, King Mathias and Queen Lamia both have the blood of gods in them?" She rubbed her temple and pulled her eyebrows together. "They are gods? And the knights are a gift to protect their Queen?"

"Something like that," I replied, totally over all this shit. "They are demigods, or at least King is. I guess when these two morons wake up, they can tell us what the fuck happened."

Chapter 36 – The Third Gift

KELLEN
DAY 17 OF THE GAMES

"Kellen Moon." A voice in the void whispered. The Moon Goddess was calling me home. "Kellen Moon," the soft feminine voice called my name. It was so calming, so comforting, that I began to search for it in the darkness.

A faint glow began to emerge from the depths of the surrounding blackness. It was warm and it pulled me in. I went to it, letting the slowly brightening light pull me in. I felt content and happy as my bones began to warm the closer I got to the ever-growing glow of luminosity.

"Kellen." The voice was a little louder, and as the darkness around me faded and turned to a cozy and agreeable brightness, I squinted my eyes, suddenly finding myself in a well-lit room.

I looked around, finding my surroundings familiar as I cast my vision over the rows upon rows of books. "Kellen!" This time the voice was abrupt. I swung around, expecting the person to be right behind me. Instead, my gaze landed on a pair of high-back leather chairs seated in front of a roaring fireplace, the flames licking out like they were reaching for me.

"Come closer." That was when I noticed a figure had been seated in one of the chairs. A hand reached out to the table in between the two seats, picking up a dainty tea cup. I began to move my feet, approaching the figure whose back was to me. Not because she said so but because I already knew who she was.

I was in the library, the same one I had seen in my and Lamia's dreams. The same one Ashe had visited Lamia in. I was not scared, but I was confused about why she was here, and why I was not meeting with the Moon Goddess who would walk me to the gates of the afterlife. I felt something warm and wet tickle my hand and looked down to find Conri, my wolf, nudging me with his nose. His silver fur glistened from the glow of the fire that danced across his moon-kissed fur.

I took a seat in the available chair, the leather warm against my bare back, and took my first look at Ashe, mesmerized by her long white, almost silver hair that hung past her waist. Her skin was as dark as the night sky, and her eyes were violet, like those of Finnegan's. She was beautiful despite her age, and I couldn't pull my stare from her.

"You are flattering me, young king." She smiled.

"Why am I here?" I asked when she said nothing else.

"Before I let you have your second gift, I must ask if you are willing to accept your third." She said, setting down the teacup, her ethereal eyes not averting from mine.

"I thought I was dead, I felt my heart stop," I said, still puzzled as to why I was here and not walking in the afterlife.

"Kellen," she smiled again, this time with pity. "Tandie gave you the gift of life; you were never going to die, not truly, or at least that will depend on the end of this conversation. Although, you did surprise me by accepting your death so easily. But this had to happen in order for you to receive your third gift."

"What is the third gift?" I put my hand out and Conri nuzzled up to me, giving me calming vibes. I didn't like how this conversation was going right now, never mind at the end of it. Ashe was confusing and spoke in riddles.

Instead of answering my questions, she asked me another one. "Are you angry with the Moon Goddess, Kellen?"

I thought about it, was I angry with her? If I had to be truly honest, then yes, I was. First, she gave me Lamia and then took her away, throwing salt on the wound and mating her to Zane. I scowled because it was the Moon Goddess who took Zane from Lamia and her unborn child, then gave her a mate she hated at first, deepening that wound and overlooking me for a second time when it was plain as day how much I loved her.

Loved. I do love Lamia still, but finding Tala had shifted that love, my heart now belonged to someone else. Or at least it did until the Moon Goddess took her away too. Did I hate the Moon Goddess?

"Despise would be a better word," I said after mulling over my thoughts and not finding a trace of the emotion of hate when I thought of the goddess. Despise, yes. Hate, no.

"What if I told you, you were always meant to be mated to Lamia?" Ashe pursed her lips knowingly, her violet eyes staring into mine.

"But we share a bloodline. You told this to Lamia." I frowned at her, not understanding what she was getting at. All these mind games were only working up the tension in my body. "You told her we were never meant to be mated."

"That's not quite true," she sighed and leaned forward, resting her elbow on the arm of the chair and her chin in her hand. "You may share a bloodline, but your wolves were always meant to be mated." She pulled her lips in a tight smile that didn't reach her eyes. "She was never meant to be mated to Zane, however, you were a possibility. Unfortunately, the gods like to play games, and they have played enough games with my children." She waved her hand in the air dismissively when she spoke of the gods.

"Are you not a god?"

"No." She scoffed, "I would be considered a demigod, but that's beside the point. Enough about me, let's talk about you." She got up and walked over to the fireplace, throwing another log on there, the heat from the flames increasing and drawing out beads of sweat on my forehead. She couldn't possibly be cold.

Ashe stood there and rubbed her hands together, and I watched her intently, waiting for further explanation. "The Morrigan sisters, Nandie, Tandie, and Andie, who you have yet to meet, are three sisters born to a goddess, a goddess who could not only transform but predict the future and give life to those close to death. Each sister has their own special... power, or gift if you prefer. Nandie gave you the gift of strength, she is also an oracle like me. Tandie gave you the gift of life, she can heal anything or anyone, and Andie... She is a shifter like you, but can take the form of any animal. She will offer you the gift of fate."

Ashe paused. Waiting to see my reaction, but I gave none.

"You have Morrigan blood coursing through veins, Kellen. That is why you were chosen to be the most powerful knight. Morrigan and Guardian blood are what makes your family royals. It's what makes you so powerful."

"If I was so powerful, how did I end up as a slave a million miles away from home?" I scoffed at her and the thought of her thinking I was so powerful. I had died. It didn't seem very powerful to me.

"How else would you meet your mate?" She deadpanned sarcastically, giving me a look as if I should have realized this. "Your mate is a red wolf; she comes from the first generation of Morrigan's. Bringing the bloodline back to its purest form can only create a generation of werewolves' unseen and uncontested."

Did she mean... our children if Tala and I were to have pups?

"Yes!" She threw her hands up in the air. "Your third gift will be to accept fate. Should you refuse, I will release you to the Moon Goddess. Should you accept - I will return you to your realm to fight for your mate."

"What do mean fight for my mate?" I stood up suddenly, defensive.

"Your mate needs you, and without you, she will be in trouble." Ashe came and sat back down in the chair. "You may be a Knight of the Queen, but that is not your sole purpose. Accept fate's gift and in many moons, you will be called upon to defend your realm. It is what the Queen carries you must protect, for the gods have already chosen. And I am afraid I cannot intervene."

Ashe paused, her gaze looked towards the fire, lost in a faraway thought. "Let me tell you the story of Inanna and Conri," she said, and began to recite a tale as ancient as she. I listened intently until she had finished. A greater understanding of our wolves and what Lamia and I meant to each other.

"How do I get back?" It was a stupid question, I knew it as soon as I asked it, but my haste to save my mate from whatever fate the gods had bestowed upon her was my priority. The rest of Ashe's words going in one ear and out the other.

She chuckled. "Open your eyes silly."

*****

My eyes shot open, my chest heaved, and I gasped for air, gulping it into my starving lungs. The first thing I noticed was the rotten stench of flesh and dried, crusted blood. I gagged and rolled to the side, blinking my eyes at the brightness. I could taste death, the smell so strong I began to puke.

Next, I noticed the pain in my back as the heat of the air hit it. I groaned, still trying to focus my eyes.

"Took you long enough, been waiting two days for you to wake up." I heard the condescending voice of a female speak, but my sight was still hazy, trying to look for the source while still emptying my guts all over... what?

My hands were grabbing something squishy, a few hard edges, and... whatever it was, was making my stomach turn over. I shook my head, still trying to get myself up. "For fucks sake, what is that smell?" I cried out when the stench was too much to bear.

The female cackled in amusement at me. Finally, my eyes began to focus, and I was able to see what it was I was trying to grab in my efforts to climb out of the goddess-awful smell. "Oh, my fucking moons!" I yelled in absolute disgust, heaving at the sight before me.

I turned my head from the very, very aged bodies, but it was a wasted effort. I seemed to be in a shallow pit of remains, some skeletons, some still fleshy, and others dried out. It was the rot on the flesh and the squishy ones that were giving off the nastiest thing I had ever smelled in my whole life. "It's not fucking funny! Help me out of here." I was annoyed that she was sitting there perched at the top of this grave site, having herself a good old time at my expense.

"I'm sorry. I can't." She said between giggles.

"Give me your fucking hand," I ordered, reaching my hand towards her. "I just came back from the dead, if I'm in here for another second the smell might kill me off."

At first, the young girl looked pissed that I had given her an order, but then her face fell, and her attitude changed when I mentioned dying.

"Well, we can't have that; Ashe has put a lot of faith in you, young king." She stood up straight with her hands on her hips and her eyes trained on me, looking very serious suddenly. "I am Andie, and I give you your third gift. Fate. By accepting this gift, you pledge to answer when you are called upon by fate. Your fate lies with your queen. Are you ready to accept your gift, Wolf King?"

Ashe said I had to accept my fate, whenever that may be. Hadn't that been exactly what I had been doing my whole life? I nodded my head. "Yes, I accept my fate. Now give me your hand."

"Oh right, okay." She giggled and offered down her dainty hand. I grabbed onto it and used her and my legs to climb out of the pit, cringing every time my foot met part of a juicy corpse.

Once I was up, Andie let go of my hand and gave herself a full body shake, making a face of revulsion.

It was almost dark. "How long have I been here for?" I asked Andie.

"Two days," I must have made a repulsed face. "Yeah, two days in that." She added, pointing to the shallow pit I had just climbed out of.

I took in Andie, she was much younger looking than her sisters, but their eyes were the same and the shape of their faces hadn't changed, just the ages they decided to display. I looked to the sky, breathing in as much fresh air as possible. I felt... different.

'*That's because we are,*' Conri awoke from the back of my mind.

"Well, have fun, it's time for me to leave. I wish you luck, young king." Andie giggled and before I could say a word, she transformed into a black raven, spread her wings, and flew off into the distance. Leaving me there not only stunned and alone, but also feeling slightly helpless.

I looked around, having no idea where I was. I saw the great wall that surrounded the palace compound, comprehending that I was outside the walls. How ironic. I would have done anything to get out of there, and now I find myself thinking about how to get back in there.

I felt a slight buzzing sensation in my head along with a scratching sensation. I tried to ignore it, thinking it was a side effect of being dead for two days and my body laying amongst the corpses.

'*I feel free,*' I heard Conri again.

I agreed, something definitely felt more... I felt lighter, like a weight had been lifted from me. I breathed in and began to try and alleviate some of the building tension in my head, which had now turned to a low thumping.

'*Conri, can you feel that?*' I questioned my wolf

'*Yes, our block is up in our mind.*' He replied carelessly.

Our block? I now questioned myself. I focused, removing

the block from my mind, taking slightly more effort since I hadn't been able to use that ability for the last three months.

Suddenly my head began to fill with voices and all their sentiments. I shut it down quickly before it was too much and concentrated on the first voice I heard. They were mumbling to me through a mind link. No it couldn't be, could it? I reached behind my head and felt for the chip. I could still feel it, right there under the skin, but if I was receiving someone else's thoughts... That must mean? The chip was inactive?

I focused on my beta's face and opened up a link to him, praying my wolf was no longer suppressed. *Mike* I said, and waited a few moments. When I got no reply, I tried again *Mike, for fucks sake if you are there...*

Holy shit! Kellen? The relief that filled me was like nothing else as my best friend's voice filled my head.

Yah, it's me. I sighed thankfully through the link, not even sure what to say. I was overwhelmed with gratefulness.

Mother of the moons, dude! I thought you had died, we all felt the loss. Where the fuck are you? Sounding just as relieved as I was, he shot question after question. I could not only hear the desperation in his voice, but I also felt his relief and the strain my disappearance had put on him lifted.

I'm in a place called Bhakhil. Jack and Oliver fucking sold me! I growled out back to him, recalling the whole ordeal on the boat.

We just landed at the port, we are two to three days away. Hang tight, we are coming to get you. He said and then added, *It is so good to hear your voice. Fuck, man you have had us worried.*

*Me too, brother. I will explain more later. Keep the link

open. Right now I have to figure out how to get back into the palace compound.*

What, why? If you are out, start heading our way... I cut him off, he didn't know what was at stake. It wasn't just me.

My mate is in there. Your future queen.

Oh, was all he said, but I didn't miss the shock in that 'oh'. Mike realized I couldn't just walk away, not from my mate, his future queen.

I was fucking elated, over the moon. Now that the inhibitor chip seemed to be disabled and I could mind-link again, shit was about to get real. Now I just needed to figure out how I was going to get back on the other side of this wall and get my fucking girl.

I stood there looking up at the gigantic wall, the barrier between me and Tala, going over my options.

'Maybe go knock on the front door?' Conri said, and it wasn't that bad of an idea. At least it was an option. 'Or wait three days,' he countered.

The story of: INANNA & CONRI

Told to Kellen by Ashe/Odeia

Many moons ago, back when the realm was still young, the gods still walked amongst the humans. In a land called Heartme, which you know as the Sea Dogs Island, the goddess Inanna wandered about the mortal realm of shifters and humans, and met a mortal king called Conrad.

Their love was forbidden, as Inanna's father had already promised her to a war god. Yet Inanna could not deny her obsession with the handsome, fierce king. Likewise, Conrad was enthralled with her beauty, falling in love with her at first sight. Her black hair and green eyes were the most beautiful thing he had ever laid his eyes on.

The gods were angry that she had abandoned her position, choosing to stay in the mortal realm in the arms of a mere human. Anu, Inanna's father, stripped her of her immortality when he found out she bore the child of a human and banished her from the realm of heavens.

When Anu cursed King Conrad the same way Zeus cursed my father. His soul would return in the form of a wolf, to be reborn over and over until the end of time. For many moons Inanna and Conrad lived happily, the king's trusted red knights protecting his goddess queen and their son. Eventually, Inanna gave birth to another, a daughter who possessed immense power. It was said that the child held the power of life and death within her blood and could shift into a wolf as silver as the moon.

When Anu found this out, he killed Conrad so he and Inanna would never be reunited again. He forgot the curse he had put in place and that the king's soul would be reborn into another.

At this time, Anu and Zeus went to war. Anu had killed one of Zeus' most precious humans; Zeus wanted an eye for an eye and set his sights on taking the demigod child. With Conrad dead, Inanna fled far away with her children and only King Conrad's most trusted knight, Cuchulainn Mac-Tire.

Inanna's mother took pity on her and granted her one wish. 'I wish for Conri,' is what she told her mother, devastated by the loss of her love. Her mother granted her wish, giving Inanna her immortality back.

The Moon Goddess, Nana, at this time, took Conri under her wing and granted him a soul mate upon his rebirth. That soul mate was Inanna.

One night on a full moon, Conrad was in his wolf form and was hunted by the humans and killed, yet again leaving Inanna alone. Inanna begged her to gift her with the spirit of a wolf so she could be reborn with Conrad for eternity.

The Moon Goddess granted her wish, but it was up to Conrad and Inanna to find each other over time. For centuries, that was what they did - each rebirth they became further and further apart until they both descended to the heavens and stayed in a prolonged sleep. One that would last until your and Lamia's births.

It is said that the great-granddaughter of the firstborn werewolf and the son of King Conrad repeated history and fell in love. Little did the gods know that the son Inanna and

Conrad had, was also born a shifter. A gift granted by the Moon Goddess to her grandson. They were fated to be mated.

That is how the story of Riocht became. It was my great-grandchild that was mated to the son of the great King Conri, and that is how you and Lamia are related. That no matter when your spirit animals are reborn; you are bound to find each other. Your wolves' spirits bonded through an endless time. They will always need each other; their love runs that deep.

Yet this time, it seems the Moon Goddess had a different plan for my descendant and her daughter's spirit wolf. She paired her with a demigod, and you to the daughter of Conri's most trusted Red Knight.

Your Queen of Shifters has already risen. Now, young king, it is your turn to rise. To protect what the queen will hold within her. Your Fate.

Chapter 37 – My Hero

<u>TALA</u>
DAY 19 OF THE GAMES

My heart was broken, shattered into pieces. My wolf had not stopped whimpering, and I had not stopped sobbing. The pain I felt was indescribable. I felt his life end, his essence fade, and I felt it to my very core. Maybe because Kellen hadn't marked me and the mating process wasn't complete was why my soul had not ripped in two.

Maybe that was the reason I was still alive. But not for long. The air in this box was running out and my breaths had become shallow. How long had I been in here? I didn't know.

All I knew was that I had lost my mate before I even knew him, but that didn't lessen the love I felt for him. All the hope I had, died that night. All that effort and planning for nothing; wasted on a whim. The Moon Goddess had taken him from me just as fast as she had given him. I could never forgive her.

I had been locked up in a small metal, coffin-sized box. Jack had dragged me down here as soon as my father gave the command for Kellen to be whipped. I had begged and pleaded for mercy, knowing this would be a torturous experience and the end of me. I had seen my father use this method of torture before. Others had only lasted a day or two at the most when put in the hot box.

I just wanted to lay there and die. There was no point in living if I couldn't share that life with my soul mate.

I had tried to mind-link Jasper and Eloise, but my wolf was weak, and they seemed to have their blocks up. Or the hot steel box was preventing me from communicating with them. I wiped my face of the now dried and crusted tears. I had no more to give. The heat had dried me up and dehydrated me to the point that I couldn't even sweat.

The image of Kellen being hung from the wall flashed before my eyes and I cringed, grasping my chest as a hot and sharp burn flared through my heart. The sound of the first crack of the whip echoed in my mind, and my wolf whimpered at my thoughts again.

I heard footsteps approaching and stilled my heavy body, listening to the steps get closer. The clang of a lock rattled, and the lid to the sweltering box opened. I squinted my eyes at the dim light and gulped in the fresh air. Two guards stood over me, ones I didn't recognize.

"You have been summoned by the Alpha," one of them said, not even able to look me in the eye. I glanced at the other whose hands moved - I noticed the gesture he made, crossing his pinkies. They hauled me up out of the box, my stiff limbs aching and my legs shaking from lack of hydration.

I was dragged back into the palace from the back of the gardens. Neither of the guards said a word, and I couldn't say anything as my lips were parched and my throat was as dry as the barren lands outside our walls. I didn't react, I couldn't. I had nothing left, I felt nothing but numb. Vargr could do whatever he liked. He already killed me. I was but a shell. The question was, why had he kept me alive? Why not leave me in the box to die? Whatever the reason was, it could not be good. Vargr was a monster, which just meant he had something worse to torture me with.

Vargr was waiting for me in his office, along with Jack, Oliver, and Beta Baron. They had a battered and bruised Teal kneeling in the center of the floor. I cast each one of them a hateful glance, willing them to burst into flames. Then I looked at Teal, whose eyes caught mine for but a moment.

The look of defeat and sadness had my heart fluttering in fear.

I cried out when Vargr grabbed me by the hair and yanked me back until I was kneeling in front of Teal. 'Where is Jasper?' Was the only thing I could think of when I tried to look around and read the room.

"Fucking ungrateful whore!" Vargr growled out, his words full of venom and hate. The slap was brutal; my head jerked to the side and I could taste the metallic blood from my split lip. I wanted to spit the blood out in his face, but instead, I licked the coppery liquid, the moisture on my tongue feeling warm.

I wasn't a coward, but I wanted to live. At least to see his downfall.

I saw Teal flinch, reacting to the scent of my blood that had coated my bottom and lip. He said nothing; he knew it could get worse. Him having an outburst would do nothing, neither of us were in a position to do much.

"I gave you a chance," Vargr ranted while pacing the room, "I was going to make you Jasper's Luna because you held alpha blood. But just like your good for nothing mother, you fucked shit up!" His voice raised an octave or two as he worked himself and his wolf up. "No matter, King Panja has a daughter. You have been replaced." He took a few paces away from me before abruptly turning back around and getting in my face again.

"You were never really my daughter," he said with disgust. "Did you ever wonder why I favored Jasper and hated you? You would have married my son." He began laughing, while I found none of this humorous and refused to give him any reaction. He had just told me Jasper was his son. I cast a side glance at Beta Baron. At first glance he looked unfazed, but a closer look showed that he was holding his wolf back. He was just as much a victim as everyone else.

"I'm feeling generous," Vargr clapped his hands together. "I fucking love a family reunion! Before you die, are there any last words you would like to say to your now slave daughter?" Vargr then laughed in Teal's face, and Jack yanked my hair again, making me look up at him.

"Tell daddy you love him, because… It's me you will be calling daddy later." He smirked, licking his lips like the disgusting predator he was. All the air left my body when Jack slithered those words out, his tone holding a promise.

Goddess, please no. I closed my eyes as any strength left in my body evaporated in that second. Please, goddess, don't let him give me to Jack. Let me die now. I have seen Jack's handy work. What he did to my mother was nothing, child's play compared to what he was capable of. I glanced at Oliver, unable to read his expression but gave Jack a narrowed looked of displeasure.

"My name is Teal Mac-Tire, Alpha of the Sea Dogs pack and Knight of the Red Branch. My wolf is Cuchulainn, who lives to serve King Conri, and he will be reborn. Tala Mac-Tire, you are my daughter and I love you." I looked into Teal's eyes. He had already accepted his death. I had not.

"NO!" I wailed, screaming and sobbing, trying to get away when without warning, Vargr plunged a knife into the back of Teal's head, and his clawed hand simultaneously punched a hole into the front of his chest, ripping his heart out.

I couldn't even put into words the emotions I was going through: disgust, hate, fear, sorrow, despair, and lastly, love. Love, as I held Teal's eyes and watched the warmth fade from them. The bright cerulean orbs had lost their gleam and their light was fading. A lone tear escaped his eye, trailing down his cheek, his face full of sorrow, the sadness drawing out my own tears as I watched his features twist with pain. I rocked back and forth, sobbing for his fate before his body, as if in slow motion, slumped to the floor.

"Arrggghh! You're a monster!" I yelled out. "All of you are monsters. May Aodh curse you all!" I screamed.

"I wanted to kill you, but Jack convinced me otherwise." Vargr's spit sprayed from his mouth as he bent down to my eye level and seethed through his clenched jaw. He clicked his finger to Beta Baron, who approached with a syringe in his hands. He stabbed the needle in my neck, emptying the vile liquid. The burn began almost immediately, and I knew he had just hit me with wolfsbane.

"She is yours," Vargr growled out to Jack. His harsh tone and bloody hand waived in dismissal, still holding Teal's heart.

Jack ripped me up by my hair and grabbed my arm harshly, his fingers digging in relentlessly, and dragged me from the room. I gave Oliver a glare, the man who said he wouldn't betray me or let anything happen to me. I was right not to believe a word he said and didn't feel anything about him, his lack of action not bothering me in the least, as it was what I expected from a man like him.

"I CURSE YOU ALL! I CURSE YOU ALL!"

I screamed over and over as I was brutally dragged down the hall toward the back staircase and then yanked up them,

Jack heading in the direction of my room. But it wasn't my room he took me to. It was a room further down the hall, one I had not been in, in a very long time.

When we got there, Jack yelled at two of the guards. "Keep these doors shut and don't let her out!" He commanded like he had some authority. The guards just nodded at him and then gave me a distasteful look. "She is mine now," he said with a cruel chuckle. He opened the door, threw me in, and slammed it shut. Leaving me alone.

I immediately began looking for a way out. My first option was to try to open the window. It had been sealed shut; there was no way of opening it. I turned to look around the room. The queen size bed lay against one wall covered in dust covers. Next to it was a dusty crib with faded blue blankets and a mobile made of stars and moons hanging over it.

Once as a child, Jasper and I had ventured into this room, playing hide and seek. Vargr had gone nuts at me when he found out, telling me to keep the fuck out or he would rip my throat out. I was nine then, and it was the first time I had ever truly seen his anger. He slapped me so hard and then kicked me in the ribs. I could never understand at that age what I had done wrong and why I was the only one punished.

As I looked around, and after reading some of my sister's diaries, I knew this was the room my older brother would have had. If he had lived. Shayna never mentioned anything more in her daries except that her younger brother had died.

I picked up the little blue ceramic lampshade and tossed it at the window, hoping it would smash the glass. It bounced off instead, and the ceramic lamp crashed to the floor, shattering. I cried out in frustration and then noticed the door on the opposite side of the room.

Opening it, I found a small bathroom with a single white sink, tub, and toilet. Immediately I turned the tap on and began gulping the water. I was so parched and weak, grateful for the lukewarm water. I began to cup the water in my hands and throw it at my face. Once I had had enough, I slumped to the floor.

'Mora,' I called out to my, wolf who stirred. *'Mora, help us.'* I begged her, my voice as I mentally spoke to my wolf was strained and full of despair.

'I am so weak.' Mora's reply came in a soft murmur. I had hoped the water would have helped, but with lack of food and being in that box, our strength had diminished. Yet again, I felt useless.

I sat on that bathroom floor for a while, head in my hands, and eventually gave up trying to get out of there. Maybe I could slip past the guards? I thought, but realized I couldn't even open the door. Jack had locked it behind him.

It was getting darker outside, and the moon had risen. The silver streams of light shone through the indestructible window. Jack would be coming back for me, I knew he would. I got up and began searching the room for anything I could use as a weapon. I tried to mind-link Jasper or anyone again, but I was still blocked, and I couldn't figure out why.

'The box had silver, that's why I am too weak.' Mora's voice filled my head. That and we had just been dosed with wolfsbane.

There was nothing here to defend myself with unless I could kill Jack with a stuffed toy. I thought about breaking the crib and using the wood to stab him with it, but that wouldn't do anything to Jack.

The lock on the door rattled and I scrambled into a corner, trying to make myself invisible. Jack's large and imposing frame filled the doorway, his eyes dark and menacing. I gulped at the sight of him. His beast was on the surface.

"I'm back to take what's mine." He growled, stalking toward me.

"Jack," I said with a lump in my throat. "Please, I have the location of the witch for you, if you…" I was cut off from my attempt to plea and bargain with him as he flashed in front of me and grabbed my neck.

His nose went to the crook, and he trailed his hot tongue up and over my cheek. "So innocent, so… sweet. I am going to ruin you, sweet princess. Over and over." He rasped in a low voice. I shuddered in fear, and he inhaled deeply again. "Fear just makes my beast want you even more. He relishes in the scent."

I squirmed. I was not going to go down without a fight, no matter how much I was trembling. I lifted my knee, clocking him in the groin. He let go of me and I took the opportunity to make a run for it. Jack was quicker and snatched me by the hair yet again, making me call out in pain, throwing me back against the wall. My head hit the stone surface with such force that I could see stars and black spots flashing before my eyes.

He threw me on the bed, pinning my hands above my head. "That is going to cost you, you bitch" He raged over me and took a clawed hand to my dress, tearing it apart. I screamed and kicked, trying to buck him off me. He punched me in the face and my body went limp as my head throbbed. His clawed hand scraped down the side of my arm, the heat was searing and blood oozed from the wounds. He let my hands go, and I heard the sound of his zipper and his pants falling to the floor.

I groaned and tried to roll away, grasping the edge of the bed to haul myself off it. His large hand wrapped around my ankle and dragged me back, flipping me over and cracking me in the face again. "If my beast doesn't kill you," he said manically, pinning my hands back over my head, "I will keep you, and every night I will fill you." He dug the nails of his other hand into the inside of my thigh and violently ripped my legs apart, seating himself between them while keeping a firm grip on my wrists.

I screamed at the pain. I screamed for what was to come. "Keep screaming, I like it when they scream." I had my head turned away and eyes shut, but when he said that, it wasn't him talking, it was his beast. I dared to look at him and what I found was Aodh, God of the Underground himself staring back at me with an evil grin. Eyes as black onyx, deep and monstrous.

"Kill me," I whispered when I felt the tip of his penis nudge my opening. His claws were digging into my wrists and thigh, his massive body pinned me, and the blood trickled from my open wounds. The stream of moonlight that poured in through the window bathed Jack's face, his black eyes glinting with pure evil as the devil shone through them. I closed mine tightly, preparing myself for what was about to happen. My wolf was clawing to come out, but she was still so weak that try as she might, she couldn't surface to defend me. My body had given up even if my mind hadn't, and I hoped to the goddess that he would kill me after.

The penetration of Jack's penis never came, but the warm flow of thick liquid poured onto my bare chest and face. I opened my eyes when Jack's body slumped heavily on top of me, then his body rolled off me. I shuddered when it hit the floor with a loud thud, and looked down at my blood-soaked naked body.

That shudder lasted, and I couldn't stop shaking. My whole body trembled, and I barely noticed the whimpers coming from my quivering lips. I had gone into shock.

Oliver.

He was picking me up off the bed, holding me close to him like a bride. I couldn't stop shaking and couldn't see for the tears, but I knew it was Oliver. I sobbed loudly and wrapped my heavy arms around his neck. I couldn't tell whose blood there was more of, mine or Jack's, there was that much covering me.

"I got you, princess. I promised I wouldn't let Jack hurt you." I found comfort in his words. He had kept his promise. I stole a look behind him and saw Jack's body on the floor. A pool of crimson surrounded him, and the dark gore was still seeping from the open wound on his neck. His eyes were wide, staring at the ceiling back to that deceiving angelic blue.

Oliver had saved me.

Jack could have killed me, or worse, he would keep me after raping and beating me beyond recognition. "Oliver." I sobbed hard, my voice shaking as much as the rest of me. But I managed to steady my breathing for a moment. "Thank you for saving me."

Chapter 38 – Adam

<u>TALA</u>
DAY 20 OF THE GAMES

Oliver had placed me in a warm bath and, after checking to make sure I was okay, left me to wash the evidence of Jack's horror off of me. I sat in the tub after refilling the water twice, scrubbing my limbs free of the red stains that had coated my body.

The bath helped to soothe my aches and shakes, and after replaying what happened to Kellen and Jack over and over like the nightmare it was, I began to feel my mind calm and sense my wolf getting stronger. I hadn't by any means come to terms with the fact my mate had died at the hands of Vargr or that Jack almost raped me, and of all people, it was Oliver who saved me.

Oliver. He saved me. Without collecting his end of the bargain. I palmed my face, trying to wash away the everlasting tension that was still wracking my body. As much as I appreciated Oliver's heroic rescue, I couldn't help but wonder why. Why would Oliver save me? Maybe because he hadn't collected his sacks of diamonds? That had to be it, because otherwise, he had no use for me.

Dawn had broken a few hours ago. I had had no concept of time, how long I had been sitting in this bathtub, or how many times I had refilled it. Making sure I washed every ounce of Jack from my skin.

As the wolfsbane began to wear off, my head started clearing and Eloise's voice filled my head. *Tala, are you okay?* Her gentle voice was like music to my ears.

Yes, I am in the old nursery. Can you get here? I asked her and added, *Can you bring me some clothes?*

She replied she would be with me in a few minutes, and true to her words, she came sliding through the bathroom door only a few minutes later with undergarments and a fresh dress. I climbed out of the tub, dried myself, and put on the clothes. My hands were still shaking slightly as I smoothed them over the blue cotton dress. My eyes began to well up as the color of the dress matched perfectly with the color of Kellen's eyes. A deep swimming blue that reminded me of the crystal clear oceans I had seen in books.

Eloise wrapped her arms around me, pulling me close, one hand stroking my hair in a motherly way like she was trying to stroke the sadness from me. "I got you, girl. You are okay now. He can't hurt you again." She whispered comfortingly to me.

"I'm not crying because of that monster," I sobbed. I couldn't care less about Jack, he was dead now. He may have shaken me up, but he would have never broken me. "Kellen" was all I had to say.

"I know, I know, but trust your best friend, everything will be okay." She stepped back and held me at arm's length. "Now for fucks sake, Tala, you are stronger than this. You will hide your heartbreak and hold your head up high, do you hear me?" I cocked my head at my best friend, not used to her being the stronger one and certainly not used to hearing her curse. She would make a wonderful Luna if she and Jasper were ever able to complete the bond. "I know about Teal," she gave me a sympathetic look.

"I'm going to kill him," I whispered to her, knowing she knew I was talking about Vargr. And I meant it. I would see his end and look into his eyes and laugh when he took his last breath. That man had taken everything from me, my childhood, my mother, my real father, my mate. And after reading Shayna's diaries, I had come to understand that he had taken everything from her too. Turning her into a dark and vengeful soul.

Vargr had so much to answer for. He used and abused his pack for decades, making omegas, hybrids, and humans slaves. Putting them into the mines to dig up his greed while they got nothing but scraps of leftover scraps. There were hundreds of pack members enslaved below the surface, forced to work down there and not see the light of day for days, starving.

Once dressed and calmed down, Eloise led me out of the bathroom. I looked around the pale blue nursery, my eyes landing on the side of the bed where Jack's body had now been removed, but the stain of his sins remained on the marbled tile. Although cleaned up, I could still see the caked red essence of his life ingrained into the grooves of the white tile.

Oliver was nowhere to be seen, and I wondered where he had gone.

"Who..." I wanted to ask who removed Jack's body, who cleaned up the blood, and where Oliver had gone. I felt safe with him. An annoyed growl came from my wolf.

Calm down, Mora. He saved us, nothing else. I chided my wolf; she thought I harbored some other feelings for the sly rogue. I definitely did not. I may feel safe with him around because of what happened, but I still didn't quite trust him, and I certainly wouldn't and couldn't look at him or feel anything more for him. My heart still belonged to Kellen. It always would.

"Don't worry about it, we have other things we need to deal with. Jasper and Cameron are waiting for us." Eloise said, patting my back as we headed out of the room. I gave it a quick once over before shutting the door behind me, wondering why this room still even existed and who my brother would have been.

"I want to see my mother first. Jasper can wait." I declared, taking off toward her suite. As we approached, we could hear shouting from her room. Eloise and I quickened our steps, hurrying towards the growingly heated words of two women in the midst of an argument.

"Oh princess, thank the gods you are ok!" Mildred, one of my mother's maids and a trusted ally came rushing from my mother's room as I heard the crash and shattering of a glass object. I pushed past her. "I tried to stop them, but..." Her words fell short as I took in the scene before me.

Alice, Jasper's mother, and my own mother were throwing curse words and objects at each other, the room was destroyed.

"For years I have kept you safe. For years I have helped you through everything your mate has done." Alice was seething at my mother, her face red and finger pointed towards the Luna. "You knew Jasper was his. He has a right to the Alpha title."

"He has no rights!" My mother yelled, her tone just as volatile. "The only reason he came to you was because I lost Adam! And do you not think I know it was you who poisoned me! It was you who drove him away in the first place! You and your goddess-damned jealousy, you tried to steal my life. Never happy with your mate, so you tried to take mine. Tell me, Alice, how did that work out for you?"

"What in Aodh's name is going on here?" I yelled, my voice louder and more prominent than either of theirs. A rush of adrenaline reared up, making the blood in my veins heat as I witnessed the two women stare each other down.

"You want to know? You really want to know?" Alice screeched like a banshee, her brown eyes flicking to me with a blaze of heat. "Your pathetic mother couldn't hold on to her mate or child. Vargr came to a real woman, a she-wolf that could give him an heir." Her words were like poison, dripping from her tongue like a drooling dog.

"Jasper may be an heir, but it was you who killed Adam. It was because of you that my wolf abandoned me. You killed my child and my wolf all in the name of greed, you shit on your mate by taking his alpha into your bed…"

"And your revenge was fucking a slave and having her?" Alice pointed in my direction.

My mother shook her head. "No, that was not revenge. That was beautiful. When Adam died, a piece of my soul died too. When you conceived Jasper, I was lost, still mourning the death of my son. When I woke up from my grief, I found the most beautiful man hidden amongst evil. His aura was strong and vibrant, everything I wanted Vargr to be. So, I took him and he gave me a princess, a she-wolf who would become powerful, a daughter who would right all Vargr's wrongs and save the people of Bhakhil."

The Luna took a step toward the Beta's wife. "You poisoned me, don't deny it. And when I shared my drink with Adam, you poisoned him too." My mother's blue-grey eyes stilled on Alice, daring her to deny her claim. "You almost killed me when you took Vargr into your bed, but when that didn't work and Jasper was born, I became so ill my wolf died.

Poisoned *again* by you. Tell me, Alice, oh great friend of mine, how does your mate cope? Does your son know? Does Jasper know Baron is not his father?"

I flicked my eyes to Eloise, who looked just as confused as I felt. Their argument wasn't making sense. I had missed something. What had I missed? "THAT IS ENOUGH!" I yelled, both women halting as the aura of my wolf came through and gave them pause, surprising them and myself at the command I rolled off to them.

How had I never noticed the hatred and animosity between these two women before? Their disdain for each other was so deep that years of unraveled tension had just surfaced, plowing up from the depths of the ground and rising like the mountains of Mint.

Jasper was not Beta Baron's son… He was Vargr's. How much more could our lives be fucked up? So many secrets, so many lies. And why? Why keep any of this hidden? Why not claim Jasper as his heir from the get-go, and why not have me banished or aborted when he found out I wasn't his? Why, why, why?

The three-letter question was making me dizzy. The more the question whirled around in my head the more it spun, faster and faster until I wanted to scream, to release the overflowing anger that would have people crawling on their hands and knees, begging me to stop.

"Alice! Leave this room immediately. DO NOT hassle Luna Mila again!" The command rolled off my tongue easily, my wolf coming to the forefront, showing her dominant side and her abhorrence of how she had treated our mother.

I watched as Alice stomped her foot, not being able to fight my wolf's command. My alpha aura poured out in waves before she turned on her heel and reluctantly left the room in a fit of rage.

"Tala," My mother called to me in a voice full of regret and grief. I held my hand up and bent over to grab my knee with my other hand, trying to steady the influx of emotions that were bombarding me.

I felt all this energy, power, and strength rearing up inside of me. I had never felt this before, this all-consuming desire to control and exert my dominance. I knew it was coming from my wolf, but why now? Why this sudden change today? Was it the trauma I experienced from Jack, the upheaval of my life as I found out Jasper and I had been lied to our entire life? Or was it the heartache and misery of losing my mate?

Either way, I couldn't place it. Eloise and my mother stood silently until I righted myself and pushed my shoulders back, placing everything I felt into a mental box and locked it up. Vargr had destroyed everything he had touched, every person he was responsible for. Destroyed the lives of people he had snatched from the streets.

"Who is Adam?" I asked my mother, not allowing her gaze to shift from mine as I held her captive with my stare.

"Adam would have been your brother." Tears welling in her eyes, my mother choked the words out. "When he died, it changed everything, Vargr became distant, mean. That's when he started to take others to bed." She said with shame in her eyes. "I was poisoned, but it didn't kill me. I let him have a sip of my tea before my wolf realized what had happened. It was too late. He died in my arms." She began to sob, and I moved toward her, engulfing her in the tightest hug I could without harming her.

"When Alice became pregnant with Jasper, I was poisoned again. That and the fact Vargr had been betraying the mate bond killed my wolf. I'm so sorry for the lies. I thought...

I thought your real father would be the one to bring him down. I was so miserable, I wanted to be loved, to have a child. So... I took it from him." She turned in my arms and went to stand by the window, looking out over the barren land outside of the walls of Bhakhil. She took a shuddering breath and crossed her arms.

"Vargr only ever wanted the wealth, my father's mines. Mate or not, he never loved me. If you married Jasper, he would have the mines and the kingdom." She suddenly turned, her red and puffy eyes now hard with determination. "Those mines are yours, Tala. They belong to me, not Vargr, not Jasper. You will inherit them. You hold the riches of this kingdom."

"Teal is dead," I told her in a matter-of-fact tone and watched her gasp, eyes widening in shock and then softening in the same breath.

"I am so sorry, my daughter, but fate is on your side. I cannot help you, but you... you can cut the head off the snake. Your real father was no ordinary wolf, he was powerful, his wolf ancient of an old bloodline. A red wolf, built to protect, built to fight. You are the same, you will see."

Teal's words came back to me. 'My name is Teal Mac-Tire, Alpha of the Sea Dogs pack and Knight of the Red Branch. My wolf is Cuchulainn, who lives to serve King Conri, and he will be reborn. Tala Mac-Tire, you are my daughter and I love you.'

"I am a Mac-Tire, not a Phelan." I looked to my mother for confirmation. She nodded, tears springing from her eyes again.

"Yes, my dear girl, you are a Mac-Tire. When you find your mate, you will feel that power, that ancient blood that courses through those red veins of yours."

"My mate is dead," I replied, choking on the words. They

didn't feel right, even saying them. Mora growled in my head. She, too, felt like the words were lies. Neither of us were able to come to terms with Kellen's death, or at least we refused to acknowledge it. If we did, it would make it all too real.

"Tala," Eloise caught my attention. I had forgotten she was even in the room, to be honest. "Jasper needs to see us. He said it was urgent." El pulled her lips in tight, looking from her Luna to me.

"Go, dear. Today is a good day. The fates will smile upon you. Of this, I am sure." I bobbed my head, agreeing with my mother. After the showdown I just witnessed, I definitely needed to see Jasper. "Eloise," my mother called out as we crossed the threshold of the door. We both turned back to look at her. "Mark your mate before it's too late, complete the bond. We have no idea what Vargr and Baron will do next."

"Yes, Luna." She replied hesitantly, wondering if my mother knew her mate was Jasper.

Chapter 39 - The Plan

<u>KELLEN</u>
DAY 20 OF THE GAMES STILL

Kellen, Lamia's sweet voice filtered into my head, and an instant calmness settled over me and my wolf. *Don't you dare fucking die on me again!* The sweetness was now gone as she scolded me, but still, the tone of relief remained accompanied by her love.

I will try not to, I chuckled back through the mind-link she had established with me. I had almost forgotten that distance had no effect on our ability to connect, and it had become much easier since receiving the mark of her knight, along with being able to link the other three knights. Again, distance did not hinder us in any way, which was why I contacted Mike as soon as I knew the barriers were down and the inhibitor chip had been disengaged.

I was still wondering how that had happened.

You died. Lamia replied, reading my thoughts. *When your heart stopped, the chip deactivated. Kellen, I could feel your pain. I felt your heart stop*

I'm so sorry I said, truly meaning it because I was sorry that she had to go through it with me, knowing how close our wolves are and that we still shared an unbreakable bond. I knew she felt everything, every little thing I felt projected onto her. Just like when she was held captive and tortured,

I felt everything except for the rape. I shuddered suddenly, remembering Zane trying to claw his heart out. The most agonizing three months of my life were when she went missing. I could only guess how she felt about me.

Come home, Kellen, soon. Mike, Tobias, and Hunji will be there in two days max. Get your mate and bring your queen home. Even though her words were soft, and they held desperation, it was a command from my queen. She wanted me home.

I promise. I have to right the wrongs in this kingdom, and then I promise I will be home with Tala I told her with purpose.

"Hey, you!" The voice of a male jarred me from my telepathic conversation.

Stay safe. Come home to see your nieces or nephews before they are born. I love you were the last words Lamia said to me.

I love you too I told her before she cut the link. I focused my attention on the approaching guard in his black pants and leather-looking vest.

"I said, you! What are you doing out here?" The man drew closer, pulling out a cattle prod from his side. Conri growled and I bared my teeth at the warrior. "Holy shit! It's you!" The man said, placing the prod back on his side and raising his hands in the air, palms out. "We thought you were fucking dead!" He looked me over, astonished and confused until it sunk in that I was, in fact, well and truly alive. Then a smile began to creep on his face, starting out small but growing until he looked like a Cheshire cat.

"Who are you?" I commanded the man in front of me.

"Goddess Aye, I am Cameron, future beta, loyal to the

future Alpha Jasper and Tala. And you are King Kellen Moon. The gladiator and Wolf King." He supplied proudly, that smile still wide and not faltering.

His eyes got glassy and like lightning, striking quick, I had him by his throat. "Who are you mind-linking?" I growled out.

"Jasper, only Jasper. Jeesh, man, I'm on your side. Tala, she thinks you are dead, they locked her in the hot box. Jasper and I have been trying to figure out how to still move forward with the plan." He spluttered and then coughed when my grip loosened. I let him go.

Conri gave a displeased growl to think they locked his mate in a box. "Everyone thinks I'm dead still?" I said, trying to push the anger away. The man named Cameron nodded in confirmation.

Rubbing his red throat, he smirked at me. "But this could be a good thing. If Vargr thinks you are dead, he will never see you coming." The smirk on his face became devious. "Let me link Jasper?"

"Yeah, then we need to get me back inside." Cameron's eyes glazed over again as he contacted Jasper.

"Come, we will enter through the west gate. I have loyalists to us posted there." He said, waving his hand and walking back in the direction he had come from. "Good job I was out on border security today and you came across me. Even though we have many allies, they may have freaked and sent a message to the Alpha about a trespasser."

*****

Cameron led me to the west gate, passing through easily, and into a different guard hut. It looked the same as the one near the barracks: a small lounge area with basic seating and necessities.

When the door opened, Jasper walked in looking like shit, and even though his future beta had told him I was here and alive, he still held the element of surprise.

"Fuck" he said after a few moments, scrubbing his hands down his face as he absorbed the reality of my return. "How?" Was all he asked, looking me up and down.

"I have friends in high places," I smirked at him. Because really, no matter the conversation with Ashe, or Odeia, whatever she called herself, and despite the three gifts from the three sisters, I still wasn't 100% sure on the 'how' myself. That was the only honest answer I could give him.

What I could gather was that this was bigger than just me or Lamia; there was something more powerful at play. Something ancient that had to do with the story of our wolves. Their spirits forever intertwined. Gods were tricky creatures, always looking to scheme on one another, and we were just their pawns.

I looked Jasper over, taking in his appearance and posture, scrutinizing him. He looked and felt like someone who could be trusted, and my wolf held no grievances towards the werewolf and recognized his aura as more than beta, possibly alpha?

"Where's Tala?" I asked, narrowing my eyes, watching his reaction carefully. Jasper's shoulders slumped as if he was reluctant to answer, and out of the corner of my eye, I saw Cameron shift uneasily. "What? Where is my mate?" I ground out with my wolf flaring in my eyes when they exchanged a look.

"She is on her way with Eloise right now, but..." Jasper hesitated. I didn't like the way he pinched his lips together lightly and looked at me in fear.

"But what?" I was losing patience and so was my wolf. I hadn't shifted in three months, and I was bristling to let Conri out just as much as he was itching to be set free. We had never gone this long without changing - the feeling of being confined for long was making us both antsy. We could seriously burst at any moment and shift right here. Not knowing where his mate was made Conri almost feral and clawing to take control.

"She uh, shit, I think it's better if she explains it to you. I haven't seen her since they put her in the hot box, but umm.... She is ok." Jasper almost stuttered out. There was obviously something he wasn't telling me that he wanted Tala to tell me.

Just then, a three-tier knock sounded on the door and Cameron moved to answer it, taking a basket and sack from whoever was on the other side of the door and then closing it again. He threw the sack to me and placed the basket on the table. "Fresh clothes and food" He gestured at the items.

"Thank you." I didn't realize how hungry I was until I smelt the sandwiches and fruit I hadn't even seen yet.

"You smell fucking awful," Cameron laughed. "You could really do with a shower. Why don't you wash up in the sink and change, then eat? Tala and El will be here soon." He suggested, cocking an eyebrow and letting his eyes scan my appearance.

I looked down at myself. Yeah, I was fucking disgusting and reeked of rotting flesh and death. It would take several showers to get this mess of shit off me and even more to rid me of the smell that had seeped into my every pore.

No sooner had I finished washing and putting on the fresh clothes, a simple blue T-shirt and white cotton shorts, than I started to dig into a sandwich. I was inhaling it like a starved man when the sweet scent of oranges with a lick of sea salt invaded my senses and the door flew open.

Tala stood there, her chest heaving as she tried to catch her breath, her eyes flicking around the room until those beautiful bright blues landed on mine. The sandwich and my hunger were forgotten, and I rose from the table, slowly and steadily - my own breath hitching and heart pounding. My gaze cast over her tiny frame, committing the way her flamed hair framed her face, her eyes roaming me like she couldn't believe I was standing there. Her pink rosebud lips parted as she whispered my name. "Kellen."

She dove into my arms, and a sob of relief sounded from her mouth as she sought solace in my embrace. I wrapped my arms tightly around her as she buried her head in my chest.

"I thought you were dead. I felt you die," she mumbled against me, squeezing her arms around my waist as tight as her little arms could. "I thought you were dead," she cried.

I leaned back after kissing the top of her head so I could look at her and unraveled one of my arms so I could lift her chin with my fingers, meeting her cerulean blue eyes with my own. "Not even the gods could keep me from you," I said before capturing her mouth with mine in a starved kiss.

It was just me and my little flame at that moment. Our lips moved in sync, caressing one another's. Nothing and no one existed in this moment of time as I pressed her body flush with mine, feeling all her gentle curves against the hard lines of mine. I licked the seam of her lips, and when they parted, my tongue delved in twining with hers, tasting her. She tasted just as sweet as she smelled and my wolf growled in satisfaction, he was unrestrained now and wanted to mark and mate his queen.

I was lost in the bliss of my mate as we fell into our own pocket of nirvana, a place of perfect happiness. I pushed Tala back against the table, looming over her, the kiss becoming more primal and my cock hardening as the scent of her arousal reached my nostrils. My hand slid down from her waist, grasping the thin material of her dress and pulling it upwards.

"*Mine.*" My wolf and I growled out against her lips, and I felt her body quake with want against me.

The sound of a cough had me pausing, followed by a gasp. "You can't mate her here!" The other female in the room said.

Breaking the kiss but not moving from where Tala was pinned between me and the little table, I turned my head to glare at the girl, baring my fangs as Conri growled at the female who dared interrupt. Simultaneously, I remembered that there were other males in the room, too, and gave them a quick sneer. My mate's body was for my eyes only. Reluctantly I let my mate go, but only for a second, taking a seat on one of the wooden chairs at the table and pulling Tala onto my lap.

I closed my eyes and reined in my wolf, tempering our primal urge to claim what's ours. I buried my head in the crook of her neck and hair, inhaling her scent until I had calmed enough to open my eyes and regard the other three presences in the room with us.

"What did I miss?" I asked when I had eventually gained focus.

"Jack is dead," Tala said with a hitch in her voice and giving a shudder in disgust as she shifted on my lap. Her ass brushed against my cock and I gave a small groan, my hands holding her like a vice grip to stop her from moving against me. It was hard enough to restrain myself before; I didn't think I could do it again. Not while her little ass ground up against my tempered length. "Oliver killed him." She took a deep breath, and I swear just hearing those names had my wolf growling for blood. "He saved me." She whispered, and I swear I could hear the faint trace of trauma in her voice. Containing Conri at this point was difficult when I could feel him surfacing again.

I had to tell him to simmer down and even though he was, somewhat, I could still sense his pacing and agitation.

"Explain." I gritted out between clenched teeth, and my hands tightened even more on my mate. At this rate, I was sure I would leave bruises, my grip instantly loosening at that thought.

"Jack, he... Vargr gave me to Jack after they let me out the box and Jack, well... Oliver killed him." I could sense her shame and I didn't know why she was feeling like that. It should be me who should feel ashamed. I wasn't there to protect my mate. Instead, the piece of shit rogue had saved her from the hands of Jack. I had seen what he could do firsthand, I knew what he had done to Lamia. "He didn't have the chance to... you know."

I swallowed hard and closed my eyes, it was a good job Jack was already dead. And even if Oliver did something good, I was still going to put his head on a fucking spike.

"They killed Teal," were the next words to fall from my mate's beautiful mouth. This time when she shuddered, the motion was for sorrow instead of disgust. I felt a great despondency at the news that Teal had met his end. He had become a role model, a father figure to me in the last few months. Without him, I didn't think I would have survived being thrown into slavery.

Without Teal, I would have lost all hope and withered in myself with loathing and pity. I had hoped to reunite him with his family after so long, but now I would only be able to tell them what an honorable and heroic man he was up until his last breath.

My little mate looked up towards Jasper, who had his arms circled around the other female, Eloise. "Do you know?" She asked Jasper.

Jasper dropped his arms from around his mate and Tala rose from my lap, standing in front of the future alpha who nodded his head, tears in his eyes. "I found out. I swear I didn't know until two days ago." Tala hugged him tight, and he reciprocated.

"You are nothing like him, you never have been, and you never will be." She said soothingly in a sisterly kind of way. "They lied to us, all of them Jasper. It is now our destiny to right their wrongs, to turn this kingdom into a pack we can be proud of. Eloise will be your Luna, and those monsters will never hurt us again."

I should be feeling jealous, having another wolf touching my mate, but somehow, I was okay with it. Looking at them I understood. I watched the reaction of Jasper's mate, who stood there with her hands clasped against her chest, tears falling from her eyes, then over to Cameron who wore a small grin on his face. Finally, I let my gaze drift back to my mate in another man's arms. It reminded me of Mike, Lamia, and me. A friendship that would last beyond the confines of mortality and time. They broke the hug, and Tala returned to sit on my lap, exactly where she belonged, and picked up the sandwich I had abandoned when walked in. She then held it up for me to bite.

Jasper cleared his throat. "The full moon is eight days away. Obviously, they will not be mating me to Tala," Jasper gave me a worried look before resuming "However, Vargr seems to think instead that I will be betrothed to one of King Panja's daughters." He scoffed and reached for Eloise. "That shit ain't happening. I have my Luna." He declared, kissing the cheek of his mate who just melted against him.

"Put me back in the gladiator barracks," I began.

"What? No!" Tala exclaimed. "I am not letting you out of my sight again, last time you died!"

I cupped the side of her face with my hand. "For two days only. I have men who will be here then - I have a plan." I looked at Jasper and Cameron. "Can you keep her safe until then?" The last thing I wanted to do was leave my mate again, but in order for the plan to work, it had to happen. Then I would never let her out of my sight.

"Since Vargr declared her a slave, maybe we could hide her in the female slave building. The madam will make sure she is not touched. Plus, the girls in there would probably be more than willing to help if they are promised freedom." Cameron supplied, Jasper nodded with him in agreeance.

"How do you know the madam will keep her hidden?" I asked. I was skeptical because I didn't know these people. I didn't know who could be trusted and who couldn't.

"Because she is my aunt." Eloise spoke for the first time since receiving a deadly look from me. "Now what do you have planned? Because the palace staff is more than willing to help too."

"We have over one hundred guards and warriors in alliance with us, and many civilians outside of these walls," Jasper supplied immediately, "We just need a plan, and if you have one Wolf King, I would be more than happy to hear it." He smiled.

"That I do, alpha. That I do." And so, we began to plot and hatch our plan that would take place in two days' time.

I hated to part from Tala again, but it was necessary; we

were going to bring Vargr and his army down. And we were going to do it from the inside.

Chapter 40 – Sealed with a Kiss

<u>OLIVER</u>

They didn't see me follow them. But that's what I was good at. Sneaking, slipping into the shadows where the darkness supplied a blanket of cover. Hiding. They didn't scent me, Jack's masking spray coming in handy once again. And they didn't notice me crouching on the roof when they left the guard's hut. Listening and watching.

The young king had lived, and I really shouldn't be surprised. With everything I have seen in this twisted realm, a wolf such as Kellen coming back from the dead makes total sense, right? Part of me, my wolf, was disgusted that the gods had favored him and was disappointed that he wasn't six feet under. The other part of me admired his strength. I envied what he had, that he grew up with loving parents, friends, and family, never having to struggle through life.

I was born a rogue. My mother was killed by his father, executed for being a rogue... so I was told by Silas. I wonder if Silas ever knew that I was his son, or if he chose to ignore it like I chose to ignore that he was my father. He made me his second in command when I shifted at fifteen, early for any wolf that didn't hold royal blood. But that's the thing, Silas did hold royal blood, being the half-brother to the late King Alexander, making Kellen Moon, by all rights, my cousin.

Unlike the blessed prince, I had grown up in poverty. Surrounded by destruction and chaos. I was taught to hate and kill, to loathe the packs and their perfect ways of life. Rogues didn't care for packs, they were greedy, but none wanted to be tamed, to conform to the laws of shifters. I bet Kellen wasn't beaten and used growing up in his palace of ivory. Not like me who had to survive every day, fight my way to the top just to be recognized and left alone.

I listened as they planned and plotted against Vargr to overthrow him. I heard that the king's men were coming, and he was able to send a mind-link. Which meant his chip was no longer active. His wolf was free to emerge at will. I gave a shiver, knowing how much more powerful he would be and what Kellen would do to me when he eventually got a hold of me. It was only a matter of time.

I watched silently, waiting like the demon in the shadows that I was. Sly and cunning, like the red fox who hunts his prey. Like the raven that patiently waits above to pick at the carcass, taking the parts less desired. Jasper and his future beta left to take Kellen back to the gladiator barracks, and Eloise lead Tala towards the whores compound.

I waited until the two she-wolves had rounded the corner and the boys had already disappeared in the opposite direction before I tactfully and silently jumped down from the roof of the small building. Landing without even the slightest of sounds and heading in the same direction as the princess.

From the first moment I laid eyes on the redheaded beauty, I felt a connection to her. Drawn to her like a moth to light. My wolf instantly felt protective of her. I didn't know if we wanted her, how we wanted her, but I knew without a doubt that I could never harm her. I could never let her be harmed. The urge to wrap her up in cotton wool and keep her hidden from the evils of this realm was beyond an urge or a feeling.

That's why I killed Jack. I hoped it hadn't come to that. Jack was a very handy person to have on your side. He may be bold and crass and was a demon in his own right, because I will not put him under any other category than a monster, but he did have value. I had tried to talk to him, even asked him not to touch Tala. I even went as far as to tell him I wanted to claim her as my own, but he wouldn't hear it. His beast was set on destroying my little princess, adamant that he was going to teach her a lesson, and once Jack and his beast had their mind set on something, they wouldn't let it go. Latching on like a leech, sucking and draining the life from their victim. That's why as soon as I saw the circumstances, I didn't hesitate to pull the knife from my boot, the blade coated in silver, and swipe it across his neck, giving the bear shifter a second smile, tearing his throat open.

Was it wrong to say I felt a sense of satisfaction when his large body slumped and naturally rolled off of my little ray of light and onto the floor? I knew Tala didn't see the glint in my eye or the way my lips twitched and twisted into a satirical and mocking smirk.

Was I any better? Definitely not. The difference between Jack and me? A conscience, somewhat.

I could walk away, but Jack could never let anything go. I have done awful, awful things. Things I was ashamed of, things I was not proud of, and when it's my time to cross into the underworld, because I have no doubt that that is where I am headed, I will accept my fate.

I sneered to myself when I thought of Jack pinning my princess underneath him. A second too late, and he would have broken her, destroying that innocence of hers that had me under its spell. So much so that I was heading to the compound that housed the slave girls just to make sure Tala was safe. I needed to see her, my wolf wanted to see her, and I wanted to offer my assistance.

As much as I despised King Kellen and his position, I had feelings for Tala. She was my light in the darkness, a beacon of hope. Hope that I could be a better person, hope that even though I had done too much damage in my life and there was no salvation for a monster like me, I could still do some good for her. Her innocence was as fresh as a petal in the morning dew, glistening from the first rays of the sun. Fresh and beautiful, graceful and durable.

She would never be mine. I wasn't under any illusion that she ever would be, and I wasn't entirely sure what exactly I felt for her. But the need to protect her, to look out for her, was so great that it out-weighed the sane side of me that told me to run, to get out of this place and never look back. This was not my fight. I had no reason to stick around. Except I did.

I waited patiently by the side of the whores building, the shadows keeping me hidden until Tala's maid, Jasper's mate as I found out, finally left. Then I snuck in when all was quiet, lifting my nose to scent which room my little princess was in.

When I found her, I stood in the door frame, leaning my shoulder against it, watching as the only light in the room was from the candle that flicked and licked in the otherwise darkened room. Casting wavering light across her milky skin as she changed into a nightgown.

I softly cleared my throat and she spun around, holding the garment to her chest. I tried not to think about how without that flimsy piece of material, she would be naked for my eyes to feast on.

"Oliver?" She whispered with a start. "What are you doing here?"

I turned slightly so she could slip her nightgown on, giving her somewhat privacy, even though I had seen her bewitching naked curves last night. Last night she needed Oliver the man, not Oliver the monster. "Our deal," I said, gulping as I pushed the thought of her bare body from my mind and again cleared my throat and shook my head free of the impure images my wolf was conjuring. "The deal was that I would help you in exchange for the location of the witch and the diamonds." Truly I couldn't care less about the witch. The diamonds I wanted, but that wasn't what was driving me to help.

"You will get your diamonds, Oliver. I made a promise, and I will keep it." I turned once I heard her shuffle to the small bed and closed the door behind me. It only took two steps to cross the room before I found myself in front of her, kneeling before the light in my darkness. I looked at her, capturing her eyes with mine, hoping I was conveying to her how I felt without having to say it.

As if on auto-pilot, my hand reached out and cupped her delicate face. "I will still help you Tala, but if it comes down to it, your mate will kill me. But I will help you both."

"Help us?" She asked quizzically, her thin red eyebrow cocked. "How and why?"

"You need a distraction; I can provide that for you." My eyes searched her face, coming back to peer into those paradise islands, ocean eyes. "As for the why? That does not matter." Fuck, I sounded like a love-sick puppy. "You provide me with my diamonds and a way to avoid King Kellen and his men, and I will never darken your life again. No one will ever hear from or about me again."

I thought I saw remorse flash in her eyes, but it was gone quickly, replaced with her usual hardness. My princess was one tough bitch, even if she didn't think so herself. She would make a good queen, that I knew.

"Diamonds and a sure exit in exchange for a distraction when we make our move?" She confirmed. I nodded, my large hand still cupping her face.

She held her hand out; she wanted me to shake on it, a gentleman's agreement. Tala was no gentleman, though. Instead, I slid my hand around to the back of her neck, lightly gripping her nape. I pushed her face towards mine. "We seal it with a kiss," I said, low and hushed, before placing my lips on hers.

They were everything I had dreamt of since the first day I had come to this goddess-awful dry kingdom. She was a breath of fresh air in an otherwise stifling place. Her lips were soft, and as I moved mine, encouraging her to kiss me back, I felt her hesitate and stiffen. When she relaxed and began to kiss me back, my wolf howled in my head.

I squeezed her neck just a little tighter and crushed her mouth with mine. She gasped, and I slipped my tongue inside her hot mouth, angling my head and deepening the kiss - relishing her taste and the feel of her soft and perfect mouth working with mine. Is this what it feels like to be wanted? I wondered.

I broke away from her before I got out of hand and leaned my head against hers. Tala's eyes were still closed, her breathing slightly ragged.

"That was one hell of a kiss, Oliver." She said, pulling back and out from my grasp.

"Sealed with a kiss. Thank you." I rasped, still lost in the moment, not moving from my position. "If I were to die tonight, I would die happy knowing I kissed the most beautiful woman in the realm, and she liked it." I chuckled and then bounced up to a standing position. "In two nights, I will give you your distraction. In two nights, I expect my diamonds and safe passage out this shit hole."

I didn't wait for her to respond. I backed up to the door and stuck my head out. Seeing that the coast was clear, I slipped out unseen, unheard, and unscented in the same way I came in, and went back to the palace to plan the distraction I would provide. I had no doubt in my mind that Tala would hold up her end of the bargain; after all, she owed me for saving her from Jack.

When I slipped back into the castle, Jasper was already there with his future beta, Cameron. I stopped when I heard their hushed voices speaking with a couple of warriors and one of the palace maids.

"Can you be ready for our signal in two nights?" Jasper asked the warriors, who told him they could. "Good, Cameron will lead the gladiators and the king into the palace. You will ensure the warriors at the gate are knocked out if our men are not posted there. We need to make this quick and fast before Vargr catches wind and raises the alarm for the army. Once he is dead, his army can do nothing but take orders from the next alpha, be that me or King Kellen."

I moved away from the door. I heard all I needed to hear. I was going to make my way to Vargr's office when I saw the beta's wife, Alice, leaning against a door frame. Was she listening to them too?

"Good evening," I said, winking at the older female who glared at me and then rolled her eyes. I had originally thought this woman to be naïve, a bit of an airhead. Yet, after everything I had learned tonight, I came to the realization she was just as much of a snake in the grass as me. I had overheard her argument with the Luna, how she had tried to kill her and ended up killing the Alpha's son. Now her own son, fathered by Alpha Vargr, would become the only heir. Did she know her son was plotting against his real father?

Did she even care?

She pursed her lips at me as I walked by her. Just as I was ready to head around a corner, her words stopped me in my tracks. "I can make it so you can stay here, Oliver. You only have to do one thing for me, and you can live with riches inside these walls." I turned to look at her. Her arms were crossed over her chest, her shoulder still leaning on the door frame, lips pursed, and her brown eyes twinkling like she held the key to my happiness and had just offered me the world. "I know you killed Jack. What would his men say if they knew you had killed their leader?"

Little did she know, I had no intentions of staying here, nor did she realize that Jack's men couldn't care less if their black-market rogue leader had died, or by who. There was always somebody willing to climb the ranks and take over his dark position of trafficking. I knew that firsthand, I had grown up in the same lifestyle as Jack. But, again, she didn't need to know this.

She didn't need to know that if it didn't benefit Tala, then I wasn't interested. "You can make that happen?" I asked with a wide grin, taking a step towards her and keeping my voice low. Playing like I wanted what she was offering. "You can… give me riches, and I would be safe here?" I looked around conspicuously like I didn't want anyone to hear us. Really, I couldn't give a shit, I was just humoring her.

The beta's wife straightened up with a coy smile. "I can." She placed a hand on my chest in a flirtatious manner. "All you would have to do is kill the Luna for me, and you could live here like a Lord." She cooed.

Under normal circumstances, I would fuck her, then either kill her or take her up on her offer. "Come with me," I said, leaning in close to her ear, whispering the words with a seductive tone. I felt the woman shiver with excitement, then I led her to one of the empty rooms on the second floor. Jack's guest room.

Well, he wouldn't need it anymore.

As soon as we entered, I pushed the older she-wolf onto the bed and lifted her dress skirt, pulling down her underwear. She was already excited and wet, and it didn't take me long to get hard by thinking about fucking her and what I was going to do to her.

I undid my pants, giving my dick a few hard strokes. I couldn't see the woman's face, her dress skirts were bunched and thrown over the back of her head as she positioned herself on all fours. That was good. When I came up behind her and rammed my rock-hard cock into her, it was easy to pretend it was Tala.

I fucked her hard and rough, plowing into her pussy. "Oliver!" She screamed out my name, and I hated how it sounded coming from her. Her grunts and moans got louder each time I plunged into her. When I felt like I was ready to come, I paused for a second and reached down to my boot, pulling out my knife. The same one I killed Jack with. I began to drive into the bitch again, harder this time. "Oliver, yes!" she cried out. I leaned over her body, ramming her hard, my pelvis hitting her ass repeatedly, and just as I was about to come, I yanked her head up by her hair. With my other hand, I slit her throat and emptied myself inside her.

My cock jerked with one last spill of my seed when she gurgled and fell forward onto the bed. Hmm, I guess it was normal circumstances tonight.

I pulled my dick from her pussy, and her body collapsed into the bed sheets that were turning dark from the blood that gushed from her neck.

"Fucking whore." I said with disgust to the corpse and

wiped my blade clean on the sheets. I pulled my pants up and replaced the knife in my boot, and then left the room to go find Vargr and his beta.

Chapter 41 – Finding Friends

<u>MIKE</u>
DAY 21 OF THE GAMES

We had arrived at the docks of Chegank, on the second continent in the country of Dre, yesterday. We had spent the whole night loading up a couple of transport trucks with supplies and weapons. I was eager to get to my king, but not so eager to leave Jonda.

I slipped my arms around her waist from behind and buried my nose into the crook of her neck, inhaling her sweet scent. Her hands came up to cover mine, and I felt her lean back into me and sigh.

"I could still come with you," she said hopefully.

I shook my head, pulling her body more into mine. "You are safer here, besides, you will be here to greet our army and help organize them. I don't want you near any fighting. I can't stand the thought of losing you, I only just found you." I said honestly. I had only known Jonda for a little more than a few weeks, but since that night at the Inn when I first sunk into her, I couldn't bear to be apart from her.

I know we were meant to wait for our mates, but I couldn't. This woman... This feisty curvaceous beauty had already captured the heart of me and my wolf, and something told us, like a gut feeling, that she had to be with us.

"When I come back with our king, will you come to New

Moon with me, Jonda? Will you stay with me?" This time it was me who was sounding hopeful and a little desperate. I think I was falling in love.

"Mike!" She exclaimed, twirling in my arms to face me. "But, what about…"

"No, shh. I want you and only you. No one else matters. I want to be with you, Jonda, I want to see where this goes. If you will have me?" I bent down and kissed her lips, lingering for a moment when her arms came up and circled my neck, pushing into me and kissing me with so much passion in a way I wanted to be kissed forever. The heat of the kiss spread warmth through me, and when her tongue twined with mine, that heat found its way to my cock. I groaned and pulled away from the kiss. "I have to go, and if you keep kissing me like that, we will only end up delaying everyone." I smiled and pecked her lips once more before removing her arms from my neck.

"That's the idea, beta." She winked. I groaned again and tilted my head back. I had to go, but her womanly ways were making it so hard.

"When I get back here, I promise you I will not go easy on you. I will have you pleading with me to stop giving you orgasms." I half-joked, but really, I meant every word of it. I was going to fuck this woman until her belly swelled with my pup. The thought made me smile and lick my lips as my eyes roamed over her lush curves, imagining her tummy swollen with our child.

Shit, I had it bad. I palmed my hard member through my pants, adjusting where it sat as it strained against the thin fabric. I was willing it to go down and mentally telling myself: when I get back; when I get back after we have saved our king.

"Okay you go play hero, and I will wait here like the good girl you know that I'm not." Jeesh, this woman was playing with me. She turned her back for a moment and rummaged through a bag in the back of her SUV. When she turned around, she handed me a large brick-like-looking phone.

I looked at it curiously. "What is this?" I questioned her, still examining it.

"It's called a satellite phone. Where you are going, there are no cell towers left. After the humans died, this continent saw no need for them. There were not enough shifters to keep them working. We use these to communicate with our captains and carriers. You can connect to a landline or a cell phone with this; you can pretty much reach anyone all over the realm."

"Huh," was all I said. These would actually be handy back in our realm too.

After another long kiss goodbye, I hopped into the truck with Hunji and Tobias. Alpha John had provided us with a few men until ours caught up with us. Also, a few local warriors from an allied pack of the Sea Dogs were accompanying us. It turns out they had had a beta stolen from their territory around the same time. Even though they were a small pack, they wanted their beta back and were more than happy to provide us with some fighters.

According to Hunji, it was almost a two-day journey to Bhakhil. I had forgotten that he was from this continent, and he had once mentioned that he traveled the realm, mostly this continent.

Two days I opened up a mind-link to Kellen and included Hunji.

*We will be waiting, brothers. And Hunji, it's going to be

a blood bath* Hunji didn't say anything, but I saw the tiniest hint of a smirk on his face.

Hunji is looking forward to it I said to him laughing. I knew Hunji didn't like to take a life unless it was necessary, but I have also seen how good he is at it. And in the throes of battle, I had seen his eye glimmer like his wolf enjoyed the bloodshed. As if there was hidden darkness behind his wall of indifference and it only peeked out when he is knee-deep in blood.

*****

It was hot, so fucking hot! I was missing the deep green forest at this point like I never had before. I was even missing the damn ocean and being on a boat. At least then I was with Jonda, and it was cooler. I opened up another bottle of water and chugged half of it down. Then passed a cold one from the cooler to Tobias, who was now driving.

We had been on the road for a day now. Hunji and Tobias had taken sides, for once, and yelled at me to shut up because I kept complaining about how hot it was here. Like seriously, I have heard the expression 'so hot you could fry an egg', but I had never really given it too much thought until now. I could literally crack an egg on any surface of this truck and have an instant fried egg.

"Tell me again why we just couldn't run in wolf form?" I asked Hunji, who turned around to face me in the back seat giving me a look that said 'what the fuck'.

"Mike, your wolf's paws would burn on the sand and dirt, plus there is nowhere for you to stop and drink and hardly any wildlife to hunt. Trust me, we are better off driving." He said, demolishing my idea. He then turned around, and I guess he wasn't finished because he swung his shoulders around again to face me. "And stop complaining! Until you have spent a week in the desert with no food or water, half dead, then you can complain to me."

That's right, it's TOO FUCKING HOT!

Tobias chuckled. "Fuck, when did you two become besties?" I jeered, hating being the one they were making fun of me. I liked it much better when Hunji and I were making fun of Tobias.

"Don't be jealous, Mikey," Tobias laughed. "We will get your bestie back too. Besides, I have mad respect for Hunji after he dropped me on my ass." He winked at Hunji. "Kinda liked it, Wolfman." He teased the Asiarian Queen's Knight, who just gave him a low growl.

Tobias was forever cracking gay jokes at Hunji, convinced he was gay because no one ever saw him with a woman. But that was by choice, according to Lamia, who said that according to Tawny, Hunji was defiantly into women.

I looked out the window. It was going to take us until tomorrow to reach the Kingdom of Bhakhil. Once we were close, Hunji would alert Kellen and he would direct us where to station ourselves until the time was right. I was hoping our troops would make their presence before Kellen made his move. I liked the idea of stability in numbers, especially as we didn't have a count on the number of Alpha Vargr's army.

The land we traveled through was vast but boring. Miles and miles of bland, flat land and sandy dirt surrounded us. I wondered how any pack could live out here. I closed my eyes and listened to the thrum of the engine as we bounced along the dirt path they called a road, Jonda in my thoughts as I tried to get some rest.

However, I had faith in my best friend. If he said he had a plan, I trusted in it. If he said he trusted this future alpha, I trusted his judgment. I also knew he would do anything to get the future queen of our kingdom out of there safely. I was excited to meet who the goddess had paired Kellen with. She had to be someone pretty darn special, I could feel it.

*****

KELLEN

Cameron and Jasper had snuck me back to the gladiator barracks, leaving me once I had entered the worn and dark building. I hated to be parted from Tala any longer than necessary, but this is what needed to happen if we were going to tear Vargr apart from the inside. I needed my gladiators in order for this to work.

When I slipped in last night, the first person I went looking for was Rogue. I found him sitting alone in Teal's area. His head in his hands and elbows resting on his knees as he perched on his cot.

"Rogue," I simply said in a hushed whisper. He shook his head like he was trying to get something out of his mind. "Rogue," I said again louder. This time his head lifted, and a look of disbelief was plastered on his face.

As soon as he realized it was really me and I was truly standing in front of him alive and well, he rose to his feet and in two big strides he crossed the small space. He brought me in for a tight embrace and clapped my back.

How is this possible, I watched him die. I pulled back stunned, my eyes searching his face. It was now me who stood there dumbfounded and not understanding.

Did he, did Rogue just speak to me through a mind-link? "Rogue did you... How did you mind-link me?" Rogue, looked at me confused.

I concentrated and opened a link. *Did you mind-link me, can you hear me?* I asked him, not feeling any resistance to my attempt at a telepathic conversation.

He jumped back a step in surprise, and I knew my voice had filled his head. *You, you can hear me?*

I smiled like a Cheshire cat, I had no idea how this was possible, but I was fucking elated. *Your voice sounds nothing like I imagined it would* I laughed at him, still conversing telepathically. *How did this happen?* I asked him.

When you died, I felt it. He looked down in sadness. *They killed Teal, one of the guards told us.*

Yes, I know I replied, just as sad but with more bitterness mixed into my tone.

Something else happened when you died that night. Rogue said, looking a little wary.

"What is it?" I furrowed my brows. "What else happened Rogue?" I spoke out loud this time while he of course used our connection to converse.

It's better if I show you, he said, stepping back and removing his shorts. To my surprise, his body began to shift, his bones quickly rearranging, and in three seconds, a large and very, very dark brown wolf stood in front of me.

"Holy shit!" I chuckled loudly and then covered my mouth, afraid someone would hear us. "How the fuck is this possible?" I whispered and hissed.

'When we died, he was already pack. When we died, his

connection broke to Vargr. When we lived, our connection lived.' Conri told me as he stirred and peered through my eyes at Rogues' large wolf form. He was nowhere close to as big as mine, but he was larger than most, pack beta size. Only just a bit smaller than Mike's wolf, Duke.

Rogue shifted back into his skin form and put his shorts back on, smiling at me. *My name is Fergus O'Brien, and my wolf is Keltar* Rogue went down on a knee and placed a closed fist over his heart. *We live to serve you, my king.*

I wasn't sure what to say, if I should be all noble and shit or just brush it off, because in truth, I was still trying to hold back a laugh at his name. "Okay, Fergus," I drew his name out with a small chuckle and his head shot up to look at me, a scowl on his face.

"I'm sorry; I just wasn't expecting that kind of old-realmy name, you know, after calling you Rogue for months." I apologized. "Let's get Corey in here and see if giving him my blood does the same thing. If it does, I want to initiate everyone tonight. Either way, I plan to take over the castle in two moons and need my gladiators in order to make that happen."

I am with you, King Kellen. No matter what, you will have my support. My wolf and I have pledged our life to you. He gave me a curt nod and stepped out of the room to go fetch Corey.

Now today was the twenty-first day of the games. Vargr had, of course, not canceled anything and things would progress as usual. I was half tempted to walk out there myself to just see the look on his face. But all day I kept telling myself: just one more day.

Tomorrow night come hell or high water, we would take Vargr down.

I had eighteen gladiators that I was able to initiate last night, and I'll be damned, but each one that became pack was able to link with me. Their chips were still active, so they couldn't shift, but whatever loophole granted us to be able to communicate mentally, I was thankful for it. I didn't have to understand it; I just had to accept it. This made shit a whole heck of a lot easier.

Two gladiators went into the ring, and only one came out. The one that died was not a great loss. It happened to be one of the men who tried to violate Rogue, one that I had not initiated and had no intentions to.

That night I sat with the gladiators I had made pack and we went over everyone's roles, and who would go where. I would be splitting us up into three groups once we reached the palace and sending an allied guard who knew the palace with them.

The idea was to sneak in and take out anyone in our way until Jasper and I reached Vargr and his beta. Cameron would be at the front gates with warriors ready to let Mike, Hunji, Tobias, and any other men they bought with him in through the front door.

Once Vargr was disposed of, Jasper would become alpha, and this kingdom would be his.

Tala would stay hidden with Eloise in the female slave barracks until the battle was over. There was no way that Jasper or I would have wanted them involved in this fight with them not having much training or experience. Eloise was his future Luna, and Tala was my Queen.

I wasn't too worried about Oliver at this moment, but I wouldn't hesitate to kill him if I came across him. In fact, I was hoping to finally take my revenge on that piece of shit for Lamia, for Travis.

I was just disappointed that I wouldn't be able to rip Jack's head off. I was still a little surprised that it was Oliver who had killed him, and jealousy reared its ugly head every time I thought about how it was Oliver who saved my mate.

Chapter 42 – The Distraction

<u>TALA</u>
DAY 22 OF THE GAMES

Yesterday was long, but today felt even longer. I sat on the bed in the back room of the female slave barracks. These rooms were much nicer than the ones the male slaves were given. The rooms actually had beds and a door, but not much else, and the only reason they had these things was for the visiting alphas, Lords, and senior warriors so they were able to visit and pay for their pleasure. Only Vargr summoned the hybrid slave whores to the palace. It was essentially a brothel. Except the girls had no choice but to be here.

Each girl here had been yanked from their home or the street and sold as a slave. There was no need to implant an inhibitor chip as the hybrid girls had no spirit animal. They were faster and stronger than humans, but nowhere close to as strong as shifters. That's why Vargr favored their race as slave whores. They could be tussled up, used violently, and would most likely recover because they could handle more. They couldn't heal like a shifter, but their bodies endured more than a human could. They could fight back, though they could never match a male shifter in strength.

"Stop stressing," I turned to Eloise when she said this and raised an eyebrow. "I can visibly see you freaking out, you are picking your nails again." I looked down at my hands that were folded in my lap.

She was right, I tore almost all my nails off to little stubs. "Says she who hasn't stopped tapping her foot for four hours." I nodded to her left foot, where her heel was still thumbing on the floor excessively.

The plan was to wait here until Jasper and Kellen came to get us once the fight was over and Vargr was dead. The boys were in no way going to let us fight alongside them. I didn't blame them for thinking that way; El was an omega, a weaker wolf, and had no training whatsoever. Me, I had some when I was younger, but not enough. I would be more of a hindrance than a help, and my presence would only distract Kellen.

The day was coming to an end, the sun lowering and dipping down behind the palace walls. With every minute I became more anxious, and with every minute Mora became more restless and only accelerated my own unease further.

Eloise and I sat in silence, me still picking my nails and El tapping her heels. Each of us let out a strained sigh every now and then when the madam came busting through the door suddenly, looking frazzled and panicked. At the same time, a mind-link came through from Jasper.

"Tala, the Alpha knows you are here! His men are coming for you right now!" The madam panted out.

He knows Jack is dead, he's coming for you, Tala Jasper's voice filled my head.

I had no time to reply or hear what else Jasper had to say as the warriors came marching through the barracks like bulls in a China shop—kicking down the doors of girl's rooms as they went. The girls began to scream from down the short corridors. I gave El a look and stood from the bed.

"What are you doing?" She hissed at me, her doe eyes wide with concern.

"I will not let them torment these girls. Vargr knows I am here, I won't fight them." I said, opening the door and facing the men who were ransacking the rooms as they went for no reason at all. "Stop!" I yelled out to them. "If Vargr wants to see me, I will come peacefully. There is no need to destroy things." I said confidently, holding my head up high and walking forward.

Two men grabbed an arm each and hauled me out the main door of the building and marched me towards the palace. I tripped on my feet as I went, trying to match their long strides. Altogether I was escorted by six of Vargr's top warriors, personally, I thought it was a little excessive just for me.

I had several stares from guards as we passed through the palace grounds and many more from the staff when we entered the palace itself. They looked more surprised and angrier than the guards, and when the warriors hauled me to Vargr's office, my mother's maid passed by us.

The look on her face said it all. She cast me one look full of putrid anger that I knew wasn't directed at me. I turned my head to watch her hurry down the hall towards the stairs that led to my mine and mother's floor.

One of the warriors knocked on Vargr's office, and his snarling voice was heard through the door telling us to come in. The two warriors holding my arms deposited me into the office, nodded at the Alpha, and left. Beta Baron approached, giving me a sorrowful look like he didn't want to be there, and placed a pair of silver-coated cuffs on my wrists. After a few seconds, I could feel the burn and itch from the coated metal as it rubbed against my skin.

Vargr sat behind his desk, his hand stroking his chin in thought as he regarded me, his eyes roaming over my body from top to bottom in a disgusting fashion. Beta Baron took up a position to his left and leaned against the door, not even giving me a glance. Instead, he kept his head down in shame. And so, he should. As a beta, he had the power to stop this, yet all these years he said nothing.

Jasper was also here. He looked worried, with dark bags under his eyes, and deep in his light green eyes, I could just detect a somber look, something akin to grief. This was not part of the plan, me being here. I should still be hidden in the female slave barracks with El. Someone had dobbed us in. I was surprised Oliver wasn't here, yet without Jack, it didn't surprise me. Oliver didn't know Vargr like Jack had. They didn't have a history.

I spoke before Vargr could. "You called for me, Alpha?" I said, puffing my chest out and chin up. He had already done everything he could to me. In my mind, there was no point in showing fear, I just had to play it cool and make sure I didn't die before Jasper and Kellen's plan was put into action. On the inside I was shaking like a leaf, on the outside I hoped I was looking as cool as a cucumber.

"How did you do it?" Vargr asked, his tone was way too fucking calm for my liking.

"Do what?" I asked, casting a glance a Jasper.

"You killed Jack and Alice. How? You are not strong enough or skilled enough." Leaning forward, Vargr narrowed his eyes at me, scrutinizing my appearance. I could almost see the cogs of his mind turning as he tried to work out how I had killed them or if I really had.

I was a little taken aback. Of course, I knew Oliver had killed Jack, but I didn't know Alice had died. Or more accurately, someone had murdered her. "I – I... Miss Alice is dead?" I looked to Jasper, understanding the emotion I saw reflected in his eyes better. Someone had killed his mother.

"Are you still a virgin, Tala?" My mouth gaped open at Vargr's question. What? "Jasper, check her. I want to know if she is still intact."

"Alpha, I, umm," Jasper was obviously embarrassed and did not want to do that. Nor did I want him to touch me like that. He looked at me, his eyes telling me to play along. That we could still do this, we just had to bide our time.

I licked my lips which had suddenly become very dry, and cleared my throat, which had also lost its saliva. "No need to go that far. Yes, I am still a virgin, not that it is any of your concern," I said, turning from Jasper back to Vargr. How I was managing to contain myself, I had no idea. Yet I still kept a blank and unbothered façade.

"Oh, but it is my business, Tala. See, I denounced you as my daughter, not that you ever were. Then the bear that brings me the biggest money makers is found dead. His throat slashed when I had declared you a whore, and you were the last to see him alive. His crew wants answers. And then... poor Alice is found dead with her throat slashed in one of the guest bedrooms. Jack's to be precise." He leaned back in his chair again, folding his arms over his chest. He gave his beta a quick glance, then his eyes were back on me.

I held his stare with a fiery glare of my own. "I'm sorry to hear about Miss Alice," I said honestly. She and my mother may have had their differences, but she was very kind to me. She loved Jasper and I knew he loved her too. "It sounds like maybe Jack killed her if she was found in his room." I was trying to blame shift, but I had no idea who had killed Alice.

"Oh, you will be," Vargr smirked. "Beta, take Tala to my room. It's time to break in a new whore."

"You sick mother fucker!" I spat at him, not believing his horrifying words.

"Oh, and Beta," he said, a wide smile creeping across his face while his menacing hazel eyes still held mine. "I command you to watch me fuck Tala. And after, I command you to fuck her."

"Alpha," Beta Baron growled. And I could hear the low growl of Jaspers wolf. This was not something we had anticipated, and I did not like it one bit.

Vargr just laughed at him and tapped the back of his neck, "Do not try to defy my order Baron. Even if the boy is not yours, I know you care for him. I can make you hurt him too if you are not careful."

Beta Baron moved from his standing position and gripped one of my arms in his large hand. "You don't have to do this, Beta. You don't have to listen to him." I said, trying to get the beta to back off. I knew he didn't want to do this; I could see it in his eyes. His wolf would follow his Alpha's commands, but not this, his wolf couldn't possibly follow that command.

"Oh, but he does. Don't you Baron." Vargr laughed. "Shayna was such a smart girl."

"Oh, my goddess!" I gasped as Baron pulled me from the room towards the top floor where Vargr's suite was. "He chipped you, didn't he?" My body twisted so I could see his face. I gave the beta little resistance. "Beta Baron, please. Don't do this to me, don't let Vargr do this. He has taken so much from all of us." I wasn't even angry at him now that I knew he had been chipped just like the slaves. How could Vargr do something like that to his own beta? The man was truly evil.

Think, Tala, think. I repeated to myself, going over scenarios in my head. "But... you can shift?" I asked because, according to Shayna, those who were chipped would trigger the inhibitor if they tried to shift and it would kill them. "I have seen you shift?"

"Orion put the chip in me; it was one of the first prototypes of Shayna's batches. It was altered and upgraded after that." The beta paused outside Vargr's room, his eyes glazed over, obviously receiving a mind link. He opened the ugly ass blue doors and pushed me in, following behind.

"How long until Vargr comes to 'break me in'?" I asked, shuddering and feeling bile rise in my throat. I vowed to fight him, them both. No man would ever touch me if I could help it. Only my mate.

"About an hour." He said, walking me over to the chase lounge and pushing me onto it to sit down. The beta knelt before me. "He told me to bring you here. He did not say I couldn't take these cuffs off you." He brought out the key and undid them without touching them, the cuffs sliding off my wrists and dropping to the floor. "He may have ordered me to watch and then…" he gulped. He couldn't even say it, he was that disgusted with the thought. "Let's hope Jasper and that mate of yours work fast."

I shook my head, he knew of the plan, he knew we were going to overthrow his alpha. "Don't look so surprised, Tala. I may have followed Vargr, but that doesn't mean I agree with him. I will help how I can, which is not much, until he dies."

An hour. I looked out the window. The sun had almost fully dipped behind the horizon now. Was that enough time? I didn't know but I hoped so.

So, Beta Baron knew about our plan. Who had told him, and why wasn't I told? I knew he didn't want to hurt me, but I didn't know if I could fully trust him, especially if he was still under Vargr's command. He made no attempt to converse with me, so we sat there in complete silence waiting for the minutes to tick by. I didn't try to talk with him either, making it a very awkward atmosphere.

It seemed like hours, but I knew it wasn't. The sun had fully submerged. The stars began to twinkle as the sky turned from an ominous shade of violet and orange to a dusky dark shade of purple until the moon rose and cast its glow across the dry land. The darker it got, the faster my heart beat. When will Kellen make his move? Could Vargr be delayed? Would Oliver provide his distraction? If the stars were going to align just right for me, please let it be tonight. I prayed that Kellen would make it in time, I prayed that Oliver would make good on his promise again, and I prayed it would be before Vargr came to 'break me in'.

Out of nowhere the bell tower began to ring. I stood up and looked at Beta Baron. He, too, stood and walked to the window, opening the French doors that led to the small veranda. The bell tower only rang when there had been a death of a higher-ranking member. I stood next to him looking out over the courtyard. A scream echoed from somewhere down below, an eerie and bloodcurdling sound that cut through the young night. The sound of the bell's chimes caused a hair-raising still to the air. I searched the courtyard until my sight landed on the twisted body of my mother, dressed in her white nightgown, her blond hair glistening under the moon's gaze. A somber and terrifying feeling came over me, and I stood stoic at the sight.

"Who... what?" I asked Beta Baron when I found my voice, turning to him, my eyes full of tears and legs shaking. I had just become an orphan. The comprehension of what had happened slowly sank into me. His eyes met mine, looking just as oblivious and grief-stricken as I felt.

"I don't know," he shook his head slowly, his mouthing pulling into a tight thin line. He ran a hand through his blond hair, not sure what he should do.

He opened his mouth to speak when suddenly a deafening boom reached our ears, causing us to both cover them as the sound rattled and shook our brains, piercing our eardrums and shaking the walls. We both dropped to the floor of the veranda, the sudden explosion scaring the shit out of us. The far end of the court was ablaze with orange flames, lighting up the darkened sky. A billow of smoke stretched and weaved upwards.

Someone had blown up the wall. A crater big enough to fit four cars full of rubble became visible as the smoke began to wisp upwards and dissipate into the night. Was this Oliver's distraction? Was my mothers death a part of the distraction?

Below people moved all around, bringing buckets of water in an attempt to douse the fire and stop it from spreading to the palace. The commanding warriors could be heard shouting orders to the guards and palace staff.

It had begun. My king was coming for me.

Despite the doom and gloom that hung over my head, I had never really known Teal and only found out he was my father a few days ago, and I had lost my mother to her own mangled mind long ago. Though I felt the magnitude of her loss and my heart ached for Teal, I could not help the smile that lifted on my face at the thought of my king rescuing his princess, who was locked in the tower by the evil villain. So fairytale-ish. But it was my fairytale. I bit my lip and gave the beta one look of defiance, and ran for the doors.

Chapter 43 – A Pack of Gladiators

KELLEN

Like a pack of silent thieves, we filed out of the barracks one by one, Jasper leading the way. He had brought six warriors with him that had all drawn a white 'X 'on their leather vests, so we knew who was a friend and not foe.

We crept through the arena and towards the palace swiftly and quietly.

My king Rogue handed me my sword, the one the old lady had gifted me. *I kept it safe* he smiled.

"You are with me, Rogue," I nodded thanks to him.

"We take out any guard or warriors without an 'X' that pose a threat," Jasper instructed before we reached the palace steps and split off into our groups. "King Kellen, follow me," he said and slipped into the shadows, Rogue and I following closely behind.

The ring of a bell had been a surprise, drawing men and a few guards away from the palace, and that's when we made our move. I held my sword tight, following the future alpha, ready to shed blood but hoping to only shed the blood of those who deserved it.

We rounded the corner of a high wall, more steps leading up to the palace doors. We paused to wait until we got the signal.

I opened up a mind-link to Mike and Hunji, *Are you in position?*

Yes, Alpha King Mike replied, using formalities. *Ready on your signal*

In position, Your Highness Hunji linked back.

I closed my eyes, opening up a mass link not only to Mike and Hunji but to the gladiators I had initiated into my pack, ready to give the signal, and we would all storm the palace. There were almost 200 fighters, which should hopefully be plenty unless Vargr calls his army. Then Jasper and Cameron said it would take them only five minutes to infiltrate and surround the palace.

I waited for a beat while a few more of the palace workers came rushing out to the ring of the bell, ready to give my signal when the thunderous boom of an explosion had us all crouching down again and covering our heads. "What the fuck was that?" I asked Jasper.

"No idea." He scowled looking as lost about the explosion as I felt. "Oliver told Tala he would create a distraction. I didn't know what, though."

More people rushed from the building, and more guards and warriors began to mobilize toward where the explosion detonated. The flames licked the sky and cast light amongst the shadows, making it more difficult to hide our movements. At least it moved more of Vargr's fighters away from the palace.

Was that your signal? Hunji asked through the mind-link

No, I growled back to him. *But it's a good cover. EVERYBODY TAKE POSITION AND MOVE IN!* I commanded through the open link, and had a chorus of affirmatives reply back to me.

*****

MIKE

TAKE POSITION AND MOVE IN Kellen's command came through loud and clear.

"The Wolf King has spoken. Take out anyone who does not bear a white cross on their uniform, do not harm civilians." Hunji told the warriors we had with us.

"About motherfucking time! Let's fuck these bitches up!" Tobias clapped his hands together and rubbed his palms against each other. He was excited for a battle, ready to dive in. This was his element. This was where he felt most at ease, his green eyes darkening as his beast came forward to show himself. I pitied the shifters he would fight tonight.

We had thought we would be waiting another two days before our troops arrived. However, once they had reached the Sea Dog pack, the chief warriors from the three units didn't want to wait, and Alpha John had them get off one boat and almost immediately onto another. And they had only been half a day behind us.

"Royal Beta, we will go in through the front gates, two of your units will go around the wall to the east and west entrance with our men." The man, whose name was Cameron, said.

He was here to meet us when we arrived. We had stayed hidden a few miles away near a rock formation until we had the cover of night, waiting for our king to tell us when to move. I looked up at the front doors of the palace, which sat higher on top of stone stairs.

We had heard the explosion and thought that was the signal, but Cameron said that was not what we were waiting for. But seeing as Vargr just commanded guards and warriors to that side of the wall, it was working in our favor.

Cameron's eyes glazed over for a second before he nodded at me. "The Alpha has left the main palace floor." He lifted his hand and made a circular motion. I did the same, and our units of warriors scuttled off to the other entrances to breach them.

We were up the steps in seconds, greeted by a small, plump, older she-wolf who opened the door for us. It was strange, the way she had let us in and then hurried away to hide. Would there be people to let in our other units? I had expected a little more resistance, but Kellen and Cameron had told us the majority of the palace workers would help us how they could.

The guards we met were eliminated quickly and quietly until we rounded a corner and came into what looked like the main hall of the palace, where there were over two dozen warriors gathered, and one of them turned to see us. "INTRUDERS!" He called out, and before we knew it, we were engaged in battle.

The clashing of metal as swords met and sounds of growls filled the air. "Find Kellen, I can handle this," Tobias growled out. When I looked at him to make sure, I saw thick brown fur sprouting over his arms and legs, his limbs growing longer as he morphed into his beast. Hunji and I took our cue and followed Cameron toward another side of the large hall.

I glanced back to see Tobias' beast let out a loud and menacing roar. The guards he was fighting visually froze at the sight of the almost ten-foot bear. We moved swiftly forward toward where we could hear the sounds of others fighting just outside. Cameron burst through a pair of double doors and halted. As did the men on the other side of the door, all with their weapons raised, ready to strike.

"Mike, Hunji!" I heard Kellen's voice and swiftly stopped the action of swinging my blade.

"Kellen!" I cheerily smiled as my best friend stepped forward to hug me and then Hunji.

"Boy, am I glad to see you guys!" He exclaimed.

I took note of his appearance: his hair was longer, his skin tanned, and he had a beard going on. What was most noticeable was his size. "Shit man, you're huge! This slavery bullshit looks like it did you some good." I couldn't help but chuckle. It wasn't the time to joke, but I couldn't help it; I couldn't, not say anything - that just wasn't me.

"Vargr is at the wall that collapsed, along with some of his army, this side of the arena." A man who was as tall as me but not nearly as built said. "Sorry, I am Jasper, future alpha." He added when he noticed me giving him a quizzical look.

"Introductions later. Let's go kill this bastard and anyone who stands behind him." I smiled at my king and gestured for them to lead the way. Seeing Kellen invigorated me, and I was ready for a fight now that we had been reunited.

*****

TALA

I watched Vargr and a few of his warriors leave the palace from where I hid, and let out a breath of relief. I didn't need to run into him, not now. Not now that I knew the fight had just begun. I could hear the distant clang of weapons and the shouting as a fight broke out down the hall. I tried to focus on my task, yet the vision of my mother's mangled body wouldn't leave. Had she done it in an attempt to weaken Vargr? Or had it simply been too much for her and she finally found a way out, and this time succeeded in taking her own life?

I rushed to the doors of Vargr's office and slipped inside, closing the door behind me. Once in, I went to the painting behind his desk, knowing the safe was behind there. I still had to fulfill my end of the bargain. Except, even as I safely got the jewels from the safe, I had no idea where Oliver was to give them to him.

The safe was easy to open. I had known the combination to unlock it for a long time. Vargr's carelessness all these years was working in my favor. Once the safe was open, I looked at the contents. Small bars of gold were stacked on one side. On the other was a large square tray holding loose diamonds. My eyes sparkled brightly, and I held one up to the light. These had already been cut, and they sparkled under the dull light of the lamps in the room. I grabbed three of the medium-sized velvet bags that were conveniently there and emptied the tray into the bags quickly, and stuffed them into the top of my dress. The jewels' weight sat heavily; heavier than I thought they would be.

I closed the safe and put the picture back, not that it mattered. If Kellen killed Vargr, it wouldn't matter that I had broken in or who knew. I guess I did it out of habit, fear of being caught by him.

I slipped out the door and ran to where Oliver's guest room was. Looking behind me, I didn't see the rogue himself and smacked straight into him. Oliver caught me by the arm before my ass could meet the floor, and I blushed when his fingers stroked the bare skin on my arm. "Princess, it's time to go," he said with eyes that looked at me sadly.

"Oliver, how did you know where I was?" I felt a little breathless, and it wasn't from running. It was the way he was looking at me. Like… a man in love.

"I didn't, but I figured this would be the best place to find you when I heard you were taken from the whore barracks."

"Oh." I said, and then again, "Oh! Here," I plunged my hand into the top of my dress and brought the three bags ."My end of the bargain, you still have the map?"

Oliver took the bags from me, peering into one before he quickly closed it and shoved all three into his pockets. "I do, where is this hidden exit mentioned in your sister's diary?" He asked.

"This way," I told him and led him to the maid's quarters. I had never known this hidden exit was here. Not until I read Shayna's diary that explained not only this, but also the location of the witch Jack wanted. I took him to the room that was a large storage closet and pointed at the shelves. "Behind there, the tunnel should take you out to the rock formation. From there, you are on your own."

Oliver slid past me and hauled the large shelving unit out of the way. He tapped the wall until he found the seam and pushed on it hard. The wall gave way, producing a small stone door. Oliver turned to me, scanning his eyes over me and then looking at the open door reluctantly. "Come with me, Tala," he said, his eyes regarding me with a pleading look. "Come with me and I will treat you better than anyone. We can live happily without any of this. We don't need a pack. Just you and me…"

He trailed off when I didn't reply and just stood there gaping at him. He was asking me to run away with him.

417

"Oliver... I can't."

"I know," he said, hanging his head in a way a child would when he was disappointed. "You found your mate and I am nothing but a criminal, nothing like a prince, but I had to ask." He took a step forward and cupped my cheek. "I have never met anyone I wanted to fall in love with," he whispered, and then bent his head to press his lips to mine.

It wasn't a kiss like last time. It was soft, lingering, a goodbye. Had I misjudged Oliver? Was there actually some good in his heart? He had surprised me. Oliver was nothing like the sly fox and monster I thought he was when I first encountered him. I'm sure he is, but he had shown me a different side to him, one that could care, one that could love. I felt sorry for him and almost sorry to see him leave. But a deal is a deal.

"Goodbye Oliver," I said when his lips left mine and he took a step back toward the opening.

"Goodbye my beautiful princess. I would say I hope to see you again, but I know if we did, it would be my death." With that, he turned and slunk into the darkness beyond the opening, closing the stone door behind him.

I would never see him again. And despite everything he has done in the past, the man he was or is, I hoped he would live the life he dreamed of, and I silently wished him well.

I stood there for a few moments, almost expecting him to come back. Did I want him to come back? I closed my eyes for just a moment until reality came crashing in on me and the sounds of a bear roaring brought me back to the now. There was a battle going on, and Vargr must die.

I ran from the storage closet, down the maid's hall, and out onto the side of the courtyard. I could hear the shouting and fighting coming from this side, close to the arena. I picked up the hem of my dress and began running toward the battle.

I had to see, I just had to. I wanted to watch Vargr die. I wanted to watch him take his last breath. I promised I would see his defeat and I would.

"And where do you think you are going?" The dark, cruel, and venomous voice spoke. Like a knife, it cut through the air and had me pausing. I knew who it was before I even turned to look the monster in the face.

"Vargr." I sneered once I had turned to face my tormentor. The man I had called father for twenty-one years. Why was he here? He was supposed to be with his army fighting against our militia.

He clicked his tongue at me, tapping his sword on his thigh. A menacing look sat across his weathered features. "Tsk, tsk, little Tala. So, the Gladiator Wolf King lives. Your mate won't be seeing you again. That I will make sure of." He laughed and lunged forward, shifting into his wolf and knocking me back down to the ground.

His wolf circled me as I laid there trying to get my bearings, toying with me, stalking me as if I was his prey. I got to my feet and tried to back away, but he growled, leaping to the other side of me, cutting off my exit down the stairs to the arena.

He shook his shaggy brown fur out and gnashed his teeth at me, making me take another step back.

Shit, shit, shit, I thought. When suddenly, I felt Mora push her way forward, and I began to shift. My shift was quicker than I thought and didn't hurt like it normally did when I had been allowed to in the past. Within seconds I was standing on four paws.

My wolf growled back at Vargr, and she barred her teeth in a warning for him to back off. He flew towards us, and she barely dodged his attack. Mora let out a howl just before Vargr's wolf turned and attacked again. This time we weren't fast enough, and he managed to claw our shoulder.

The cut was deep and burned, but that didn't deter my wolf, she was ready to fight. When Vargr's wolf attacked again, she flew forward meeting him head-on. I wasn't in control, my wolf was, and Vargr's wolf was too big for Mora to take on, yet she bravely defended us. I knew she wouldn't go down without a fight.

Chapter 44 – His Red Wolf

KELLEN

More of Vargr's army had turned up and we were now engaged in a full-on battle. Metal clanked, and growls were heard as some of the opposition began to shift, their wolves attacking my gladiators who could not shift.

"We're outnumbered!" I heard Jasper call to me from my left.

I cut down a soldier, his body dropping like a heap of rocks, and darted my eyes around the arena. He was right, we were outnumbered. I smirked because even though it looked like we were at a disadvantage, I knew we could win this. "Maybe, but his army doesn't have the skill my Elites have."

I looked to Rogue, who was on my right, fighting beside me. "Rogue, keep the gladiators fighting with the non-shifted," I yelled to him while plunging my sword into another soldier's chest, knowing that the gladiator's chips were still active. They couldn't shift or else they would die.

"Hunji!" I called to the man in red, who was taking down man after man and dropping wolves like they were vermin. "Show these soldiers what an Elite army can do!" I thought fast and began to redirect our troops strategically.

"Yes, Your Highness, with pleasure." And the fucker actually smiled and rushed forward, calling out commands to ours and Jasper's fighters, knowing exactly what I was thinking. After all, it was Hunji who had trained me back at the academy. We were lucky to have a man of his skill and experience fighting alongside us.

Just then, I heard the howl of a female wolf. I felt a tightness grab my chest, and my heart sped up in fear. *'Mate,'* Conri growled. I didn't need him to confirm it, in my heart I already knew it was her wolf who had called out. My mate needed me, she was close. I saw Jasper freeze, his eyes locked on mine - wide and fearful.

"Tala." That one word, made me shiver. The growl of a much larger wolf each our ears. "Fuck, Vargr has Tala!" No. I would not let him hurt her again.

Mike, I'm going for my mate. I don't see Vargr but kill him on sight if you get to him before me I linked him when I didn't see him. Then called out to Hunji that I was going for Tala.

Without another second to waste, I took off in the direction I had heard the howl of my mate's wolf, tearing down anyone who got in my way. I bounded up the stone steps that led to the courtyard, the same ones I had descended not so long ago. Reaching the top in seconds, I saw a large brown wolf looming over a smaller red she-wolf at the other end. He had her cornered and looked ready to attack.

My mate. Her red fur was just as bright as Tala's hair.

My heart stopped for a second when the red wolf stood on all fours and growled at the much larger brown wolf. He was big, Alpha sized. This must be Vargr.

"HEY!" I yelled, running forward to catch his attention. The brown wolf halted and turned its head toward me. Saliva dripped from his muzzle and the red wolf leaped onto him, digging her teeth into his shoulder. He knocked her off with a harsh shake and had the time to give me a wolfish grin before his hind legs came up and kicked the red wolf so hard that she hit the wall. The small wolf slumped down the wall and laid there with labored breathing.

I felt frozen, unable to move an inch, worried about my mate as she lay there unmoving. That fear quickly turned to anger, and a storm full of endless rage built inside me. I was ready to unleash that fury onto the brown wolf.

The Alpha wolf shifted when I was twenty feet from him, and there stood Vargr in all his glory. It really wasn't a nice sight to see. An older Alpha who had let himself go. I stopped when he began to laugh. My eyes were still on the little red wolf behind him who moved. She seemed to be okay other than getting knocked out and now coming to.

"Vargr!" I hissed.

"Wolf King, it surprised me that you had lived, but you are still the underdog in this figh.t" He chuckled.

"Is that so?" I questioned him, ready to tear this fucker's head off. "Then fight me like an alpha and we will see who the underdog is."

"Fight you?" He laughed. "I don't need to fight you to win." He laughed again. "*Shift.*" He commanded me and my wolf.

He still thought my inhibitor chip was active? Stupid fool. "I don't think you want me to shift." I said, trying to hide my wry smile.

"*Shift.*" He commanded again, with a little scowl.

"I had hoped to make you suffer, but you leave me no choice if you insist on me shifting," I smirked.

"I SAID SHIFT!" Vargr was becoming more perplexed by the second, and it was only fueling his and his wolf's anger. It was obvious I was ignoring his command, he should have had an inkling then when he had to repeat himself. He visibly began to shake with rage before he shifted back into his wolf. And lunged toward me.

Within seconds I had shifted into Conri. His silver fur glistened under the light of the moon, and his giant form flew up to meet Vargr's much smaller wolf in mid-air. Claws and teeth locked as we tumbled to the ground and rolled.

If Vargr thought this was going to be an easy fight for him, then he must have definitely lost a few loose screws somewhere along the line. We broke apart and I could see his wolf tremble with fear when he looked up at Conri, who bared his teeth and snapped at him. Yet the fool still came at us, snapping his jaws and wildly growling, looking like a rabid animal.

Conri thought about ending him in one swift move but changed his mind at the last second and whirled around, knocking him over with his butt. Vargr's wolf got up snarling and challenged us again.

'End this Conri.' I told my wolf, wanting this shit show to be over so we could get to our mate, who I could see was stirring from behind Vargr's wolf.

'With delight,' he replied with a cheesy growl.

The brown wolf was waiting for us to make the first move, so Conri stalked forward, teeth showing and a low rumble from his chest. The wolf crouched and then attacked. Conri caught him mid-air, latching onto his neck, and violently shook him, tearing chunks of fur and flesh as he did.

We threw the Vargr to the ground where he stayed, not attempting to move like the weak, pathetic shit he was. My wolf lorded over hi, when the weak alpha shifted back into his human form, grabbing his open wound. I shifted back into my skin form and bent down to a crouch in front of him.

"Is he dead?" I turned to see my mate, naked as the day she was born, come to stand next to me glaring at Vargr.

"No, would you like the honors, my queen?" I asked, standing from a crouching position to face her.

"No," she said softly with a slight shake of her head. "I just want to watch as he takes his last breath. End this, my king."

"Wait, Tala... you don't..." Vargr began to talk, but his words were just noise. There was nothing he had to say that either of us wanted to hear.

I crouched down next to him again, bending and taking his head in my hands. Before I broke his neck I whispered to him, "You fucked with the wrong gladiator. You are nothing. You die as nothing." With that, I twisted my wrists and snapped his neck, hearing his spine separate from his skull as I did. I let go of his head, his body limp, and his eyes open and dark from death. I stood up next to my mate.

"I wanted to laugh in his face when he died, but I couldn't do it," Tala spoke quietly. Her words had a befuddled tone to them. Like she couldn't figure out why wasn't laughing or why she couldn't, she stood there staring down at the dead alpha.

I took her in my arms, pushing her head into my chest and kissing the top of her head. "I don't think we ever act the way we think we would or should in the face of death," I said, dropping another kiss on her head. "Death is disturbing and dark; it creates emotions we didn't think we would feel. Do not trouble yourself over his death."

"Your Highness!" Both Tala and I turned toward Jasper as he ran towards us. I growled and pushed Tala's naked form behind mine, warning him to not look at my mate.

Jasper dropped his eyes to the ground but flitted them to

where Vargr's lifeless form lay and let out a huge exhale of breath, the visible tension rolling off of him when he saw he was dead. It was then I noticed the silence in the blood-soaked air. The fighting had ceased. They had all felt the connection to their alpha snap. The fight was over.

"Princess! Princess!" The maid who had opened the front door came running towards us with a blanket. Wrapping it around Tala as soon as she was close enough.

Tala hugged the old woman, who began to stroke her hair, "Shh, it is over now," she told her.

"My mother?" Tala asked still hugging her. "She, she..."

"She took her own life. She heard what Vargr was going to do and jumped from the bell tower, hoping it would create a distraction and weaken him so you could get away. She did it for you Tala. I am so sorry." The old woman began to weep. "Your mother was too sad to stay in this realm any longer."

Tala moved from the old woman's embrace and nodded her head. She had no tears, but I could see the mortification she held in the way her posture curved. "I know," she sighed. "What now?" She asked, looking at me and then Jasper.

"Here, stop showing off your title," Mike chuckled, throwing some shorts at me as he just turned up to the scene. "Hunji and Cameron are rounding up Vargr's army."

"They surrendered when they felt the link to their alpha snap," Jasper said while I slipped on the shorts and moved over to take Tala from the old woman's arms and bring her into mine, where she belonged.

"Now Jasper cleans house and starts putting this kingdom back together. The way it was meant to be." I answered my mate's question, holding her tight against me. I was never letting her go again. I was never going to let her out of my sight again. I almost felt sorry for my mate. Now that I had her, there was no way my wolf nor I wanted to be away from her ever again, that possessive alpha instinct kicking into full gear.

When we walked into the palace, the old woman leading the way, Jasper already had men cleaning up the remaining bodies and bloodied floor, and I could smell food being cooked in the kitchen.

"Princess, the kitchen has already started preparing food for all the men. Once things have been settled, it will be laid out in the main dining hall for them to eat as they please." The old woman told us once we had reached the main part of the palace, where a grand staircase stood leading up to a few more floors. "Also, we have made provisions for the King's army to bathe and rest. My husband will make sure they know where to go."

"Thank you, Mildred, for everything," Tala said, giving her a slight nod of the head.

"Why don't you and the king go wash up before the meal is ready." She said, winking at me and my mate.

It seemed strange that there would be a happy vibe in the air, that no one was mourning. If I hadn't been here myself, I would have never thought that this palace had just had a battle and lives had been lost. Was Vargr's rule that bad, that people were actually happy he had died and would celebrate? The staff here had organized and prepared for victory.

"Okay." She giggled back at the old maid, her cheeks holding a slight blush. "This way, my king," she smiled, taking me by the hand and leading me towards the stairs.

Tala brought me to a modest-looking room with simple décor, a queen-sized bed, a dresser, and a vanity. The walls were white, but the bedding was in light shades of blue and pink. I was guessing this was her room. It was confirmed when she shyly asked, "I hope you don't think I was being too presumptuous by bringing you to my room?"

I smirked, turning it into a fully-fledged smile as I pulled her by the hand I was holding and brought her up against me. "That depends on what you are being bold about, my little flame." I rasped, looking into those striking blue irises of hers, licking my lips.

She bit her lip, and her pale skin flushed with color. When she tried to avert her eyes from me in embarrassment, I caught her chin between my finger and thumb and tilted her head up towards me. Her tiny frame quivered, and I felt goosebumps break out all over her arms that held on to the blanket tightly. "Those are my lips to bite," I told her, and then stooped down to capture them with mine.

Her mouth parted immediately, welcoming my tongue as I deepened the kiss and angled my head so my tongue could delve deeper into her sweet-tasting mouth. I felt her breath hitch, and she let out a little moan at the heated and passionate moment we were sharing.

I growled when the scent of her excitement reached my nostrils, my cock hardening in the thin shorts, ready to claim my mate. My hands moved to play with the edge of the blanket, ready to unwrap my prize when Mike's voice invaded my thoughts. *Kellen, you need to come back down here,* he said.

Not now! I'm busy! I growled back. I wanted time alone with my mate to worship her, to explore her, to claim her. I had waited long enough.

I'm sorry, man, you know I wouldn't interrupt if it wasn't important...

*Fucking deal with it, Mike. There can't be anything that's

that...*

Tobias found Oliver.

"*Fuck!*" I groaned aloud, starling Tala and making her jump. I didn't realize I had growled too. "I'm sorry, I didn't mean to scare you. My beta just mind-linked me that they found Oliver. I have to deal with him." I reluctantly let go of my mate, internally scolding myself for not putting up a block. "Wait here for me, I will be done with that snake quickly."

We had been looking for Oliver for three years now. There was no way I was missing this opportunity to rip his head off. I didn't rip Vargr's off, only because Tala was standing there; otherwise, I would have and then put it on a fucking spike in the middle of that dang arena. I pecked Tala on the lips and then left her room. Pissed, might I add.

"You seriously have bad fucking timing!" I chastised Mike as I got back down to the courtyard where Mike, Hunji, Jasper, Rogue, and Tobias stood. Tobias was holding a very defeated and sorrowful-looking Oliver by the scruff of his neck.

"Wolf King!" Tobias greeted me with a wide grin. "Look what I got for you. Almost killed him myself. Went out of the palace, back to where our trucks are sitting, and look who came crawling out of a rock. Like really came crawling out from under a rock," he laughed.

They already had him in silver cuffs, but he didn't look roughed up at all. "I thought about beating the shit out of him, but... I figured you owed him all fun. Call it an early birthday present." Tobias answered my unasked question, ending the sentence with a wink.

"Oliver, Oliver, what to do with you?" I sneered. "It would be so easy to rip your heart out, or your head off. I could slowly torture you?" I contemplated how I wanted to kill him for a moment. "Maybe you would prefer torture? I know how much you enjoyed that when you and Silas held MacTire."

"Do what you will, King Kellen. I deserve it." Oliver didn't even try to plead for his life. He obviously knew that this was how it would end: me and him, a million miles from where he killed my parents, and I would still get to kill him.

Oliver wouldn't look me in the eye, keeping his head low, accepting his fate as he should. It had been a long time coming.

Chapter 45 – A Fate Worse than Death

KELLEN
DAY 23 OF THE GAMES (early morning after the battle)

Rogue handed me my sword. I turned it in my palm a few times, debating whether to just end Oliver or start cutting little pieces off him. I still hadn't made up my mind when my little flame came running towards us, now wearing a light pink dress. "Kellen stop! No, please! Don't kill him!" She cried out, stepping between me and the soon-to-be dead shifter.

Protecting Oliver.

I ground my teeth together, not wanting to argue with her, but she didn't understand. Like a slithering snake, the jealousy of her choosing another man over me crawled over my skin because that's what it felt like, what made it worse was that it was fucking Oliver! The man I dreamt of killing for three fucking years. The sly fucker that always got away.

"Listen Red, he is the most wanted man by four kingdoms in the first continent, after Orion and his bitch Shayna." Tobias retorted behind Tala, his hand securely gripping Oliver's neck. I rolled my eyes back and held my breath. Tobias seriously needed to shuck the fuck up. Conri began pushing forward, trying to force me to shift. He saw the bear shifter, our friend, as a threat toward our mate and I tried to calm my wolf. He was simmering just below the surface.

I tried telling him to calm, controlling my own violent urges and Conri's were proving difficult.

Tala spun around, placing her hands on her hips. I couldn't see her face, but I could tell she was staring Tobias down. "Listen here werebear, that bitch Shayna happened to be my sister and you don't know shit about her!" Then she turned to me, and I was right, my little flame was burning bright with hot anger. "I don't give a shit what he has done in his past, he saved me! He killed Jack and saved my ass twice!" She snapped, pointing behind her at the snake in the grass Oliver. "You promised you wouldn't kill him," her tone was just a tad softer.

Is she fucking kidding me? She just pleaded for his life? This kidnapping, raping, murderer? My mate just pleaded for the life of the man who committed the biggest crimes of our realm against the Queen of Shifters. My temper flared, and my chest started to rumble with Conri's low growls. I was angry that my mate was naïve to Oliver's ways. It was like he had charmed her, made her believe that he wasn't all that bad, just a lost soul.

'*Kill*,' snarled Conri, stirring at the precipice of my mind, ready to push me off the edge. The jealousy flared, mixing into a dangerous concoction with the slowly boiling temper Conri wanted to unleash on Tobias.

"You have no idea what kind of wolf this man is. He wouldn't think twice to rape and kill you. Do you think Jack was bad? He is no better." Tobias spat back at my mate. I gave him a low warning growl that he was stepping over the line. He had no idea how close he was to me killing him right now.

A low whistle came from Mike, who didn't want to get involved but was just as eager to see Oliver's death. "Lamia is going to love her," he chuckled.

"Who is this... Lamia?" Tala asked, still with a pout and frown on her face.

"The Queen of Shifters, the woman this ass wipe kidnapped and committed a... a horrible crime against." I noticed Mike changed his answer, not wanting to air our best friend's dirty laundry in front of everyone or give Oliver the satisfaction of hearing it. Not publicly, not here. It was difficult for Mike to talk about; he was the one who had taken her out of the cell, him and Tawny.

Tala's mouth formed an 'O', and she cocked her head at me. I didn't miss the sharp sting of jealousy, she hid it pretty quickly, and my eyes moved to Oliver. I let Conri come forward through my eyes, and I knew they were going black. Like a shield, a protective film slips over my eye, and a power like no other feeling starts resonating throughout my body to the beat of Conri's eerie growls he has aimed at Oliver.

"Might I suggest something?" Hunji stepped forward, cutting off the building tension, the ever-present calmness to his tone, and lack of emotion.

I slipped a look at my little flame and was pleasantly surprised that she was looking at me lustfully. Conri's attention averted from 'kill' to 'Tala'. Just the thought of his mate subdued him for now. I scrubbed a hand down my face, nothing was ever easy. "What do you suggest, Hunji?"

"We take him back to MacTire, let Travis handle him however he sees fit." Hunji's suggestion was a good one. A fair one. I knew we all wanted a piece of him, but when it came down to it, Oliver may have killed my parents, but it was Lamia and Travis who really had the right to determine his fate. "I think this would bring some closure to Travis." I had to agree, Oliver didn't just torture Travis amongst other things, Oliver was the one who almost killed Travis with his silver arrows and helped kidnap Petra.

I noticed Tala stiffen at the word MacTire and look at Hunji with curious eyes. Had she heard of that place?

I saw Mike's eyes glaze over, and then he connected the four knights and Lamia in a mind-link. *Lamia, we have captured Oliver, Hunji has suggested we bring him back to MacTire for Travis to decide his fate instead of us killing him right here and now.*

Finally! That scum deserves to die! Her sweet voice carried through my head. *Rhett, what do you think?* She asked the fourth knight, Travis's gamma.

Bring him back here for sentencing. He will be tried for his crimes in court. It was the right thing to do, even though we wanted him dead. The law states we are to hold a trial, and Rhett was the head of the enforcers, upholders of the law.

It was settled; little did Oliver know that it would be a fate worse than death. I could only imagine what Travis would do to him, and it would be nothing less than what the scumbag deserved. "Oliver will be escorted back to MacTire, Alpha Travis and Gamma Rhett will try him for his crimes and decide on his fate," I said. "Jasper, can your men escort Commander Tobias and the prisoner to your cells?"

"Of course," Jasper agreed and called a few of his men over.

Tala turned back to Oliver, "I'm sorry, Oliver. I had hoped you would have been far away and got to live the life you wanted. Free... of all this." I hated the tone she used towards him, it was regretful and remorseful. If only she knew what he had done.

"It's okay, princess, I deserve no less." He lifted his cuffed hands and stroked her cheek with his fingers. And the fucker had the balls to look into her eyes longingly! Mother of the

Moon Goddess, my mate didn't want me to kill him, but she was making it really hard for me to keep my word. Hunji, Mike, and even Tobias looked worried and shared a look between them. Tobias yanked Oliver away, realizing his mistake. Maybe Oliver did know that handing him to Travis would entail more than a quick death?

"Get him out of here, I growled. Another second of him looking at her like that and touching her, I would snap. I was truly holding on to Conri by a sun god's fucking thread right now. I couldn't imagine what my face looked like at this moment because it felt all kinds of screwed up to me. I wanted to snap his fucking head off.

I clenched my fists and drew in deep breaths, trying to hone in my building temper and jealousy. Those two emotions were a recipe for an explosive reaction. I was so much stronger after receiving the mark of a knight. Even stronger now that I have been here and come back from dead, it was hard to control all this built-up energy after Conri had been confined for three months.

Tala noticed I was having a hard time controlling my wolf. At first, she looked a little frightened, the look disappearing and a new one emerging. One full of lust and want. One that craved her alpha, her king. Tala slid over to me, her body hot beneath my palms, a light sheen of sweat coated her forehead, and wrapped her arms around my waist. Instantly I began to feel calmer as the mate bonds magic did its thing.

Tala's hands began to explore my naked chest and she started scenting me, her nose going from my torso up to my chest. Her tongue poked out of those petal-kissed lips of hers, trailing along as Tala slowly let her nose brush against my skin, tasting with the flicks of her tongue. She had no idea what she was doing to me. Every second her arousal got stronger, and her scent became overpowering. I just wanted to bury myself deep inside her.

"Tala, stop!" I said harshly, pulling her from me. If she didn't, I would mate her right here and now, in front of my men, and stake my claim on her for all to witness.

"Kellen," she pushed herself towards me, her hand reaching for my engorged cock. "I want to fuck you," she seductively spoke. The precipitation building on her skin, her scent musky and...

"Shit, she's in heat!" Jasper groaned out just as I thought it.

Well, at least we had defeated Vargr before she went into heat. I picked my mate up like a bride, her hands twining around the nape of my neck, fingers twirling with my hair. Soft lips found their way to my shoulder. My cock hardened painfully when she started nibbling on my shoulder and then kissed each spot she bit.

"Shit, Tala," I moaned, moving with inhuman speed to get to her room. "You are really testing me, I don't know if I can hold back from you. I won't let another man touch you. Ever!"

"Kellen, I was going to let you have me earlier. Now I just have you to myself longer." She said between sweet nips and licks now near my marking spot. Moons, this woman... Fuck, she could hate me later. I wasn't strong enough to hold back. She had already marked me. I couldn't say no. Hell, I didn't want to say no. The sparks I felt between us were hot and fiery, and her just saying the words, knowing she wanted me as much I wanted her had me losing all rational thinking.

We made it to her room; I think it was her room. I took a quick look around. Yep, it smelt like her in here and it looked like hers. Good enough. I put her down on the bed, and she scrambled out of her dress. Quite quickly. She was a she-wolf in heat, craving to be mated. I was an alpha, a king, and she need to mate with me, her wolf demanded it. She felt the bond and the attraction much more with us both having alpha blood, and once in heat, it could last anywhere from two to five days.

Tala was up on her knees reaching for me. I let her pull me forward, and her hands played with the band of my shorts, her fingers dipping down and hooking the band, sliding them down. Her eyes followed and widened when she freed my cock and licked her lips. She looked up at me with wild, hungry eyes.

I looked down at her, drinking in her porcelain skin, teardrop breasts, and down to the firm curve of her ass. All basic instincts told me to pounce and sink into her warm center, where my eyes were now glued to her pussy, bare except for the thin strip of red hair. She already told me no man had ever touched her before, her words echoing in my head as my lustful eyes roamed her perfect body.

The sun was just coming up, and a golden stream of light poured through her window, dancing across her skin and illuminating her hair, making it look more like the hot flame of a fire than it already did. I pushed her back onto the bed and crawled over her, her legs parting for me. I captured her lips in a bruising kiss, a show-stopping kiss, one that would have me bending at the knee and agreeing to anything for my little flame.

When she panted for air, I began kissing down her neck, past her collar bone, slowly moving down until I reached her breasts and sucked one of her already hardened nipples into my mouth. Her back arched, and she moaned out a sensual sound of pleasure when her erect bud popped from my lips. I moved to the other breast administrating the same action, this time sucking harder and taking more in my mouth. Her hips lifted and her opening brushed against my cock.

All I wanted to do was sink into her, but not yet. I trailed sweet kisses between her breasts, moving further down and over her flat stomach.

"Kellen, please." She moaned wantonly. She had no idea what she was asking for - her heat driving her to mate.

I slipped a hand between her thighs, between us. My middle finger caressed her opening. She shuddered and bucked when I spread her wetness over her and found that tight little bud and let my finger roll it before pushing that finger inside her and watching her eyes roll back, lips part, and a ruttish sound escaped. I slowly plunged my finger in and out, watching her reaction before adding another. She was so tight around my fingers, her channel squeezing - I could only imagine the feeling of her wrapped around my cock. I crooked my fingers and found that soft spot, rubbing over it, her breathing becoming more labored.

"Dear goddess, don't stop!" She wailed, letting me know how close she was to falling over the edge.

"I don't think I could ever stop wanting you, Tala." It was the truth.

I slowed down my movements and brought my face over hers, diving in for a short but promising kiss. My fingers still slowly stroked her while my tongue ran down the length of her body until I reached her hip and moved between her legs. I let my tongue lick from her opening to her clit and sucking it in, then gave her a quick nip.

Tala squirmed in ecstasy as my mouth latched on, my tongue delved to her clit, and my fingers pumped in and out. Her moans got louder, and when she clamped around my fingers, her legs shook and she went off like a firecracker. Her ragged breathing and whimpers echoed into the room. I tasted her orgasm that spilled into my mouth and lapped her juices up, growling at the taste, which only made me want her riding my cock even more.

I slid up her body and she pulled me to her, kissing me. Tangling our tongues, she moaned out in greed when she tasted herself on me. "I need you inside me, Kellen," she says between nipping my lips.

"Your wish is my command," I growled and moved my hips so my cock was seated right at her entrance. My intentions were to go slow, it was her first time, and I didn't want to hurt her any more than it already might. I pushed the head of my rock-solid, throbbing length into her entrance, watching her, making sure my little flame was good to go. She lifted her hips and wrapped her legs around me tight and impaled her pussy onto my cock, taking all of me in one go - her back lifting off the bed as I filled her. Her sultry moan had me making my own sounds of rapture.

I stilled, catching my breath before I blew my load. Tala's hand reached up, and her nails softly slid down my chest, leaving a trail of prickled skin as the sparks ignited all over me. This was nothing like I had experienced before. Being connected to Tala felt like home. A place I never wanted to leave.

"Kellen... Please," she moaned breathily and circled her hips, grinding against me.

I opened my eyes only to meet hers, locking our gazes and finding ourselves in a moment of utopia. I pulled my throbbing cock from her heat and pushed back in slowly. "More," she begged, and I plowed into her.

"You are mine, Tala. Say it" I growled, still keeping a steady pace, moving in and out of her.

"Yours." She heaved as I thrusted into her roughly.

"Say it again. I want to hear you."

"Yours, my king. Yours!" She cried out, and I slammed my cock into her.

Plunging into my little flame over and over, I hooked my arms under her shoulders and leaned back on my knees, holding her tight against me. My hips bucked into her, seating my cock deep inside while she held on to my shoulders. My gums began to tingle, and as if sensing it herself, Tala tilted her head.

My canines descended and pierced through her skin, right where her neck and shoulder met. She screamed out, her orgasm rocketing around me, milking my cock for everything it had and squeezing me to my own release. I released my bite and emptied my seed into her, throwing my head back as I did and howling at the feeling of completing the mate bond.

I let go of my grip on her and ran my tongue over my bite, lapping at the small amount of blood. Her body went limp in my arms, and I laid her down in front of me, her legs still hooked around my hips.

"Again," she said with her eyes closed. I laughed. I most certainly would take her again, I just needed a moment and so did she.

Chapter 46 – Why the Witch?

<u>TALA</u>
WHAT WOULD HAVE BEEN: DAY 23 OF THE GAMES

Kellen was angry. I could feel it and I knew some of that anger had been directed at me when I defended Oliver. His jealousy crept off of him, I could almost see it, like dark tendrils of shadows reaching out to me and twisting across my flesh. How dark his aura was, was frightening; words were unfit for the Wolf King's thoughts. Kellen stared down his men, then landed his frightening eyes on Oliver. Obsidian black eyes, the only white showing was the white mark of the knight, bright against where his pupil would sit - If you could see them.

It was an eerie sight to see and feel. I could almost taste his strength and see how hard he was trying to rein his wolf in. His wolf was magnificent. There was a painting in my mother's room that depicted a goddess walking with her wolf. Kellen's wolf was the spitting image of the one I grew up seeing every day. The look of primal carnage on his face and those vines of jealousy wrapping tightly around me made me hot. Light perspiration coated my skin as my desire heated up.

I needed to feel him. I wanted Kellen to consume me, and the desire bubbling inside began to surface to an immeasurable boil.

I wrapped my arms around my mate, scenting his spice

and masculine natural smell, my tongue tasting him as my senses consumed themselves in him. Bathing in his muscular and ruggedness. My body was craving him. Mora was whimpering her lust, the need for her mate to claim her was great. When he pushed me away a little, it surprised me when the words 'I want to fuck you' came flying out of my mouth.

I didn't even care if he took me right then and there. I needed to mate him and needed it now. There was an ache between my legs, pulsing and hot, and I was dripping with desire.

I barely registered Jasper saying I was in heat when Kellen swept me off my feet. I couldn't keep my hands or lips off him, nipping and kissing the skin I could touch. I wanted him to touch me.

*****

I woke later that morning encompassed in large, strong arms, still craving my mate's touch. My hunger for him was insatiable. I felt sore between my legs, yet for someone who was a virgin less than a few hours ago, my craving had not been satisfied. The heat had died down, but I still wanted more. Recalling the memory from earlier this morning when I had demanded Kellen to fuck me again. And he had - Over and over.

I lifted my hand, my fingers going to my neck where Kellen had marked me. Little pleasurable sparks ignited when I touched the area, remembering the feel of his teeth sinking into me and his cock buried deep inside me. I was barely conscious after coming down from the high and my own orgasm when I told him, 'Again'.

I smiled and relaxed back into the safety and warmth of

my mate's strong hold. A place I never wanted to leave.

"Good morning, gorgeous," I heard Kellen's voice, deeper from waking up. The husky sound stirred up all those sexual desires once again.

"You mean afternoon," I giggled, and he sat up, pulling me with him so I was tucked into his side.

He sniffed me, his nose delving into the crook of my neck and taking a big gulp of my scent. "You smell like a mixture of you and me, I like it." I could feel his smile against my neck. He softly pecked the tender skin, his lips barely grazing me, but all the same, he still left me shivering in delight.

"What happens now?" I asked, turning into his arms and wrapping mine around his neck. His frame pushed me down until I was lying crooked beneath him, his large masculine frame leaning above me.

"Now we go home." He smiled.

"Your home?" I gulped. The truth was, I didn't want to stay here and hoped he would say yes.

This place no longer felt like home, it never had if I truly thought about it. My mother had taken her own life, Vargr was never my real father, and he consequently killed the man that was. My sister had died under the influence of Orion, and that was just the tip of the shit show. Poor Jasper had been lied to just as much as me. I wanted a fresh start.

"Yes, I have a kingdom I need to take care of, and I have been away far too long." His eyes studied my face with concern. "I don't want to rush you Tala... but,"

"I understand, and I want to go with you. My place is beside you. The only place I will ever want to be." I told him exactly what I was feeling. I didn't want any more lies in my life. No more.

I knew I had said the right thing when his face lit up like a lantern and he beamed a wolfish smile at me, making me melt over again. It was crazy to think how much I had fallen for him without even knowing him at all. The mate bond was doing its thing, pulling us together, weaving its threads around us, and bonding our souls together for life. Now that Kellen had marked me and wore my mark, I didn't even want to think about the possibility that we would ever be apart.

Kellen bent his head, his lips pressing against mine firmly and capturing me in a slow, passionate kiss. A kiss that made my heart stop and my breath catch. A kiss that had my toes curling and sent me dizzy. A kiss I found myself lost in.

All too soon, he had broken away from me, leaving my lips puckered, waiting for more, and I pouted from the loss of him. "Where are you going?" I asked, sitting up as he rolled to the side and clambered out of the bed.

"You need food and I want to get shit sorted out here, and to be honest," he looked at me lovingly, "I want to go home, Tala. I want to take you home."

I nodded at him, feeling a little disappointed that he didn't want to spend the day in bed with me. I also knew it must have been so hard for him, being stuck here against his will. Thinking of him being kidnapped and sold into slavery brought my thoughts to Teal and my mother, and I felt the unshed tears brimming at the surface. I took a shaky breath, willing them to stay where they were while I got my emotions under control.

"Baby, what's wrong?" Kellen had noticed my discomfort and came back to my side, sitting on the bed and wrapping his arms around me. I leaned into him, needing that calmness the mate bond supplied, providing me with the love and comfort I needed at that moment.

I shook my head, "I'm being silly."

"No, you are not. Tell me what's going on in that beautiful head of yours?" He soothed, pinching my chin lightly and raising my head so our gazes could meet.

"I understand why my mother took her own life, she had been ill for a very long time. I understand her death." I shuddered out a breath. "It still hurts but... Teal, I, he said something to me... right before he died." And I felt the streak of wetness glide down my cheek.

Kellen swept the tear away with his thumb. "What did he say?" Concern etched across his face.

So, I told him verbatim, because those last words of his would be forever etched in my mind. "He said his name was Teal Mac-Tire and that he was the Alpha of the Sea Dog pack. What I found strange was he told me that he was a Knight of the Red Branch and that his wolf Cuchulainn would be born again to serve his King Conri. Who is King Conri?" I asked, searching my brain for if I had ever heard that name before.

'He is my mate,' Mora stirred in my head, and at the same time, Kellen frowned and said. "Conri is my wolf."

"I never knew Teal's family name was Mac-Tire." He looked perplexed, a little withdrawn as if he was lost in his own thoughts.

"Does that name mean something to you?'"

"It does," he slowly nodded, still staring off into space. "MacTire is a kingdom on our continent. A long story, and I'm not sure it's mine to tell." I could see the information had slightly rattled him or at least put him in deep thought. I didn't want to push it; I figured he would tell me in his own time. We had the rest of our lives to learn about each other, and I, for one, was okay with that. I didn't care how long it took us to get to know each other, as long we were together. My wolf hummed in happiness and agreement.

*****

Later that day, after showering and another round of Kellen's glorious cock filling me up, a large number of us piled into the large seating area on the ground floor of the palace. No one wanted to go into Vargr's office. I was surprised to see Beta Baron there, standing close to Jasper. He was looking solemn and a little afraid at the larger-than-life shifters in the room, and kept sliding worried glances towards the bear-shifter, Tobias.

"I want to leave as soon as possible," Kellen stated. "Jasper, what do you need from us in order to get this kingdom to a place you can begin to grow and the people start trusting your leadership?" I loved that he took charge just like that, diving in to get all the necessary facts so he could make a decision, and more importantly, he took into consideration the pack members.

Jasper slid a look to me. "I need to pull the slaves from the mines, make an announcement that all slaves are free, and I would like to give them and their families compensation." He smiled at me. It was something we had talked about before, what we would do when he became alpha. "Also, we need to hold some funerals for deceased pack members."

Eloise, who was standing beside him, also smiled, with a proud look on her face for her mate. My eyes went wide when I noticed the mark on her neck that she wasn't trying to cover. I looked at Jasper, who smiled even bigger at me, and as if knowing what my expression was for, he raised his hand and pulled the collar of his shirt to the side so I could see his mark too. The thought that those two had finally completed the mating bond made me so happy I started crying.

"Tala," Jasper said worriedly.

El went to move towards me but I waved a hand at her, telling her to stay put. "I'm just so happy for you guys. I didn't," I swallowed hard trying to find the words, "I'm just so thankful it worked out for you guys. I love you both so much!"

I felt a little silly crying in front of all these men, in front of Kellen's men, who one day I would be their queen. It wasn't my strongest moment.

"I think any of the slaves who had been brought by Vargr, should be offered to stay and find a place here, or be given the means to go back to where they came from," Jasper carried on, doing me the favor of ignoring my happy tears so as not to embarrass me.

"With my son's permission, I would like to stay on as an advisor. We have not had council members in this kingdom since before Vargr's reign," Beta Baron supplied. I watched for Jasper's reaction when he called him son, and when Jasper didn't flinch, just bobbed his head, I knew they would be okay. No matter what blood ran through his veins, the old beta still considered him his son, and Jasper still considered him a father.

"Beta Baron, my only father, was as much as a victim as the gladiators. Not only had he been subjected to an inhibitor like the gladiators, but he was also under the influence of Vargr's commands and a cheating mate. He has enlightened me about much since Vargr died and the chips became inactive. He will be staying and acting as a gamma as we begin to bring this kingdom back to a place the people can be proud of. There is much to accomplish, and in time, I believe we will win back the trust of the people of Bhakhil."

I was so proud of Jasper, and I really wanted to believe that

Baron was a good person and any wrongdoing he committed was down to Vargr's influence.

"We also have another issue," Beta Baron looked at Jasper with concern and with hope in his eyes when he regarded Kellen. "King Panja of Asiarian was mobilizing his troops as of last week. After news of Orion's death, kingdoms have begun to start fighting. There was a gap left with his absence, and now larger kingdoms are looking to take over and claim even more territory and cities. Panja is particularly interested in our mines."

A scoff came from the dark wolf, Hunji. "The old man was always a greedy bastard. Are they not still the richest kingdom this side of the water?" He asked, but I didn't think he was looking for a reply. Beta Baron's remark had physically upset him, his eyes had become impossibly darker, and I could see the vein in his forehead throbbing.

"Yes, and he also has the largest army. Our army is big and trained well, but we will lose if it comes to war. The only reason he has not attacked before was because of Orion. He feared Orion like everyone else." Beta Baron explained.

"He also has many children refusing to complete the mate bond, and keeps many mistresses." I looked at Jasper, shocked. How could someone deny the mate bond for so long and keep a harem of women in front of her? I had never met King Panja, and I hoped I wouldn't.

After discussions about the future of Bhakhil and me announcing that I would be handing over fifty percent of the mines to Jasper and Eloise so they would have the funds to put into the pack, Jasper, Cameron, and El left to go make announcements. One of the announcements was that the Gladiator Games would cease, effective immediately. Instead, a celebration would be held on the full moon to solidify a new beginning and a new Alpha and Luna.

I was a little sorry I wouldn't be here to witness Bhakhil's new beginning. However, I was more than excited that I would get to travel and see the outside realm through my own eyes instead of through the pages of a book. That, and I was anxious to see my mate's home, my new home.

"I think we should leave tomorrow. It seems as though Jasper has things under control and we won't be needed. We could leave a few of our Elite warriors to help train the army in case this other king does come looking for a fight." That was Kellen's beta, Mike. A handsome and large male, he seemed to have charisma surrounding him and a face that said he could be a handful but was a kind and playful person.

"You just want to get back to your little obsession." The large bear shifter said while laughing at the Royal Beta.

"Obsession?" Kellen laughed, but looked at Mike quizzically.

"Yep, Mike fell on his knees, literally, for the Sea Dog pack Alpha's sister. Pretty sure he almost cried when he left her at the docks." The bear shifter laughed some more.

"Shut it, Tobias." Mike warned the bear shifter whose name I just learned, and then turned to Kellen with a serious look. "Her name is Jonda, and she is coming home with us."

Kellen stared at his beta, their eyes locked like they were having a private conversation. I was right when the beta looked at me, stunned. "Well, I'll be damned!" He chuckled, "It really is a small realm."

It took me by surprise when the large wolf shifter named Hunji spoke again, hearing his voice for the second time. His deep voice, somewhat husky, matched his outer persona: dark, quiet, but dangerously handsome. His tanned skin, onyx eyes, and long hair made him look like one of King

Panja's Royal commanders. Intimidating, wild, and savage. "I will not be returning with you, King Kellen." His voice almost commanded the room.

"Why not?" Kellen asked him with a frown, those beautiful blue eyes darkening.

"Queen Lamia sent me on a mission. After finding you, I have been tasked with a quest to go looking for Finnegan's sister, she has supposedly been locked up for years because of her witch background. Her last known location was somewhere close to Andora," he remarked, and I jumped up from my seat on Kellen's lap.

"The witch? The witch is Finnegan's sister?" I said with a little too much excitement because I actually knew something they didn't. This was all too much. "Jack wanted the location of a witch, and I gave Oliver one of my sister's diaries that told him the location, or at least the last known location of the witch. It was part of the original deal we made. Jewels and the location of the witch and he would help me. She recorded everything, but the diary didn't mention a specific location, just that she was in Andora, and no name was mentioned either. I don't think Orion let anyone near her or wanted anyone to know who she was." I explained to them.

"Why is everyone after this witch? What is so important about her?" I was curious. I had heard of witches, we even had some shifters in our pack that had ancestors that were witches. Witches were healers. They sometimes had intuition and could manipulate plants and herbs, otherwise, there was nothing more to them. They were essentially humans.

Chapter 47 – A Painting of Old

<u>KELLEN</u>
WHAT WOULD HAVE BEEN DAY 24 OF THE GAMES

"The witch is called Morgan. She is Orion's daughter, Finnegan's sister. Supposedly she has been locked up since she was fifteen years old when her gifts became known." Hunji began explaining what he knew. Mike and Tobias did not seem surprised, though I was sure they were privy to this information. Of course, I had been enslaved here, so everything he was saying was new to me.

"I had no idea Finnegan was still alive." I scowled, "I would have thought Mathias had executed him." I was a little baffled that he had been allowed to live. After all, he was not just Orion's son, but I thought he was his accomplice. His actions at the battle of Riocht were unexpected, and Lamia had protected him from being killed right there and then, but I was sure that once he had given them information, the King of Shifters would not let him live.

"No, Your Highness, it seems he was in as much of a mess as you were. Xander and Damon were able to remove his chip, and he was locked in the Clan Mansion's cells for a while. If it wasn't for him, we might have never figured out where exactly you were." I looked at Hunji, a little astonished at the turn of events. Although knowing Lamia, if he wasn't dead, there was a reason.

"That and we were able to retrieve this from a very willing

source of information," Mike's hand went into his pocket, revealing a shiny object and holding it out to me.

"My watch!" I smiled, thinking I had lost that forever. I turned it over to read the inscription: 'Our Bond is as timeless as our friendship and love. L'. A small smile spread on my lips. After Ashe's story about their spirit animals, I was more than convinced that everything Lamia had endured and everything I had gone through was not wholly about us, but our other halves.

It was about Inanna and Conri. It was their story we were living. Everything from Lamia losing Zane and their pup to her being a Dire wolf and Lycan hybrid. Even how our wolves initially rejected each other, and she became mated to the Bear King. It all started making sense. Me, ending up here and meeting Teal, becoming mated to Tala; it all meant something. It seemed like things were coming full circle, and now Hunji was sent on a quest to find the sister of the Bear King's surprise brother.

I couldn't help feeling like something bigger was coming. The gods were playing a game and we were all entangled in it together. Ashe had warned me about the god's efforts to control and how they saw us as pawns. Even MacTire had a role, just like Riocht. Finding out Teal's last name was MacTire had been a real head-scratcher, and why did he state his name, rank, and lineage to Tala? And what was a Knight of the Red Branch?

Conri had been silent when I asked him about it, only telling me 'not yet'.

"I think Lamia would kick your ass if you returned without this." Mike chuckled at me.

"From what Mathias said, she has been hell-bent on us finding you, even kicked his ass a couple of times. He said she seems to be drawing strength from the babies." I looked at

Tobias, cocking my head.

"Did you just say, babies?" I asked, wanting to make sure I heard him right.

"Umm, yeah," he looked around at Hunji and Mike. "You didn't know she was carrying triplets?"

My eyes just about fell out of my head, and my mouth hung open, gaping. "Seriously?" The guys all laughed at me.

Congratulations, you will be an uncle Rogue's voice rang out his congratulations in my head. I spent many a night and day telling him about Lamia and Mike, so he knew how close we all were.

"Thanks," I said out loud, "I feel sorry for King." I gave a half-hearted laugh and squeezed my mate, who was still sitting on my lap, a little tighter and kissed her cheek.

"Don't go getting any ideas," Tala said playfully, swatting my arm. I gave her a look; her heat had only lasted one night, which probably meant I got her pregnant on the first try. Did she not realize she was probably baking me a little pup right now?

"Is that so," I said to her with a coy smile. "I might have to work on that, practice makes perfect you know." There was no way I was going to tell her, I would let her work it out on her own. But really, she had to know, right?

Mike shifted uncomfortably every now and then, his eyes darting to my mate and glancing over her. Not in a lustful way, it was more of a curious look at how things would go once Tala met her half-brother and sister. We had discussed Tala and Teal privately, and when Tobias mentioned Mike's new love interest, I put the pieces together. Jonda was Tala's half-sister, Teal's daughter, and Alpha John of the Sea Dog pack was Tala's half-brother, Teal's son. I wondered how she would be received by them, and Mike knew that if they held any animosity toward my mate, he would not be bringing his new love interest back to New Moon.

"Alright, so we leave for the port in the morning. Another two-frickin'-day drive in this goddess awful heat! Hunji, you are staying here to go hunt for some bear shifter's witch sister?" Mike looked at the reserved and stoic wolf with a raised eyebrow.

Hunji nodded back to him. "I will stay here for a few days in case I am needed. Then I will go to Andora and see if I can find where she is being held. I would like to speak with our prisoner before you leave, if I may?"

"Yeah," Mike said, running a hand down his face, obviously exhausted like the rest of us. I could tell he was anxious to be home too. The months of stress and sleepless nights my disappearance caused had taken a toll on Mike, and now everything was catching up with him. "Take Tobias with you. As we have seen, he has very useful interrogation skills if you need them."

"How are we going to fuel the trucks out here? I didn't see anything resembling a gas station out here or on our way." Tobias grimaced.

"Oh! No need!" Tala said, now standing up and leaving my arms empty. "We don't run our cars on gasoline here." I think we all looked at her like she had grown two heads.

"Then how do you fuel your cars?" Tobias asked, just as confused.

My mate smiled brightly, "We run them on corn oil, it burns just as good. A little smellier, but just as effective and has a good burn time on engines too."

"Huh," was all Tobias offered her.

"This continent is definitely different from ours. In some ways, it is very far behind and lacking, and yet in other ways, they are further ahead in technology than us." I could see Mike's brain ticking over.

"As far as technology, yes. But their way of thinking, they are still very primitive, especially in Asiarian." We all looked at Hunji when he made that statement. Of course, he would know, that's where he was born. We knew this from the very little information he had given us about his background.

My little flame made her way back onto my lap, wrapping her arms around my neck and giving me a soft kiss on my cheek. I breathed in her delicious scent, an instant peace descending upon me. We could get to know each other more on the ride to the port, and I was excited to learn all about her, just knowing I would love every little detail about Tala. I looked forward to discovering all her quirks and kinks.

The meeting ended and I sent Rogue with Mike, I wanted them close. I wanted Rogue to learn from my beta, and I hoped they would get on and become friends. Also, at the moment, Mike was the only other person Rogue could mind-link with.

I was going to take Tala back to her room so she could pack up and then have some time with her friend Eloise before we left tomorrow morning.

"Wait," Tala said suddenly, tugging my hand and leading me away from where her room was and down another short hall. "I want to show you something." Her wide smile and excitement indicated it was probably something I would like.

Tala led me into a very feminine room and stood at the end of the bed, waiting for me to join her. At first, I thought she wanted to get it on in here, so I slid my arms around her waist and nuzzled her neck.

"Silly king," she chuckled, pushing me away, much to mine and my horny wolf's annoyance. "Look," she said, holding up her hand and pointing at the adjacent wall.

I wasn't prepared for what I was about to see, and no words could ever describe how I felt about the painting I was looking at. I took a seat, perching on the end of the bed and covering my mouth with my hand.

"That... That's impossible." I sat there stunned. "Who? Where did this come from?" I asked Tala, not able to draw my eyes from the painting.

"I don't know, but I do know it had been in my mother's family for centuries. At least that's what she said. When I saw your wolf, the first thing I thought of was this painting. It was strange because, at that moment, I felt like I had been seeing you all my life." She sighed and sat beside me.

"No, Tala. You don't understand." I scrubbed my face with my hands. "That is me. And that woman with the wolf is Lamia."

It was true. I was staring at a painting that stretched across almost the entirety of the wall. Depicted was a large wolf, silver in color with blue eyes and standing tall and proud. The wolf was enigmatic, but whoever the artist was captured the powerful beast in such a way that made you want to bow to it. The wolf was standing on a large rock accompanied by a woman, tall and in a long green tunic dress with gold embroidery. Upon her head of golden and onyx streaks sat a crown twisted like ivory with green jewels to match her striking emerald eyes. The goddess-looking woman exuded power. In her right hand, she held a magnificent sword, poised and ready to strike down her enemy. Her left hand sat on the silver wolf's head, whether it be in comfort or protection it didn't matter. Again, the artist captured the bond between the beauty and beast.

The painting told the story of a battle scene; the sky was illuminated by a half-moon that clouds swirled around. Behind the woman, below the mound of rocks, sat three wolves, bent so their snouts touched the ground as if bowing to the pair. Behind the Godly Wolf were four more wolves, the largest being a red wolf, looking almost as powerful as the silver wolf.

"There is an inscription on the back. I have never seen it, but I was told the painting was of the Goddess Inanna and her lover after they had defeated her father, Anu. The wolves surrounding her were her knights, and the other four were a king's most trusted warriors, also knights. The inscription on the back says: As it was once before, it shall become again. The goddess Inanna and King Conrad."

I looked at my little flame, lost for words. I knew what I wanted to say, but I wasn't sure how to begin. "It's all true," was what I managed to say, my voice low, speaking more to myself. I mean what else are you meant to say when you are shown a painting that depicts you and your friend from centuries ago and coming to the stark truth that everything a white-haired lady had told you was true?

It was no coincidence that the sword in the painting was one of Lamia's. There was no denying the main figures were Lamia and my wolf Conri. "I would like to take this painting with us. It means so much to you, and you have no idea what this painting means to me." I turned to her, almost asking but mostly telling her. Once she met Lamia, she would understand better. Right now, I couldn't even fathom how to explain the very obvious coincidences and similarities.

'We are born again each time, but this time it is different. This time the Moon Goddess fated us to another.' Conri said, his wolfish voice sliding around in my head. His slight disappointment was obvious, but when my sight landed on our mate, I could feel his contentment and happiness mirroring mine.

For a long time, it was my thought that the Moon Goddess had done us wrong, had cheated us out of our girl. I used to think that Lamia should have always been mine, but as we stand before the beautiful piece of artwork with Tala, I came to realize that I never lost Lamia, I was never cheated. Instead, we were both given a second chance. Instead of repeating the past, the gods gave us a path to change the future and determine our fate. I couldn't be happier with the outcome, disregarding the way we got here.

I would always love Lamia, but she was not mine. Tala was mine, and that thought made me smile and take my mate in my arms, wrapping them around her waist from behind and pulling her back against my chest. Both of us quietly stared at the painting in front of us while my chin rested on her shoulder. She was my happiness.

Did it mean everything would be okay? Did it mean things were falling into place? I didn't know, but this was my fate and I had already accepted it. And so far, it had been one heck of a ride.

"I will ask the maids to pack the painting up for us. I'm so glad you love it." Tala turned in my arms with a jubilant smile, snaking her hands up my shoulders and around the back of my neck, pulling my head down until our lips met. "I have always felt as if it called out to me, is that crazy?"

"No, not at all. It's fate, my love." I said, tucking a piece of her bright red hair behind her ear and placing a soft kiss on her lips. "We were meant to be," I whispered before taking her lips again for a more heated kiss.

"I've already fallen in love with you, Kellen," Tala gasped

when she broke the kiss for a moment, her cheeks pink and heated from her arousal.

"The feeling is mutual," I said, lifting Tala in my arms so her legs could wrap around me and carrying her out of the door towards her room, not breaking the passionate and needy kiss once.

I took Tala back to her room and laid her down on the bed once we got there. Savoring each kiss like it was our last. This woman had no idea how much she meant to me.

"Kellen," she moaned as I peeled her clothes from her ivory skin and let my kisses trail over her body.

I quickly took my own pants and shirt off and climbed back over her. Her legs parted for me so I could rest between them. I kissed her as I moved up her body, my hands exploring her soft curves and my fingers relishing the skin beneath them.

I sunk into her with a groan, filling her up and feeling her tight pussy clench around me once I was fully seated. I began to move slowly, pulling and out and pushing back in. This time the need to make love to her was great, unlike the primal need when she was experiencing her heat.

Her moans and gentle sighs that matched the rhythm of my thrusts were dangerously close to making me end this before it was even started. I kissed her and thrust harder, gaining a squeak of pleasure from her. Her hands roamed my arms, caressing each trembling muscle as I held back on the beast that wanted to claim her roughly. Up over my arms and shoulders, her nails trailed. Then down my back, her tiny hands descended until they reached my butt, and she squeezed, pulling me deep into her on my next plunge.

"Fuck you are so beautiful," I groaned. Changing my angle and moving in and out of her at a quicker pace.

I felt myself building, and I moved a hand between us to find her swollen bud, rubbing it hard. She moaned and her walls clenched my shaft. I began to pound into her harder, knowing she was on the edge of release.

With two more pumps inside her, Tala screamed my name, "Kellen!" Her nails were digging into my back as her orgasm gushed around me, her toes curling and back arching.

I was right there with her, burying my cock deep inside her and releasing my seed. "Fuck, I love you, Tala. Now and forever." I growled, placing a kiss on her lips when I had emptied my essence into her. I took my time before I pulled out, not wanting this connection to be broken. I would stay buried inside her all day every day, if I could. She was my everything.

Chapter 48 – The Sister

<u>MIKE</u>
2 DAYS LATER

Tala was sweet and funny, she genuinely laughed at my jokes and was eager to hear stories about Kellen and me growing up. The closer we got to the port, the more I worried about Jonda's reaction. What would she think of Tala when they met and she found out that they were half-sisters? That her long-lost father, who she had never met, did indeed have another child.

We were able to bring back Teal's body under Kellen's orders; he wanted Teal to be returned back home. Albeit, this was not the way Kellen had hoped to reunite him with his family. Luckily, we were able to preserve his corpse and find a box that would keep his body cool on the journey.

Rogue decided to ride with Tobias to help keep an eye on Oliver as well as escort Teal's body. I felt a little bad for Tobias, traveling with the criminal and a wolf with no voice. At least he had two other warriors riding with him whose ears he could talk off.

I used the satellite phone to let Jonda know we were on our way back and with how many men. She had been excited to hear my voice, and I could hear the tension lessen in her tone when I told her I was fine and that we had gotten everyone out.

Kellen was sitting in the back of the truck, his arms

securely wrapped around Tala. It had been a while since I had seen Kellen happy, years in fact, and it made me happy for my best friend. He had found his mate, his love, and I could already see how much he cared for her. And Tala seemed super sweet, she was good for him.

The first person I laid eyes on when we pulled up to the port was Jonda. She was standing there in cut-off shorts and a light red tank top, a huge welcoming smile on her face, and she waved excitedly as we got closer. I parked the truck and hopped out as soon I had turned it off and rushed, almost ran, to my love. Her auburn hair fluttered in the light breeze and her hazel eyes met mine.

"I missed you so much," she declared, jumping into my arms and planting kisses all over my face until she finally found my lips and dove in to give me a hungry kiss, telling me just how much she missed me.

"I missed you too," I said between kisses, the feeling mutual. I did not like being separated from her and welcomed the igniting passion between us. I kissed her back, licking her lips until she allowed me entry, and I twined my tongue with hers, holding her up above me, her legs wrapping around my waist and her dainty hands caressing my stubbled jaw.

We broke the kiss and I let her down to the ground gently, still keeping her in my arms, not yet ready to let her go. Kellen had cleared his throat and was standing with Tala looking unsure how to make introductions.

"Jonda, this is King Kellen Moon and his mate Tala," I said, facing them.

"It's a pleasure to meet you, Your Highness." Jonda gave Kellen a modest bow and then turned to Tala.

I might as well rip the band-aid off now, so I added, "Tala

Mac-Tire, your half-sister."

Tala pinched her lips together and her face flushed red, her body sinking into Kellen's side and her eyes glazed over with tears. Jonda stood there staring at her, her hands clenching my wrists that sat firmly around her waist. A moment of awkward silence until Tala stepped out of Kellen's protective hold.

"It is nice to meet you Jonda. I did not know your father well, but I can tell you he was respected, brave, and a good man." She offered Jonda a small smile and stepped back to Kellen. Jonda did not reply to her; instead, she took in Tala, not glaring but not welcoming either.

"Let's get stuff loaded up," Kellen said. "Jonda, how soon can we leave?" He asked my love after a long beat of silence.

Shaking her head from whatever thoughts were swimming around in there, she directed her attention to the king. "We can leave as soon as everything is loaded," she smiled.

"What up, feisty girl!" Tobias smiled cheerily as he came striding across the dock, Rogue next to him with Oliver, who was flanked by two warriors.

"Tobias," Jonda smiled at him and then furrowed her brows, looking around. "Where is Hunji?" She asked with concern, her eyes still darting around as if he was going to magically appear.

"He stayed behind, Queen Lamia had a special mission for him. He was sent to go find the daughter of the witch who cursed you." I told her, and her head snapped towards me.

"What?... Why?" The genuine concern could be heard in her words.

"Because the queen asked him to," Kellen said defensively

and matter of fact. "She may be able to reverse your curse, amongst other reasons," he added a little more lightly.

Jonda and Tala didn't speak, neither of them attempting to converse at all. Truthfully, I think they just didn't know what to say, and instead of either of them putting their paw in their mouth, they decided the awkwardness between them was easier to deal with. There was an air of tension, just a silent self-consciousness and awareness. They would have to deal with this at some time or another, especially if they were both going to be living in the palace.

*****

We had finally settled into the cabin after loading the boat and placing Oliver below deck in a holding cell, and getting some food inside of us. I was lying on the small bed with Jonda in my arms, caressing her naked back while her body curled up on top of me, resting her head on my chest. Things just seemed so easy with her.

"She didn't know Teal was her father for a long time, only finding out recently. She was a product of rape." I said, filling the silent cabin with my voice, my fingers trailing over my love.

"Are you saying my father raped her mother?" Jonda sat up with a scowl on her face, daring me to say it, a fire in her eyes at my implied accusation.

"No, the opposite," I took a deep breath. "Her mother raped your father. He had been imprisoned for over twenty-two years. From what Tala and Kellen told me, he was taken from here the night your mother was cursed by Orion and his witch and sold to Vargr. He stayed there under the influence of silver until Vargr's eldest invented the inhibitor chip and they tested it on his own beta first. Once modified, they implanted it into your father, and he became a Gladiator slave. He couldn't shift, he couldn't mind-link. One night, Tala's mother drugged him and took advantage of him, thus producing your half-sister."

"Are you kidding me?" Jonda asked, shocked.

"I wish I was. That's how Kellen met Teal and Tala, his fated mate. Your father knew about Tala from the beginning, but Tala... she had no idea until a couple of days ago. Tala has not had an easy life from what Kellen has told me. She is your sister Jonda, wanted or not. I think you should at least give her a chance, she is a good person and cared for the people of her kingdom even if her hands were tied." I explained everything I could, everything I had been told by either Kellen, Tala, or Jasper. I wanted Jonda to understand that Tala was not to blame, and neither was her father, Teal.

"Is it wrong that I am jealous that she at least got to know him more than me? Even if it was just a little?" She sighed and scrubbed a hand down her face.

"No, it's not wrong, love. I think it is quite normal to have those feelings. All I ask is that you try to see it from her side before you decide to hate her."

I watched as Jonda swallowed a lump, her gaze drifting off to the other side of the tiny room, lost in thought. There was no need for me to say anything more. I could see she was thinking about it, so I just offered my gentle and comforting touch, letting my fingertips caress her pale skin. That was the only resemblance between Jonda and Tala, they both had pale skin. Jonda's hair was auburn, whereas Tala's was bright red. Tala had bright blue eyes, and Jonda's were a soft hazel with flecks of green. Both were small and dainty, but Jonda definitely had a much larger rack than Tala.

After a while, Jonda spoke in a whisper, laying her head

back down on my chest. "She looks like him, you know. From the pictures I have seen of my father, she looks so much like him. She and John have the same eyes." I listened to her, letting her talk and after a while, she drifted off to sleep.

*****

TALA

The journey from Bhakhil to the Chegank port was long, but luckily not boring. Kellen and I talked a lot, and Beta Mike was funny - filling in the silent gaps with stories from their childhood and making me laugh more times than I can count. We got to know each other so much more, and I felt like I had also formed a good relationship with Mike.

I don't think it mattered what his home would look like. I was sure I would feel just at ease there as I did in the presence of my mate and his best friend. I was definitely curious to meet Lamia as she was also a huge part of their stories. I hoped I would not feel intimidated in front of the Queen of Shifters, and I truly hoped that she and I would like each other as I could see how important she was to these two wolves.

We had taken a large boat to an island, and I was mesmerized by the vast expanse of the ocean. Its crystal blue depths had me wanting to jump in. The smell of the salt water tickled my senses, and I felt so at ease breathing in the fresh air. So different from the dry, stagnant air in Bhakhil.

For two days, day and night, I stayed on deck watching the sunset and the moon rise over the ripples of water and occasional waves. Kellen stayed by my side, offering his strength and a shoulder to lean on.

They had put Oliver below deck, chained up in silver, and as much as I wanted to go see him, I couldn't bring myself to leave the view of the waters and the dolphins that would occasionally swim alongside the boat.

I hadn't spoken to Jonda or seen her. She and Mike hid themselves away in a cabin for the duration of the trip back to her homeland, the Sea Dog pack and Island. I think she was still trying to decide how she felt about me. Suddenly finding out you have a bastard sister whose mother raped her father to conceive me was a lot to process. Jonda hadn't been mean or rude, and I didn't get the impression that she outright hated me, but I could see the distrust in her eyes. I don't think she knew what to make of me, so she kept her distance, focusing all her energy on the Royal Beta.

*****

<u>TALA</u>
2ND DAY ON THE BOAT (4 days later)

I had become quiet since arriving at the docks. Far from the place I grew up and far from my friends. If it hadn't been for Kellen, I think I would have felt lonely. I wasn't as excited to discover new lands and the outside realm as I was when we left Bhakhil. I was enthralled by the beauty I had seen so far, however, I now was unsure of how Kellen's people would receive me. Would they all look down on me as the girl whose father stole the king and was a bastard daughter to an alpha? At least I knew my place in Bhakhil. Not now, though. Now I didn't know anything, and I was scared that I wasn't enough for Kellen.

According to the captain, we were close to arriving at the island, Teal's home. The sun was coming up over the horizon in the east, its first rays of light dancing across the wild waters, creating glimmering flecks of light over the small breaks of waves. It was so peaceful, so quiet and serene.

I hoped for many more days I could spend on the ocean; I felt at ease with the wide-open space. It was hard to think only days ago I was surrounded by sandy dirt and barren land. What would the New Moon Kingdom look like when we got there? I hoped I would like it as much as I did the open waters of the ocean.

I placed my hand on my lower belly. I wasn't stupid, my heat had only lasted that night. The king's child was growing inside me, and I didn't dare say anything to him. I didn't need my wolf to confirm it, I just knew. What if when we arrived at his kingdom, his people hated me so much that he rejected me? What if he wasn't ready to be a father and resented me because it was too soon?

"Tala, my little flame, please tell me what's wrong. I can sense your worry and it is driving my wolf crazy." Kellen spoke gently to me, taking my hands in his. When I didn't lift my head, his hand lifted my chin so I had nowhere else to look but into his eyes. Those blue irises scanned my face and tried to figure out what was going on in my mind.

I sighed and reached up, brushing my hand over the beard he had grown. It was so thick, unlike the first time we had met when his face had seemed so clean and young. "I am scared," I admitted. His face turned into a frown and had me turning from him, no longer able to look in his eyes. "What if, what if your people don't like me? What if they don't want a foreigner as your queen, what if I'm not good enough, Kellen?" I said, my sentence trailing off to a mere whisper.

Kellen whirled me around, holding my face in his hands, the concerned look etched across his whole face and a hint of anger. "If you are good enough for me, you are good enough for my people. I love you, Tala, with all my heart. You are mine and I will never let you go. Do you understand? You are my family, my only family, and I will never have another mate. You are it for me." He then kissed me, pouring all his love and emotion into that kiss, sweeping me off my feet like he did the first night we met in person in the slave barracks.

All my worries and self-doubt melted away with the way his lips caressed mine. He wanted me, I could feel it, I knew it deep down. I was his and he was mine. I could endure anything with him by my side. After a few moments, we broke apart, both of us breathing heavily. I wanted to rip his shirt off and take him right there and then.

With locked gazes, I remembered the promise I had made to myself and Jasper. No more secrets. And without thinking, "I think I'm pregnant," I told him.

"I know." He replied, his gaze not wavering and his eyes only intensifying on me with a burning desire.

The sound of the boat's horn startled me, and I jumped in the air into Kellen's arms. We both began laughing at the timing of the loud intrusion into our personal moment. Turning together, we looked out over the vast body of water to find a shoreline a few miles ahead, becoming closer.

We had arrived at the Sea Dog pack's island.

"I only want to stay for one night, enough time to give Teal a traditional Alpha send-off, then I want to take you home."

"Are you in a rush, my king?" I asked curiously as to why he would be in such a hurry to get on another boat so fast. I loved being on a boat, but the amount of traveling we had already done in the past four days had tired me out. And staying awake this whole time was taking its toll on me now. I had been too excited to sleep.

He chuckled, "Yes and no. I have been gone for too long

and I am anxious to be home, but I also made a promise to Lamia. Every year we have made it a tradition to spend the first minutes of our birthday together. For the last two years, she never showed... for personal reasons. But I promised her I would be home for our birthdays and before her children are born."

A glint of admiration sparkled in his eyes when he spoke of Lamia. I had certainly underestimated their relationship. He had said they were close, but how close? He had told me I would understand once I met her. I hoped I would.

Chapter 49 – Luna Siobhan

<u>MIKE</u>
4 DAYS LATER

We stepped off the boat. Alpha John was there to greet us upon arrival and immediately he came to us, first acknowledging the king. "Welcome back, Your Highness, it is a pleasure to finally you meet you." He offered his hand to Kellen, who took it enthusiastically.

"It is good to be back in the kingdom, Alpha John. I have heard many great things about you, and thank you for not only your hospitality to my warriors but also for your help in bringing me home." Tala stood by his side, looking down at the ground, her hands fidgeting until Kellen spoke her name. "This is my mate, Tala. Although I was enslaved for a while, the Moon Goddess blessed me with finding my fated." He said, pulling Tala close to him.

"A pleasure to make your acquaintance, future queen. I am sure…" Alpha John's words died on his lips as Tala lifted her head to greet him. He looked at his sister, he and Jonda sharing a look and mind-link. When he finally turned his attention back to Tala, I could see tears in his eyes, the same cerulean blue as Tala's. There was no mistaking they shared a family trait, the unique eye color they shared spoke volumes.

"Brother," Jonda spoke softly, stepping forward. "Meet our sister, Tala Mac-Tire." I think I almost cried when Jonda took Tala's hand and smiled at her, accepting her.

Alpha John was five years old when his father had been captured and taken, so he somewhat remembered his father. He looked from Jonda to Tala and then, to everyone's surprise, he engulfed Tala in a hug, squeezing her tight. "Welcome home Tala Mac-Tire, I look forward to getting to know you."

"Thank you," Tala said with a short breath as if Alpha John was squeezing her a little too tight.

"Let her go, John. You are squeezing the poor girl." Jonda swatted her brother's arm, and he released Tala's tiny frame.

"You look so much like him." Alpha John stared at Tala, reaching up to touch her red hair. "Your eyes, your hair..." He cut his words off, still looking at her like it was unbelievable.

When the warriors carried the simple coffin-like box off the boat, Alpha John stood up straight. His eyes grew dark with sadness as he watched the men put the box with his father's corpse into the bed of a truck.

"I am sorry. Teal, your father, is someone I will always look up to. Without him, I don't think I would have survived mentally or physically. He wasn't just a friend but a father figure to me while we were held in captivity." A sense of pensive sadness spread throughout the group, and an air of melancholy surrounded him as Kellen spoke of the late, missing Alpha of twenty-two years.

"Thank you, Your Highness. Your opinion means much to me and my family. Now come," Alphas John's attitude suddenly took on a lighter tone, "I have food set up in the main pack house for everyone. I know you have had a long journey, and I want to hear everything about my father and our new sister before we send him off to the Moon Goddess tonight."

Jonda walked with her brother, who spoke with Kellen and Tala on the way there. I hung back with Tobias and Rogue. Oliver trailed behind, still escorted of course. I thanked the gods he had not tried to communicate with Tala or talk to any of us. I still didn't like that he had been left alive and was listening to our every word. His very presence made me feel uneasy.

"Take him to a holding cell and watch him closely," I commanded the two warriors, who nodded in acknowledgment. As soon as we could, I would have him transported to MacTire and then Travis could do what he wanted with the shit bag.

Please tell me we do not have to take another boat I chuckled at Rogue when he spoke to me telepathically. He and Tobias shared the same seasickness.

"Rogue wants to know if we have to take another trip on the water," I laughed, speaking to Tobias who turned to Rogue with a sickly-looking green face to match his.

"Brother, I'm so sorry, but yes. Yes, we do, and you look about as happy as me right now," he groaned. "But I promise after that, all land."

Rogue rolled his eyes and kept step with us, following the king and alpha.

The pack house was a modern structure made of heavy dolomite stone that gave the building a dark look, almost medieval-looking like MacTire's castle. Inside, as we walked through the main entrance, it had a much brighter and cheery atmosphere with light yellow painted walls decorated with paintings of the beaches. The décor was white wood for the furniture and light-colored hardwoods. The place had a fun yet peaceful vibe to it.

We were led into the main dining hall that held four large tables, each being able to seat sixteen to twenty people, and along one side of the wall sat a long bench-type table that held buffet trays. I could smell the food wafting through the room and my stomach grumbled. I felt like I hadn't had a decent meal since I left Lonely City that dreadful morning when Kellen disappeared.

"Please come sit and help yourselves to food, there is plenty." Alpha John gestured to the large table that sat horizontally to the other three tables.

We all scrambled for food and found our seats, the Alpha sitting at the head with Kellen next to him and Tala right after. Jonda sat on the Alpha's other side but left a seat vacant between them. I was happy to see they actually had meat choices, and I wondered if this had been provided because Jonda knew I was not a fan of seafood.

The room suddenly went quiet, the chattering stopped, and all eyes turned to see why the Alpha and his sister had suddenly quieted. "Mother," the Alpha smiled and stood from his seat, followed by Jonda.

"I would like to introduce you to my mother and current Luna until I meet my mate; Luna Siobhan." The Alpha's proud smile fell short when his mother's eyes landed on Tala, who shrunk back in her seat.

Jonda moved to hug her mother, who replied to her daughter with an equally enthusiastic embrace, yet her eyes did not leave the king's mate. I felt the air turn cold and looked at my best friend and then at Tala, who looked embarrassed to be there. The comfort and acceptance she was given by Jonda and her brother at the docks had suddenly vanished.

The Luna stepped around the table until she was closer to

Tala. "What is your name child?" She asked her, quite calmly.

"Tala, Luna." She said, standing up to face the older Luna.

"What is your last name?" Her questions were short and demanded an answer.

"My name is Tala Mac-Tire, Luna. I am so sorry." I watched as Tala's eyes filled with tears and her mouth turned down, a visible look of remorse on her face and a little bit of fear of what this woman would say to her. She looked down just as the Luna spoke.

"You are Teal Mac-Tire's daughter, yes?" Shit, this Luna was scaring me at how composed she was facing the illegitimate daughter of her late mate.

"I – I am, Luna. I am sorry my mother put you through hell, and I am sorry Vargr took your mate away from you for so long. I am sorry my family made you suffer for so long." The tears streamed from Tala's eyes, and Kellen made a move to comfort his mate when the Luna put her hand up, keeping Kellen in place. A very bold move.

"Is it true what my daughter has told me? Your mother took my husband's seed and now she is dead?" Tala nodded her head. "And is it true you had no idea Teal was your father until recently?" Again, Tala nodded her head. I figured Alpha John must have mind-linked his mother, giving her a heads-up about Tala. That was the only explanation I could think of for the older Luna knowing these details. I truly felt for Tala, she was going to get verbally roasted and she was going to stand there and take it because she thought she deserved it.

I remember Jonda telling me her mother had felt the betrayal of the mate bond only once, and her mark had still been present. My eyes searched her neck, and I could see her mark, slightly faded. I wondered if she had felt the break in the bond when her mate died. She did look tired, despite her appearance. She couldn't hide the dark lines under her eyes.

"Look at me, child." The Luna spoke softly, and Tala lifted her head, showing her tear-stricken face. I heard a low growl come from Kellen, upset that his mate was sad and that the Luna had made his mate cry, yet he did not move to comfort her. "I have no idea what you have gone through or what kind of family you came from, but you are Teal's child. A Mac-Tire. You are family now and I will welcome you as one of my own."

I felt a warm wet tear slide down my cheek, moved by the moment and the compassion the old Luna was showing her mate's other child. I quickly swept it away and looked around to make sure no one had noticed, but I found several people with unshed tears in their own eyes, including the Alpha and Jonda, and even Kellen.

"Thank you, Luna." Tala sobbed as the Luna took her in for a hug and stroked her hair like she was her own child. "Thank you so much, your kindness and words mean everything to me."

"Dry your tears, child, let us eat and remember my alpha and husband before we say goodbye. Then maybe we can get to know each other better, hmm?"

Now Kellen chose to stand and bring Tala back to the table. Instead of her sitting in her own seat, he placed her in his lap and pulled her plate in front of them so she could eat.

*****

KELLEN

It was a full moon tonight, and I stood to the side of the pyre as they carried Teal's body down through the streets from the morgue where the family had been able to go see him and say their final goodbyes. Tala had asked to join them, so I accompanied her. It was a somber moment to watch Teal's estranged family cast their eyes on him for the very first time in over twenty-two years. For Jonda, it was the first and last time she would ever see him in person.

Much like now, the atmosphere was somber. Many older folk who remembered the Alpha came to pay their respects, and many of the younger generation stood to support their current alpha and pay homage to the once-lost alpha.

I walked up to the makeshift podium, the Luna had asked me to speak, and I had humbly accepted. It would be my honor to pay tribute to Teal.

"Members of the Sea Dog pack, it is my honor to be asked to speak and pay homage to your late alpha. I stand here not as a king nor an alpha, but as a friend and a companion and, more importantly, as a gladiator. In the next few weeks, you will hear stories about Alpha Teal, where he had been, why he had been gone for many years." I looked towards Luna Siobhan, and then at his two eldest children. "Alpha Teal spent many years away from his beloved pack and family, and on many nights, he told me of his son and Luna. And how he wished he could meet his daughter, who had yet to come into the realm before he was savagely ripped from his home.

"I cannot tell you all that happened to him in the twenty-two years he had been away; it is not my story to tell. But I can tell you about the man I met and the man I came to know. Teal became a mentor and father figure to many who were enslaved. Without him, I believe I would have lost myself to my own mind. He was there at a time I needed someone, at a time I had lost everything. At a time when I felt no hope, Alpha Teal became my strength. His wisdom and perseverance gave me the courage to take action. He gave me back my will to keep fighting. My only regret was that I could not save his life and reunite him with his family."

That was when the tears began, I could no longer hold them back. Looking at the faces of his family, I thought of my own parents. The brutal way they died and how Tala explained Teal had died. In a way, my words were not just for Teal but also for my father and my mother. When we sent them to the Moon Goddess, I did not have the words to speak. But now I felt like these words fit, and they meant more to me than just the simple dialogue I was saying. As I grieved for Teal, I grieved for my parents, the true effect of their loss finally hitting me after all these months.

There wasn't much more I could say, and I was about to step down when Rogue's voice filled my head, *Live or die we fight*

"Live or die we fight!" I called out, looking at Rogue.

"Live or die we fight!" Tala echoed.

Only the three of us knew what that truly meant, and how the words that were chanted in that arena brought us all closer together and fueled us to fight for our lives.

I stepped down and Luna Siobhan took my place. Immediately Rogue and Tala were by my side. Tala's small hand curled around mine, and Rogue's hand sat on my shoulder. Our memories played like a vision in our heads as the Luna spoke.

"For many years I waited for the return of my husband. Every day I prayed to the Moon Goddess, and she has finally answered my call. I have always known Teal as a strong and kind alpha, a man with morals beyond his peers, and I thank the king for his words today, solidifying that no matter what, my husband was able to keep his truth and remember who he was and where he came from. Sometimes people change with their circumstances, their paths blurred by evil and hate. King Kellen has proved that no matter what, Alpha Teal had kept true to his spirit. He fought to stay alive with the hopes of coming home. He helped those in need and led as an alpha should. May the Moon Goddess receive his spirit and his wolf's spirit. May they forever walk amongst the stars until we are reunited in the afterlife, and he can walk in the presence of his three children: John, Jonda, and Tala Mac-Tire."

The Luna then stepped down, and Alpha John took the first lit torch and placed it on the pyre, followed by Jonda, then Tala, myself, and Rogue. The warriors began to howl the melody of crossing over, as they would until the last flame died and Teal's spirit animal had been received by the Moon Goddess.

We stayed for a while, watching the embers float into the darkened sky. The full moon's beam shone directly on the pyre giving the flames that licked up into the night a pale yellow glow. After a while, Mike came up beside me, laying a hand on my shoulder where Rogue's was earlier.

"It's time to go, Kellen if you want to be home by your birthday. Lamia is waiting at the palace." He said sympathetically.

"Of course, let us say goodbye. I will meet you at the docks, have Tobias and Rogue take Oliver to the boat and secure him. Tala and I will say goodbye. Is Jonda coming home with us?"

"She is. I'm in love, Kellen." That was all Mike said to me, and I did not say anything else. I didn't know if he truly was in love or if this was something to occupy them both until they found their mates. After all, you couldn't run from fate.

For a second, I watched the clouds drift over the moon.

Today would have been the 28th day of the games, also the night Tala and Jasper were meant to be mated and married. My gaze found Tala, how differently things had turned out for both of us, even for Jasper and the Kingdom of Bhakhil. A better, different, and more promising future.

Chapter 50 – The Queen of Shifters

TALA

We arrived at a port on the mainland a day and a half later. Both Tobias and Fergus, I refused to call him Rogue, were more than happy to be on dry land again, and much to my amusement, they both bent down and kissed the ground.

"It wasn't that bad." I laughed at them, "You just need to find your sea legs."

"Easy for you to say, princess, you were born with sea legs. It's in your blood." Tobias pointed at me, giving me a non-amused glare.

"I was born in a desert, Tobias, no matter who my father was. I had never even seen a body of water, especially the ocean, since I left Bhakhil. Just because my real father was a Sea Dog, it doesn't mean anything."

"It means everything. I, personally, am a mountain bear. I prefer the cold weather and the streams full of fish, not on a vessel in the middle of nowhere, floating for the sharks to come eat."

I rolled my eyes at Tobias. "Stop being a big baby," I jested to the overly large bear shifter who was friendly and, when he wasn't throwing up on the boat, was a lot of fun to be around. A little flirty, and Kellen had to give him a few warning growls every now and then, but otherwise, he seemed like a good person.

It was to my understanding that he was second in command to the King of Shifters, also known as the Bear King. And despite his playful demeanor, Mike said he could be a scary bastard in battle or interrogation. I hoped I would only have to take his word for it and not ever have to see him in 'beast mode', as Mike called it.

There were cars waiting for us and a big transport truck with blacked-out windows. This is where we parted ways. The six of us, Kellen, Tobias, Fergus, Jonda, Mike, and I, would be going to the New Moon Palace.

Half a dozen warriors would be escorting Oliver to the Kingdom of MacTire. A place I desperately wanted to visit, if only because it held Teal's family name. I looked across at Oliver, where he was being escorted into the transport truck, catching his eye. He gave me a weak smile and a wink. I hadn't been able to talk to him since Bhakhil, and even if they all held animosity towards him, I couldn't. The wolf had saved my life and he had kept his word.

"I want to talk with Oliver," I said, turning to Kellen who scowled, and I could hear the low vibration of a growl from his wolf.

"Why?" Was his short and annoyed answer.

"Because Kellen, despite his wrongdoings, he saved my life. He killed Jack to save me." My voice pleaded with him. If Kellen said no, then I would not, but it was important to me.

"Fine." He grunted out and turned his back on me.

"Hold up, I want a word with the prisoner," I told the guards as I neared the truck they had just shoved Oliver in the back of. They made way for me but didn't go very far for security reasons.

"Princess!" Oliver beamed at me, showing his pearly

whites off. He didn't look distressed or worried at all.

"Oliver, I'm sorry..."

He cut me off, shaking his head. "Do not pity me, princess. This was always my fate... I had just hoped to avoid it. This is how things were meant to be. This is goodbye, though. After I reach MacTire, Alpha Travis will have me executed. You will not see me again."

"Oliver," I sighed, feeling tears brim, "Thank you for saving me from Jack. And thank you for showing me who you really are, not what you were made to be."

My words must have hit home. His eyes shifted from side to side like he had been found out, and he lowered his head, but not enough that I couldn't see the remorse and guilt hidden in those beautiful eyes of his. "You are the only person to see me for who I truly am. For that, I will be forever grateful, princess, and will carry our kiss to the grave and cherish it as I take my last breath. Thank you for really seeing me."

"Times up, we need to get moving," one of the guards said, shutting one of the double doors.

My eyes stayed locked with Oliver's. "I will pray to the Moon Goddess for you, Oliver." I called out as the second door shut, closing off my view from him. I stood there for a few moments until the warriors climbed in and drove away. A strange empty feeling sitting in my heart, as if I had just lost a friend or a brother.

My relationship with Oliver was a complicated one to describe. We didn't start off trusting each other; I thought of him to be like-minded to Jack. Oliver never pretended to be anything more or less than just himself. Maybe because he was the first outsider to be honest with me, maybe it was because I knew he felt something for me. Something more than I could ever feel for him, but still, I trusted Oliver when it came to me, and perhaps I was the only one that ever could and would trust him in his whole life. He hadn't had it easy, this much I knew. Maybe that's why we connected; two lost souls who had understood each other at a pivotal point in time.

*****

The drive to the New Moon Palace took a little over two hours. I had drifted off almost immediately and woke to Kellen's gentle kisses and him calling my name softly. I stirred, smiling when the pleasurable tingles lit up over my arms as fingers caressed them up and down, "Tala, wake up. We are almost there."

I sat up and wiped my lips free of the drool that had leaked out while I slept, noticing a wet patch on Kellen's shirt. I blinked a couple of times before my eyes widened, enamored by the lush and vast scene of greenery. Trees that kissed the clouds lined the hard black road we traveled. The sky was a brilliant blue, but unlike Bhakhil, the clouds were white pieces of tuff dotted in the sky instead of wispy streams of haze.

I rolled the window down and inhaled a huge gulp of foreign scents. One, in particular, excited me. "Stop the car!" I shouted excitedly, and the driver pulled over. No sooner than he had, I opened the door and ran toward the nearest tree, looking like a crazy person as I sniffed at it violently. It smelled like my mate. That spice and other heavenly smell I could never name, this was it. "What is this?" I asked Kellen as he joined me by the tree.

"It's a tree," He chuckled bemusedly at my actions and question.

"I know that, but what kind of tree?"

"It's a pine tree, they grow almost everywhere in our kingdom." He hesitated, "Tala have you never seen a tree?"

"Only palm trees in person and in books but this…" I inhaled again, "This tree smells like you. Pine. Spice and pine, that's what you smell like to me." I turned to him, still as excited as a kid with candy. "I didn't know what your scent was, just that it was divine, and I like it. Now I know."

"Come on, let's get back in the car. You can scent me all you want, and when we are settled, we can let our wolves out and run through the forest."

I let him take my hand and guide me back into the car, "We can shift and run in the forest?"

"Yes, whenever you want." He cocked his head.

"Vargr never let me shift. When you saw my wolf fighting him, it was the first time I had shifted in a long time. I didn't even know if I could that night." I sighed, watching the trees pass by, looking out the window.

"Vargr, didn't let you shift?" He asked, surprised.

"No, after I shifted on my sixteenth birthday, he commanded me to never shift again unless he said so. So, once a year I got to shift and run in the palace gardens. I don't know why." I could hear my own sadness in my voice, so I was sure Kellen hadn't missed it.

"I'm sorry, Tala. I'm sorry you had to grow up like that. Things will be different now, you can shift into Mora whenever you want now, and we can run together. Conri and I can show you all our favorite places, and we can explore new ones together."

"I would like that." I smiled to myself. Just the thought of running through these lush forests had my wolf excited and wanting to come forward. Mora couldn't wait to be set free, so much so that I worried she might never want to shift back.

Soon enough, the car turned off the black road and onto a more worn road, and the trees began to thin out, giving me a look further past forestry. "Is that your palace?" I asked when I spotted a huge white building on top of a hill, a small city surrounding it.

"Yes, that's our palace," I heard him chuckle.

The car neared the outskirts of the city, and the closer we got, the more I noticed how different this kingdom was. Not just because of the greenery and dense forestry, but there was no wall around the palace, and the streets were busy with newer-looking vehicles and shifters walking around. Their clothes were different, jeans and shirts as opposed to summer dresses, tunics, and togas. We passed by some small huts and gates, where warriors stood in black uniforms embroidered with blue patches and the crest of a moon and a silver wolf's head. No brown leather vests, no cattle prods. Some had swords, but none looked like they needed them.

Buildings in different sizes, shapes, and colors lined the road, and people stopped to watch the car pass by. All waved, and I wondered if they knew it was the king returning. The people here looked well fed, and I didn't see one person begging as we passed through.

We pulled up into a gravel driveway that led into a huge circular courtyard and stopped in front of some steps. There were several people waiting for us, for Kellen, and I suddenly became very nervous again. The car Jonda and Mike rode in pulled up behind us with Tobias and Rogue in it too.

"Hey, they are going to love you." Kellen took my hand in his and lifted it to his mouth, planting a kiss on my knuckles.

I bit my lip, I wasn't too sure. The Sea Dog pack had been kind to me and welcoming after a rocky start. Could I get that lucky again? After all, it was my sister who helped Orion try to destroy these people's lives. Kellen got out of the car first and then offered me his hand to take. He was all smiles and full of energy. The adrenaline of being home made him almost bounce on his feet. Taking his hand, he led me out of the car at the same time Jonda emerged from the car behind me. We shared a look, this was her first time meeting Mike's family, but I was sure I was more nervous than she was.

We took the first steps up and a heavily pregnant woman, no older than me, came wobbling down the steps, ignoring me and flinging her arms around my mate. "Welcome home! I missed you so much," she cried.

I was taken aback as my mate hugged her just as hard and long. His shoulders began to shake, and I could just hear his and hers murmured sobs as he held on to each other tightly. Mike had already taken Jonda up the steps to meet everyone else, and I stood there not knowing what to do when suddenly a large dark shadow was cast over me.

I looked up and further up at the mountain of a man who stood before me. His silver eyes were frightening, dominant. This giant was huge, and I felt like a small mouse. His stern dark features bore into me when to my surprise, his lips parted, and his face broke into a large smile. I was dumbfounded by his rugged beauty and enormous muscular stature.

"They may be a while," he gave a deep chuckle. "I am Mathias, and you will get used to how close our mates are," he grumbled.

Holy shit! I was standing in front of the King of Shifters himself, and the pregnant woman who was still holding onto my mate like he was her lifeline was Queen Lamia. I blinked a couple of times trying to find my voice, the rumors did not do this pair justice.

"T-Tala, Your Highness," I managed to fumble out. I had never felt so intimidated in my life.

"Don't let this big teddy bear scare you. Maybe once he was big and bad, but he was tamed the moment Lamia showed up." Tobias slapped a hand on the king's shoulders. I thought Tobias was big, but standing next to the king, he looked average and not so... big.

I felt arms wrap around me and knew it was Kellen right away. Immediately I felt secure and safe, even with the towering herculean man in front of me.

"Tala, I'm so sorry for hogging your mate like that. I am Lamia, and Kellen better have told you about me" I turned my attention to the pregnant woman, ready to greet her and put on a fake smile, instead my jaw dropped.

Her strawberry blonde, black-streaked hair was so familiar, and her green dress also looked the part. "W – wow," was all I managed. The vision in front of me was the spitting image of the goddess from the painting. Her human form and my mate's wolf form. Kellen said it was all true. I just dismissed it as he had heard the stories. But no, they were the living, breathing personifications of that painting.

"I told you would get it once you met her," Kellen whispered in my ear, giving me a kiss just below it.

"Umm, I'm sorry, you must think me an idiot," I stumbled, shaking my head. "It's nice to meet you finally, Your Highness." I managed to gather my wits and pick my jaw up off the floor.

"Uhh no," she said sternly. "You will not call me anything but Lamia, you are my best friend's queen. We are equals, and hopefully, we will become good friends." She smiled at the last part, and instead of shaking my hand, she reached out to give me a very awkward hug. Not only was she super tall, but so very very pregnant that I ended up just patting her shoulder.

Once we broke apart from the strange greeting, she took my arm and we walked the rest of the way up the steps together. "I am so excited Kellen finally found his mate, maybe now he won't get himself into too much trouble. Because I swear to the moon, if he lets himself get kidnapped again, I will personally hunt him down. I would have been there, but King wouldn't allow me anywhere. I had to threaten him just to let me travel here."

Lamia chatted away until we came to the top of the steps, "This is Delta Marcus and Vivian Langley, my parents," they both greeted me with hugs, "...and this duo is Beta Michael and Olivia, they are Mike's parents. Kellen and I call them Aunty and Uncle. I am not sure how much the boys have filled you in, but I will answer any questions you have." She leaned and whispered, "I know all their secrets and have no problem exposing them."

I laughed at her, liking her already. She seemed so genuine and down to earth for someone who was a queen, Queen of Shifters at that.

"Lamia," Mike called out and caught her attention. "I would like you to meet someone very special." Mike pulled Jonda forward and I sympathized with her intimidated look, which I was sure mirrored my own. "This is Jonda. Jonda, this is my best friend, Lamia"

"Your Majesty, it's a pleasure..." Lamia cut her off with a click of her tongue.

"Jonda, I'm going to tell you the same thing as I just told Tala. As Mike's mate, we are equals, and please call me Lamia, we are family now."

"We are not mates," Jonda said, confused, and I watched as the queen's face morphed into one of confusion and she cast a glance at Mike. I swear it looked murderous, but was quickly wiped off her face and replaced with a smile.

"I'm sorry, I didn't realize," Lamia said, turning back to Jonda and ignoring Mike. "Still, if Mike thinks so highly of you, and you must be someone special for him to bring home, then you are still family to me." She gave Jonda a big welcoming hug. I could see my half-sister go stiff, and finally, she brought her arms up to pat her shoulders the same way I did. The hug was just as awkward as ours.

The beta and delta family we were just introduced to crowded around Kellen, giving him hugs and pats, all parties obviously happy to have their king home.

"I want to introduce you all to Rogue, he was enslaved with me, and he is now pack and family. He doesn't talk much but he can mind-link with everyone who is part of the New Moon pack." He waved Fergus over and began to introduce him.

"Okay, let's break this step party up. We have food and wine inside, and the kitchen staff have been working all day, excited to have their king return. Tonight, we get reacquainted, tomorrow we work." Vivian, Lamia's mother, clapped her hands and started rallying us all towards the large wooden doors into the palace.

"Fuck!" We all heard Lamia cry out, followed by a splashing noise.

"Lamia! Language!" Her mother began to scold her until she turned to face her daughter, and her face paled.

"I know great timing, arrggghh!" She cried out again and doubled over. "King!" She reached for her mate, who was quickly by her side.

"Shit, call the pack doctors. We have babies on the way!" The king panicked.

Vivian rolled her eyes, "Take her to our suite, she will deliver there. Olivia, do we have everything ready?" She asked the beta's mate.

"Yep, ready for anything," she smiled. Then the older woman jumped up and fist-bumped the air. "We are having babies!" she yelled out, super excited.

I somehow figured that living here was going to be very exciting. Never a dull moment. Jonda and I looked at each other. "How can we help?" I asked.

"Ladies follow me, the more hands the better. We will be bringing three little shifters into this realm." Vivian smiled.

"Hey, Lamia!" Kellen called out to her, the king stopped midway up some stairs, and Lamia glared at Kellen over his shoulder. "I came home in time for the babies to be born," he laughed.

"Asshole!" She ground out through another contraction, but also managed to give him the finger.

Chapter 51 – The Next Generation

<u>KELLEN</u>

We were all currently gathered in the beta's suite that was on the opposite end of the hall to the delta's suite, where Lamia had been in labor for several hours now. Our women, along with several pack doctors, had been coming in and out of there gathering all the necessities to deliver the triplets.

They were concerned about the third baby, it was so tiny, and the doctors worried about the child being underdeveloped and not making it. They wanted to take her to the pack infirmary, yet moving her could endanger the smallest child, or worse, rupture something in Lamia. So, she would be giving birth here.

I, like the other men who gathered in the beta suite, for some reason thought this would be quick. We were all concerned for Lamia, but it gave us all a chance to talk and catch up, keeping the business conversation light and focusing on the more meaningful conversations, yet subjects would come up and I couldn't ignore my duty for long. By tomorrow I would be back to being a king, and I had not just a pack and business to run, but I also had a kingdom I was responsible for.

What I really wanted was more time with Tala, just her and me on our own. Just for a little longer, we hadn't had our time yet. I had barely had time to explore my mate. Sure, we got to know each other better throughout our journey, but we were constantly surrounded by people. In truth, I needed some downtime, some peace, some time for us to reflect on the past and more importantly our future. I wanted to do this with Tala. She and I, no one else.

Unfortunately, that time was not now.

"Where are you, son?" My thoughts were interrupted by Uncle Marcus.

I focused my sight on him, drawing it from the corner of the wall where I had been staring for a few moments. I gave a smile, one that didn't meet my eyes, and I didn't intend to hide my stress. I was not ashamed to cry in front of the men in this room, but I held my tears back. My best friend was in there and there was a high chance she could lose another child or worse, we could lose her too.

Being this close to Lamia stirred up a myriad of emotions, my wolf and I tuned into hers and we were experiencing what she felt, not the labor but her emotions. Not to mention the influx of nerves and excitement coming from my mate. I just wanted quiet. I just wanted to be with Tala.

Instead, I pushed all those emotions down deep and tried to lock them away, even pushing my wolf to the darkest corners of my mind, and then responded to Uncle Marcus. "Thank you, all of you. For taking care of this kingdom and not giving up on me."

"For fucks sake, son! Come here!" Uncle Marcus motioned with his hand as he stood up and came to me, despite his words. He pulled me up into his arms. For a man in his late forties, he was still built and strong, his huge arms squeezed me in a fatherly hug.

"We were so scared," he whispered against my face, kissing my cheek. "We thought we had lost you too. I was not okay with that." The next thing I knew, both Mike and his father,

Uncle Michael, were also hugging me. "None of us were okay with that. Don't you dare do that to us again! Do you hear me?" Uncle Marcus's words were harsh and forceful, but they were full of gratefulness and relief and so much love.

"We got him, we got Oliver," I barely mumbled above a whisper. "I want him to suffer for his crimes." I cried.

"And he will, son. He will. You did good, real good. I'm so proud of you, and I know your mother and father are too." I cried onto the shoulder of Lamia's father, no longer able to hold back. Every emotion, every feeling, came crashing down on me like a tidal wave carrying a ton of bricks.

"I died, I fucking died... the gods brought me back. Ashe, she brought me back. Lamia felt me die." I sobbed harder than I had ever sobbed in my whole life. I cried more now than I did for the death of my parents. It was too much, everything was just too much. So much for remaining calm and pushing the emotions down, the floodgates had opened, and I didn't know how to stop.

I wasn't ashamed of crying, I was ashamed because I felt weak. Not once did Lamia break down, not once did she crumble. With every hardship she has encountered, she stood back up and pushed back. Yet here I was, a mess and being selfish. I was selfishly crying to my family when Rogue stood there in the room with me. He had endured just as much hardship. And only so many feet away was my little flame that had probably faced more trauma than me, and neither of them were even close to being as traumatized and grief-stricken as I felt.

I couldn't tell them with words how I felt, but I knew each one of them was feeling it. Eventually, I calmed down, my breathing easing, and only then did Uncle Marcus release me. I stepped back and wiped the streaks of salty water from my face and took several deep long breaths.

"I'm sorry for being a wuss," I found the energy to smirk. "Especially to you Rogue, you have faced just as much as me."

I didn't die, Kellen. You saved me, offered me hope when I had none. I did not suffer the way you did. You saved every one of us, and you saved your mate. You may not see it, but you are the Gladiator Wolf King.

"What the fuck is going on here?" Mathias' deep voice cut into the quiet room and through my mind, blocking out Rogue. He picked up a bottle of rum and began taking out glasses and pouring the thick liquor into them.

"Kellen believes he is selfish because he cried and is suffering from PTSD." Leave it to Tobias to just throw it out there regardless of the timing. He could read the room, he just chose to ignore it.

"Don't be stupid," Mathias grunted and handed me one of the glasses, then proceeded to pass out the rest until everyone was holding one. "Everyone cries, every man in here has cried. Except for me." He knocked back his drink, and at the same time, Tobias scoffed.

"You cried your ass off when you thought Lamia wouldn't forgive you. You didn't touch a drink for months." Mathias glared at Tobias. Tobias pointed at King with a knowing look and a cheesy smirk plastered on his face.

"Fuck off," he aimed the insult towards Tobias. "Here's to Kellen's return. I for one am grateful, now I don't have to listen to Lamia whine about you." He lifted his glass to his lips, hiding the upturned corners of his mouth and downed his drink.

"To the king's return," Mike said, and everyone downed their drinks.

Mathias observed Rogue, giving him a once-over with his

cold, stone-colored eyes. "What's his deal?"

"Mute, had his tongue cut out when he was a kid." I thought I would save Rogue the trouble of having to explain. People would have to get used to having to converse telepathically with him because he was here to stay.

"Well, that's fucking annoying. Is he your pet?" God's, King could be a real asshole. I had forgotten how much so. With that statement, King stomped over to him and grabbed his chin, "Open your mouth."

Rogue looked at me, frowning. I nodded my head, not understanding what Mathias was doing. It was just better to do it than have Mathias make you. He was a good man and treated Lamia like a goddess, but he was a brute in all senses of the word. Rogue opened his mouth, and King moved his head from side to side looking inside. After a few seconds, he grunted and let go of Rogue's face.

"What do you think, King?" Tobias asked with a serious tone, his eye following the king who walked back by the bar.

He poured himself another drink, swigged it back, and stared down the former gladiator. "Possible, but I'm not sure," he replied, peeling his eyes from Rogue and landing them on his best friend. "I'll think more on it after my children are born safely and my little wolf is recovering." He left then, going back to Lamia's side.

"What the fuck was that shit?" Mike asked Tobias, throwing his hands in the air and grimacing at how the king just manhandled Rogue.

"Lamia isn't the only one who has healing blood." Tobias tapped the side of his nose and winked.

"Since when did Lamia have blood that could heal?" Uncle Michael asked, looking pissed that he didn't get the memo and giving the delta a scowl.

"Don't look at me!" He raised his hands in defense, "I had no idea and she's my daughter!"

"Fucking Lamia." Uncle Michael chuckled with a sigh, an everyday phrase he had been saying since she turned fourteen and got her wolf.

"Kellen, we don't want you coming back for a couple of weeks. You are home now. Just enjoy being here and connecting with the pack again, everything else can wait. Show Tala the New Moon Kingdom. You too, Mike" Uncle Michael had his arms crossed and looked very serious. There was no changing his mind, his words were final. I was actually very grateful that they didn't want to throw me back into everything so soon.

"Thank you," I replied, still wondering if Mathias could really give Rogue his tongue back. The injury was old, and I knew their blood could heal, but could it grow back his tongue? It's not like it's a limb, but still, I would be shocked if he did make it happen.

A growl so intense suddenly shook the walls, and less than a second later, my mate and her sister came running out of the room, both looking flustered and sickly. We all stood up at once. "What happened?' Uncle Marcus' face pinched in concern, worried about his daughter and grandchildren.

"She, umm, we couldn't stay in there." Looking perplexed and scratching her head, Tala gave Jonda a strange and awkward look. The next thing we knew, Aunt Olivia and Vivian came out of the suite followed by the doctors who were sweating profusely. The only person who hadn't come out of the suite was King. "They both need to calm down."

I quirked an eyebrow, not understanding what was going on.

"Lamia was unable to control her aura and it started suffocating the doctors. Mathias tried to use his to overpower her, but that just made her angry, and then we all started feeling sick. We can't go back in until those two calm down," sighed Aunt Vivian while palming her face, also frustrated.

"Kellen and Marcus could go in there."

"NO!" Both I and Uncle Marcus quickly shut down Uncle Michael's suggestion. There was no way in hell I was going in there. No not in a million years.

"You can come back now." We all turned to look down the hall. From where we sat with the door open, we had a straight line of sight to the delta's suite, and we could all see King leaning out the door to call to us. "She crying because you all left." I could physically see the strain on his face as well as hear it.

"Very well, let's go, ladies. Doctors," Aunt Vivian stood up, smoothed down her skirt, and motioned for everyone to follow again. My mate and Jonda followed behind, and their excited expressions returned.

Around another hour later, all ears perked up when we heard the first cry of a baby. For a bunch of strong shifter males, I had never seen more crybabies in my life. A few minutes later came another cry, this one distinctly different. Baby number two had been born.

Waiting for that third cry was the worst thing I had ever experienced. We all sat in silence with bated breath, hoping, praying that we would hear the wail of that third child and soon. After ten minutes, it didn't come, and we began to worry. I was holding Uncle Marcus' hand in a vice-like grip.

After another five minutes, it seemed as though the gods had not favored the third child, and we had given up hope. Whenever so softly, the faint sound of a soft cry could be heard - if we hadn't all been so quiet thinking the worst, we might have missed it.

Yeah, there wasn't a dry eye in this room full of males as each one of us let out our held breath. The mournful weight that was sitting heavy in the air lifted like a gust of wind clearing the clouds.

"Two boys and a little girl," Uncle Marcus breathed out, patting his chest. "I'm a granddad!" He said and repeated it a few times in a shocking state of disbelief. He obviously received the news from his mate.

Uncle Marcus' eyes glazed over again, and when he refocused, I don't think I could have witnessed a more vigorous and elevated smile than what was plastered on his face. "My daughter wants me to come in."

Mike poured us all drinks again while we waited until we could go see Lamia. It was a while before Mathias emerged holding two little bundles in his huge arms, grinning from ear to ear, followed closely by my Tala, who also carried an even smaller bundle in her arms. We all stood as they entered the suite. "Boys, I would like you to meet your niece, Amali Kellyn Artos," King proudly announced.

Tala placed the small child in my arms. I felt awkward at first, scared I would break her. "You named her after me?" I asked in a daze. I looked down at the beautiful little girl in my arms who already had some light blond hair cresting the crown of her head like a halo. Words escaped me as I smiled down at her. She was perfect.

"Mike, meet Maximus Michael." He held out one arm and Mike took the larger child from him, more comfortably than I had. "And Tobias, my best friend, this is Zachary Tobias."

"Fuck dude, I don't know what to say." He took the largest little boy from Mathias' arm and I saw the tears drop from his eyes. "He is going to be the best looking, just like his uncle Toby," he smiled. The big bad bear was actually crying after giving us shit earlier.

It was so humbling to see how three tiny little creatures could reduce such big strong men into a ball of nerves and emotions. I kissed the top of Amali's head and scented her. I already felt a close and protective connection with her, and I had only met her for mere minutes. I wished Hunji was here to witness this. I would bet that even he would be an emotional mess right about now.

"Alright give them back. Just because they carry your names, they are still mine," Mathias growled out, taking the boys back from Mike and Tobias and then nodding to Tala to take Amali from my arms. And then they disappeared back into the delta's suite.

I sat back down to wait with Mike for our mates to come out. Tobias and Rogue decided to retire for the night as it was late. The omega staff had already prepared rooms for them, and Uncle Michael walked them to their rooms a floor below.

"I can't wait to have pups," Mike said out loud with a little pep in his voice. "I mean, not right now, but I would like a few. We all grew up as close as siblings, but it's strange how our parents only had one kid each, ya know?"

Indeed, it was strange, but that was the case with most high-ranking shifters; they never had any more than two children usually. That way there would be less fighting over titles and positions. Lower ranking families like gammas and omegas would, in most instances, have at least two to four offspring.

"I may be a father sooner rather than later."

"No! Really? You think Tala is with pup?"

"Her heat only lasted that one night, so if we go by standards, very possibly." I couldn't help the grin when I thought my little flame might be carrying our pup, a vision of her belly swollen with our baby. I hoped she was. And even if she wasn't, I was going to keep trying, every single chance I got.

Starting tonight, when she eventually came out of the room.

Chapter 52 – Happy Birthday

KELLEN

My watch read 11.45 PM. I lowered my arm, exposing the moon high above me; she looked like she was smiling tonight. The birth of triplets had probably pleased the Moon Goddess. The chosen queen had done well, and at only two days old, they were able to determine their races.

The eldest and biggest, Zachary, would have the spirit of a bear, taking after his father. Maximus, the second eldest and only slightly smaller than his brother, was a wolf. The smallest and prettiest, Amali, also smelled as if she would be a wolf, but her scent was different from her brothers. Perhaps she would be a Dire Wolf like her mother, or a Lycan - also from her mother's side. Of course, she could just be an ordinary werewolf too. But I didn't think so. She was special, maybe because she held my name, and I was biased?

I would spoil all Lamia's children, but mostly her. Both boys had been born with the mark of a royal, their little crown birthmarks sitting on their hips just like mine and Lamia's.

I was lying across the stone bench, the same place I would come to every year on this very same night. For the last two years, I had been alone, and I was sure I would be alone again tonight. The cupcakes sat on the ground below me, the warm air was sure to make them start melting soon. I scoffed, thinking that if I was Bhakhil, they would have been a puddle of icing and soggy cake already.

"It's a beautiful night." The sweet melodic voice of Lamia startled me, making me jump up. I hadn't heard or smelt her enter the Royal Gardens or approach me.

"Lamia," I smiled, pleased she was here. "I didn't expect you to come out here, I figured you had your hands full." I knew three babies was more than plenty to handle, and I wondered how I would be as a father at the same time.

"Yah, that's what husbands, parents, and aunts are for," she giggled, coming around and taking her place on the bench next to me. "It seems like another lifetime since the last time we were here together." She mused.

"Almost three years, but yes, it seems like forever ago. Would you change any of it? If you could go back and change the past three years, would you?" I asked her, wondering if I had the chance, would I? It was a question I had asked myself many a night, and I found myself spacing out and thinking about it during the day.

She sat there, obviously thinking about it, doing that cute thing she always did when in deep thought and scrunching up her nose. Up until recently, I had always thought my answer would be yes, I would change so much. But now, finding my mate, meeting Tala, and dying, the answer was no. No, I wouldn't change it because then I wouldn't have found her.

"I don't think so, I mean, there are some things I definitely would leave out." She squirmed, and I could guess what those things were. "Honestly though, Kel, if we were able to and did change things, would we be where we are today?"

I didn't think we would. Would we accept whatever fate we changed just as easily, though?

"I really like Tala. She is special you know, I can feel it. And the way she looks at you, the way her eyes light up in your presence or just the mention of your name... She loves you."

"I love her too," I admitted.

Lamia scooted sideways and propped her legs up over mine. The shorts she was wearing rode up, and I could see the deep scars from her first fight with a rogue bear. It seemed like that was the beginning of everything. "I have a scar like that too," I said, and lifted up the leg of my shorts to show her the marred skin where the lion had left his claw marks on me that last day in the arena.

Funnily enough, my back should have been scared from the whip, yet when I awoke in that pit of death, they had reduced to nothing but thin white lines. Some were a little raised, but they were hardly noticeable. But the Lions marks had stayed, like a badge of honor, depicting a story.

"I swear to the Moon Goddess, we should have been twins." A chuckle mixed with her sigh. "I didn't get you a present this year, just so you know. I was kind of busy."

"You gave birth to three healthy babies, you gave me two nephews and a niece. I think that's the best present ever." I rubbed her bare leg in comfort and noticed the faint tingles spark on my fingertips and I frowned at the all too familiar feeling.

"I feel them too," she whispered, "I don't think they will ever go away."

"They won't," I replied and, after a beat of silence, I added, "I didn't get you a present either, I was a little busy myself."

"Fucker, your home and alive. That's the only present I need." She swatted at me, and I feigned hurt, giving her a smirk.

"Hey, weren't you and Tawny supposed to head up to Lonely City and party for your twenty-first like we did for Mike's?" I was half teasing but also quite curious that Tawny wasn't here, after all those two were just as close as we were. Lamia hadn't even mentioned the werecat.

"Ahh, well Tawny is dealing with her own mate problems right now, and I wasn't due to give birth for another couple of weeks. She is going to be super pissed she missed the birth. I called her yesterday."

"What she say?" I was truly interested. I had missed Tawny and was gutted when she decided to stay in the Werecat Kingdom and not come back home.

"You know, I'm not sure it's my place to tell you. She's tough, though. She can handle it and I am sure once she gets the message that I gave birth, her ass will be straight over to Riocht." Again, Lamia let out a small chuckle and I joined her, knowing she was right. That feisty little cat will be majorly pissed she wasn't here for Lamia.

"Wait, Riocht?" I asked, her words just sinking in.

"Yeah, it's not quite finished, but that's where we have decided to settle. I will be leaving in the next few days with Mathias and Tobias. Mom and dad will be moving there too, and momma Amitola will visit, but she wants to stay at the Clan Mansion to help Ria become Den Mother."

"Ria, Den Mother?" I swiped a hand down my face. "Ha! About time they completed the mate bond," I shook my head, I truly had missed a lot in the few months I had been away. The thought left me feeling a little more detached. I would also be losing Uncle Marcus, a man I had been as close to as my father, closer than I am to Mike's father. "It's a new era and you just gave birth to the first of a new generation. I feel like life is moving too fast. I don't want to slow down, though, in case I miss the important parts. But at the same time I pray for peace and quiet."

"I know exactly what you mean. We are about to turn twenty-one and I already have three rug rats and have had two and a half mates." I wondered if I should tell her about meeting Ashe in between my stasis of life and death. I had a feeling she already had an inkling, so I didn't.

Instead, I lifted my watch up again, 11.58. I bent down and picked up the box, settling it on Lamia's legs, and pulled a lighter out of the box I had already put in there, and lit the two cupcakes. Once lit, I gave her one and took the other for myself.

"Happy birthday, beautiful." I told her.

"Happy birthday, handsome." She replied, and we blew out our candles, both closing our eyes and making a wish.

We sat there for a good while munching on our cupcakes, sometimes speaking, sometimes letting our own minds think, and sometimes we shared a glance. Just being with each other was enough comfort for both of us. There was no need to make conversation.

"Hey, you want to go for a run? It's been a while since I have been able to shift into my wolf form. I could morph into my beast while pregnant, but my skin felt way too itchy and uncomfortable." She shuddered, wiggling her shoulders like she physically remembered the sensation.

I stood up. "Race you!" I yelled and shifted into Conri in a matter of seconds, and he took off towards the tree line.

"You're going to need a head start, cheater!" I heard her yell behind me before the sound of her giant paws padding heavily against the forest ground reached my ears. I sped up, knowing I couldn't outrun her, but loved the idea of competition anyway.

Our wolves ran and played for what seemed like hours, they had missed each other too, until we found ourselves by the side of the lake, a favorite spot for the three of us growing up. Lamia shifted back into her skin form and dived right into the lake. "What are you waiting for?" She laughed as soon as her head emerged to the surface.

I shifted and dived in, swimming under to grab her legs. Only the moon provided us light, and we splashed and played like little kids until the position of the moon told us it was time to head back. We both walked out of the lake, stark naked, and for the first time, I didn't have those lustful thoughts when I glanced at her womanly body. Her healing abilities had put her back to the way she was before being pregnant.

"It's weird, isn't it?" She asked. "Being able to look at each other naked and not wanting to jump each other's bones. That's the mate bond for you."

"Mmm," I hummed back, not thinking she needed me to answer. We ran back to the palace, slipping on some spare clothes we had stashed in a box by the entrances. We parted ways on the stairs with a kiss on the cheek and a simple goodnight.

I entered the Royal Suite quietly so I wouldn't wake Tala, and crawled into bed next to her. I gently pulled her into my arms and spooned her, inhaling her scent. She was my home, my happiness, and I couldn't wait for our lives to begin.

I went to sleep that night feeling more like myself than I had in a long time. And I knew things would be okay, life was going to be good. All I needed was my little flame to help light the way.

"I love you," I whispered to her before my eyes closed.

*****

The next morning after making love to Tala and then ravishing her again in the shower, I found myself at the training grounds, meeting up with Rogue and Mike. Mike was wearing a permanent grin on his face, and I wondered if the wind changed, would his face stay like that?

"What are you laughing at?" Mike questioned me, grin still in place.

"Just wondering if your face hurt from wearing that stupid look you've had since we came home." I laughed at him.

You have that same stupid grin Rogue scoffed at me through the mind-link, including Mike in it.

"See, I'm not the only one." Mike chuckled.

"Why are two idiots smiling like you won a golden egg?" Mathias' deep baritone voice cut into our bantering. Like the shits we were, Mike and I just kept smiling back at him. "I take it you both got laid last night," he grunted, knowing full well we did, well, me this morning.

"You," he pointed at Rogue, "Let's go see if we can fix you." He said, giving the former gladiator a measured look, his silver eyes putting the moon to shame. "This could make you sick, and I can't guarantee it will even work."

Mathias stomped off, Rogue giving us a worried glance as he ventured to follow the king.

You will be fine I linked him.* He is really a big teddy bear*

If this works, chocolate for everyone! He laughed, and I laughed along with him, being reminded of how he ate his piece when the rest of the gladiators used their pieces of chocolate to pay tribute to me.

"What do you want to do with Rogue?" Mike asked as soon as they were out of earshot. "We already have Tyron as the next gamma."

"Let's see what King can do first, if he can do anything. Rogue is a good fighter, smart and quick, and he has strength. I don't think he was born to be a rogue, more like a beta. His wolf is almost as big as yours." I hadn't decided where Rogue would fit in, but I hated to waste his talents and give him a warrior position. Unfortunately, his lack of speech was a hindrance, despite his skills. It was okay to mind-link, but he needed a voice if he was going to communicate with pack alphas or other kingdoms.

"Jonda said she and Tala were going to visit with Lamia and the babies today."

"That's what I heard, between all her moans this morning." I waggled my eyebrows at my best friend.

"I'm glad Jonda decided to give Tala a chance, and I am really happy they are making an effort with Lamia. I know she can be intimidating, and for Tala, everything is new."

"Me too, I think the three of them will become really good friends in time. Let's just hope Tawny doesn't feel shoved out. I'm a little concerned that she is alone in Cambiador, and I really miss her."

"I know exactly what you mean," Mike's smile dropped just for a second as he thought of Tawny. "You know though, she is not the scared little girl Lamia rescued three years ago. Besides, if Lamia didn't think she was okay, do you really think any of us would be sitting here right now? Hell no, Lamia would send her army down there and fuck shit up for the little kitty." He laughed, and he was right.

Still, Tawny had become part of our family and I wanted to make sure she was okay on my own. I knew I would be making a call later on, but right now, "Are you ready to get your ass kicked?" I half-jested with Mike.

"Get my ass kicked? Please! I'm not the one who has been on vacation, sitting on my ass for three months." His words were playful, but he knew full well my time away had neither been a vacation nor had I been sitting on my ass.

"Whatever, have you seen how big my arms are now?" I threw off my shirt and flexed my muscles for Mike, making a show of it.

"Put that shit away before you embarrass yourself!" He chuckled, pulling his own shirt off, twirling it around his finger, and then flinging it at me. "I missed you dude."

"I missed you too, big guy." I winked at him playfully, earning fluttering eyelashes from Mike. Fucking Mike.

The both of us laughed at each other, stepping into the sparing ring, noticing a small crowd of warriors that were already here gathering around. "See that, they all came to see their king kick your ass."

"No, they came to see the beta put his king in place."

"Game on, brother!"

After some time of grappling and throwing punches, we took a break. "Holy moons, man, you are not even sweating," Mike exclaimed as he panted from our workout.

"I told you, I have never trained and fought so hard in my life than my time as a gladiator. I eat, slept, and shit fighting."

"TMI, definitely, I don't need to hear that again." He shook his head, making a disgusted face at me. It was nice that we could just fall right back into our friendship, that he didn't have to tiptoe around me. I guess that's one of many reasons why I loved him.

I had come back bigger, stronger, and wiser. I had left a boy, a lost prince, and I had returned a man, a Gladiator Wolf King.

Chapter 53 – Blood Lust

<u>OLIVER</u>

How ironic that Alpha Travis would have me put in the same cell that I once had him held in for months. It took us four days of traveling to get back to MacTire. At first, I laughed that they would take me back to the place I grew up in. I knew every single inch of that castle, every nook, every cranny, every secret passage and tunnel. It would be easy to break out of their cells and leave the dungeons; I knew the mechanisms by heart.

How wrong I was.

I realized it was idiotic for me to think they would not have made upgrades and changes to the castle. I understood that as soon as the guards led me down below and into the dungeons, bringing me to Travis' old cell. There were new barred doors, and the floor had been painted with silver, leaving a small strip for a prisoner to walk on. I was stripped down and hosed down, then given a pair of thin shorts and shoved into my new home.

There was no way I was breaking out of this cell. A cot, a chair, and a bucket were all that furnished the dark and damp 6x6 cell I would now call home while I waited to be executed. I sat on the cot, my toes burning when they touched the edge of the silver-lined floor. A guard came and provided me with a meal. Not scrapes or porridge, but an actual meal with meat, potatoes, vegetables, and a bottle of water.

I was apprehensive about eating it and cautiously sniffed it for any poisons, fully expecting it to be at least laced with wolfsbane or something. It was not, which made me nervous. For a man who was about to have his heart ripped out or his head chopped off, they were treating me rather well. Too well.

I ate, picking at the food, mulling over the why. There was no doubt I deserved to be here after everything I had done. I would accept my fate like a man. I would pay my penance for the crimes I committed. I truly wish it hadn't come to this and I had been able to escape and live the life I had dreamt of since I was a little boy. Alas, that future was not in my cards. A cunning fox always meets his end, and I had run out of luck. Like a cat, I had used up my nine lives, and now it was only a matter of time before death met me to guide me to the pits of the underworld.

For three days I was fed, and for three days I wondered when I would receive sentencing. It was the night of the third day when finally, I was visited, and not just by a guard bringing me food or exchanging my bucket. I knew it was someone with ranking when I heard the slow and heavy steps approaching from the far corridor.

My wolf began pacing and growling in my head. He, too, was ready to accept our death. Less happy about that me, as he knew all too well that most of our crimes, the worst, were unavoidable. I had no idea what time it was, but it was late into the night, a time when most members of the castle would be tucked up in a comfortable bed sleeping. No demons to keep them awake, no echoing screams of their victims filling the black void or their minds. No, those people would be sleeping peacefully under the protection of their alpha and the warriors that patrolled the main pack grounds and surrounding villages.

The steps came closer until a large figure stood in front of my cell. He had changed. No longer was he the mildly toned wolf with soft brown eyes and an aura of good around him. No, instead, a man who had put on muscles and looked to have grown several inches since I held him in the cells stood in front of me. His shoulders were broad and his arms thick; a neatly trimmed bread and short, freshly cut hair with his dark eyes gave him that rugged and imposing look. This wolf had been broken and put back together, yet when he was glued back together somewhere, a piece was missing.

"Hello, Oliver. Welcome home." Travis, now the Alpha of MacTire, said with an all too deceptive smile that spoke volumes. "I have come to tell you that your execution will be held the day after tomorrow."

I nodded, understanding and not expecting anything less. The dark alpha looked down at the food still on my plate and scowled. "You need to eat, old friend. I need you in good health." This time it was me who drew my eyebrows close together, not understanding his meaning. His words were too friendly for a man I spent months torturing.

He laughed. "Do you really think I would execute you so fast? No," he looked up at me through hooded eyes, his hands clasped behind his back, and a shadow covered part of his face giving him an eerie and crazy presence. "No, the man who will die is a rogue. Everyone will just think it is you. I would not give you up so easily now that I have you." He turned his back on me and drew in a deep breath, letting it back out just as slowly. "I remember how much you liked to play games, Oliver. I have many fun games we will be playing together. Enjoy your food."

The heavy fall of his steps faded as he left the corridor where my cell was - the furthest corridor from the stairs that led down here. I gulped and closed my eyes. So, this was how it was meant to be. Travis had no intentions of killing me, yet. Instead, I could only imagine all the things his games would bring. After all, I had played most of them with him. I picked up the wooden plate with the food and threw it as hard as I could at the wall.

I laughed loudly, the sound echoing through the cell and down the corridor, bouncing off the stone walls. I laughed some more and couldn't stop. Death would have been too easy. Why did I even think it would be that easy? Of course, it wouldn't be. I was now Travis' play toy, just like he was mine once upon a time. The only difference was - that the dark alpha was doing this for himself, nobody was giving him orders or commanding his obedience. He was going to repay the favor because he wanted to - not because a dominating and superior alpha was commanding him too.

I suppose this is retribution for complying, yet I could not deny that my wolf and I did enjoy part of what we had done. I still hated what we had become, but the blood lust had always been there, and it seemed someone else had also begun to crave it.

I don't remember much of my mother, but I could still see her angelic face when I squeezed my eyes tight and concentrated enough. I tried to do that now, but my vision filled Tala's face instead.

My mother died when I was still a young boy. I wish I could say a happy young boy, but that was never the case.

I had always lived here or in the village. I had only known this place to be filled with rogues, dangerous men who cared for no one and nothing except their greed. Some only wished to survive. The women in the village were not here by choice except for the select few who were just as mentally damaged as the men. Most women were stolen, kidnapped, or born into the life of a rogue pack of delinquents, criminals, murders, and people whose wolves had craved for a pack.

I grew up fighting for scraps of food, my mother taking different lovers just to put food in my belly until one day, she wasn't there. Gone to the New Moon Kingdom, where they executed her in cold blood without a trial.

Silas had told me she went there to beg for a place in the pack and that the king had given no attention and ordered her death right there on the border. I was there, supposedly. In my mind, I remember it, but my wolf does not recall it. It was shortly after that I became a servant to the Rogue King, and a few years later, I grew strong and joined the ranks. It wasn't until I shifted did Silas really start to take note of me and eventually named me his beta after showing him loyalty. I didn't follow him because I wanted to, I followed him for survival. Then it was out of duty once I was properly initiated and became the Beta to the Rogue Kingdom.

When the Dire Wolf killed Silas, I felt a weight had been lifted from me, his death freeing a part of me. I was scared, I had nowhere to go - I was left in a void, and I wasn't ready to die for that bastard.

I blindly followed Jack and found myself too deep in Orion's charades. I should have left, he was much worse than I could ever imagine Silas to be. Yet, I didn't. I fell into step in fear that I would become one of the creatures, so instead, I showed my loyalty again and even helped lead the Crawlers into battle, transporting them to each town we attacked and letting those monsters loose.

I killed for Silas, and I killed for Orion. I took my pleasures out on women and a few men. It was the only way I knew how to placate my wolf, who craved a mate but would get carried away in his primal desires, then hate the person we fucked because we were not who they wanted and kill them. A bad person like me would never be blessed with another half by the Moon Goddess; she did not give gifts to murderers like me.

I had come to the conclusion, in my short twenty-six years of a life full of violence, that the Moon Goddess had never given me a chance. From the moment I was born, I was cursed. A child of the moon, hated from the first breath I took. She didn't favor me or any of the children born to rogues. Instead, she turned a blind eye to our misgivings. There was no hope for a child born in the life of a rogue's world.

*****

TRAVIS

I left Oliver cell feeling smug and excited. I didn't know what to expect from myself when I would finally once again come face to face with the man and wolf that caused me so much pain.

For three years, I had dreamt of killing Oliver. For three years, I imagined what it would be like to hold his life in my hands. Now that I finally had him, I didn't want to kill him. I wanted to inflict the same pain on him as he had done to me. It wasn't revenge I wanted to serve that man; when I lived not once but twice after he had deemed to kill me. This was retribution. There's a fine line between the two similar acts but a whole different way of serving my repayment. Revenge would have me taking his life and executing Oliver like I said I would. Retribution would be dishing out his punishment as fate best saw it.

I walked away from Oliver's cell with lighter steps and an air of pleasant darkness surrounding me. I shook my head with a chuckle aimed at myself. How could darkness in someone's soul be considered pleasant? Yet mine was, and my wolf Janus relished in the growing power we both felt.

I came up the stone steps that led to the back of the castle and emerged close to where the omega quarters and kitchen were located, and started humming a tune that belonged to a song I didn't remember.

"Uncle Travis, did you go to see the prisoner?" My self-absorbed, tainted happiness was broken with Petra's interruption.

My wolf growled. "Not now, Petra, I'm not in the mood," I barked at her and walked past and began to hum my tune again. I could feel her heated stare at my back and hear her little growl. She was a feisty one, that little she-bear. She already had a deep growl, and her spirit animal would not even emerge for another three years when she turned fourteen. Reminding me that her birthday was coming up in just a few short weeks, turning eleven.

I stopped before reaching the door's entrance, my hand pausing to push it open. "I'm sorry Petra," I said with my back still towards her. "Uncle Travis just needs some time," I told her, feeling guilty for pushing her away and brushing her off. I had been doing that a lot lately, and she didn't deserve it.

Petra had chosen to stay with me instead of heading to the Clan Mansion and Bear Kingdom with Lamia, Ria, and Mathias. And when they would finally move into Riocht, Petra still wanted to stay with me. The night Hunji received the mark of the knight had scared her, and I don't think the fright had ever left her. Even though she loved him, she would never see him in the same light again.

From the first moment I met this little girl, she captured my heart, and knew I would always be there to protect her. It cut me to pieces when Orion orchestrated her kidnapping. My heart had stopped when Finn held her in his arms, the scent of fear rolling off of her. I can only thank the heavens and whatever god she prayed to that Finn turned out to be a good man and protected her with his life. If he hadn't, Lamia would have taken his head for herself.

If only Petra knew of the darkness slowly growing inside of me.

I felt little arms come up and circle my waist, trying to squeeze me. "It's okay, I still love you. Even if you are grumpier these days."

I finally turned around and bent down to her level. "Give me a couple of days and I will be back to my old self again. I promise." I ruffled her hair and headed towards my office, leaving her in the kitchen. Not even questioning why she was up at this hour when she should be tucked up in bed safe and sound.

It turns out Petra was not the only one up at this hour. I found Rhett sitting in my office waiting for me. Another night owl. "Rhett," I acknowledged him and came around my desk, sitting in my chair across from him. "What can I do for you?"

I liked Rhett, he was honest, brave, and different, but right now his genetic makeup was a mystery. He could grow fangs and extend claws, move with inhuman speed, and had far more strength than that of any human. Yet he had no wolf. And like the rest of us, even if he bore the mark of a knight, we could not understand how that was possible. By all rights, he was a hunter, but no hunter could half-shift as he could. They had strength and speed, and some even healed better than humans. Rhett was indeed a mystery.

"We have the execution of Oliver set for the day after tomorrow. Is this still the plan?" I nodded at his question.

"Yep, he is in cell three in the first corridor. I want his head covered and chopped off." Lies, Oliver was not in that cell. He wasn't even in the same corridor. The man in cell three was a rogue criminal, but I had beaten him so badly that they wouldn't be able to tell what his face looked like. He would do as a decoy.

Was it wrong that I didn't even feel the slightest bit of guilt for lying to the gamma? I didn't even care if Lamia or Kellen found out that I hadn't killed him. They had given him to me to decide his judgment, and I had decided to take my time serving his punishment.

Part of me thinks Lamia should have let me die on that hospital table that night. When I woke up, something had shifted inside, not just with me but also with my wolf. I dismissed Rhett, he was making my wolf uncomfortable. That's the thing about Hunters, they have a sense of justice and smell a lie if given enough reason to suspect you. And Rhett was very good at his job as an enforcer.

Once he left me alone, I opened up my laptop, pulling up the now-forgotten pictures someone had taken of me and Lamia in the throes of passion. My cock twitched and Janus whined, remembering the feel of her. We craved her sometimes, and sometimes the craving was so intense that I wondered if our obsession was for lust or her blood. This crazy reaction to and for her had only started a few weeks after she saved me.

I thought it was a normal side effect of her bite, but I came to realize nothing was normal or healthy about how much I wanted her, how much my wolf lusted after her blood.

Chapter 54 – The Road Traveled Before

<u>HUNJI</u>
1 WEEK LATER

"Congratulations again, Your Highness. I look forward to returning and meeting the three of them." I ended the call with Lamia. I was still trying to wrap my head around the fact the young queen had given birth to triplets and was thankful the little girl had survived.

I shoved the satellite phone into my backpack, along with the power bars, two bottles of water, and a change of clothes. My swords were already attached to my back. It wasn't much for the journey I was about to embark on, but then I was hoping to make quick work of finding Finn's sister and bring her back in as soon as possible.

"Do you have everything you need?" Jasper asked me, walking into his office.

"Yes, alpha, as much as I need to carry." I zipped up the bag while replying to him.

I had spent a little over a week here, helping the new alpha and his Luna adjust. Kellen had left a handful of his warriors here, and a gladiator named Corey had decided to stay in Bhakhil now that it was under the rein of a new alpha.

A few other gladiators had also stayed and decided to

join the warrior ranks and quickly found themselves in leadership positions thanks to Kellen's training during his stay. The majority of the gladiators found they had nowhere else to go; either home was a faraway dream, or they had no home.

Xander was able to provide Luna Eloise with the specifics to remove the inhibitor chips safely, so every shifter who had one was now free of them.

"Hunji, I cannot thank you enough for everything you have done here for me and our people in this short time." I heard Jasper's words, but I let them drift in one ear and out the other. "Is there anything we can do for you to make your journey easier? I could send a few men with you…"

"Thank you, alpha, but they will only slow me down."

"I have maps, so you know where you are heading…"

"That won't be necessary, I know this land." I wish I didn't know this land so well. It had been a long time since I had traveled this continent, but it was still fresh in my mind after all these years. I hated being here, all it did was remind me of my past and the place I grew up.

"In that case, I can only wish you a safe journey and good luck." Jasper sighed. "Please be careful, I hear wars have started breaking out in numerous kingdoms, and Andora is not a stable country right now. King Panja started mobilizing troops through Bashenstan in an attempt to claim more kingdoms. We are not sure how far his army has reached or if it has affected the surrounding countries, including Andora."

"Thank you for your concern, alpha. This is one reason why I am best to travel solo. I will not draw too much attention myself."

"Very well." He gave me a curt bow out of respect and probably because I outranked him. He may be an alpha, but I was second in command to the Queen of Shifters, which gave my wolf and I a much higher position, if not above than equal to any alpha, excluding King Kellen.

I walked out of the palace, escorted by Alpha Jasper, his Luna Eloise, and Beta Cameron, who wished me well yet again. I climbed into the beat-up truck, threw my bag and swords onto the passenger seat, and started the engine. Destination: Andora. Operation: find the witch and bring her home.

My eyes were on the sandy dirt road, but I looked in the rearview mirror, watching Bhakhil's Palace get smaller and smaller until the dust from the road hid it from my vision.

"The one place you didn't want to end up again, and here you are, foolishly sent on another quest." It was just me and the road right now. I only had myself to talk to. As long as I could stay away from Asiarian, things would be fine. Just being this close to that country and kingdom put me in a bad mood. That was the good thing about heading to the western continent, I was further away.

I hated this continent. More so, I loathed the idea of being so close to my home country. I had avoided it and its rulers for thirteen years, and I had no desire to even come anywhere close to that goddess-forsaken place. Bad memories, too many memories, ones I didn't want to see again.

It had taken me a long time to get where I was today. A lot of self-discipline and courage. So many days I wanted to give up, but the priestess's words stayed with me. I found myself repeating them more and more often these past few years.

'He who walks amongst death and lives to tell the tale shall preview life and its coming attractions. Sometimes we need a wake-up call from fantasy so we may survive reality.'

That kooky old woman never did make sense, yet I still

found myself spitting out verses she had told me. I bet the old crone was still alive, sitting on her throne of gold, pretending she still believed in prayer and teaching others to pray to their gods. She must be 200 years old now if she still lived.

I pushed thoughts of my old mentor and savior from my head and was going to concentrate on the road again. But the road was deserted, and the road was just a worn path on the dry ground. There was nothing to concentrate on.

Ever since we had set foot on this continent, old forgotten memories began to rear their ugly heads, memories I had buried deep down a long time ago. One's that I wished had stayed forgotten. It was only months ago that I had vowed, yet again, that I would never step foot on this continent.

Yet here I found myself, traveling a road I had been down before. The stagnant air and smell of the desert, a forgotten familiar, now stirring up those lost echoes of a life left behind long ago.

'Get in, get the witch, and get out.' My wolf Ruda grumbled. He too, was not keen on being back on this side of the realm. My past life was stirring up his own bad memories, after all, he almost died along with me, and together we had felt and endured the worst pain a shifter can fathom.

Our place was beside our queen, not out here in the desert. Except our queen had sent us on a quest, and we had pledged allegiance and our life to her. Refusing her request would hurt us, we were fated to protect her. Sent to another new kingdom to find her and stay by her side. I hadn't figured out what was so important about this young witch called Morgan yet, aside from being Finnegan's sister and having been locked away most of her life.

Maybe our queen felt for her or felt sorry for Finn. Whether Lamia made a promise to King's half-brother or not, I was still a little sour on why it had to be me. I had no issues coming to find Kellen, he was a brother, a knight, and I knew how bonded he and Lamia were. If he had truly died that night, I'm not sure she would have recovered.

I don't think she would have died herself, but Lamia would never have been the same. That I was sure of.

If I remembered correctly, I had two days of travel time by car or just under. I would reach the border of Andora by then, and then hopefully, I would be able to find her in the heart of the country. Tala's sister, Shayna, hadn't quite disclosed her exact location, but she did describe the large white-marbled mansion she visited with Orion. There was only one place I could think of in Andora that was made of all-white marble: The Megaron.

A large mansion-type structure consisting of an open porch, a vestibule, and a large hall with a central hearth and a throne. It was the only place Orion, who thought of himself as a king, would reside. It was also on a secure site, sitting above the rest of the city, and was home to hidden chambers beneath the stone structures.

I had never visited it, but I had seen pictures and studied their culture during my time with the priestess. I would head there first, it was my best bet and most obvious place to keep a locked-up princess.

"Hmm, a princess." I thought out loud. If Orion was a king on this continent, and her half-brother was the King of the Bears, she would actually be a princess. More so than Tala. "A witch princess, a princess witch." Now that was a title I never thought I would hear myself saying. For all we knew, until Orion's appearance, all the witches had died out long ago with the fall of the human race.

The shifters had survived with only a handfull of the

human population. The disease had wiped them out and left our realm to be ruled by were-folk once again. Then came the shifter wars, each race and each kingdom trying to take control. The shifter race had been less in numbers than the human race to begin with, so we filled in the gaps, taking over businesses and politics and reshaping the realm to fit us.

Things the humans once took for granted became lost relics, like flying machines, and in some parts of the realm, things like technology were lost. Packs and clans relied on telepathic communication and basic primal needs, while some things from the old realm survived and thrived, other things became null and void. Useless in our lives, no longer needed. And with the fall of humans, witches fell along with them. Unlike shifters, they were not immune to diseases.

Shifters could still have bad hearts and failing organs, those were genetic malfunctions from impure bloodlines. But simple things like flu, Ebola, and the pox, did not affect us. We could be poisoned by silver, wolfsbane, or some other highly potent drug, but general poisons would not harm us. It took a lot more for a shifter to fall. Our genetics allowed us to heal faster, some faster than others, but even then, we could be exhausted and die from deep cuts induced by silver or other potent positions. We were not invincible, just more robust.

I groaned out loud at myself. Once again, I was lost in my own head, thinking of things that bore no consequence to me. This was certainly going to be a long journey. Another reason to get the witch, get out, and go home.

I wasn't a fan of music, I preferred silence or books, but it was at this point I wished the radio in the truck worked. I fiddled with the dials anyway. Static and more static. Either the radio truly didn't work, or the East still hadn't figured out how to work transmitter towers. I had been spoiled living in the West with all the technology, food, lush greenery, and better transportation. This continent was mostly desert. Only the outlying countries closer to bodies of water had vegetation.

If wasn't for the desert heat, I would have run in wolf form. Unfortunately, the sand and dirt would have burnt my paws, there was nowhere to stop for water, and there was little to hunt out here. Running in wolf form would have consumed a ton of energy and we would need to eat. Not to mention I would die of heat exhaustion before I could even cross the wastelands.

*****

Day two into my Journey, and I will have to do what I was trying to avoid in the first place. I had pulled over last night to get some shut-eye, waking up at dawn. The heat from the sun stirred me awake as its first rays reached the windows. I turned the key in the ignition and was met with a whirring sound. I tried several times until the engine said 'fuck it' and wouldn't turn over.

I grabbed my pack and attached the swords to my back. Luckily, I was wearing the suits Lamia had commissioned and just took off the pants, shoving them into the bag, the whole time huffing and grunting, moaning to myself about having to run in wolf form. Ruda wasn't happy either, he missed the forests and mountains of MacTire.

I shifted into my wolf form and picked up my bag, hooking it to my back teeth, and let Ruda take over. We had already looked at a map and knew the direction we needed to take; we were close to the rocky hills that began before the borders of Andora.

Ruda had a great sense of direction, and now that we were

in wolf form, we didn't need to follow the road. We could stay close to the mountains that were a few miles away. We should reach them in a few hours. Although, it may take us a little longer to reach the outskirts of Andora and even longer before we hit a city.

This wasn't the first time we had made a journey like this in these conditions, and I doubt it would be the last time. I huffed and I puffed, still annoyed at the situation I had found myself in, and then Ruda took off heading south, keeping a steady pace so he wouldn't wear himself out too fast or too soon. We at least wanted to make it to the low-laying mountains, where we would find shade and maybe some fresh water if we were lucky. If not, I still had the power bars and a couple of bottles in my bag.

By nightfall, we had reached the mountains, finding a small opening to rest in for the night. I shifted back into my human form and took one of the power bars and bottles of water, scoffing the small meal down in two bites and then sipping the water.

I missed my bed in the castle and the hot steaming water of a shower. I had truly been living a life of luxury these past few years. Far from the mat and pillow I had at the sanctuary. I pulled on my shorts, laid my swords beside me, and put my pack under my head. The nights could get cool here, temperatures dropping down to what would feel like near freezing. They weren't, but after being out in the dry heat of the desert all day, I would feel the cooler air much more. If I was human, I would probably have sunstroke by now and a fever.

I felt an itching at the back of my mind and lifted my block only to hear Lamia's voice filter through. *Hunji,* she spoke softly. I rarely heard her yell or screech unless she was pissed or in battle. *I just wanted to check in with you*

I should reach Andora sometime late tomorrow I replied with my eyes closed.

Okay, but how are you? Did she sense my apprehension at being back in this goddess-forsaken continent?

Fine, I will find the witch and bring her home as soon as possible I know it pained her that I never opened up to her, but I had nothing to say. If I told her about my past, my history, she would only look at me with pity. Not with the respect she looks at me with now. I cared for Lamia, more than I could say I did anyone else. She was akin to a little sister and still, I kept my emotions at a distance from her when she had no problem confiding in me.

Okay. Just please be careful and come home safe. If you can't find her in the next week, just come home. We miss you, stay in touch I could hear the sincerity in her voice, but I still mentally scoffed.

How could anyone miss a broken wolf like me? I had cut myself off from emotion and personal contact for so long that I didn't know how to socialize or open up anymore. Tawny came close to breaking that wall of mine down, once. And I had pushed her away too.

Will do, Your Highness, I will check in with you in a week I cut the link. As a knight, there was no restriction to distance for us to mind-link, but it could be mentally exhausting and drain us of our energy. I needed to conserve that energy right now seeing as I had run on all fours.

Fucking truck.

Chapter 55 – What Future Might It Hold

<u>KELLEN</u>
3 WEEKS LATER

"Ready?" I asked Tala.

"Yeah," she squeaked excitedly, bouncing on her feet, hardly containing her excitement.

We had been out on runs together several times over the last three weeks, but for some reason, today she was overly excited.

Lamia, King, Tobias, and the babies had left a week and a half ago, permanently moving to Riocht. Unfortunately, that meant Aunt Vivian went with her, and Uncle Marcus was going to follow behind them once he had everything organized here. I was going to miss them. The palace would seem even emptier now.

I had spoken to Tawny. I didn't like her position, but she was tough, and she knew what she was doing. She could handle herself, and when she needed me, I would be there for her. It satisfied me to hear she was planning on heading to Riocht in the next coming days to meet the kids. It warmed my heart knowing Lamia and Tawny had formed an unbreakable friendship, that no matter what, they would always have each other. Thinking of them had me thinking of the relationship that had me smiling.

Hunji's situation was a little concerning. He had gone dark and was blocking all our attempts to mind-link him. We were getting to the point where we were ready to go back to the other continent to find him. Lamia had more faith in him, though, and told us to wait it out. I didn't like it, but she knew him the best and knew he would come home. For now, she wasn't overly concerned but still checked in to see if we had heard from him. The last time she had spoken to him was a week and a half after she had left. Supposedly he had found Finn's sister.

Tala and Jonda had found common ground after assisting with Lamia's birth, immediately bonding. Now the two are inseparable, and Mike and I never have to wonder where the other is, only what they are up to.

The energy pouring off of Tala right now was almost too much. Waves of her elated enthusiasm were rolling off her, and I couldn't help but laugh at how her body twitched with the urge to shift and run.

We had reached the edge of the forest just outside the back end of the palace. I started stripping my clothes off once we were in far enough, and, faster than I could get my shorts off, Tala had peeled her dress off and discarded it over her shoulder. She had already shifted into her magnificent red wolf before I had even gotten both legs free.

"Someone is super excited!" I said, watching Mora hop around on all fours, waiting for me to shift.

I shifted into Conri and approached her, rubbing my muzzle against her soft fur. I swear her wolf purred just like a cat at the gesture. She began yipping at me, waiting for me to take off. I told Tala I was taking her to the lake today. We hadn't been there yet, and if she knew where it was, I was sure she would have been halfway there by now.

Conri's tail wagged and he licked her snout and then barked at her, turning to run towards our destination. Mora was a sleek and fast wolf, so I didn't need to slow down too much for her. She had no problem keeping up with my larger wolf.

Our wolves frolicked and played along the way giving each other loving, gentle nips, sometimes tackling one or the other. It was the beginning of August, so it was still pretty hot out during the day and cooler in the evening, like right now. A perfect evening for a run.

We reached the lake, and usually, I would shift back before jumping in it, but my mate had other ideas. Mora stopped for a second just to take in the scenery before running full force towards the water, leaping high into the air and diving into the water. She was the only wolf I knew that would willingly submerge her whole body and head under water.

Conri growled when she didn't come up for a few minutes and was ready to go save his mate when Mora's furry red head bobbed up over the surface and then dived back down, emerging this time in her skin form.

"The water is wonderful!" Tala shouted out to me.

I shifted back into my skin form and took a running jump into the water right near her and popped up behind her, grabbing her arms and pulling her to me.

"Come on, I want to show you something," I gestured with my head and started swimming towards the far bank where there was a rocky cliff. "Take a deep breath and follow me."

I dove below the surface and swam under the rocks, taking a quick glance behind me to make sure Tala was there. I swear if she wasn't a wolf, she was a mermaid in a previous life. She had never swam, she had never even seen the ocean or a lake before. There was a large pond in one of their gardens, only being able to wade in it, but that was all she had until she came here. She was a natural swimmer; even her wolf naturally took to the water and could probably outswim one of our divers amongst the elite warriors. Tala just had a natural relationship with water. I was sure it had something to do with being Teal's daughter; the ocean was in her blood.

A minute later, we were able to surface on the other side of the rock into a small subterranean lake. A hidden cave in the cliff. There were not many people who knew about this place but Lamia, Mike, and I would come here often. As we got older, we would actually camp here in the cavern, mostly during the summer. The water was high enough to cover the entrance, and we only had to dive down a few feet, coming up on the other side into a cavern with a pebbled shore.

The lake itself was big, stretching for hundreds of miles and then splitting off. The idea of being able to give her this moment, and knowing she would cherish it forever, filled my heart to the brim. All this was new to Tala, and seeing her face light up like was right then was a special moment shared just with me. This moment was ours. The mate bond allowed me to experience how she was feeling, and I could see the cave through her eyes as if it were the first time finding a place that felt magical.

Natural light shone in from somewhere, just enough to be able to see. That light cast across the pool of water and reflected on the cavern's ceiling. I never realized how romantic this setting was until now.

Tala stepped back to me, gently turning as her eyes still wandered over the beauty of the cave, taking everything in until they landed on me, locking in place with mine. "This is beautiful, Kellen, it's the most beautiful place I have ever seen!"

"I wanted to share it with you and I am so glad I did. You make me happy when your eyes light up with excitement, and your smile... it makes my heart beat a little bit faster." I swallowed and shifted my eyes from hers for a few seconds and then brought them back to her again, meeting piercing cerulean eyes. My heart thumped harder in my chest. "I love you Tala and I want to make you happy..."

"Shhh," Tala put her finger on my lips. "Did Conri tell you?"

I tried to connect with my wolf, but he shut me out. Whatever it was that he knew, he wasn't going to tell me. I mentally cursed Conri. I could feel my face screwing up into a scowl. Frustrated that my wolf was withholding information from me; it was one of my pet peeves.

Tala was standing there with her hands on her hips and a finger on my lips. If she realized she was naked, she didn't show it or just didn't care. Of course, my eyes scanned down her body as soon as I focused on the sight of her, and something else started taking note too. My cock hardened at the vision of beauty before us. Her long red hair, bright in the dim glow of the light, hanging over her shoulders and flowing over her breasts, was driving me crazy. The way the pool reflection shimmered on her ivory skin, patterns danced across her, and she looked like a textbook definition of a mermaid.

Bewitchingly beautiful. My hands reached out for her, full of lust and want. I wanted to hear her moans echo through the cavern when I made love to her.

"Mora confirmed it today." Tala declared, making me freeze and raise an eyebrow at her statement. I was missing something.

I halted in my tracks, not getting it. What was that

supposed to mean? Her declaration made me pause from confusion, but by the look on her face, I might as well have just slapped Tala. All the romantic vibes and lustful wanting died at the moment right there. The mood was ruined.

"What did Mora confirm today?" There was so much hesitation in that one sentence. I didn't know if I was asking the right question or if I was digging a deeper hole to put myself in. Because I was definitely in the dog house, I just didn't know why.

*****

TALA

It's as if we had swum into a whole other realm; one made out of fantasy, where pirates and fairies and mermaids existed. It was the most beautiful place I had ever seen. I couldn't smile any wider, I was so entranced with the cavern. The only thing that would have made it better was if there was a chest of treasures like the adventure books I loved to read.

The pool of water we swam up from was surrounded by rocks except for the far end, where the water had created a pebbled and sandy mixed shore over the years, and I could walk up and out the water to sit on it.

Earlier today, minutes before we went out for our run, Mora had confirmed that we were with pup. Pregnant, just like we had thought. I was so excited I had been bursting at the seams from the moment she told me, taking the decision to wait until we got to the lake to tell him. Then, Kellen had me follow him into this cave, and it couldn't have been the most perfect place to tell him.

I could hear Kellen talking next to me, I wasn't really listening though. I was trying to figure out the best way to deliver the news, so I decided to just rip the band-aid off. I lifted my hand and pressed a finger to his lip "... and I want to make you happy..." I cut him off.

"Shh," I hushed him. "Did Conri tell you?" I was thinking maybe Conri had already discovered the news; maybe my scent had already changed. "Mora confirmed it today." I guess I could have said it in a more romantic and softer way than just blurting it out. I was really just so excited that I just had to get it out right then and there.

Kellen froze, his face morphing into one of confusion. His blue eyes darted over my face, searching like my eyes held the answer. I held in the sigh I desperately wanted to let out at him. He was being completely dense. I put my other hand on my hip, with my finger still on his lips as I waited for the fleeting panic in his eyes to pass and for him to work it out.

"What did Mora confirm today?" Holy moons, he was killing me! I had to bite back a laugh, rolling my lips, just staring at him, waiting for the coin to drop. The romantic mood was absolutely ruined. I wasn't sure if there was any way to get it back after this. I should have waited or chosen my words better.

I was ready to open my mouth and tell him, 'I'm with pup!', when finally, the realization set in his eyes and he stooped down to catch my line of sight, making sure he could see my eyes. "Yeah?" he asked, suddenly a little breathless.

I dropped my finger, letting it slide down his chin to his chest. "Tala, are we having a pup?" He bit his bottom lip, and it made me swoon, wanting to taste him. I nodded, eyes still on that simple action.

"Tala... Yeah?" He asked again, getting in my line of sight again. His knees bent, not quite believing it and brimming with excitement that threatened to explode. His eyes slightly glowed with his wolf and his lips hinted towards a smile. "We're pregnant? I'm going to be a dad?"

"Yeah," I nodded my head, bobbing it up and down with a slow up-turn of the lips. "Mora confirmed it today."

"You just made me the happiest man in the realm!" He swept me out of the water by my hips, securely holding them and lifting me high, spinning around, the water splashing around his calves. "Fuck! I'm going to be a dad. Do you have any idea how happy I am?"

"I could take a wild guess," I giggled. He lowered me until I could wrap my legs around his waist, my face level with his.

"I love you so much... thank you for being mine." His hot breath against my lips made my body shudder and my tummy flutter, bringing those pleasurable sparks to life and dancing over my skin.

"I'm yours, my king, always yours," I rasped with a desirous voice. Our close proximity and his enthusiasm turned me on, making my body thrum with pleasure and wanting. Kellen's cock grew rock hard under me, brushing against my ass.

I wiggled against his stiff manhood, teasing him, tempting him because I wanted him. I found myself being pinned against the smooth surface of a rock; Kellen unlocked my legs from his waist and lifted me a little higher, then slid his body between my legs, placing my legs over his arms and spreading me wide open until his head was between my thighs.

He dove right in, licking my slit to my swollen clit and sucking on it. I cried out in ecstasy and rolled my head against the rock. His tongue swirled and his lips sucked, driving me insane and building up heat in my core. I felt him push a finger inside me, and my pleasure echoed around the cavern, giving me a few pumps before adding a second.

I moved my hips, wanting to grind my pussy against him. The feel of his freshly shaven face against my skin was sinfully erotic and I cried out for more. "Kellen, don't stop," I pleaded.

I was on the brink of exploding when he stopped and removed his fingers. The frustration immediately built at not being able to reach my release. Then his cock was brushing up against my entrance, and he lowered me back down to the floor carefully. "Turn around and put your hands on the rock." The previous vexation melted away, and I obliged. The magnetic pull of our bodies wanting us to join together won.

I turned around and placed my hands on the smooth rock face and moaned, sticking my ass up in the air as an invitation. "Open your legs wider, Tala." The dominance of his order drove my wolf wild and my pussy wetter; I was weeping for him.

Then the thick end of his cock was nudging its way through my lower lips to my pulsing entrance. The slow burn of a needful moan slipped passed my lips when Kellen began to fill me up, the moan lasting until he was seated deep inside me. I could feel his heaving breaths and hear them in my ear as he leaned over me, placing his hands on the rock face just above mine. I was still holding my breath, scared that if I let it out, the intense pleasure I was feeling would go with it.

"Breathe, baby," he soothed in my ear. No sooner had I let go of that breath - Kellen began moving slowly in and out of me. "You are fucking perfect," he groaned. "You make me so happy." His long length stroked me with each movement in and out, my walls fluttering around his cock. Without warning, my body trembled, and an orgasm ripped through me. The position and angle were deeper, more filling, and it wasn't taking much for me to go off.

"You like that baby?" his husky voice vibrated by my ear, sending ripples of pleasure through my body.

"Yes, my king... Harder, my king!" I shamelessly begged and received.

Kellen's pace changed, pumping into me faster and harder. He moved his hands from the wall, one at a time, the first going to my hip to hold me steady, the second snaking around the front, between my legs, finding and pressing on my clit, circling it. The sensation of him pumping in and out of me and his finger flicking that oh-so-sensitive bundle of nerves had me screaming out his name as I flew over the cliff and clamped my pussy's walls around him.

"Stay with me, little flame, were done yet." My legs were shaking as I came down from the high, unable to catch my breath when Kellen's tempo changed again, and his cock began to ravish my pussy relentlessly.

His pounding reached new depths, and the burning heat began to build again. I couldn't control the noises of pleasure that left my tongue. Kellen thrust hard and fast, his hands holding me up as I lost traction with my own, and they began to slide down. Still, he thrust hard a few more times until I was seeing stars and both pairs of my lips were quivering, and my orgasm flooded around his cock. No sooner had I reached my peak than Kellen's cock swelled, and he stilled his thrusting, his hot seed spilling into me.

"Tala," my name was but a whisper on his lips. He pulled me up against his chest and held me tight until we both caught our breaths. Leaving kisses on the exposed skin he could reach.

I had found my happily ever after. The fairytale I never thought I would have. Kellen turned my nightmares into my fantasy. He set me free from the moment I laid eyes on him in that arena.

My heart would forever belong to my Gladiator Wolf King.

*****THE END*****

Chapter 56 – EPILOGUE-ISH

<u>MIKE</u>
6 MONTHS LATER

"Are you shitting me, Rhett?" I growled down the phone, gripping it tightly and wanting to crush it. I was dangerously close to losing my cool. Who was I kidding, I had already lost it about two hours ago.

"Ahh come on, Mike, you're my favorite turd. I wouldn't shit you." He laughed.

"Fuck you, Rhett, this is not cool. Can't you handle it? The fucking crowning ceremony is ruined, and now a fucking murder? The party hadn't even started, for Goddess's sake!" Yep, I had most definitely lost my cool. "Fine, Jonda is on her way here. I'll leave once she gets here. I swear to the moon, this better not be something one of your enforcers couldn't handle. If I miss this, he will never forgive me!"

"Trust me, I wouldn't call you if it wasn't bad. We have two bodies in the safe room." I hung up with Rhett, resisting the urge to throw my phone across the hall. I resorted to jumping up and down, waving my arm around, and stomping my foot like a madman.

"Fuck. Fuck. Fuck. Shit Goddess-damn it!" I let out a string of curses and only stopped to the sound of my love's voice.

"You look a little stressed." She chuckled and leaned against the white wall in front of where I was having a tantrum. My shoulder slumped when I looked at her. "You look beautiful," I was now full of disappointment that she had spent hours organizing the event and on herself. She looked like a vision, a goddess in her flowing floor-length purple dress. Her hair curled to frame her face and her lips were painted in the most fuckable color I had ever seen. "I have to go," I pouted, standing in front of her and cupping her cheek, staring into those mesmerizing green-flecked hazel eyes. "There has been a murder."

"No! You're shitting me?" She gasped, "Tell me you're fucking with me?"

I grimaced, shaking my head. "I wish I was. That's why you saw me hopping around like a deranged nut job, I just got off the phone with Rhett."

Pinching the bridge of her nose, she closed her eyes. "Can this night get any more fucked up?" She sighed with her rhetorical question. I pressed my lips to her cheek, and she dropped her fingers from her nose. "Can't the enforcers take care of this?"

"I asked the same thing, but Rhett told me he needed me there. You know he wouldn't even bother me with this if it wasn't urgent. I don't think he is disclosing the full details over the phone, so it must be bad."

"Fine," Jonda sighed out. "I know duty calls."

"I will be back here as soon as I can. I promise." I bent down and kissed her, lingering longer than was necessary. I needed the reassurance, though, and I needed to calm the fuck down before I arrived at the crime scene. "I love you."

"I love you too," she called out as I made my way down the

hallway.

*****

I pulled up to the crime scene. I removed my tie and jacket, dumping them onto the seat next to me, and got out of the car. I took note of the already growing crowd and Rhett's enforcers doing their best to secure the scene and perimeter, keep the nosy, beady eyes of guests away. The guests had gathered and were trying to take a peek inside, trying to find out what had happened, standing behind the yellow tape and wondering if the rumors they heard were true.

Ducking under the bright yellow tape, I heard a guy telling a civilian to back off. I nodded to one of the enforcers. "Rhett?" That was all I had to say, motioning with my head in the direction of the vault room, and the guy gave me a quick nod and replied yes.

I lifted my nose, catching a perfumed scent of peaches, very light, hardly noticeable when mixed with the flowery smells of the other women. I then proceeded to go find the man who had pulled me away from my nephew's birth.

It had started out as an awesome day, waking up and making love to Jonda, I had been sporting a smile all day. Even when we were running around like headless chickens to make sure everything for tonight was in perfect order; guests had been allocated suitable rooms, the halls decorated, the food catered. Everything was running perfectly and smoothly. Until it wasn't.

Until Tala decided to go into labor an hour before the crowning ceremony - her crowning ceremony. The baby had decided to come two weeks early. We knew we were cutting it close, but we didn't realize how close. Then this shit happened, like the queen in labor wasn't enough?

I made my way through the jewel room, passing the old armor on display and pieces of expensive jewelry locked behind reinforced glass, making my way to the back where there was another room, the vault room. This room held more expensive pieces, also displayed behind heavy glass. Then there was the inner main vault that was home to the crown jewels.

Rhett was standing just at the entrance, speaking low with a female; she was taking notes while he talked. He was still dressed in his suit, and like me, the tie was gone and the top few buttons of his shirt were undone. "Hey," I said, catching their attention.

They looked up to see me, Rhett's visible tension on display and permanent lines formed over his face. "Sorry to call you away, Mike. I was truly hoping to meet Jonda tonight, but..." Rhett ran a hand down his face, stressing. "We found two bodies inside the main vault room, one is an alpha's son."

"Shit..." I tipped my head back, this was not good. "And the other?"

"An unknown wolf." He waved his hand and walked into the vault room. Sure enough, two bodies were laid out over the marble floor. I bent down next to one, the alpha's son by his scent. He had been stabbed multiple times and his neck was snapped. I looked at the other body, another male lying only feet away with no stab wounds, but his neck had also been snapped. I lifted my nose, sniffing, but I couldn't get any scent off the second body. Strange.

I stood up and wandered around the room, nose still twitching and eyes searching to see what was out of place. "Do you know what they were after?" I asked Rhett, still walking around the large room.

"No, can't see anything disturbed, nothing missing from

this room or the front room." Rhett sounded just as baffled as I was at the moment.

I could smell the faintest whiff of peaches again, "What about the cameras and the third person?"

"Cameras had been disabled... and what third person?" He frowned, notably not catching the fact that there had been three people in here. I assumed the third person was the one who had killed the two men and fled.

"There was a third person here, I can smell their scent. It's fading but there was definitely another person here. Most likely the one who killed these two." I replied, thinking nothing of it. My senses were much more heightened than Rhett's, but a tracker should have caught it. "Did you have any trackers in here?"

"Yah, just one. He could only scent the alpha's son and got nothing from the unknown. He detected no other scents." I could feel his frustration and curiosity from the other side of the room.

Hmm, my fingers rubbed my lips in thought. "There was a third person in here, no doubt. Nothing was taken?" Then my eyes fell on the door of the inner vault, a room that was fortified by steel walls and a steel door. The only way to get in was to enter a nine-digit code for the door to open, and less than five people had that code.

I had a strange feeling and walked over to the door, punching in the code. The sound of clicking and a long beep was heard, and the control panel lit up before the door unlocked and could be pulled open. The lights came on automatically and I stepped in, standing in the middle of the much smaller room. My eyes scanned every corner. The scent of peaches was much stronger in here.

"The bodies were discovered around ten minutes before I

called you. Dana, here, suspects they had already been dead twenty minutes before we were called to the scene." Rhett began giving me details while standing at the entrance of the door behind me.

My eyes landed on the empty pedestal, the one that should have held Tala's crown. Something Kellen had commissioned especially for her for tonight's ceremony. "Fuck," I sighed, catching Rhett and Dana's attention. "They stole the queen's crown. How the fuck did they get in here?" I groaned, annoyed.

Tonight was definitely turning into more of a shit show than it already was.

I turned to face Rhett, "We are now investigating a double homicide and a theft. I am assuming whoever took the crown was also the one to kill the unknown wolf and the alpha's son." I thought out loud. "I want to know where the alpha's son was and who the last person to see him was. Try and get an identification on the second body and have all other cameras in the palace checked. Alpha Jacobson is going to want answers."

If I was correct, then the scent belonged to the third person who was in this room, and that person was not only the jewel thief but also the murderer. It would take a highly skilled person to not only break into the inner vault, but also someone strong enough to take down the two men in the room outside. I had smelt the same soft scent of peaches when I arrived at the scene, so it hadn't been that long ago. The scent was fading, but seeing as I could smell it, I could track it. They shouldn't have been able to get that far.

"Rhett, get your men to secure this scene, grab a couple of trackers and warriors to follow me. We have a suspect and I'm going after them." I turned to look at him with a serious expression. "The hunt is on."

I left the vault, walking back outside to the hall with a new goal in mind. I could hear bystanders whispering, trying to guess who it was that had been murdered. Word traveled fast, and I could only assume a member of staff had opened their mouth and now the guests were making their own assumptions.

"And have someone tell the guests to stay in their rooms for the rest of the evening," I said, needing the gossip mills shut down, then walking out, letting my nose guide me. The scent led me outside towards the forest line, my footsteps hurried, and with no regard for my suit, I shifted into Duke. The suspect couldn't have gotten that far, but I should be able to catch up before the scent completely fades.

Duke took off at high-speed, weaving between the trees and bounding over dead branches and logs, emitting a low growl once in a while as we tracked down the scent of the jewel thief and murderer, honing in on the fruity scent.

I heard the sound of paws behind me and Rhett's light feet running with the wolves. I was much faster than Rhett, even if he had shifter speed, and I was much faster than any of our trackers or warriors. Being a Queen's Knight came with added bonuses. Everything about us was heightened, our sight, smell, hearing, speed, and strength, just to name a few.

Follow my scent I sent a mind-link to Rhett, and my wolf sped up, hurdling forward now that he had a good lock on the suspect's scent.

We ran and ran, my wolf taking us close to the border of the pack's territory. Whoever this culprit was, was fast, but we were faster. The scent was getting stronger as we pushed forward. It didn't matter where they ran now, how far, or how fast. My wolf had a lock on them, they couldn't hide.

I'm getting closer, how far behind are you? I asked Rhett.

Trackers are ten minutes behind you, I'm about fifteen He replied, panting.

Duke began pushing himself harder, determined to run down the suspect. The scent got stronger, and I could conclude the scent definitely belonged to a female. Confusing me even more at how a female would be able to take down not one male wolf but two.

Bounding through some trees and into a small clearing, Duke let out a menacing growl and slowed his pace slightly. We were close. My wolf's head snapped to the side, noticing a movement, zeroing in on it, and turning direction to pursue. We had been running for an hour now, chasing down the criminal.

From out of the bushes darted a sleek brown wolf. She was quick and nimble but not fast enough. Duke leaped towards the female wolf, giving chase. The pretty wolf dodged and weaved, but despite her quickness, it wasn't enough. Duke ran her down, catching her back leg in his jaws and throwing his large, superior body onto the smaller wolf.

We rolled across the dry ground and tumbled into the base of a tree halting our roll. The she-wolf let out a whimper. I shifted back to my human form, quickly grasping the wolf in my arms tightly. "SHIFT!" I commanded. The female wolf trembled against me.

"SHIFT!" I commanded once again, getting irritated. The wolf's bones started to shift, and her fur began to recede. A petite, slender female formed in my arms, her back flush against my muscular chest, and my cock grew impossibly hard. Pleasurable tingles spread across my body everywhere I was touching her. The urge to mate the woman locked in my grasp was so great that my chest began heaving and my heart raced.

I pushed her away and flew to my feet, looking down at the female in front of me. She quickly scrambled back against the tree, pulling her long dark brown hair over her slender shoulders to cover her chest, trying to cover her nakedness and wrapping her arms around herself. I pounced forward, pinning her against the tree so she couldn't attempt to escape. My manhood was straining towards her and rock hard, the contact of my hand on her arm had sparks flying over my nerve endings.

'Mate,' Duke whispered in awe in my mind. The one word I had been dreading to hear.

Her wolf must have called the same thing as she lifted her eyes to mine, wide with shock, her full lips parting and letting out a little puff of air. I growled and stepped back from her, the taste of her peachy breath enticing my wolf. I was truly pissed that my mate turned up now when I was already happy and in love.

Fuck. Jonda is going to be pissed. My love was the first person I thought of, not my mate who was standing naked as the day she was born in front of me. I let go of her and took a step back, creating some distance. My eyes wandered, traveling down her shaking form, unable to help wanting to look and touch her again. I admit she was beautiful, with long dark brown hair, an olive skin tone, and a slender body. Her breasts were a perfect size, not huge but not small either. I clenched my fists at the thought of my hands cupping them. Her honey-colored eyes held golden flecks, and she watched me with worry. She was scared, her fear mixing with her delectable scent of peaches. No wonder I was the only one who could smell her.

How close are you to me? I linked Rhett, wanting him to get here as fast as possible.

Five minutes. The trackers should be there sooner. He replied immediately. Good, I thought, the less time I am in her presence the better. The Moon Goddess must be laughing right about now, except the joke was on her.

I didn't want my mate, despite my body's physical reaction. I was in love with Jonda, and I had already decided to take her as my chosen mate. We had just talked about this, this very morning. The Moon Goddess had paired me with a female who was a thief and a murderer; this she-wolf would be executed once tried for her crimes.

I snarled at the mate, disgusted with her. She was a criminal. I would have no problem rejecting her. The she-wolf shrunk back under my fiery stare, and her large eyes filled with tears. My wolf whined at her discomfort, urging me to take her in my arms. I shut him up. That would not be happening again.

Luckily for me, I heard the paws of wolves and the trackers emerged from the tree line, coming to a halt as soon as they saw me. A few were in wolf form, and the ones that weren't cast their eyes over the suspect lustfully. I growled out a warning. "Turn the fuck around! Don't look at her!" I snapped at them.

Just then, Rhett came running onto the scene, stopping in his tracks and assessing the situation. "Give me your shirt," I ordered him. He quickly took it off, not asking any questions and handed it to me. I threw it at my mate. "Put it on, now," I growled at her.

"This was the third person in the room. Have her taken to the cells and interrogated. Only mated wolfs around her or you." I barked out. I glanced over my shoulder at the woman who was wearing Rhett's shirt now. "She is your problem now."

I walked away from the group of trackers and Rhett, feeling their stares on my back. *You okay, man?* Rhett asked me privately.

*No, she is my fucking mate. * I growled back through the mind-link. *I'm going back to the hospital and to talk to Jonda.* With that, I shifted back into my wolf form and ran all the way back to the palace to grab some clothes before I went back to the hospital to meet my nephew and tell Jonda what the fuck happened tonight.

I would have to reject the criminal before she was executed anyway. I had chosen Jonda as my mate the moment I laid eyes on her. We decided to wait and mark each other after the crowning ceremony and after our nephew had been born, which was all meant to happen tonight. I was in love with Jonda, and nothing was going to change that. I wanted a family with her, and I wanted to grow old with her by my side.

Tonight was a huge inconvenience and disruption in our lives, yet there was a hidden blessing. Maybe the Moon Goddess planned it this way, giving me a criminal as a mate, one that was fated to die for her crimes.

Chapter 57 – Epilogue 2

KELLEN

I stared down at the little bundle in my arms, his eyes struggling to open and his mouth straining to yawn. I welcomed the smile that spread across my face as I took in his wrinkled face and hands. His eyes blinked open, and only being a few hours old, they were already brilliant pools of blue. Somewhere between the color of mine and Tala's.

I stole a glance at his mother, who looked at us with adoring eyes that sparkled with love and happiness, mirroring my own.

"What shall we name him?" Tala asked, adjusting her position to sit up a little better. I sat on the side of the bed, cradling our son in my arms. Jonda had come in to meet her nephew and stepped out when Tala had dozed off after giving birth to give us privacy and to call Mike, who was on his way back here.

"I'm not sure," I spoke gently. My eyes were trained on him, still enamored with my son and his small movements.

It's strange how I thought I would never feel love like I did for Lamia, then, in one crazy turn of events, I was whisked away from everything I loved and knew and thrust into the unknown. Only to find Tala and fall so head over heels in love that nothing else mattered except for her. Now I hold this guy that she and I created in my arms, who I only just met, and could not even fathom a life without. "I love you so much, thank you for our son." I said to Tala but not looking at her.

"You know he is my son too!" She giggled, reaching out for him. I laughed and reluctantly placed him in her arms. "You will have to share him." She beamed down at him while tucking him against her chest.

"I hope he has your love for water." I thought about how much Tala loved water and the day she told me it was definitely with pup, when I took her the cave. Ever since that day, we had gone there as often as we could. Tala was a natural in the water and could hold her breath longer than any other shifter I had ever come across. I swear she was part mermaid.

"Knock, knock." The soft sound of Jonda's hushed voice filled our ears. "Look who I found downstairs," she smiled, opening the door more and coming inside. Mike was behind her, dressed in jeans and a t-shirt instead of the tux he had previously been wearing.

I scowled when my eyes met his. He looked shaken, worked up, his eyes darker than usual which meant his wolf was on the surface. I knew tonight hadn't gone as planned, but I didn't think it was that big of a deal.

It was meant to be Tala's coronation tonight, but our little boy decided he wanted to come early and be the main event, stealing his momma's spotlight.

What's going on? I mind-linked Mike, worried because he truly looked frazzled.

All good, we can talk later He replied, but I could tell something was definitely bothering him. "Finally, I get to meet my nephew!" He grinned widely and came forward, stretching out his bulky arms and giving Tala a grabby motion for our son.

She placed our son in his arms with a laugh, knowing how much Mike loved kids and that he was still a big kid himself. "So, what are we calling the monster?" He asked while rubbing his nose on the baby's.

"We hadn't thought of a name yet," I replied, looking at Tala and raising my eyebrows as if she had a suggestion. "I like the name Connor," I told her, thinking of my wolf Conri and the story Ashe had told me. He was just as proud of a father as I was right now with his chest mentally puffing out.

"I like that," Tala replied, her lips pursing as she thought. "How about Connor Alexander Teal Moon?"

"That's a lot of names," Jonda laughed from the end of the bed, still wearing her gown. Obviously, she had not had time to go home and change. "I like it, though."

"Me too," Mike supplied while still cooing at the baby. "Hi little Connor," he spoke softly to him, "I'm your uncle Mike, the only one that matters and your favorite uncle."

"You just want to be the favorite uncle to all the kids!" Jonda laughed at Mike.

"I sure do, and I will be the best dad in the realm when we have our own pups." He said smiling, not breaking his eyes away from little Connor. Jonda's eyes snapped to him, full of love but a hint of concern mixed with her adoration. "Now I hate to give you back to momma, but I have to talk with your dad for a few moments. I promise we will see lots more of each other." I smiled at my best friend as he spoke to my son and reluctantly handed him back to Tala.

I gave Tala a quick kiss, promising I was just stepping out for a minute. Then followed Mike out the door in the corridor, noticing he had not given Jonda any attention, which was very unusual for him. He couldn't keep his hands off her usually, those two in the same room together were worse than King and Lamia.

"What's going on?" I asked as soon as we were clear of the room, crossing my arms and staring Mike down, who ran a hand through his hair and then down his face several times before looking me in the eye. Those actions told me alone he was stressed beyond what he wanted to deal with.

"I will give you the cliff notes because we have it handled... for now." He puffed out a large breath before carrying on. I stood and waited. "Someone broke into the main vault and stole Tala's crown," I went to interrupt, but he held his hands up to let me know he wasn't finished yet. "Two bodies were found. An unknown wolf whose identity we are still trying to figure out and the Alpha Jacobson Summers' son, Scott, was also found dead with multiple stab wounds. Both in the outer vault room."

"Okay," I nodded my head, processing the information. "What else?" I asked. I knew there was more to this, his actions and demeanor indicated as much.

"And I found my mate... Right now, she is the main suspect for the theft and murders."

"For fucks sake!" Now it was me who wass swiping their face roughly. I didn't know what to say to him. "What are you going to do?"

"Rhett is handling the investigation as well as the integration with the suspect, and we already have Damon going through security feed, we..."

"About your mate Mike! What are you going to do about that?"

"Nothing!" He gritted out through a clenched jaw, his fists curling tightly by his sides. "Nothing, until I talk to Jonda." He said, a sullen look came over his face and his voice softened. "I will need to reject my mate before she is executed for her crimes." He looked like he was reasoning with himself, and I could see his wolf flash in his eyes at the mention of rejection.

I knew how much he loved Jonda, but I also knew how strong the mate bond was. "Are you sure this mate is the murderer?" I question him.

He bobbed his head slowly, "Pretty sure. Rhett will find out more but as it stands, her scent was all over the place, including the inner vault where she took the crown from. I will have a report typed up and on your desk by tomorrow."

He turned towards the room my mate and brand-new son were in, halting his steps, and turning to face me again. "Congratulations, Kellen, he is a strong boy." He clapped me on the back and brought me in for a bro hug. "I'm sorry this night didn't turn out the way it should have."

"Dude, Tala gave birth to our perfectly healthy boy. How can this night not have turned out great for me? For you, I'm sorry. I know how much you love Jonda and know how much she loves you. You will get this figured out. And don't forget that I am here for you."

We broke the hug and I grabbed him by the shoulders. "I mean it, Mike. Before anything, we are brothers, and I will stand by you, whatever happens, whatever your decision is. Keep Rhett on the case, but I will need you to talk to the Alpha; he will want answers on what happened to his son. Alpha Summers is an arrogant asshole, and I am sure he will create problems not only with other packs but also with the council. He has been after having me removed from the throne before I even turned eighteen, and he has quite a few followers."

"Let me grab Jonda and take her home so you can be alone with your family. This night is already fucked up, no need for me to make it worse." He says, forlorn.

A few hours after Mike and Jonda had left, Tala slept while Connor slept in the provided crib by her bedside. I leaned back in the chair and propped my feet up on the side of the bed, just watching my mate take small light breaths as she slept.

I couldn't help but think how much I loved her, how not so long ago I never thought I would have this. Have her, my son, and already be the King of the Werewolves. It took some time before I was comfortable enough to fully step into my role, but with the help of Uncle Michael and Uncle Marcus, the transition was seamless. My father had taught me well.

My chest tightened a little as I felt the loss of my parents, how my mother would be fussing over my son and Tala. How much they would both love her. How my father would look at me with pride and clap me on my shoulder telling me a job well done.

With those thoughts, I began to reflect on my time in Bhakhil, on Teal. Both Tala and I were orphans now, but we were happy, and each day I grew more in love with her and each day she made me proud with how well she had fit into our kingdom. She embraced the life here, and the people love her. I knew how disappointed the royal pack was that her crowning ceremony was halted, but I also know how excited our people would be to welcome a new prince.

Mathias, by some kind of weird magical blood he has, was able to restore part of Rogue's tongue. I still refused to call him Fergus. He could now talk, but his speech was a little off, especially forming some words, and he remained quiet most days unless he was amongst friends. I wanted to make him my Royal Delta, but he refused the position and asked to be placed as Tala's personal bodyguard. He was now the head of the Queen's security and took his job very seriously.

Rhett had been spending less and less time at MacTire and

more time traveling the continent. He wanted to establish more enforcer locations and seek out more Hunters to join him while he builds a better and fairer justice system that benefits Humans, hybrids, and shifters. He was going to bring to life Lamia's vision of a new era.

I had yet to figure out how us four knights played into everything, but Ashe's words echoed through my head on a daily basis: 'You must accept your fate when the time comes, it is what the Queen carries you will need to protect'.

Hunji believed something was coming and we all agreed. Until then, we could only enjoy what lives we have, savor every waking moment, pave the paths of the future for our children, and pray that what we do in our time will make a difference when it is their time.

I was startled from my thoughts when a gentle knock came on the door. I turned as the door slowly creeked open, and jumped up smiling when I saw bright orange hair and yellow eyes peek around.

"Tawny!" I yell out, then realized Tala was sleeping. "Tawny," I said quieter, "I had no idea you were in town!"

"Hey big guy," she moved in to give me a hug, her tiny frame engulfed by me. "I just got here and came straight to see the little guy. I'm sorry I didn't call, I wanted it to be a surprise."

"Last I heard, you were visiting Lam's and the trio?"
"Yep, I was ready to head back to Cambiador but decided to take a detour. Looks like I came at the right time." She was smiling big as she leaned over Connor's bassinet. "May I?" She asked, giving me a quick glance, her eyes sparkling with excitement.

"Of course," I said. No sooner had the words left my lips, she was picking the tiny bundle and holding him to her chest, whispering sweet nothings to him.

Tala woke up shortly after, and after wiping the sleep from her eyes, she beamed at Tawny. "You must be the elusive werecat princess I have heard so much about?"

"Tawny, nice to finally meet you. And congratulations, this little guy is so handsome!" She extended her hand to my mate.

"Tala, and yes, hopefully he will be just as handsome and caring as his father."

We sat and talked for a while, and I couldn't believe how easily Tawny and Tala get on, almost as if they have known each other their whole lives. It made me so happy that my friends had accepted her so easily and that Tala fit right in with our family. Finally, Tawny handed Conner to Tala and said she needed to be on her way. I offered to walk her out.

"So," I said as we reach outside the hospital, "I hear you have a mate?"

Tawny scoffed, placing a hand on her hip and cocking that and her head to the side. "Not have, had." She said, a slight sneer gracing her dark pink lips. "I actually came here hoping to run into Hunji," she said sheepishly.

"Oh yeah?" I asked, curious as to why she would be seeking him out now. "I haven't seen him months, he's still in the Kodiak Kingdom. Did Lamia not tell you this?"

She nodded, her eyes looking at the ground and her toe tapping. "She did, but he said he was heading this way. I was hoping to see him and... I don't know, talk to him." She let out a big sigh. "I miss him. I miss all you guys, but I miss him the most and I just." She straightened up and looked me dead in the eyes. I could see hesitation staring back at me. "I don't know what I want, I don't know what I would say to him, but I just feel like I need to see him, Kel."

"So, are you going to head up the Bear Kingdom then?" I asked, hoping she would say no because I don't know what she is after or thinking, and I don't think it would be a good idea for her to go up there right now.

"No." She shook her head, and I feel relief wash through me. "I have to go home and sort my mess of a life out. Just tell him I really want to see him, please."

"I will, Tawny. I promise." She gave me a hug and I wrapped my arms around her tight, holding her there for longer than necessary. I wanted her to know she was family, and we would be there for her, whatever she was going through. "You know you can talk to me, right? Mike and I have your back not matter what."

"Thanks," she said, stepping out from my arms and craning her head to meet my eyes. "When I figure out exactly what it is I'm doing, I will let you know," she laughed. A car pulled up and honked. I leaned down to look who was driving and saw Mason, a werecat who used to be one of Lamia's top warriors at MacTire, but when he left to escort Tawny to the Cat Kingdom, he never left her side. I wondered if that was who her mate was. For whatever reason, Tawny seemed to think she need to deal with shit on her own and didn't want to bother us with whatever shit storm she was dealing with. She was tough and grounded and, try as we might, she had expressed that she had it handled and would say nothing more to us.

I asked Lamia, but she told me it wasn't her business to tell and when Tawny needed us, then Tawny would let us know.

"I gotta go, my ride is here." She hooks her thumb at the sleek black car behind her. "It was great to see you, Kellen, tell Mike I said hi."

"Don't stay away too long, Tawny. We miss you around here." I said honestly. I wanted her to come back, I felt like she was getting further and further away from us. We all had our own lives now, but Tawny, it just seemed as though she was purposefully distancing herself from the rest of us. Maybe that was why she wanted to see Hunji, for his advice or comfort. Maybe she was looking for a way to find herself again.

I headed back up to the maternity ward after I watched my friend drive away. I loved seeing Tawny, but I was ready to resume being in my little bubble for a little while longer until my mate and son got to come home, and we would have to resume our duties and fall back into the rat race.

BONUS CHAPTER FOR BOOK 4 – HUNJI A BROKEN WOLF & the witch of Andora

Chapter 1 – Andora

<u>HUNJI</u>

Day three of the quest I had been given by Queen Lamia: Find the witch Morgan, Finnegan's sister, and bring her home.

I was already a day behind. The truck I had been given by the now Alpha Jasper of Bhakhil broke down yesterday morning, causing me to run in wolf form, find a cave in the foothills of the Andora Mountain range, and rest for the night. At first light I shifted into my wolf, letting Ruda lead the way once again.

Some hours later, well into the late afternoon, we had made our way to the first city, only a couple hundred miles outside the capital where the Megaron was situated in Bozgvol. I shifted back into my human form behind a house on the outskirts and threw on the loose pair of pants I had stuffed in my backpack, fastening the retractable vest that held my swords.

It had been years since I had traveled through Andora, nine to be exact. Andora was a beautiful and rich country, surrounded by a border of low-laying mountains rich with quartz. Most structures were made with sandstone, but the richer cities were built using granite and imported marble from their neighbor.

Andora was home to many shifter races, all living in harmony. It's where the entrepreneurs and traders gathered, making their way to the capital to sell their goods to the scholars and rich. Nine years ago, I had come here under orders in search of the chosen. My mentors believed that if the new queen had been born, it would most likely be in this country. I had wasted over a year looking for her here, only to find her four years later on the first continent in an academy for alphas.

I remember the first day I laid eyes on her. Lamia Langley. Barely seventeen and taller than most she-wolves; strawberry blond hair with a black streak that stood out. Her eyes were the most captivating green I had ever seen, like the purest of emeralds from the richest of mines. When she smiled, you couldn't help but smile back at her, the warmth of that smile seeping deep into your heart. Even my cold dead heart had reacted. My wolf, Ruda, had whimpered at the sight of her, mentally rolling over, ready to comply and do anything she asked. We immediately knew who she was, immediately felt protective over her, drawn to her. Don't ask me how or why because that didn't matter, and I couldn't give myself or anyone that answer.

I was twenty-eight at the time, eleven years her senior, and for the longest time, I confused my connection to her with something more than just being protective. I thought I was in love with her. Both my wolf and I looked forward to spending every day with her, the reason we convinced ourselves to get up in the morning and suffer the pretense of being a teacher. Letting the Academy Deans and other professors think we were something we were not.

Until it was time for her and the prince to leave the academy earlier than expected. I left with them under the disguise of protecting the prince, Kellen, when truly I was there for her.

It became apparent to me early on how strong she was; how capable and fierce she could be. Yet, as tough as Lamia was, she had a kindness about her, a sense of justification, a love she would give to anyone and see them for who they were. That's what scared me about her, that her innocence could be taken advantage of, and her ability to forgive would be used against her. The more I got to know Lamia the more I realized I wasn't in love with her, I just loved her. A simple love akin to an older brother or an uncle, but never like the way Mike and Kellen loved her. Their threesome was impenetrable, and her bond to Kellen was something I was jealous of. Maybe because I knew I never could or ever had that type of bond. Not even with my mate.

Three years later, Lamia has now been crowned Queen of Shifters, and her now mate Mathias, the King of Bears, is crowned alongside her as the King of Shifters.

When Kellen went missing, she had asked me to accompany Beta Mike and King Mathias' second in command, Tobias, to go find him and bring him home because she couldn't. She trusted me with the job she couldn't do and then gave me the task of finding a witch. Morgan. The sister of Finnegan, the half-sister to Mathias, and all three are the children of the now-dead Orion, who was killed by Mathias's own hands in the battle for Riocht.

I was the old man of the group and no matter how much they valued me, I would never be a part of them, Knight of the Queen or not. I was the expendable one, the one that shouldn't be there, and the one that shouldn't be alive. By all accounts, I should have died thirteen years ago. A question I always asked myself, every time my eyes opened, was: why am I still alive? Why did the gods let that old priestess find me so many moons ago and bring me back from the dead? Why did they allow me to live?

I still wondered what my role will be in this story, and believe me, there is more to this story than any of us know. I can feel it, see it unfolding, almost taste it. The last three years have just been a prelude to something bigger, something yet unseen and unknown. Lamia and Mathias may be the main characters, but we all had a role, an important part to play. Unfortunately, the script of our lives had been hidden away, or maybe it just hasn't been written yet.

So there I was in Andora, in a city on the outskirts of the country. Looking around, I saw a sign for a bed and breakfast. It was late in the afternoon, too late to carry on my journey to Megaron, and could do with a good night's sleep.

I pushed the old heavy wooden door open, casting a glance around the place. A young woman was seated behind the front desk, and her head immediately popped up from whatever held her attention. Her eyes met mine and roamed over my stature before bringing them back to my face and giving me a wide smile, her face slightly flushing in appreciation. By the way she was chewing on her bottom lip, she liked what she saw.

"Can I help you?" The hopefulness in her eyes told me she would be more than willing to help me with more than just a room. But I ignored the way she looked at me, her pink cheeks, and the way she pushed out her breasts in an attempt to catch my attention.

"I need a room, just for the night," I said, not meeting her stare, not wanting to engage any more than getting a room key and paying her.

"Of course, sir. Will it just be you?" When I nodded, I caught a glimpse of her eyes widening with excitement. I looked away quickly. I didn't want to go there, and couldn't be bothered with turning her down. So, I ignored it and kept my face stoic and impassive.

"That will be 50 coins," she said, sliding the room key across the desk to me. I took out the bag of money Alpha Jasper had given to me before leaving Bhakhil and threw down two silver coins. Reaching for the key, the girl's hand landed on top of mine. "I would be more than happy to help you relax sir, or if there is anything else I can help you with." It wasn't a question, she was offering herself up on a silver platter for me, offering me her body.

I cringed and finally lifted my eyes to hers and held them. "Just a room, thank you." I said it slowly, making sure she got the gist. She didn't because her fingers were gently stroking mine. I whipped the key and my hand from under hers, holding back the shudder of disgust I felt from her touch.

The girl was human and pretty, but I could smell several males that had already been all over her. If I had been interested, the scent of other males was enough to put me off. The girl was obviously a prostitute. If not, then she had serious commitment issues. "Is this a brothel?" I asked her seriously. Her head jerked back in surprise, and her eyes narrowed and glareed at me with disdain from my insult.

"No!" She scoffed.

I bit my tongue, but it didn't help. The words just spewed out. "You certainly smell like one." Her eyes widened with the realization that I was a shifter, and she snatched her hand back from me so quickly that I thought she was going to throw her shoulder out.

"Your room is on the second floor." She spat out, now angry that I had called attention to her promiscuous ways.

I nodded a thank you and headed for the stairs I could see just behind the desk. Finding my room, I unlocked the door and glanced around at the simple furnishings. A double bed sat under a small window with a light green quilt covering it, a white nightstand sat beside it, and a matching dresser was on the opposite wall behind the door. On the far left was another open door leading to the bathroom. Looking in, there was a sink and bathtub that housed a shower. Simple. Plain. I didn't need anything more for just the night. This was a luxury compared to some of the places I have been in my lifetime.

I threw my bag on the bed and stripped my clothes, heading back to the bathroom and turning on the shower, stepping in before the water had even warmed up. The coolness of the spray quickly turned warm as I began to wash myself down using the provided soap.

I didn't want to be here. I didn't want to be on this quest Lamia had sent me on. I wanted to go home, where I had been comfortable and stable. Where I had thought I had finally found my place. I knew home would no longer be at Mac-Tire. Instead, I would be moving to Riocht with the king and queen, still serving as the queen's second in command, and Tobias would be serving as the king's second. It was never the 'where' that made it home, it was the 'who', and Lamia was my home. I would follow her through the gates of the underworld if that's what it took.

My hands scrubbed down my body, lathering the soap across the planes of my chest and abs, going lower until I reached between my legs, palming my dick and running a rough hand over it to clean it. It had been years since I had touched a woman and given in to my desires. I came close three years ago, and I almost took what I so desperately wanted, almost. I just couldn't do it, no matter what my urges were.

I gripped my dick tighter when the vision of Tawny filled my head. She had been so young then, so innocent. She wanted me, and I wanted her, but I turned away. I wouldn't allow myself to get lost in her to take her innocence. I should have because almost every day since then, I thought about that moment in the motel room. Trapping the little kitty against the door and scenting her arousal had me twisting in knots wanting more than anything to fuck her.

The grip tightened around my now hard shaft, and my hand began to stroke faster as I remembered Tawny's yellow eyes looking up at me, her chest heaving and her heart racing. She licked her lips as her gaze roamed down my body which was only covered by a towel around the waist.

"It's been a long time since I have tasted beautiful," I growled low into her ear. It took all my strength to walk away from her, slam that bathroom door, and get dressed.

I braced my hand on the wall, pumping my cock through my calloused palm harder. I imagined that moment going differently. Instead of turning away from her, I should have dragged her to the bed and torn her clothes off. Licked her gleaming black skin from head to toe, bit her nipples, and listened to her moan my name. I should have sunk my dick deep into her virgin pussy while she squirmed and begged me for more.

My balls tightened, and the heat in my lower back seared as I gave myself a few last strokes before coming all over the shower wall. "Tawny," I whispered her name as my dick jerked in my hand with its last stream of seed spilling out into the open. I gave myself another quick rinse before shutting off the shower and snagging a towel that had been provided on a shelf above the toilet.

What woman would want this? I questioned myself, staring at my reflection in the half-steamed mirror. My eyes settled over at the angry scars of my past that littered my chest, back, and further down my legs. My whole body was covered in scars, and it was one of the many real reasons I haven't touched a woman in years. Contrary to popular belief, not all scars can be healed on a shifter.

A reminder of the love I cherished, the love my mate couldn't return. The reason for my other scars – was the punishment placed on me before my exile. By order of the king, my father... My eyes settled on my dick, now hidden beneath the white towel, where the evidence from the lick of the whip dipped in silver and wolfsbane marred my junk. It disgusted me most of the time when I felt the three raised welts that still lingered there, a reminder that I could have been less of a man than I already felt.

Over the years, I had learned to forgive, not forget. Never forget. I had almost paid my penance with my life, almost with my wolf's life. I sought my redemption for a long time. I forgave myself, forgave my mate, and even still, I knew I would never be forgiven in the eyes of the Moon Goddess. Despite what the priestess had said to me, I knew my crime was not justifiable. There was always another way, things I should have done differently, ways I could have controlled the situation. If I hadn't given into my wolf's anger, his madness and vengefulness that had seeped into me, maybe things would be different now.

I shook my head and turned away from the mirror. There was no point wondering the 'what ifs', no point contemplating my earlier life choices. The past was just that – the past. There was nothing I could do to change it, and through the years that followed, I understood that I didn't want to change it.

It took me a long time to come to terms with that thought. After many years of healing, many years of studying, and many years of training, I finally understood myself. I was given a purpose, reborn, and given a new name and a new life.

That purpose and life have brought me where I was today. The first time I laid eyes on Lamia Langley, I knew she was special, the chosen one. I knew I would follow her, protect her, serve her in any way she asked, in any way she needed. Lamia, Kellen, Mike, and Travis had become my family. I looked over them like the big brother, like I did long ago for my sister.

It didn't matter that I was more than ten years their senior. They respected me, but not because I was their teacher and mentor. It was in spite of those things that they had become my friends and then family.

When I first arrived at the Alpha Academy just over three years ago, landing there in my search for the chosen one, the Queen of Shifters, I had still been lost in myself. Alone. Still trying to find my place in my new life, where I belonged on that new continent. The world there was vastly different from the one I grew up in. The second continent was far behind in some ways yet advanced in others.

I came from a kingdom where automotives were for the rich and powerful, where horses and buggies were still used, and where were-folk only shifted in battle or extreme circumstances. The fashion was old realm-y compared to the casual jeans and tees they wore there. There, were-folk shifted all the time. They didn't just rely on their weapons or hands, they embraced their animal counterparts and would let them out to run for fun, not because they were in battle or fighting for a title.

They had a council there, a justice system. Not just one man's command.

That was the reason I found myself looking for the sister of Finnegan Artos, the last true witch in Andora. For Lamia, for my queen - no one else. It was because she asked that I came searching for a girl no one had seen, with only Finnegan's description and the diary of a dead woman to guide me.
Find her and bring her home. That was all I had to do.

About The Author

J.w.g. Stout

Jessica Stout is the Author of The Delta's Daughter, the sequel Rise of a Queen, book 3 – The Gladiator Wolf King, and the latest in the series Hunji: A Broken Wolf & The Last Witch of Andora – book 4.

Born in the USA and raised in the United Kingdom, she is now a wife and mother of two, living back in the USA, with a passion for writing and animals.

Before becoming a full-time writer, Jessica was an entrepreneur with her own printing business. She enjoys spending time with family and friends and most of all curling up with a good book and her three dogs Venus, Apollo Creed, and Atlas.

Books In This Series

The Delta's Daughter

The Deltas Daughter - Book 1

Rise Of A Queen - Book 2

Hunji: A Broken Wolf And The Last Witch Of Andora - Book 4

The Crimson Grimalkin - Book 5

The Beta And The Jewel Thief - Book 6

Made in the USA
Columbia, SC
03 November 2023